New York Times Bests

Vivian Arend

"If you've never read a Vivian Arend book you are missing out on one of the best contemporary authors writing today."
~ *Book Reading Gals*

"The bitter cold of Alberta, Canada, is made toasty warm by the super-sexy Coleman brothers of Six Pack Ranch."
~ *Publishers Weekly*

"Brilliant, raw, imaginative, irresistible!!"
~ Avon Romance

"This story will keep you reading from the first page to the last one. There is never a dull moment..."
~ *Landy Jimenez*

"I definitely recommend to fans of contemporaries with hot cowboys and strong family ties.."
~ *SmexyBooks*

"This was my first Vivian Arend story, and I know I want more! "
~ *Red Hot Plus Blue Reads*

"In this steamy new episode in the "Six Pack Ranch" series, Trevor is a true cowboy hero and will make any reader's heart beat a little faster as he and Becky discover what being a couple is all about."
~ *Library Journal Starred Review*

New York Times Bestselling Author

Vivian Arend

Six Pack Ranch
Rocky Mountain Heat
Rocky Mountain Haven
Rocky Mountain Desire
Rocky Mountain Angel
Rocky Mountain Rebel
Rocky Mountain Freedom
Rocky Mountain Romance
Rocky Retreat
Rocky Mountain Shelter
Rocky Mountain Devil
Rocky Mountain Home

Thompson & Sons
Ride Baby Ride
Rocky Ride
One Sexy Ride
Let It Ride
A Wild Ride

Adrenaline Search & Rescue
High Risk
High Passion
High Seduction

DreamMakers
All Fired Up
Love Is A Battlefield
Don't Walk Away

A full list of Vivian's paranormal print titles
is available on her website
www.vivianarend.com

Rocky Mountain Devil

Vivian Arend

Rocky Mountain Devil
Copyright 2016 by Vivian Arend
ISBN 9781535405485
Edited by Anne Scott
Cover by Angela Waters
Proofed by Sharon Muha

Prologue

February, Rocky Mountain House

RAFE COLEMAN sat on the tailgate of his truck and stared into the slate-grey winter sky. He had a six-pack of beer beside him, a borrowed suit on his back, and a shit-ton of guilt raging inside.

Right then organ music was probably playing softly in the church. Background noise as everyone in Rocky shuffled in to settle on the hard wooden pews, awaiting the main event.

If they wanted him there, they'd damn well have to wait a little longer.

Made sense this day would be cold as hell and colourless—washed out and empty. The bitter void fit his mood nicely, and he was pretty much ready to sit there for as long as he could, thank you very much.

Except it seemed the world, meaning his Coleman family, wasn't going to allow that option. His cousin Trevor's truck rolled down the snowy driveway, big tires sliding through the deep snowfall of the previous night.

Rafe eyed the truck with suspicion. Trevor alone wouldn't be strong enough to move his ass, but if he'd brought Joel, or a few of the other cousins, Rafe's rebellion could be over fast.

Only it wasn't Trevor, or Joel, or even his brother Gabe.

It was Laurel Sitko, fire flashing in her eyes as she glared out the window, fishtailing to a stop beside him. She dropped from the cab, her petite body freefalling for a foot before she hit the snow. Her feet slipped on the traitorous groundcover, and Rafe stiffened his spine to keep from leaping to her rescue.

She marched right up to him then planted her fists on her hips. Her pale blonde hair was pinned up neatly, and a warm but stylish winter coat covered most of her dress. The only thing about her that didn't look as if she should be prancing around in a castle like a princess were the oversized work boots on her feet—she'd probably found them in the truck when she'd borrowed it. Her breaths turned to a cloud of steam on every sharp exhale into the frigid winter air.

Rafe picked up the beer beside him and lifted it toward his lips.

She snatched the bottle from his fingers. "Don't you have somewhere to be, Coleman?"

"Yup." He grabbed the bottle back, taking a good long drink before looking into ice-blue eyes filled with sorrow and frustration. "Right here."

Laurel's gaze narrowed, and before he could stop her, she'd nabbed the bottle again, twisting on the spot to fling it against the narrow strip of fencing beside them. The glass shattered, the explosion echoing like the lake during spring breakup. Shotgun sharp, cutting like a razor.

She moved like a whirlwind, stealing away the rest of the six-pack. She sent it flying into the deepest snowdrift within tossing distance before turning back to face him. Cheeks red, body shaking.

"You're going to that church, right *now*," she informed him.

Didn't look so angelic when she got pushed too hard. She looked fiery, and passionate, and Rafe hopped off the tailgate and stepped into her personal space.

She tilted her head so she could keep glaring. "You don't scare me," Laurel snapped. "Get your ass in gear."

He raised a brow at her curse, but her sheer determination and vibrancy just made that icy blade of fear in his gut stab harder. He was one second away from losing her, and there was nothing he could do about it.

Rafe closed the distance between them, dragging their bodies together. He lifted her until their heads were in line so he could stare into her eyes.

If this was goodbye, he was going to take *everything* one last time.

He caught her by the back of the neck and brought their lips together in a searing hot kiss—

Chapter One

September, Rocky Mountain House, sixteen years ago

THE SECOND week into kindergarten, she arrived.

One minute Raphael Coleman had been sitting alone in the sandbox and the next, a beautiful angel stood next to him, and somehow he knew his life would never be the same.

He'd heard about angels, of course. In Sunday school, and from his mama, usually when she was warning that *his* guardian angel was getting a workout.

More than that, he'd been called one for as long he could remember. *The Angel Colemans*. To make them different from the other three Coleman families in the area. He'd never been sure what he and his big brothers, Mike and Gabe, had done to be ranked up there with shining creatures with wings, but it was the way things were.

Although, his daddy? Daddy teased him to stop being a devil child and get to work.

Yes, angelic beings had been discussed regularly in his world, but he'd never seen a real angel until now, and she *had* to be real. Her wings were hidden, but she shimmered with the light of the sun behind her, and he

4

waited cautiously for her to speak, to be sure he didn't scare her away. Around them, the children from his kindergarten class ran and screamed, laughing and burning off energy before they got pulled back into the portable trailer that was their classroom. But here in the sandbox he'd found a quiet refuge.

She tilted her head to one side, long white-blonde hair in pigtails glowing in the sunlight as she examined him. Her pale blue eyes sparkled, and she nodded firmly as if happy with what she saw.

And then she spoke, and even her voice was different than the other children's. Sweeter, and kinder, and perfect.

"Want to build a racetrack?"

Definitely an angel. A mere girl would have suggested making a castle, or something equally silly.

Rafe held his hand up, his two favourite Hot Wheels offered like a sacrifice. "Want one?"

Her eyes widened and her smile threatened to blind him. But instead of taking one of his slightly battered toys, she reached into her pocket then settled next to him in the sand. Rafe waited as she lifted her hand and showed him two more vehicles. "I'll trade."

They both considered carefully before exchanging—her black truck for his green one. Then they worked together, shaping the sand into circles for the track and racing their new trucks loudly over the course.

Everything went well up until Jacob MacHalden, the biggest boy in the class, plopped down in the middle of their most exciting race yet. Plopped down and deliberately kicked everything apart with his feet before offering an evil grin as if daring either of them to complain.

Something in Rafe went hot, then cold, then hot

again.

He'd spent years begging to go to school like his brothers, and the first days had been a lot like he'd expected. His mama had said there'd be lots of kids for him to play with, which was true. His brother Mike, who was ten years older than him, had warned Rafe might not always like the other kids, which was also true.

After a week, Jacob was already on Rafe's limited but growing do-not-mess-with list.

His brother Gabe, who was eighteen and all grown up, had told him sometimes people wouldn't be nice, but it was up to him to not lose his temper. And that throwing tantrums was for babies, and that he expected Rafe to deal with troubles without ever throwing a punch...

Gabe had a lot of things to say, but that was okay. Rafe kind of worshipped him. He'd do *anything* to make his biggest brother proud.

So all those things were running through Rafe's mind as he glanced at the angel beside him and saw her lower lip quiver. What he wanted to do was punch Jacob, hard, for ruining their fun. What he *should* do was something else that would make Gabe happy.

But as he watched, an expression came into those pale blue eyes he hadn't expected. Between one moment and the next, his angel grew claws, leaping from his side to land her slight, delicate frame on top of the class bully, her shrill scream echoing through the playground.

Her name was Laurel Sitko, and she was the new pastor's younger daughter. He found *that* out when they were both hauled into the principal's office and their families had to come get them.

He didn't remember much about that visit other than standing close enough to Laurel the back of their hands brushed. She secretly caught his fingers in hers and squeezed before letting go.

Oh, and he remembered she refused to apologize.

"But he was *mean,* Daddy, and happy about it," she told Pastor Dave in front of Jacob's mom, the principal, Gabe and God, because God had to be there since the pastor was.

"We still don't punch people, even if they're mean." Pastor Dave looked stern, but he hugged Laurel tight after she'd promised to not punch Jacob again. Although, she looked pretty satisfied that the bully's right eye was already turning a dark shade of blue.

That was the beginning of a beautiful friendship.

June, twelve years ago

Rafe was tight inside from trying not to cry when he spotted her. Laurel stood in the hallway outside the church hall after the funeral, fingers clutched. Seeing her lips quiver didn't make it any easier, and he clenched his hands into fists and fought for control.

The past three days had been like nothing he'd ever experienced in all his eight years. His ma hadn't said much because she was busy crying. Mike—he wasn't saying anything because he was dead. They'd had birthday cake for him, and a couple nights later Mike had gone out, and Rafe had gone to bed like usual, and that was the last time he saw his brother.

"A terrible accident" and "taken far too soon" people said over and over and over until Rafe wanted to scream.

His big brother Gabe, who was twenty-one and past grown up, had knelt beside him and choked out that if he wanted to cry, that didn't make him a baby...

For once Gabe didn't have a lot to say.

Neither did his dad, or anyone, except for Laurel's dad who had just said a bunch of words during the funeral about how Mike was gone but he'd sure shone bright while he was on earth.

While he liked Pastor Dave, Rafe hadn't wanted to listen to anyone talk about Mike right then. He wanted his brother back, but he was old enough to know that dead was dead.

Laurel glanced both directions before grabbing Rafe by the hand and pulling him after her into one of the side rooms off the main hall.

Looking at her still made him think of angels, only now they'd gotten into trouble too many times over the years at school for him to believe angelic looks always meant well-behaved.

She closed the door before taking a deep breath. "Gabe is leaving."

He stared at her. "What?"

"I heard him. I snuck up because it looked as if something interesting was happening. He was talking to one of your cousins, and I heard him. He's leaving, Rafe. And he isn't going to tell you, so you need to talk to him before he goes. Or you'll be sad, and so will he."

Gabe wouldn't leave. Not while everyone was crying over Mike.

But it was true. As soon as the whole, horrible graveyard visit was over, Gabe offered to drive him back to the church. Rafe waited for him to speak, but they sat in silence the entire trip. Gabe parked back at the church, took a deep breath, and then let it out without mentioning a thing.

Only when he glanced over briefly, the expression on his brother's face told Rafe that Laurel was right.

"You're leaving me," he accused.

Gabe jerked in surprise. "Where'd you hear—?"

"I don't want you to go," Rafe interrupted.

His brother gripped the steering wheel tightly as he stared out the window into the sad, grey sky. "I don't want to go either, bucko, but I have to."

"You're a grown up. You can do whatever you want."

Gabe turned a sorrow-filled face toward him. "Sometimes what we want to do and what we need to do are two different things."

"Will you ever come back?" Rafe got out before his throat closed up completely.

"Maybe," Gabe offered. He wrapped a hand around the back of Rafe's neck and made Rafe look him in the eye. "I'm not leaving because of anything you've done—don't you *ever* think that. You're one hell of a great brother, and I know you're gonna miss me. I'm going to miss you too, but right now, this is what I've got to do."

Sadness welled up past his breaking point, and Rafe escaped from the truck, dashing across the churchyard. He didn't know what he was running from, just that he needed to get away.

He ended up standing in the backyard of Laurel's house, leaning against the massive apple tree in the back corner. He put his face against the cool bark and let the rough texture dig into his cheek as he stood there, confused and hurt.

He was going to lose both his brothers, and it wasn't fair.

Soft fingers brushed his, but he didn't move. Just let Laurel lean her head against his back as she slipped her arms around him and hugged him tight.

She didn't say anything. Only stood there crying

quietly with him, and for him, and it was exactly what he needed. She'd known that. Somehow, she'd known, exactly like a friend should.

September, study hall, eight years ago
"Get out. Seriously?"

Rafe dragged a finger over his chest in the shape of an X before motioning for her to be quiet. "You're going to get us detention first week of school, Sitko," he whispered.

"It's my turn. Last year it was your fault," she muttered back, glancing at the teacher's aide pacing the library where the eighth-grade class was supposed to be filling in their homework agendas for the next month.

He and Laurel had their class calendars open on the tabletop, and their notebooks out, but they were more interested in discussing his date from the previous night.

Which might have seemed a strange topic, but not for them. They shared about everything. Ever since kindergarten they'd been thick as thieves, and people rarely blinked at seeing them wandering the school halls together.

No one taunted, either—there wasn't any use. Rafe would have fought the teasers, but Laurel simply raised a brow in the most haughty way the first time any newcomers tried to poke fun at them.

"Why on earth should we care what you think?" she'd ask in all seriousness.

There'd never been a good answer to that one, so Rafe had grown accustomed to the fact his best friend at school was a girl.

And now that they'd reached the age where everyone was thinking hard about the opposite sex, it seemed pretty natural to talk about *that*. Laurel wasn't allowed to date, and until recently Rafe hadn't done more than look, between chores at the ranch in his out-of-school hours and no way to slip into town to meet up with anyone. But now that his big brother Gabe was back, so many things had changed.

Not his friendship with Laurel, though. That was solid as ever.

Laurel pushed a piece of paper in front of him and pretended to point to something as she leaned in close. "So you kissed her? That's it?"

Rafe thought back to the previous night. "We held hands in the movie theatre for a while."

"Holding hands is good."

"Yeah, but awkward. I'd bought us a supersized container of popcorn."

"Awkward *and* disgusting. Go, you."

She snickered as she pulled away, muffling the soft sound, but unable to stop her body from showing her amusement. She rocked hard enough her shoulders quivered. Rafe glanced at the room monitor, then back at Laurel who looked on the edge of a seizure, she was shaking so hard.

God, she drove him crazy.

His mom said he had to buckle down and not get in trouble as often this coming year. His dad grumbled and cussed, but not about Rafe. He just grumbled and cussed and drank too much at times because *everything* was terrible, according to him, but at least ever since Gabe had come back, Ben hadn't lost his temper with anyone.

Gabe said Ben had "issues".

Whatever. Rafe thought his dad was a jerk, and he should grow up and act like a dad again.

Thinking about girls was far more interesting

11

than analyzing the tension at home.

He poked Laurel in the side, and she shot upright, covering her mouth with a hand to stop from shrieking.

"What's so funny?" he demanded.

She made a big fuss over straightening the things in front of them, and didn't answer. Uh-oh. Avoidance, which meant she was trying not to have to lie. She was a truly shitty liar.

He rapped his knuckles on her head. "Earth to Laurel...what is your twisted sense of humour doing in there?"

"Mr. Coleman. Please keep your hands to yourself and leave your study partner alone."

The aide directed a warning look at both of them, and Laurel had a coughing fit as Rafe smiled politely. "Yes, sir."

They waited until the TA was on the far side of the room before leaning toward each other. "You *sure* all you did was give her a kiss?" she asked.

"Duh. You'd think I'd know." He pulled back, slightly worried now. "Why? What'd you hear?"

"Third base."

"Hell, no," Rafe shouted in surprise.

Their classmates, including the young lady he'd been playing tonsil hockey with the night before, twisted on the spot to watch as the aide bore down on them double-quick.

"Oops," Laurel muttered, gathering their books into two piles. "Your fault, again."

Rafe bit the inside of his cheek to stop from laughing out loud as the TA snapped up a hand and pointed toward the door. "I assume you two remember the route to the principal's office?"

Laurel waited until they were out the door and on

the stairwell landing before turning to him, and wearing her most innocent expression, sweetly asking, "Shall we go straight there, or take the more scenic *road to hell?*"

She smiled from ear to ear then let her laughter loose. Rafe joined in, because the fact they had names for the trip to the office was beyond stupidly funny. He had to prop himself up with one hand on the wall to keep vertical as they both laughed until they were gasping, stomachs hurting, in spite of being in trouble.

Or maybe because of it—best friends who did everything together.

June, three years ago

Lights sparkled off the shiny disco balls hanging over the school gymnasium floor, sending twinkling flashes over fancy dresses and borrowed suits and tuxes. Stars spun overhead, hung from long threads, and the entire room looked like a throwback to some cheesy eighties movie.

Rafe leaned on the nearest wall and watched with amusement.

Graduation night—small-town style. As the youngest in the Coleman clan, he'd heard stories from his cousins who'd experienced it before, some many years before him. He'd compared their memories to what he'd seen on TV and in the movies, and come up with a pretty realistic set of expectations.

Grad in Rocky didn't run to rented limos or extravagant hotel banquet halls at an expensive hotel. There was no sneaking off to check into hotels with prom dates to have sex...

Heck, their classmates who wanted to have sex were already having it, and the holdouts wouldn't bother trying tonight when everyone would be on the lookout for anyone going wild.

His amusement lingered as he searched out one feminine figure, making sure she was having fun and didn't want to leave.

Pastor Dave's ban on dating still stood, but for once Laurel's argument that they were just friends had made a difference. Rafe had gotten permission to pick her up and bring her home, and he was not going to do *anything* to mess up at this point. Not with Laurel going away at the end of the summer.

She was off to school, and he would stay in Rocky to help his brother, Gabe, with his new fiancée, Allison, hopefully turn around the Angel Coleman ranch troubles by going organic.

A whole lot of years of friendship were about to come to an end, and there was a knot in his belly as he considered it. A sense of sadness.

She was spinning in a circle, holding her friends' hands, the girls a tangle of laughter and joy. Heads thrown back, bright happiness pouring off them.

Rafe stepped forward, unable to resist being a part of it.

Bad timing on his part, or maybe it was brilliant. The music changed as he took her hand, pulling her close for a dance. A slow ballad filled the air—something that called for their bodies to be pressed together as they swayed under the flickering lights.

It wasn't unexpected for his body to react. Especially when Laurel looked up at him, nibbling on her bottom lip, eyes full of trust.

Rafe went hot everywhere.

"Stop wiggling like that," he ordered. "You're turning me on."

She snickered. "Stupid man hormones. You get

14

turned on in a high breeze, Coleman."

He wondered if it was more than just *stupid man hormones*. At this point, thinking about her turned him on, but he knew better than to push it. He eased away, trying to create some room so his cock didn't rub up against her. She didn't cooperate. Instead, she stepped closer with that determined expression in her eyes.

"Devil woman," he warned, forcing her to a safer distance as they danced. She gave in to his superior strength, finally going back to the modest clutch that he found just as tempting without being deliberately seductive.

Even him getting a hard-on around her on a regular basis hadn't messed up their friendship. It's not as if they were fooling around. Laurel could be pretty blunt when it came to talking about sex—like she was blunt about everything. And he appreciated it, he really did, although sometimes he wished...

He didn't even know what he wished.

They were in his truck, and he was driving her home when she dropped the bomb.

"I'm going to Bible College in September."

"Knew that," Rafe said, taking the long route. The one that took them all the way around Rocky, because he wasn't ready for the night to end.

She sighed. "You don't know I'm going on a mission trip first."

He tightened his grip on the wheel. "Where?"

"Belize. They had a last-minute opening, and I was on the wait list. I'll be doing volunteer work in an orphanage for two months."

He did the math and ended up with an aching pit in his stomach. "When do you leave?"

She laid a hand on his arm. "End of next week I

15

head to boot camp."

"Fuck."

"Rafe..." Laurel chastised.

"Damn?"

She laughed, but her heart wasn't in it. "I know. Me too."

Rafe had known it was coming, but he'd kept hoping it wouldn't really happen. "Will you be at home at all before you start school?"

"No."

Such a simple word. Such a damning, horrible, heart-and-soul-killing word.

Impulsively, he pulled into the parking lot at the wilderness center, stopping the engine so they could sit in silence and watch the sunset paint the nearby Rocky Mountains with gold and red as he tried to deal with reality.

His angel was flying away. It had to happen. She'd leave, he'd stay—friends knew the world went on. Friends didn't expect forever.

Rafe turned to face her. "Going to miss you."

She nodded as if unable to speak, her pale blue eyes filling with tears.

Damn it. They'd talked about this, but now that it was real, he couldn't accept it. He caught her in his arms and pulled her close, hugging her as if that could change anything.

She clung back, fingers on his shoulders, the soft scent of her filling him more and more with every breath he took. Warmth and connection growing.

Changing...

As they cuddled together in the growing darkness, he found himself playing with her hair. His fingers teased her fancy up-do until it came apart in his hands, and silky seduction draped over his fingers. A shiver took him as he imagined the long strands sliding over his naked skin.

Rafe went cold, then flaming, wickedly hot.

She lifted her chin and stared at him with wonder in her eyes.

It was wrong. Completely and utterly wrong, but everything right between them until now had led to this moment.

"I'm going to kiss you," he warned.

She opened her mouth slightly, and the soft sound of longing that escaped ricocheted through his system, hitting all his *on* buttons and shoving them to *high*.

They both leaned in, and their lips met.

Sweet.

Brief.

A brush together, then apart. Yet with one taste, he was lost. He curled his fingers into the hair at the back of her neck and gripped tighter.

He went in for another kiss, this one deeper. Longer. Totally and utterly blown away by the fact that everything they'd ever joked about while watching their friends *fall in love*—like seeing stars and feeling the earth shake—all of those hokey clichés were true.

They fumbled in the dark, kissing harder, moving together until she was straddling his lap and he had his hands sliding up her bare legs, under her skirt. He cupped the soft fabric covering her butt and dragged her closer, putting heat and pressure over his fully engaged cock.

She'd untucked his dress shirt and was frantically undoing the buttons, her bare palms bumping his abdomen as she worked, and he was going to die because they couldn't do this—

And there was nothing he wanted more.

He caught her wrists, trapping them beside their hips. It forced him to stop groping her as well, and they shifted their torsos far enough apart they could catch their breaths. Chests heaving as they struggled for control.

"We shouldn't," he whispered, "but I have never wanted anyone the way I want you right now."

"Me too." She took a deep breath and blew it out in a long, steady stream. "So, what do we do?"

For some stupid reason his brother Gabe's words rolled in. *"Sometimes what we want to do and what we need to do are two different things."*

Laurel wiggled her wrists and he released her. She caught the front of his open shirt, tugging until she could smooth the fabric over his chest.

Even with a layer of material between them, her touch scalded him.

"I bet what we need to do is cool off with a walk by the river before you take me home," she offered.

"Cool off with a jump *in* the river, you mean."

Rafe groaned as she lifted herself up and settled on the seat beside him, their hands brushing lightly. His body was a burning mass of need and guilt.

Walking together beside the water in the moonlight was all kinds of perfect and terrible. Rafe held her hand and wished for a way to go back to what he'd felt before, even as he never wanted to give up what was churning inside.

They turned in unison toward the old tree hanging over the water, the surface of the curved trunk worn smooth by time. Laurel crawled up and sat demurely, arranging her skirt carefully before lifting her face toward him.

"When you leave, you live every day to the fullest. Don't wait for me, you hear?" Rafe ordered.

Laurel's eyes were shining pools of moonlight, a thin line folding between them as confusion drifted in.

"I mean it. You're going away, and you get to date for the first time—heck, you might fall in love. If that's what's waiting out there for you, you've got to take the chance. Life's too short to be put on hold, but..." he caught her by the chin and poured every bit of himself into the words, "...but if you come back, and we're both single, I'm warning you right now, you will *never* get away from me again."

"What if I want to wait?" she asked.

Even though her words gave him a thrill, he shook his head. "That's not living. You're my best friend, Laurel. How could I want you to put everything on hold for years when we don't know what might happen tomorrow?"

The lesson he'd learned from Mike's death. Don't wait, don't waste a minute.

She nodded before pressing a hand to his cheek. "You're right. We don't know—so when I leave, you need to live too. You need to date, and maybe fall in love." A burst of laughter escaped her. "Hey, don't make that face. Not after you finished trying to boss *me* around."

"That's different," he attempted, only to have her cover his mouth briefly with her palm as she leaned in close and glared.

"Don't push it, Coleman. I have it on the *best* authority I'm the devil to deal with when I want to make a point. No, you *will* do all those things that mean you're living, including not letting your father make you bitter."

"He's a jackass—"

"Yes, I know, but that doesn't mean you get to—"

Laurel interrupted herself, eyes flashing. "Not having that conversation. Not here. Not now. Now is for *us*."

He leaned their foreheads together. "For us."

They stared at each other for the longest time. Rafe stood between her legs, the warm summer breeze tangling around them as they silently said goodbye, thank you, and everything else words couldn't say.

Then between one breath and the next, she took his world and changed it forever.

"You're right, Rafe. There are no guarantees, and we don't know what might happen tomorrow. So if you promise to live, then so will I." Laurel stroked a hand down his cheek, "But if all we've got for sure is today, I want everything."

She wrapped her arms around him and pulled their bodies together...

Chapter Two

June, current day, Rocky Mountain House

Shhhhh
Lies, Deception and Why We Keep Secrets

LAUREL STARED for a moment before rolling her eyes then moving the library cart toward the nonfiction section. Books were wonderful. Books were amazing, and some of them had double the entertainment value the author intended.

An entire book on why people keep secrets. Umm, *duh*? Because it was no one else's business? Try that one on for size.

"Laurel, when you're done, I'm going on break. Man the desk?" Wendy Tomes—unfortunate name for a librarian—stood beside her, pressing a hand to her baby-full belly. "I need to get off my feet for a minute."

"Go now. I can finish this later," Laurel offered, pushing the rolling cart back toward the front desk of the Rocky Mountain House Public Library. "Did you ever consider keeping your maiden name?" she asked suddenly.

Her supervisor snickered. "I don't think so. Tomes is an improvement over Ripper."

"Ouch. Yeah." She pushed the swinging gate aside for Wendy. "Good decision."

The other woman grimaced as she pressed a hand to her back and stretched her baby bump forward. "Dawn is starting the Reading in PJs program in a few minutes, so you're on crowd control as well, okay?"

"No prob."

Laurel resisted the urge to hum happily as she surveyed her almost brand-new kingdom. Returning to Rocky Mountain House after three years away was an exercise in joy and sorrow.

Joy, because this was home. Sorrow, because not everything that had happened while she was gone had been perfect, and there were deep hurts inside she had to learn to deal with.

The front door opened and a familiar face marched forward, and for one breathless moment, she thought Rafe had walked through the door. Then the man took off his cowboy hat, revealing hair that was far too dark, and she forced herself to take a few slow breaths and dig for calm.

Helping one of the Coleman cousins find a book brought her back to here and now instead of drifting into daydreams about her friend who she hadn't seen or heard from in a long, long time. They hadn't kept in touch through texts, or emails, or anything.

Rafe had suggested a clean break would make it easier to do that "live life to the fullest" stuff. She'd teased him it was more because he was too lazy, but she had to agree it'd been the right decision. The total cutoff from him had been hard. *Real* hard, but she'd gotten on with her life, and now...

Now she was back in Rocky.

The temptation was strong to ask Trevor Coleman if he'd seen Rafe recently. The words were nearly out of her mouth before she restrained herself. It was too dangerous to ask that personal of a question in case the answer made her sad.

Rafe could have moved away. He could be in a relationship—they'd said they weren't going to wait around for each other.

Passing over a copy of the children's book Trevor wanted, she slipped away for a moment, waiting for her racing heart to settle to a normal pace. She replaced books on the shelves automatically as her thoughts turned to the real question.

What if Rafe *was* with someone?

What if—?

No. She wouldn't do that to herself. If he was with someone, she'd be fine. And if he wasn't, maybe they'd be able to pick up their friendship.

She refused to let her brain go to the section labeled "more than friendship" for all sorts of reasons, the strongest of which—she wasn't sure exactly what she wanted.

On the other side of the stacks, someone spoke sharply, followed by an even louder *hushing* noise. Little children thinking they're being quiet.

Laurel moved quickly toward the children's area where moms and their toddlers were gathered on pillows on the floor, listening to Dawn read out loud, the oversized book twisted toward the group to show off the pictures.

Her gaze drifted past what looked to be an unusually well-behaved gathering of little people toward the magazine section. Trevor was there, but he wasn't alone. He was talking with a blond-haired Coleman, and this time there was no mistaking who it was.

Rafe spoke loudly. "Shut. Up. Not here."

The entire group of toddlers turned and pressed a finger to their lips. "*Shhhhhhhhh.*"

He glanced up, and his gaze met hers, and for a split second she thought she saw hunger before his face twisted into a familiar expression. The same one she'd seen far too many times before—his sweet *who? innocent me?* fake-o one he'd whip out in the hopes whatever trouble they'd gotten into, the punishment would be reduced because they'd *meant* well.

Her feet felt light, and she wanted to dance across the room.

She should have expected it. He would show up and it would be like they've never been apart, only now they were both old enough and smart enough to know what type of trouble they were getting into.

Oh, the trouble they could get into...

Heat rushed in as she moved toward the men. Her cheeks were blazing hot, and she deliberately looked Trevor in the eye before turning to face Rafe.

He winked.

She jerked her gaze away before he set her off giggling. "Would you guys take your conversation outside, please?" she asked primly.

Two could play the innocent game.

Trevor demanded her attention, cocky smile in place as he held forward the *Winnie the Pooh* books she'd found for him. "No problem. Can you help me check these out, first?"

It was as good an excuse as any. She snatched them from his hand along with his library card then all but ran to escape. Behind her, the guys spoke a little more, but quietly enough she didn't need to kick into librarian-police mode, which was good because she probably would've burst out laughing.

Rafe walked out without saying goodbye, which was also a good thing. It let her keep her cool while explaining something inane about how to get a library card to Trevor.

By the time he left her cheeks were cramping from holding back her laughter.

Luckily, Wendy came back on shift right then. Laurel grabbed the shelving cart and fled to the back of the room, hiding in the farthest corner of the library where tall windows stretched from floor to ceiling. She pressed her face against the cool glass in the hopes it would lower her temperature.

It had been three years and she'd never forgotten what he'd said.

Never forgotten what they'd *done*.

Fortunately, some of the items on the cart actually belonged in that corner of the library, so she wasn't completely wasting time as she forced herself to concentrate and accomplish some work. All afternoon she kept waiting for Rafe to return, and being thankful when he didn't.

She left at five o'clock sharp, slipping into her little car and taking the first full breath she'd gotten since spotting him.

Tucked under her windshield wiper was a folded note.

So much for breathing. She jerked open the door and grabbed the note, ripping it open.

Do you want to build a racetrack?

She headed to the schoolyard, heart pounding.

Rafe sat at a picnic table on the edge of the playground. He'd rested his elbows on the tabletop as he stretched his long, jean-clad legs in front of him. She took her time walking across the field to appreciate the view, from the sturdy cowboy boots all the way up to his hair that stuck out slightly from underneath his cowboy hat.

He needed a haircut.

Or maybe not. The slightly ragged length looked good. It fit, and it fit the rest of him as well as she continued admiring him.

Since she'd left, the boy had become a man. The muscles pressing the sleeves of his T-shirt were far more solid. His face had matured to sharper angles, his high cheekbones and square jaw just that much more defined now that he'd moved into his twenties.

The expression in his eyes was the same as she remembered, though. Hell-bent on mischief, and one hundred percent on her side.

Laurel came to a stop a few feet from the table. She didn't quite know where to put her hands. "I missed you."

He rose instantly, not one bit hesitant about where to put his hands. He wrapped her in a big hug, lifting her off her feet as he swung in a wild circle. His hat tipped off backward as he buried his face in her neck and squeezed her close.

She clung to him tightly, wondering how this could feel so much like coming home and still like the beginning.

He lowered her to the ground, leading her to the picnic table to sit. "Couldn't believe it when I heard you were back."

"And I can't believe that nobody stopped in to tell me everything about you," she returned, crawling up on the tabletop. "I figured the minute I hit town, the entire Coleman clan would be in my back pocket, giving me the rundown on everything you've been up to for the last three years."

Rafe shrugged. "I don't think anybody except your family, my mom, and the people we went to school with really remember we were that close."

"That makes no sense. The sheer amount of time we spent in the detention room together means somebody should've noticed."

He laughed. "Yeah, but we're younger. Nobody looks that direction. They were all focused on their own stuff and the people they're chasing." He ignored the rude noise she made. "You know I'm right. It's like hiding shit in plain sight, or above people's heads. Heck, by the time we hit junior high most of my extended family had graduated, and they didn't give a damn about what was happening back in school. We were two years behind my nearest cousins, Lee and Lisa, and three years behind the Six Pack twins. And compared to *them*, we were saints."

"Still think it's weird."

He smiled, stroking his thumb across the back of her hand, and a shiver rolled over her. "Being invisible isn't a bad thing. It means we get to deal with us on our own timing."

"Us?" The word came out a little squeaky.

"*Us.*" He slid his hand over hers, and heat sizzled up her arm. "You're single?"

She nodded, heart in her throat.

"Me too."

Somehow in the past ten seconds every nerve in her body had gone from tingling in anticipation to full-out electric storm. "Oh, boy."

"Right?"

She wanted to move to the next thing very *very* much, whatever that next thing was, but there were enough other things going on, she was worried.

"Rafe... What if I need some time?" A burst of laughter escaped her. "That sounded stupid. It's been three years, and I think I want to...whatever it is we're going to do—"

"Date. We're going to date."

She nodded firmly. "Right. But I'm just back from school and need to figure out some stuff. I'm worried about dealing with my parents, even though they're mostly great, but it's still—"

Rafe soothed her, placing her hand on his thigh before leaning in closer. "I've got bad news, too. I'm going to be gone most of the summer. Just before I heard you were back, Gabe asked me to do pickup and deliveries all over Western Canada, and I promised I would."

Disappointment rushed in, along with relief. "All summer?"

Rafe nodded. "I'll be home only a few days at a time, and none of them with much warning."

It wasn't exactly what she'd been hoping for, but the instant decrease in her stress level told her a lot. "I've been gone for three years, and this is the first time I've held a full-time job." She made a face. "Maybe it's good you won't be around to distract me or get me in trouble."

"Ha. Look who's talking, kettle." He brushed the hair off her face. "God, I missed you. I missed talking to you, getting lectured by you, and the way you blurt out ideas soon as you think of them."

"Gee, thanks. You like all the awkward things about me."

He leaned forward and looked up into her face with a brilliant smile. "Yup, I sure do."

It didn't seem right they were sitting there in the middle of the playground, with three years to catch up on, and she was obsessing over the feel of his thumb against her skin. "Speaking of awkward things, I don't quite know *how* we're planning to do this."

Do this. It sounded far too sexual.

She glanced up to discover his eyes had gone dark with desire.

Oh boy.

As usual, Rafe had far more control than she did. "I don't want you to have to put up with the Coleman Inquisition, so I suggest we wait."

"Wait for sex?" Drat. She didn't miss his sharp intake of breath. She couldn't see his face, though, because she'd buried her face in her hands. "Go, Laurel. Silver-tongued as usual."

His soft laughter slid over her. He put an arm around her shoulders, squeezing briefly before letting her go without offering anything more intimate. "September sixth."

She checked his expression closer, pretty sure he wasn't suggesting that as the date for sex. "Go on."

A slow, heated look rolled over his face. "We met September sixth, so how about we wait until then to start over?"

"You'll be done traveling?"

"And you'll have time to settle in without anyone giving you grief about me popping in and out of your life like a broken jack-in-the-box."

"I don't care what people say," she insisted. "It's not that."

"I do," he snapped back. "About this? About *you*? I want it clear from the first minute we're together that you're *mine*. No one will take me seriously if I'm gone ninety percent of the time, not even you."

Too many questions shoved forward. Did his resolve to be taken seriously have something to do with recent events? Three years was a long time. A lot could have happened...

A lot *had* happened.

Laurel gazed across at her best friend who had no idea what had shaken down in her recent life. The only way to know if they had a future, though, was to try.

She nodded firmly in acceptance. "September sixth? It's a date."

His smile widened. "Hell, yeah, it's a date. I'll pick you up."

"Wait—" She hesitated to mention it, but... "What about Trevor? He saw you in the library. He knows something's going on."

Rafe's grin morphed back to his *aww-shucks* one. "I told him I was lusting over you, but too chicken to ask you out."

Her jaw fell open, and she hurried to snap it back into position. "You? *Chicken?* Does he even *know* you?"

"Not as well as he thinks." Rafe's smile faded.

Definitely things to relearn about each other.

She eyed him for a long moment, wondering what was the right move next. Did she shake his hand then head home? Hug him farewell?

Kiss him passionately the way she really wanted to?

"Not only have you failed to learn how to lie, you've got a terrible poker face." Rafe cupped her chin. "I want to kiss you too, but we're waiting, remember?"

She flushed. "Then why even mention it?"

"Because I want you to think about it all summer while we're apart. Think about how the next time I see you, we won't be waiting anymore." The deep velvet of his voice stroked her as surely as the motion of his thumb over her lips. "When I see you in September, I'm going to take a hell of a long time relearning how you taste, and what makes you moan, and what makes you scream."

The temperature seemed to have soared in the past few minutes.

Laurel made a show of fanning herself if only to distract him from how hard her pulse was beating—had to be nearly loud enough he could hear it. "Good job, DC."

Rafe raised a brow. "Devil child? Wow, I haven't heard that one for a long time."

"If the shoe fits..." She rose to her feet, walking at his side back to the parking lot.

"It doesn't fit," he insisted as she crawled into her car. He lowered himself beside her, reaching across her lap to do up her seatbelt. The movement squeezed them together for a brief instant, and she sucked for air.

"I'm not a child anymore," he informed her clearly. He pressed his lips to her cheek then murmured, "I'm all grown up, and I can't wait to prove it to you."

She had trouble swallowing as he stepped back, offering a cocky smile before sauntering away.

Chapter Three

September 5th

THE SKY overhead was robin-egg blue, with not a single wispy cloud anywhere to be seen—a typical Alberta fall day. It was warm enough Rafe had his window rolled down as he traveled the final miles along a familiar gravel road.

He pulled to a stop at the top of the hill to stare over the Angel Coleman land. From his vantage point, the new buildings he and his brother had raised the past couple years shone in the midday sun. Bright red barns with cheerful white trim turned the pastoral scene into something out of a magazine. There was no sign of Gabe's house, though, except for a welcoming thread of smoke rising from the thick forest hiding it from the road.

The log building might be out of sight, but Rafe knew behind those trees sat a house full of warmth and laughter.

His gaze drifted farther to the west where the original Angel homestead lay on a small rise across from Crown land, the buildings worn by time. The ravages of neglect were clear even from this distance.

As he restarted the engine and headed toward Gabe's, the contrast between what his brother had and what Rafe had to look forward to hit hard. Back at the homestead there would be no welcoming fire, no homey goodness to anticipate. At least not yet...

It had been good to be away for the summer. Hard, because he was itching to get together with Laurel, but after twenty-two years in the same place, two months on the road had given him a new appreciation for coming home.

Home meaning the people he loved, not the building he'd grown up in.

Time away from Ben had been good as well. Didn't matter that he knew his father was a bitter old man, it still took a lot of energy to avoid falling into doom-and-gloom mode after working around him.

And considering that imitating the man was the last thing on earth Rafe wanted—he refused to give the bastard the satisfaction—joining him in asshole-hood was out of the question.

He pulled into the yard at Gabe and Allison's, admiring the additional changes they'd made over the summer.

His sister-in-law hurried out of the house, waving at him before adjusting his nephew who was balanced on her hip.

"Glad I caught you at home," he called out the window.

"Been waiting for you. Gabe had to go into town, and he figured you'd like to know where to drop those animals." Allison marched up to the window and offered a warm smile. "Good to have you back. We missed you."

He reached out the window and rubbed a hand over Micah's soft brown hair. "Of course you did. I'm charming, a hard worker, and the best babysitter you've ever had."

"Modest, as well."

"That goes without saying."

She chuckled as she passed on the instructions.

He pulled the trailer around to the new barn, transferring the stock into the pens his brother had prepared. Their organic farm status was growing more viable every year, and all the Angel ranch gains were because of Gabe and his brilliant wife.

Rafe took a moment to lean on the fence and watch the load of breeders explore their new home.

"Sturdy-looking animals," Allison said, joining him at the side of the rail. She wore a kid carrier—the type that let her carry Micah on her back and keep her hands free. The little guy had a thumb in his mouth, but his eyes were wide as he leaned to one side and reached his free hand toward the sheep.

"They cost enough. Hopefully they turn out to be worth it." Rafe gave the backpack a wiggle. "That's a neat contraption."

"Micah loves it, which has made getting chores done a whole lot easier. Ten-month-olds don't understand the concept of 'in a while'." Allison twisted beside him, staring up at his face. "You look tired."

Rafe shrugged. "I got up early. I was done with being on the road and wanted to get home."

She hesitated before asking, "You sure you want to go back to living over the garage at Ben and Dana's?"

The concern in her eyes was there for a good reason. Yeah, he didn't want to admit it, but his impulsive move out of the place he'd been renting with his cousin might not have been a good decision. "I'm pretty sure my old place is gone—Jesse's probably found a new place or roommates. I don't plan to stay at the apartment long term, but it's good enough for a while."

"You know our door is always open."

Which would make things worse between him and his dad—bad enough he agreed with the changes Gabe and Allison had implemented. If he moved in with them, the gap between the generations would widen even further.

He offered Allison a quick hug, surprised again to discover he was now bigger than her. "You guys are awesome, but I need to figure out the next thing on my own."

She nodded but offered a mild scolding. "You go ahead and figure it out, but you are *never* on your own. Not in this family."

"Because Angel Boy Coleman always has something to say?" he teased. If he'd been called a devil by his friends, Gabe had always been the opposite.

"Because your brother has two ears and he likes to listen even more than he likes to talk," Allison answered. She walked with him back to the truck. "Come for supper if you'd like."

"Later this week? I'm pretty sure Mom will insist that I—"

"Oh, shoot." Allison put a hand on his shoulder and twisted him back toward the barn. "Can you load up a half dozen of the goats and take them to your mom's? She asked if I'd bring them over, and I nearly forgot."

Rafe didn't bother to hide his smile as he headed out willingly. "You're getting forgetful in your old age. And what the heck does my mom need goats for?"

Allison pulled to a complete stop and looked utterly confused. "You know, she didn't say. Or I can't remember if she did."

"Definitely going senile."

She stuck out her tongue. "Sleep deprivation. Just wait. Someday you'll get to experience the joy of parenthood as well."

He loaded the goats into the massive trailer then pulled out from the yard and headed over to the homestead, his amusement fading as he prepared himself for whatever he found there.

A night-and-day difference hit as he drove the long approach to the house where he'd grown up. Faded paint had begun to peel off the shutters, and the barns were past that point where they looked weathered and well used. These looked weathered and edging toward falling apart.

Huge potholes greeted him on the drive, along with a nasty crop of wild thistles thriving on either side of the entrance. Another shit job on the to-do list already—he got to deal with noxious weeds as well as break out the tractor and level the road. Maybe call in for some extra road crush.

His father had insisted he wanted to be in charge of the road, but obviously over the summer he'd failed to keep up with what should be a normal maintenance task. If it wasn't done soon, they were going to end up with damage to their vehicles.

Frustration hit harder. If Ben was going to do a job, Rafe didn't know why he didn't do a thorough job of it, considering that's what he'd always demanded of the boys back in the day when all three of them worked side-by-side.

Rafe noted with some satisfaction his dad's truck was missing from the yard. Probably hanging out at the coffee shop with the rest of the old timers, bitching about how much life had changed and what hassles their kids were.

The less he saw of his father, the better. He might've decided he was going to have a good attitude about a bad situation, but it was decidedly easier to keep from falling into pissed-off frustration when he was nowhere near the man.

Rafe parked by the barn, hurrying toward where the doors stood open. An old ranch truck and trailer they rarely used anymore were backed into position where he least expected it.

He rounded the corner to discover his mom, her tiny frame wrapped in a coverall, attempting to corral some of the lambs into the trailer.

"Hey," he called out in warning.

Her head snapped up and she jerked back for a moment before offering a smile, fingers tightening in the woolly coat at her feet. "Rafe. I didn't expect to see you yet."

He stepped forward to stop the three lambs already loaded from escaping, strong-arming them into place and putting up the low gate that was ready at hand. He raised his voice to be heard over the loud bleating. "I made good time. I figured a nice lazy Sunday afternoon off would be better than hanging out on the highway. What're you doing?"

"Community fair this afternoon. The Baptist church is running the petting zoo. I promised we'd provide the animals." Dana glanced away. "Just a few."

"I don't care how many. Why're you out here by yourself?" He scooped up the lamb and placed the noisy creature with its siblings behind the gate. "Where's Ben?"

She shrugged. "He must've forgotten. It's not a big deal. I can get them there by myself."

37

Rafe folded his arms and looked down from his additional inches, feeling a little as if he were the parent and she were the child who hadn't quite thought this through. "Sure you can. And once you're there, you can also safely wrangle a half dozen sheep plus whatever else you plan to bring along, all by yourself."

His mom had the grace to look guilty.

"Especially since there's going to be a whole lot of kids running around, probably screaming their heads off and wanting to touch. Jumping up and down, rushing the animals—yeah, I can see how it makes perfect sense for one person to do that all by themselves."

Dana rolled her eyes. "Sarcasm doesn't become you, son."

"Was I being sarcastic?"

She ignored the question, speaking over her shoulder as she headed into the back of the barn. "I made a commitment, and I'm getting the animals there. And I'm not foolish. Your cousin Karen is meeting me. She's bringing some horses, and I was going to let her help."

"Great. Between the three of us we should be able to—"

"Rafe," she scolded loudly from behind the pen wall. "I don't expect you to give up your afternoon to help me."

He could out-stubborn her. "I didn't really have anything else planned, and as you said, you made a commitment. What else do we need to round up?"

Dana reappeared around the corner leading their old, placid donkey, Homer. "Three or four goats. I asked Allison to drop them off—she should be here soon."

"I've already got them." He grabbed the donkey's head rope and guided the beast into position inside the trailer, coming back for a pitchfork to load hay to quiet the animals. "I need to get changed first, though. Even if we're working with the animals, I doubt everyone at the picnic will appreciate my current state of aroma."

"There's time," his mom assured him. "If we get everything set up by two o'clock, that works. Scoot. I'll finish pulling everything together."

Ben forgetting about the commitment he'd made was par for the course. Of all the things Rafe worried about helping his mom with, the fair was an annoyance, nothing more.

He hurried to the long staircase that led to the great room over the garage where he once again hung his hat. His things were still in boxes—he'd moved quickly during a single twenty-four-hour period he'd been back in Rocky at the start of summer. He'd wanted to be close enough that if his mom needed him, he'd be there.

That had been before the whole traveling-all-summer bit had registered.

He hurried to the shower, scrubbing away the dirt and dust of the road. Of course, *while* he was in the shower was when it hit that he would probably end up seeing Laurel at some point today.

It was a thought he really should avoid while naked and wet.

His recent daydreams were close to being possible. Considering how many of his ideas were dirty, it was amazing he got out of the shower as quickly as he did, hurrying as if he were headed back to school in the fall, eager to catch up with his friend.

His mom chatted the whole way into town about pretty much nothing, excited to be able to tell him everything she was working on.

They made it to the fairgrounds where his mom pointed out the tents and makeshift corral at the side of the parking lot. By three o'clock the parking lot was full of cars, and the designated area where they'd set up straw bales covered with burlap sacks was full of families.

His cousin Karen had corralled her younger sister, Lisa, to come out as well.

Lisa offered a pleased smile as she sauntered in and took over helping the kids take turns climbing up on the bales to crawl onto Homer's back. "Look who's back. Hey, cuz."

"Hey, Lis. You doing good?"

"Doing great. You know me—always one step ahead of trouble."

"Makes me think you're the one causing trouble and leaving it in your wake," he teased.

"Shh. That's a secret." She gave Rafe a wink as she led the old beast around the blocked-off area designated for them. Karen was with the horses in a nearby pen, and Rafe...

Well, he stood ankle deep in lambs, goats and kids with his mom, helping toddlers to "pet the pretties" without the kids, human-type, getting bumped out of the makeshift pen by some too eager critter.

People wandered everywhere. Music blasted in the background as the temperature soared like on a summer day. He kept looking around for Laurel without admitting as much to himself, but her blonde hair was nowhere to be seen in the crowd.

Instead, Rafe spotted her father first. Pastor Dave marched through the crowds, nodding in greeting to the families he passed, but he kept moving in a straight line obviously aimed at Rafe.

Guilt and a healthy allotment of apprehension percolated in his belly.

The man had to be close to Ben's age, but his neatly trimmed beard and mustache were shot only with the faintest hint of silvery white, and ample smile lines decorated the corners of his eyes. He was nearly as tall as Rafe, looking him in the face as he approached. Everything Rafe knew about the man put him firmly into "not Ben" territory.

He was still the leader of his mom's church, a place where Rafe hadn't willingly stepped for over seven years, *and* he was the father of the woman he intended to get involved with.

Not to mention the other guilt-inducing bits of history, secret and not so secret. Nope, it wasn't fear Rafe felt, but there were a whole lot of ways this could go awkward, real fast.

Fortunately, the man nodded briskly as if delighted to see him before offering a firm handshake. "Rafe Coleman. Thank you for taking time out of your day to help us out."

"No problem. Glad to help."

"Still appreciated." The sound of laughter and music swelled for a moment, pulling their attention to the crowds even as Pastor Dave continued. "When your mom offered to supply the animals, I wondered if I'd see you. And look, here you are."

Here I am. Rafe kept his smile firmly in place. "Yes, sir."

"You're welcome to join us, any time. Not just when there are animals to manage."

"Yes, sir."

The other man smiled. "I know. I know. You've got other things going on." He clapped Rafe on the shoulder then seemed to remember something. "Hey, I wanted to mention. We've got a new candidate visiting. Nice young man, only a few years older than you. We're considering hiring him as a youth pastor, but he'd also help with College and Careers members. If you remember, that's the people about your age." He gave a self-depreciating chuckle. "Sitting and listening to me ramble isn't on everyone's to-do list, but this fellow is pretty sharp. I bet he'll get some great activities going. Nonchurch-y ones. You might want to take part."

Rafe wondered briefly if they had a quota like the police did when it came to handing out tickets. Like—so many nonmembers they had to try to pull back into the fold on a regular basis. Only the invitation was said with such sincerity, he couldn't get upset, or respond rudely.

Besides, his mom would tan his hide if she found out he'd been impolite to the pastor. Didn't matter if she was a foot shorter and a hundred pounds lighter.

And that didn't even take into consideration Rafe's plans for Laurel...

"Think on it," Pastor Dave admonished.

"Yes, sir."

It was an honest answer. He had every intention of thinking on it, but he already knew the answer was *hell no.*

Thankfully, one of the goats made a break for it. Rafe tipped his chin briefly then turned away to deal with beasts and babes.

It took a solid hour before the area was less noisy and most of the wiggling children had left, and Rafe had time to look around. There were people from the church as well as a lot of family and friends dropping in to take part in the picnic. Rafe counted no less than nineteen family members over the course of the afternoon.

Suddenly he was looking at an angel. He caught hold of the bale in front of him with both hands as if that would stop the instant response of his body.

Two months had been far too long, and he took in every detail hungrily. Laurel had left her long blonde hair down over her bare shoulders, the silky strands so pale in the sunlight she seemed not of this world. Jean shorts and a plain black tank top covered her curves, and her feet...

Shockingly pink runners that made him grin.

She wasn't wearing anything too revealing, but his imagination was more than adequate to fill in the details. Imagination, and the fact he'd been daydreaming about her the entire summer. Small pert breasts and sweet curves were balanced over long legs that he'd woken up dreaming about far too often.

Yup. Rafe was one-hundred-percent fool when it came to Laurel Sitko, and it was about time everybody found out he was carrying a torch.

Their gazes met across the distance and—

He'd heard of people who'd been struck by lightning losing the ability to move, as if their feet were glued to the ground. It was like that for him. Nothing worked right, except his heart that took off into a racing tempo that left him breathless and lightheaded just looking at the woman.

She'd frozen the instant their eyes met. The sudden stop left her partially off-balance, and she had to scramble to keep herself upright. Rafe laughed, not at her, but with her, feeling the same stunned sensation that had obviously hit her.

Instead of returning his amusement, her tongue slipped over her lips, and her head tilted downward as her gaze stayed fixed on his. As if she were praying and her heavenly requests had come true.

The weeks and months and years they'd been apart vanished, and all he could think about was marching across the yard, sweeping her up and taking her back to his place to disappear for a few weeks.

His place—a one-bedroom apartment in his parents' yard...

Oh hell, he hadn't thought that part out very well.

Rafe kicked his own butt as he broke the eye lock between them and focused on the kids, animal-type, that were trying to eat his shirt.

Now that he knew she was there, their reunion was inevitable. He found himself checking on her as she paced through the crowd. They darted glances at each other, offering flirty smiles.

He was so ready to get rolling on the next stage— and not just fooling around. He'd *missed* her over the past years, dammit.

Because he was being a busybody, Rafe spotted her father stepping away from a group of what had to be church elders, a well-dressed young man at his side. Probably the youth pastor he'd been told about. Rafe's age, or slightly older. The fellow was handsome enough and held himself as if he might actually survive a day's hard labour.

Not that Rafe was looking for a new best friend.

Only because he'd been watching so closely did he see it. Laurel's gaze caught on the potential youth pastor.

Rafe shot to his feet, moving before he realized it. Even across the distance it was clear all the blood had drained from Laurel's face. She swayed for a second before stumbling to the nearest upright post to clutch at it.

What the heck?

One broad leap took him over the low fence surrounding the animal pen as he raced toward her, the urgent need to protect screaming to the forefront.

Oblivious to his approach, she took one more frantic glance at the young man then turned her back, marching steadily toward the parking lot as if she'd remembered an urgent errand.

Rafe raced the final few steps to catch her by the arm and turn her toward him as he checked her over worriedly.

"What's up?"

She didn't answer, yanking herself free from his grasp then taking another couple steps.

"Laurel." A masculine shout carried in their direction.

She didn't glance over in acknowledgment. Instead, it seemed her pace increased, widening the distance between them as rapidly as possible.

"You know him?" Rafe demanded in a whisper as he hurried at her side.

"Later, Rafe," she snapped.

Screw this. He tugged her around the corner behind the cookie-and-coffee tent, holding her in place as he caught her by the chin and looked her straight in the eyes. "Laurel. What's wrong?"

Her mouth opened and then closed tightly, lips pressed together.

It was probably twisted and wrong, but he needed to do *something* to snap her out of whatever was causing this reaction. His first instinct was his *only* instinct. The only thing he wanted to do.

He pulled her against him and kissed her.

Chapter Four

FOR A brief second, an entire battalion of emotions struggled for headline billing. Confusion, and disbelief—that couldn't actually have been Jeff Lawson she'd spotted in the crowd at the Rocky Mountain House Fall Fair.

Frustration and guilt and old-fashioned anger joined the party as another bolt of agony shot through her, only...

Well, there was a whole lot of history she didn't want to be thinking about, so it was a good thing she had something *else* to concentrate on at that moment. Something like the fact that Rafe Coleman was kissing her senseless. Tall, solid and handsome Rafe, who she'd been dreaming about all summer even as she'd tried to settle into town.

It'd helped her work ethic not to have him around. She could now do her job at the library in her sleep, and she'd met new friends. Established some routines.

But the entire time there'd been an aching Rafe-sized hole in her life.

His mouth against hers was better than a dream because it was real. Firm and commanding, Rafe teased with his lips as his hands took control of her body. Laurel was pretty sure they weren't supposed to be doing this. Not here, not now, but it was so very wrong, it was right.

He held her in his strong arms, one hand pressed to her lower back to bring their bodies together tighter. She regretted the layers between them even though she was hanging out in shorts and a tank, and he wore his typical jeans and flannel shirt. The thin layers were far too much. She wanted skin. Lots and lots of naked Rafe.

Scandalous, yes, but true.

If she wasn't able to feel the finer details of his firm shoulder muscles under his shirt, she had nothing to complain about the connection between their lips. His other hand cradled the back of her head and held her in place as he traced his tongue over her lips and went in for another kiss. Tender, yet not. Careful, yet still on the wild side. It didn't seem as if Rafe was worried about overwhelming her, but more as if he was holding himself on a tight leash.

Which, man-oh-man did she ever want to experience him going for it at one-hundred-percent.

He stepped forward, pressing one leg between hers. It felt like the most natural thing in the world to move in closer, when reality kicked in with a vengeance.

They stood only feet away from a whole lot of people who would not consider making out in public an appropriate activity for them. For her.

And that wasn't even considering Jeff—

Oh no. *Jeff.*

She jerked her hands down to Rafe's chest, pushing him away as she sucked in a deep breath of air.

His gaze darted over her face as he tucked a stray strand of hair behind her ear. Utterly calm and relaxed, as if there was nothing else he was supposed to do right then except hold her in his arms and kiss her.

She liked that idea far too much, which is why it surprised her when her words snapped out sharper than expected. "What're you doing?"

"Kissing you."

"I noticed that, but I mean *why* are you kissing me?"

Rafe leaned his shoulder against the post next to them, arms draped around her. "Because I wanted to. Because it looked like you needed it."

"I can't deal with this right now," Laurel muttered, wondering if she had time to escape around the backside of the tent before Jeff found them. He had most definitely been headed her direction.

"Because of that fellow your dad was telling me about?"

"Who?"

"The guy you were running away from."

Drat. He wasn't supposed to have noticed. "Jeff."

Rafe raised a brow. "So that's his name."

Laurel shook herself, trying to make sense of what was going on even as her brain continued to whirl. Next attempt. "Rafe, what are you doing?"

"You asked me that already. I told you. You okay to stand on your own?"

Embarrassed, she realized she'd been leaning against the long, hard length of him. She went to retreat, but his arms remained firmly in position, holding her in place.

"Want to let go?"

"Not particularly."

She narrowed her gaze. "Rafe Coleman, let me go this instant."

He did, stepping to one side.

Disappointment shouldn't have been her first emotional response. Laurel told herself to be quiet and do the next thing, which the plan book said was escape.

Stupid timing.

Jeff appeared around the corner, his glance taking in her and Rafe with a great deal of curiosity and a bit of concern. "Everything okay back here?"

Rafe used the hand resting on her hip to pull her against his side. "No troubles. Welcome to Rocky. I'm Rafe Coleman."

He held his free hand toward Jeff who shook it briefly as he introduced himself.

"Jeff Lawson. Good to meet you." He turned his dark brown eyes on Laurel, looking her over carefully. Intimately. "Hey. Long time."

What did she say? What did she do?

What she'd *like* to do was haul back and plant her fist in his smug face, but that probably wouldn't be very appropriate.

Instead she answered with as little emotion as possible. "Years, actually."

He had the grace to look uncomfortable, as he very well should, and right then she was kind of happy Rafe had her propped up against him as if they were already an item.

She twisted her head to offer Rafe a lover-ish smile as if this was old hat to her. If they could procrastinate for long enough, maybe Jeff would get bored and leave, and she wouldn't need to talk to him one on one.

No such luck.

"I should get back to the animals before someone decides to try goat wrestling." Rafe placed his mouth near her ear and lowered his voice. "You want to come with me?"

He was a darling for trying to give her an out, but leaving was impossible. She checked her watch. "I'm due at the face-painting station in a few minutes."

"I guess our kissing break is over then," he joked, offering Jeff a cheeky smile. "They're never long enough in my opinion."

Jeff didn't say anything.

She had no idea what he thought about Rafe's comment because she refused to look at him. Her face was hot, and her heart was pounding, and she was very thankful when Rafe tugged her with him into the open area in front of the tent, Jeff following like a ghostly annoyance.

"See you later, hon." Rafe squeezed her fingers. "Same place next break?"

"*Rafe*." Her cheeks flashed even hotter at his sexy laugh. He gave her one final cocky grin, then tipped his chin at Jeff and left.

She was back in the safety of the crowd, only Laurel didn't feel safe. She'd lost that the moment she laid eyes on the last person she'd ever wanted to see.

Somehow she had to get through the next few minutes, that's all. Laurel dug deep for something to say. She hoped for casual, but what came out was anything but. "I didn't know you were coming to Rocky."

"It was a new development. Came up pretty quick." Jeff folded his arms, glancing over to where Rafe was stepping back into the animal pen. "I didn't know you were involved with anyone."

"It's a new development. Came up pretty quick," she deadpanned.

Understatement of the year. Her lips still tingled, and her entire body was hot. She couldn't pull her gaze away from Rafe, and her heart leapt into high gear when she discovered his eyes on her, mouth twisted into a wicked grin.

What had she done? Now Jeff would think for sure she and Rafe were involved. Which, they totally planned on happening, but not at the speed of light. The inevitable questions from her family were a bit of a panic inducer, but in a way, she was glad to have something else to worry about other than why in the world Jeff Lawson was hanging out in her backyard.

The deep pain in her chest that had finally faded to a dull, constant ache over the past two years flared, stabbing like daggers as she looked him over. "Why're you here?"

"Isn't it obvious? I'm candidating for a position."

No. Way. God, tell me he's joking. He's got *to be joking.* "Seriously? At my father's church?"

"It's not your father's."

Even though she'd promised a long time ago to stop punching people, the temptation was very strong at that moment. "You know what I mean. I can't believe you think that's a good idea."

She could've sworn he was about to reach for her before choosing instead to adjust his coat.

He offered his patented understanding smile. "Obviously, I do think it's a good idea. I was asked, and I'll go where I'm called to serve. I always loved the descriptions you shared about Rocky Mountain House. I think we could have a lot to look forward to once we put the past behind us."

Only there was no moving past some things, and explaining that to him—she didn't even know why she should have to try. Luckily, with a whole lot of the community milling about them, this wasn't the time or place.

"I need to get going." She turned away.

He caught her by the wrist before she could escape. "Not even an 'it's good to see you' for me, Laurel?" He caressed her with his voice.

Laurel jerked her hand free, mad enough to spit nails. What an asshole move on his part, for so many reasons. He was married, and he was practically begging her to fawn over him? She wasn't sure why she was surprised, though—it was always all about him. He had a far too healthy sense of his own importance.

"I've never been a very good liar," she reminded him. And then before he could speak, she delivered her parting shot. "I won't keep you from your duties. I'm sure I'll see you and *Jessica* sometime in the next few days."

Her feet moved fast enough to be a run, escaping quickly to where she could surround herself with little people as a wall of protection.

There were a lot of good things she'd enjoyed since coming back to Rocky at the start of summer. Family. New friends. And now that Rafe was here, she had even more to look forward to.

Jeff...complicated matters. Sent her happy thoughts into an emotional spiral she was desperate not to return to.

Rafe tracked her down before he left. The hour she'd had to cool off while painting cat stripes and whiskers on toddler faces had done wonders for her nerves, and seeing him striding vigorously toward her gave her the final push she needed to adjust most of her attitude to a better place.

Most...not all.

He caught her by the arm, fingers curling around her biceps as he squeezed lightly. "Are you feeling better?"

"I wasn't sick. And if I was, ick, it's kind of gross you decided to up and kiss me."

His lips twisted into a grin. "I have no germs you need to worry about."

Frustration lingered. Jeff was certain to say something to her father. Maybe ask about *Laurel's boyfriend*, and while they had plans, that kiss Rafe had given had been wonderful *and* complicated things. "Did you take leave of your senses? There was no need for you to storm over there and put me in an impossible situation."

Shock flickered in his eyes. "You looked scared to death."

"You were rescuing me."

"Only a little." His smile widened as his hand drifted down her bare arm. "Mostly I was kissing you."

Laurel felt like stomping her foot on the ground. "Can we stop talking about that?"

"We can stop talking about it if we want to go somewhere so we can do more of it. I'm good with that scenario."

She rolled her eyes. "Rafe. How about we slow down to something a little more manageable?"

"We did slow down. All summer long." He stepped closer, stroking his fingers through her hair. "It's time we get things rolling."

While she mostly agreed, she was exhausted and confused, and what she really needed was to get away from the people glancing at them with curiosity. "I can't do this now. I know you were trying to help, and I was a little shaky for a while there, but I'm okay. Let's plan to get together tomorrow."

His amusement faded, concern rising in its place. "My mom's waiting for me, and I have to drive her home, but how about I stop by your place a little later?"

It was like a flashback to high school when he'd get on a topic and hound her over and over until she caved. Not this time. "The sheep must've been really loud this afternoon."

He eyed her. "Not particularly, why?"

"Because you've obviously lost your hearing. I said not today. It's not even the sixth," she pointed out triumphantly. "So, text me or something. I've got to go."

Laurel twirled on her heel, head held high, ready to...

She grumbled in frustration. Her departure couldn't be nearly as impressive as she'd intended. She desperately wanted to avoid meeting up with Jeff, or her father, or her mother or—anyone, really.

So instead of marching away like a strong, determined woman, she ducked into the coffee tent and took the long way around to where her car was parked, crawling into the tiny thing to escape as quietly as possible.

Of course, checking in her rearview mirror she discovered Rafe stood there in plain sight, waving after her until she turned onto the main road.

WELL. THAT wasn't what he'd expected from the afternoon.

Rafe drove his mom home and unloaded the animals, heading back to his place bemused by the whole situation.

Obviously there was some history between Laurel and Jeff, and he couldn't wait to get to the bottom of it.

He didn't feel guilty for having deceived the fellow about Laurel and him going out. He might have rushed the truth a little, but who the hell cared? It was time they both did something for themselves. She'd make him happy, and he'd make her happy at the same time.

Rafe hurried through another shower while scrolling through the long list of things he needed to deal with as soon as possible.

He should drop in at Gabe and Allison's to catch up with his brother regarding plans for the next few weeks. He should touch base with the cousins he'd been ignoring all summer, especially Jesse and Trevor. The memory of him feeding Trevor a cock-and-bull story earlier that summer about how dating Laurel was an impossible dream flashed back and made him laugh. He couldn't wait to see Trevor's face when he realized he'd been played.

Yeah, there were a whole lot of things he should do that night, but what he needed most was to see Laurel and make sure things were clear between them.

Still, he couldn't toss off everything entirely. He hauled out his phone and sent Gabe a text.

Rafe: *I'm back. Obviously. What's on for this week?*

The answer came not a minute later.

Gabe: *Glad you survived the summer, bro. Sleep in. Stop by the house for lunch and we'll get caught up.*

Rafe: *Deal. Want me to grab anything?*

Gabe: *Nah. We've been saving leftovers for you for weeks.*

Rafe smiled as he put away his phone, able to focus on his more immediate plans. Laurel. There was one way to approach this—full steam ahead.

Only in light of having gotten her back up, even though he'd been trying to help, Rafe made a slight detour before parking on the street and making his way to the stairs that led down to her small basement apartment.

He carefully made his way down the stone steps to the entrance to her basement suite. There wasn't even a peephole in the door.

Thankfully when she opened to his knock, only a thin crack of light appeared as she peered at him past the security chain. "Rafe?"

He held forward the batch of flowers. "It's September sixth somewhere."

Laurel rolled her eyes but then smiled, pushing the door closed. An instant later the chain dropped with a rattle, and she opened up and let him in.

"I should make you stand out there until it's the sixth on Mountain time, but I want the flowers."

Rafe snickered. "I've got chocolates, as well."

She slipped over to the small kitchen area and brought out a jar for a vase. "I bet you eat more than half of them," she teased.

He put the box down on the table, standing beside the counter she was currently hiding behind. "You're in a better mood than before."

"I figured you'd show up." She took a moment to arrange the flowers, fussing over them more than expected. When she lifted her eyes to meet his, she wore a rueful smile. "This afternoon was not about you. I got surprised, and it threw me. I'm sorry I was rude."

"Surprises can do that to you." He avoided mentioning Jeff's name.

She leaned on the refrigerator, folding her arms as she looked him over. "I'm glad you're here. And the flowers and chocolates are a nice touch."

Her smile warmed him. "I never used to buy you that stuff."

Laurel shrugged. "We weren't dating."

There was a moment as they just stared at each other, a little bit awkward but tangled up with a whole lot of anticipation. "We weren't. But we were close."

"Real close." She stepped toward the tiny living space where an old couch and single chair faced an even older sound system and TV.

He wasn't surprised when she sat in the armchair.

He settled on the couch, looking her over and making no attempt to hide the attraction he felt. "But it's been three years, right?"

She nodded, her ponytail swaying. "The good thing is we've got a solid foundation, so dating should work."

Rafe felt his lips twitch. "I'm pretty sure dating will work just fine." Awkward. Hesitant. So *very* awkward, and while it made total sense, he needed to fix it. "Want to go for a walk?"

She shot to her feet. "Perfect."

"Almost as perfect as suggesting we build a racetrack."

She grabbed a light coat from a hook beside the door, smiling over her shoulder. "Almost, but I don't expect you to reach my levels of awesomeness immediately. Pull the door closed after you—I've got keys."

She led him to the front walkway, and they headed down the sidewalk side by side. It was early enough there were still kids playing in the street, and lights were just beginning to shine in living room windows.

"How'd your summer go?" Rafe asked. They had to start somewhere, and that seemed safer than bringing up Jeff and her reaction to the man.

"Pretty good. I've settled in at the library. No problems there. Wendy and Dawn are good to work with, and they've got some neat programs that are fun. It makes work enjoyable." She bumped her elbow into his side. "What about you? Any idea how many miles you did?"

"God, I don't even want to figure that out. A lot. I think I visited every remote farm in rural Saskatchewan and Manitoba, and I now know exactly which roads I shouldn't ever drive while hauling a trailer."

She snickered. "Had to do some creative manoeuvering, did you?"

"I had to back up for a good mile one time. Remember when I was teaching you how to drive, and you got stuck between the barns at the Moonshine Ranch?"

"You promised to never bring that up again," Laurel returned. "Seriously, that bad?"

"Worse. It was dark." He got a laugh out of that, and suddenly things between them felt a little more comfortable. "How's your family?"

Laurel pointed across the road to where a trail led toward the outskirts of Rocky. "Leslie and her husband are slightly less delighted that I'm back than they were at first because I'm not willing to instantly show up to be super-sister babysitter at the drop of a hat. My mom slapped my name back up on the schedule for playing piano at church so fast even I was surprised."

"You still play?"

She made a rude noise. "Not nearly as well as I used to, especially since they've added new songs to the list." She lifted her eyes to meet his and offered a mischievous smile. "First week they had me in, I played the classic version to a song instead of the modern variation. The old-timers were delighted."

Rafe laughed. "As long as you're having fun."

And as long as she didn't expect him to join her anytime soon.

He glanced over, suddenly realizing his non-participation might be an issue. It hadn't been when they were friends, but now that they were dating, did she expect him to become a full-fledged member of the church? Because that wasn't on his agenda, but it wasn't something he wanted to talk about that instant, either.

Changing the topic seemed prudent.

"What else did you do this summer?"

They were in a nicer residential area now, a new development on the edge of town. Laurel seemed very focused on the houses passing by. "I got invited to go dancing, and to a party, and speed dating. Plus I had lunch out a whole bunch of times."

Curious how quickly an uninvited sensation struck. "Trying to make me jealous, Sitko?"

"Me? Never." She turned innocent blue eyes his direction. "Is it working?"

"More than you think."

She patted his arm. "Don't worry, I didn't do the speed dating, or the dancing, and for the rest of the time my date was Nicole Adams."

Interesting. "She's quite the wild child for you to be hanging out with."

"Not really. She's been seeing Troy Thompson—" Laurel jerked to a stop. "Oh no, you probably didn't hear yet. Troy was in a pretty bad accident a couple days ago."

"Shit. He gonna be okay?" Troy was one of the sort-of-related-by-marriage people in town—they needed a record book to keep track of all the Coleman players— and he'd hate to hear things were seriously wrong.

"Yeah, he'll be fine. He's already itching to get out of the hospital. Nicole was pretty worried, but it looks as if Troy was pretty lucky."

They talked a little longer about other people they both knew. Laurel mentioned who else she'd bumped into over the summer, and Rafe caught her up on their classmates who'd moved away during the previous years.

They deliberately avoided any more delicate topics, but by the time they got back to Laurel's they were a lot more comfortable than they had been. More like getting together those first days after a long summer break when they hadn't seen a lot of each other.

Rafe stopped her before they could descend the staircase. "I'm not going to come in," he warned.

This time Laurel smiled. "That's probably wise."

"No probably about it." Rafe moved in closer, resting his hands on her hips because he had to touch her. "Dating, but at a proper pace. That's what you said this afternoon."

"Just because I said it doesn't mean it's really what I want to do," Laurel whispered, her gaze darting over his face.

"Me neither, but it's not even September sixth here in Rocky."

She snickered before nodding in agreement. Her hands drifted up his body until she was playing with the hair at the back of his neck. "You know, there's a lot of things we didn't talk about yet."

"We've got time. Now let me kiss you good night before my good intentions vanish."

She lifted her lips, and it wasn't the first time that they'd done this, but damned if it didn't feel special. She was warm and willing, and she kissed him back eagerly.

By some miracle they kept space between their bodies, but their lips and tongues danced. Pleasure passed between them, and Rafe told his body to behave itself because, yeah, he was getting turned on, but this was about *more*.

More than the sweet friction and tantalizing taste of her. More than the little sounds she made that went straight through him and sent chills up his spine.

Kissing like this meant pushing their relationship to something more than they'd been for years, and the change was something to cherish.

When they backed apart, her cheeks were flushed and her lips were swollen, and mischief danced in her eyes. "Well, Rafe Coleman, I guess Jenna Ireland wasn't lying back in the day. You *are* a fine kisser."

He squeezed her one last time then somehow let her go. "You already knew that," he pointed out.

"Always good to have backup confirmation. It *has* been three years."

"I kissed you this afternoon," he grumbled.

"Didn't count," she said primly, walking down the steps to her apartment.

"It didn't count? What the hell're you talking about?"

She unlocked the door then smiled up at him. "We weren't dating then."

Troublemaker. He let her have this one.

"Call me," he ordered. He watched until she closed the door and locked it, then wandered back to his truck whistling happily.

Yeah, there were all sorts of things they needed to figure out, and tonight they'd pretty much ignored anything big that needed to be discussed. But it still seemed as if it'd been the right thing to do.

They'd needed a dose of *them*. A time to remember they liked each other as people. As friends.

Yup, it had been a fine evening, and a good start to the next stage of their relationship. Rafe ignored all the things that needed to be done back at the ranch. Instead he headed back to his apartment and crawled into bed feeling pretty damn satisfied.

Full steam ahead. That was the plan.

Nowhere in the fucking plan was someone supposed to knock on his fucking door at six a.m.

Rafe stumbled out of bed, cursing lightly. Odds were it was his father, because Gabe didn't expect him to be up. It had to be Ben, and Rafe grumbled his disapproval. Pissed off and angry was *not* the way he wanted to resume interaction with the man.

Except, waking up someone who thought they got to sleep in was kind of the perfect way to get the *pissed off and angry* results.

Rafe didn't bother to pull on any clothes. Just stomped his way to the front entrance in his boxers and yanked the door open, ready to offer his opinion on the bullshit situation in no uncertain terms.

62

"What the f—?"

He nearly swallowed his tongue to stop before he said more, because it wasn't Ben standing on the steps.

It was Jeff Lawson, Laurel's mystery man.

Chapter Five

JEFF HELD forward a familiar red Tim Hortons cup, extra large. "Coffee?"

Rafe stood there, not quite believing his eyes.

"I brought cream and sugar. And doughnuts." Jeff lifted his other hand, a paper bag in his grip.

Confusion set in harder. Rafe was a little iffy on whether he was awake or dreaming. "Did I know you were coming over?"

"No. I thought it would be a good idea to get to know some of the people in the community."

"And you decided to start with me."

Jeff nodded, seemingly not one bit concerned at having shown up unexpected and uninvited. He waited patiently as if him being there was the most logical thing in the world, which meant he was either the stupidest man on earth, or the smartest son of a bitch.

Rafe shrugged, then turned his back and retreated into his apartment. "Come on in."

He ignored his guest and headed to his bedroom, grabbing jeans off the back of the chair where he'd tossed them the previous night. It only took a second to haul a dark T-shirt over his head before dragging a hand through his hair and returning to the living room.

Jeff had made himself at home. Well, as much as he could considering everything Rafe owned was in boxes except for two wooden chairs and an old wooden table that were so decrepit he hadn't bothered to take them with him in the first place.

Still the man was happily setting out the food as if on fancy china. "I brought a bunch of breakfast sandwiches, as well. Figured you probably hadn't eaten yet."

"Not yet." Rafe didn't see much reason to be polite. "By this time most days I'd already be in the fields, but since you caught me on my morning off, appreciate it. I guess."

Jeff looked slightly uncomfortable. "I didn't realize. Sorry."

His distress vanished almost instantly, and he offered another one of those "reassuring" smiles. The kind Rafe remembered seeing far too often on people who hoped to get something from him. The guy was going to be disappointed if he was barking up that tree.

In the meantime, Rafe wasn't about to turn down the offer of a free meal.

He popped the lid off his coffee cup and drank deeply, letting the scalding-hot liquid sink into his system and take the edge off his annoyance. He unwrapped one of the bacon-and-egg sandwiches, and Jeff did the same, and the two of them sat quietly, eating, drinking and eyeing each other.

Finally it was too awkward to stay silent any longer, even by Rafe's standards. Might as well satisfy some of his curiosity.

"Where're you from?"

"Toronto. Lived there my entire life—my father is the senior pastor at the Central Baptist Church."

Ahhhh. The plot thickened. "Following in your father's footsteps, I take it."

Jeff smiled proudly. "Don't most sons?"

Buzzzzzzzz. Wrong answer. Rafe reached for another sandwich, balling up the wrapper and tossing it into the open box he was using as a garbage bin before answering. "Some. Some set their own path."

The other man hesitated before nodding. "We all have to do what we're called to." He found his stride, straightening and looking Rafe in the eye. "That's part of why I'm here."

The caffeine must have hit Rafe's system. He was awake enough to deal with this strange situation. "If you're looking for information about the church, I'm afraid I can't help you. My mom's a member. While I have no beef with any of you in particular, it's not really my thing."

"I'm not here to talk to you about the church. I'm here to talk to you about Laurel."

Of course he was.

"Awesome woman, isn't she?" Rafe leaned back in his chair and took another long drink as he watched Jeff closely. "Me and Laurel, we go way back."

Jeff dipped his chin briefly. "She mentioned you while we were at college. Said you were pretty much the best friend she'd ever had."

Wow. Rafe wasn't sure what surprised him more. That Laurel had been talking about him at Bible school, or that Jeff had admitted it. Only it wasn't *their* past that was important right now.

She hadn't been happy when she'd spotted Jeff yesterday. Rafe circled the wagons and put up as much protection as he could. "That's part of the reason why us being together now is so perfect. We've got all that history."

There was a pause as Jeff played with the empty sandwich wrappers in front of him. "Yes, well. The Bible says that when we're young, we think as a child, and speak as a—"

"If you don't mind, Pastor Lawson, let's skip the Bible recitations." Rafe folded his arms over his chest. "Like I said, I've got no beef with the church, or with the Bible, but if you want to talk to me, I'd prefer the words coming out of your mouth were your own."

Jeff seemed shocked by the request, but he gave a quick nod then gathered his garbage together and put it in the now-empty bag. "Why don't we go do some work while we keep talking? That might make the conversation flow a little easier."

He'd obviously forgotten the part earlier when Rafe had said it was his day off, but hey, if the man wanted to volunteer as free labour? Rafe was not about to deny him the privilege.

"Sure. Just let me pull on my boots."

"Oh, and call me Jeff." The man followed Rafe toward the door. "Pastor Lawson is my father."

Rafe jammed his feet in his boots and his hat on his head before pulling the door open for his guest. "After you, *Jeff.*"

Out of the tasks he might have picked to inflict on the man, the first one that popped to mind was all sorts of wrong. Temptation was far too strong, and Rafe grabbed a scythe from the shed along with a rake before marching them up to the front of the drive.

He turned and assessed the man. "You comfortable working with the blade, or you want me to do the cutting?"

"I'm good for whichever." Jeff's chin rose as if this was a challenge he wasn't going to fail. "Just show me a few practice swings so I can see how it goes."

Rafe swung low and hard, letting the weight of the sharp blade do most of the work. The green stalks of thistles with their massive purple heads fell in batches as he mowed about him with the scythe, stepping in an easy rhythm, arm held stiff against the cool metal handle. "It takes a little getting used to, but I'm sure you can do it."

Jeff accepted the tool, his arm dipping slightly at the unexpected weight. He took a first swing, and the leading edge caught at a bad angle, dragging the scythe to a halt, tangled in the thick stalks.

"Happens to the best of us," Rafe offered in support. "Hold the blade a little farther in front of you. That's it. Now, try again."

This time some of his target fell, and Jeff glanced up with a pleased expression. "I did it."

Rafe refrained from chuckling. "You did. Now keep going, I'll rake behind you."

He waited until the other man was a few feet ahead. Jeff was a far better sport than Rafe had expected, but since he didn't know what had set Laurel off, he wasn't ready to become bosom buddies at this stage of the game.

"You knew Laurel at college?" Rafe asked, returning to the most important topic.

"We did a year together, yes." Jeff kept his eyes on the blade in front of him as he spoke. "She's a lovely young woman."

"We can agree on that." Rafe shook weeds off the rake head, watching Jeff's shoulders move under his light jacket. His solid frame was thick enough—he might be able to hold his own if it came to a fight.

Not that Rafe was thinking about knocking him over and dragging him through the dirt.

Much.

The other man wore runners and cotton pants—sturdier than dress slacks and fancy shoes, but not thick enough to protect him completely. On every step his shins and knees brushed the tall thistles on the deeper side of the ditch as he cut the layer in front of him. Rafe wondered how evil it was that he didn't warn Jeff to be more careful.

"Yes, Laurel is lovely, and we found we had a lot in common. We dated, in fact."

Rafe was suddenly glad he hadn't said anything about the thistles. "Really."

"She didn't tell you?"

He wasn't about to admit they'd barely had time to say hello, let alone talk about anything serious since he'd gotten back to town. "Nope. I guess she figured it was in the past, and it didn't matter."

Jeff paused, glancing over his shoulder. "I care about her a great deal," he informed Rafe. "And while you might have a friendship that goes back a long ways, I hope that like me, you'd want what's best for her now."

"Yup," Rafe agreed. "Which is why I'm dating her."

The other man gave Rafe his back as he returned to swinging the blade. "It's good to have confidence in our abilities, and it's good to have a positive self-image, but it's also good to be realistic."

Bunch of starched-shirt bullshit. "What's that supposed to mean?"

"Just that the most important relationships in our lives, the ones that count, need to fit where we come from *and* where we're going." Jeff turned, setting the blade head on the ground and leaning on the shaft as he spoke seriously. "I came to Rocky to consider serving the church, but I won't lie. I also came because I knew Laurel was here."

Rafe had to give the man credit for being blunt. "She's here, but she's mine."

Jeff raised a brow. "See, a comment like that is what makes me think you're really not the man for her. I can only imagine how well that would go over with Laurel. To be claimed as someone's possession."

Sudden anger slid in, partly because the bastard was right. "She knows how I feel about her."

The other man's shoulders lifted in a soft shrug. "And that means she'll be able to make an informed decision when it's time."

"I think you should leave now." Rafe held his hand out for the scythe, his sense of humour vanishing abruptly. "And you need to think twice before getting in Laurel's face, because it was pretty clear she wants nothing to do with you."

"We'll see," Jeff returned evenly, looking Rafe squarely in the eye as he handed over the tool. "You have a great day."

Rafe bit his tongue to keep from shouting something rude after the man, but it didn't keep the curse words from popping into his head. The last few minutes of conversation had been as good as a declaration of war. One that Rafe had no intention of losing.

He stood there until Jeff left, a rush of satisfaction hitting as the car bottomed out in a deep hole just shy of the main road. The screech of rock against the undercarriage was the *fuck you* Rafe hadn't permitted himself to offer in person.

Well. That changed things.

Last night with Laurel he'd gone slow. Taken his time. But if Pastor "I have an opinion and it's full of shit" was sticking around, Rafe wanted the whole story ASAP. Like today.

Only it was barely six thirty in the morning, and he could hardly tromp over to Laurel's to demand to know what was going on.

So instead, Rafe tossed the rake aside and took aim at the noxious weeds around him. He laid into them with a great deal of enthusiasm as he imagined mowing down Jeff at the ankles then piling everything into a massive bonfire and burning it all to hell.

**

Laurel took the early lunch slot and arranged to meet her friend Nicole for a quick catch-up. The past few days had to have been exhausting, and Laurel was worried about her and Nic's boyfriend.

She ran the last few paces to nab her arm before Nic entered the café.

"Hey, how're you doing?" she asked as she caught Nicole in a firm hug.

"Okay." The dark shadows under Nicole's eyes were new, but she smiled as they grabbed a table. "Troy's champing at the bit to get out of the hospital already. Looks like maybe even tomorrow."

"Wow, that's fast. I mean, that's great, but..."

"I guess he's banged and bruised but only partially broken, so yeah, four days and he'll be out."

Nicole pushed aside the menu on the tabletop and leaned back in the booth. She covered her mouth as a yawn escaped. "I'm taking a couple days off. Troy insists on moving in with me, so I want to try and get as much done before he's home, or else he'll overdo it."

"I can give you a hand," Laurel offered. She squeezed Nicole's fingers. "There's a whole lot to celebrate in what you just said. The fact he's healthy enough to want to do *anything* is a miracle."

"I know."

They gave their lunch order then Nicole turned on her with a stern look. "And now *you*. What the heck is going on, girl?"

Oh, me? Just dealing with a new boyfriend, and an old one, and a whole lot of other baggage.

She didn't say that out loud, though. It was far too much to drop at one time, especially since Nicole was facing her own troubles. Instead Laurel shared the part Nic was probably most interested in.

"Rafe Coleman's back in town."

"Yes... That's part of the news I heard. I was wondering more about the kissing booth you were running at the fairgrounds yesterday."

Laurel snorted. "Nice try, but there was only one kiss, and it was just a welcome back between friends."

Instant reaction. Her face went so hot she was sure her cheeks were fire-engine red.

Nicole tilted her head to one side and looked across the table with amusement. "So *that's* what happens when you lie."

"Shut up."

"Awww, you can do better than that." Nicole rested her elbows on the table, eyes bright with interest.

"Tell me all the dirty, dirty details. You and Rafe? I never would've guessed."

"We're just starting to date." Curiosity struck again. "Rafe and I have been friends since way back. High school and before. Didn't you know that?"

Nicole looked slightly embarrassed. "We're good friends now, but back in school, I didn't really know you were alive. Or that you were cool."

"I've always been cool," Laurel insisted. She pointed to her face. "See? No blushing. Therefore, not a lie. Therefore, I am cool, and always have been."

Her friend laughed, looking a whole lot less stressed than even moments earlier. Nicole smiled as she spoke, the words tinged with amusement but also sincerity. "I'm glad you're dating. I was getting worried there for a while that you were pining after *me*."

"Well, if I did lean that way, you'd be the first to know," Laurel told her seriously. "But since I don't, you no longer have to worry about trying to set me up."

"Huh." Nicole pretended to pout. "But I've got a perfectly good twin brother who's single. What am I supposed to do with him?"

Laurel shrugged. "I thought you were trying to set me up with that handsome firefighter you're keeping on a string."

Nicole waved a hand. "Back to the more interesting details, tell me about Rafe."

"As if there's anything I could tell you that you don't already know." Still, Nicole waited patiently, so Laurel went on. "He's the youngest in the Coleman clan. He works at the Angel Ranch, and we've been friends since we were five. There's not much else to say."

"What about he's tall, blond and built?" Nicole's grin widened. "Yeah, I see that smile on your face. He's one *fine* young man, and I approve."

He *was* mighty fine. And he was a good friend.

"What's that big sigh for?" Nicole asked.

Laurel blinked in surprise, waiting until the waitress had finished putting their plates in front of them. "Did I sigh?"

"Hugely." Her friend glanced around the café then lowered her voice. "Something else is going on that you're not telling me."

"Turn in your accountant badge for a detective one. Something shiny, just like you."

"That's not a denial," Nicole pointed out.

"Right." She picked up her hamburger and took a big bite.

"*Laurel...*"

She took her time swallowing. "Yes?"

Nicole eyed her. "This whole strong, silent thing doesn't work for me. And it's totally not you."

Maybe it hadn't been her this summer, but she'd had more than enough practice staying quiet over the past three years about all sorts of things.

Credit where credit was due, though... "You're right. You bring out the noisy in me."

"I bring out the *best* in you, and don't you forget it." Nicole looked her over carefully. "You know what? After Troy's home we need a night out. Girl time—I'll make sure he's happy with Netflix and junk food, and we can take off and talk until we're sick of each other."

Even though Laurel wished she could sweep everything under a rug and forget, it probably wasn't a good idea. She wasn't sure how much she wanted to share, but bouncing a few of her concerns off someone she trusted couldn't hurt.

She nodded firmly. "Deal. You need me to help move stuff tonight?"

Nic shook her head. "Mike offered to box everything up first because I'm going to the hospital, so tomorrow and the next day we'll move it and unpack."

"I can bring something for supper tomorrow, then."

"Sounds good. I have potluck planned for everyone who's coming to help. If you bring your red velvet cupcakes for dessert, I'll love you forever." She batted her lashes.

Laurel smiled. "Five thirty?"

"Perfect."

They chatted about inconsequential things as they finished their meals. Nicole hugged her tight before they headed off in different directions.

Laurel was struck by how much the world changed in a blink of an eye. For years she'd lived in the same town as Nic, crossing paths and never thinking anything of it, yet after one chance meeting three months ago, they'd become really good friends.

Rafe. He'd been a rock and a safe place to her forever, but the way she'd thought about him had changed in an instant.

And...Jeff. The whole situation with Jeff.

Another example of when one moment to the next, her world had changed.

Some changes were good, some not, and yet there didn't seem to be any way to control the outcomes of those small, all-important moments. All she could do was the next thing. React, and hope she picked the right path at each fork in the road.

Laurel returned to the library, clinging to the good sensations Rafe had sparked the night before. Chatting quietly with him had been like old times. Comfortable, fun. No unanswerable expectations.

He was Rafe—she *knew* him. A slow peace returned to her soul.

Peace, plus a whole lot of quivering anticipation for the next time they'd be together. Thinking about his kisses and his touch wasn't a bad way to distract herself and pass the time until she could go home and make official sixth-of-September contact.

It was totally working. Most of the afternoon passed before she rounded the corner of the stacks to discover her father at the front counter, chatting quietly with her coworkers.

He glanced up as she approached, and that's all it took for her calm to evaporate. She knew that look. It was the same long-suffering expression she'd seen every time he'd been called to the office after one of her and Rafe's scrapes had landed them in hot water.

Funny. The world could change in an instant, but some things? Like instantly reverting to feeling like a naughty child about to be chastised?

It seemed *some* things never changed.

Chapter Six

NEVER HAD a day passed so slowly.

After his wake-up session with Jeff that morning, Rafe ended up wandering over to Gabe's far earlier than expected. There hadn't been enough weeds to destroy, and he was still uptight, and he stomped his way across the barn floor to where Gabe was measuring feed into bags.

His brother stood, offering a hard hug and a firm pat on the back. "Good to see you. I figured you wouldn't show up for another couple hours."

"Had a rough morning," Rafe admitted.

"Shit." Gabe caught him by the shoulders, worry on his face. "What did Ben—?"

"Not him this time. Although it's pretty sad I have to say that."

"Yeah, well." Gabe returned to his task, Rafe slipping into position to hold the sack open. "We both know how it is."

"Has it been bad this summer?"

"No worse than usual." Gabe shrugged. "In fact, he's been out of sight more often than not. I hired a few extra hands to help, and we've been trading off more tasks with the Six Pack and Moonshine clans, and neither of those choices sat well with him."

"But you got to make them, right?"

Gabe nodded. "You know he signed control over to me years ago, so there's nothing he *can* do except be miserable about it. I give him a list of tasks to help with every week like always, and he does them or not, depending on his mood."

It was screwed up, and it was wrong, but like Gabe said—it was just the way it was for them in the Angel clan.

"Mom okay, though? I worried about her all summer."

"She's fine." Gabe hesitated. "Miserable, but fine. Allison goes over as often as she can, but Ben scares her, and she really doesn't like having Micah around him, either."

This was more than screwed up, to have a family like this. "How can he stand to have his own daughter-in-law frightened of him? How can he stand having his sons barely able to look at him?"

"I have no idea what goes on in that stubborn brain of his, but I know this." Gabe tied off the final bag at his feet and gestured Rafe toward the door. "I refuse to let Ben be more than a passing thought. I've got too many things to be thankful for to get dragged under by him and his issues. You need to do the same. Get out of that yard, Rafe. We might have to work with him occasionally, but the less we see of him, the better."

"Funny. I'm sure you were the one to suggest I move into the loft."

"You were seventeen years old at the time," Gabe snapped, "and it was better than living under his roof."

"And now it's better that I'm close enough to be there if Mom needs me," Rafe bit back before taking a deep breath. "Enough—this is not what I came over here for."

Gabe caught him by the shoulder again and squeezed. "Me, neither. I missed having you around, bro."

"Didn't miss you one bit," Rafe lied. "Or Allison. Or that kid you guys found under a cabbage leaf. He seems to have doubled in size since I left. What the heck are you feeding him?"

"Organic growth hormones," Gabe gibed, but he positively beamed with pride as he led Rafe toward the back of the barn. He paused, tilting his head toward the second barn where they kept the horses. "Want to go for a ride? I can tell you most of what we're working on while we're out. I need to check a few fields."

"God, *yes.*" That was exactly what he needed to settle his soul.

They saddled up quickly then met in the yard. Rafe patted Belle's withers fondly before mounting and following Gabe up the narrow trail leading to the ridge.

Even after Gabe's comment about catching him up on what needed to be done, they rode without speaking for the next fifteen minutes or so, just taking in the morning. Brothers who had worked together for most of their lives, sharing a time of wordless communication. They alternated taking the lead. Gabe dismounted to open a gate. Rafe walked Belle through, Hurricane bumping his nose into Belle's flank as he followed along so Gabe could close the gate behind them.

His brother swung into the saddle, his eyes flashing for a moment as he glanced ahead. Rafe clued in fast enough—both of them still silent, but the challenge was blatant. They were only a few steps away from the path that led to the lookout, and a shot of good-natured competitiveness flared.

Gabe oh-so-casually tapped his fingers on his thigh. Rafe didn't bother to hide his grin, counting down with each motion.

Three, two—

The instant Gabe's fingers struck *one* they both shifted forward in the saddle, urging their horses into a run as they took off over a path they'd raced more times than Rafe could count.

That was when he knew everything would be okay. That moment when he felt almost weightless, Belle's muscles bunching and stretching beneath him as they flew up the trail.

Rafe gripped tightly with his thighs as he leaned over Belle's neck, no longer glancing beside him, completely focused on his forward flight as familiar territory whizzed past in a blur. The cool morning air brushed his cheek like the stroke of a lover.

As if the Coleman land were personified and caressing him, letting him know this was where he belonged.

They reached the finish line together, pulling to a walk to allow the horses to cool before descending into the coulee where the Whiskey Creek meandered.

Rafe rocked in the saddle. Comfortable, easy. "We have an amazing place, don't we? We're lucky to live here."

"Luckier than a man can explain." Gabe's low rumble was tinged with emotion.

Rafe stared across at his big brother, the fierce sensation of hero worship toward him as strong as it had always been. It wasn't that Gabe could do no wrong, but that he kept trying, and he'd been rewarded because of who he was deep inside.

"I really want what you've got some day," Rafe shared.

"You'll get there," Gabe said seriously before his face twisted into a teasing grin. "Except for the *annoying little brother* part. That's my joy to experience, not yours."

"Shut up," Rafe muttered without heat. He was glad to be Gabe's little brother, annoying or otherwise.

They picked their way along the creek as cool air swirled around them, talking through plans for the rest of the month. It was pretty much familiar territory, which was fine by Rafe. Familiar didn't mean boring.

A loud whistle drew their attention across the creek where a group of three horses broke clear of the trees. Their cousins Karen, Lisa and Jesse waved, pulling to a stop on the opposite bank.

Gabe and Rafe forded the creek at the shallowest part, joining the group on the other side. The horses settled next to each other with soft nickers and head tosses.

"You running trail rides on our land now?" Rafe asked Karen. She'd been using the Whiskey Creek horses in a camp in the Rockies for the past couple of years.

"Once you crossed Whiskey Creek you hit our land, but now that you mention it—" Karen winked. "Are you offering to be trail cook if I do?"

Rafe shrugged. "Better me than Jesse. I at least know the major food groups."

"Beer, beans, steak and tequila," Jesse drawled, lounging lazily in the saddle, his smile wide.

"Good breakfast menu—what's for lunch?" Rafe taunted.

"If it ain't broke, don't fix it."

Rafe made a rude noise. "Yeah, that explains so much about you."

"Why I'm so awesome and worshipped by all I meet?"

"I was thinking about the smell." Rafe leaned forward and sniffed. "Yeah. Explains so much..."

"Jerk," Jesse offered with a grin.

"Stinker."

"Asshole."

"Butthead."

Karen rolled her eyes. She pulled a wallet from her back pocket and handed over a twenty to her smirking sister.

Gabe snorted in amusement. "What was the bet?"

Lisa put the money away. "That the children here would end up exchanging single-word insults within five minutes of seeing each other."

"Children? I'm older than you," Jesse complained.

"And it's oh-so-obvious by your behaviour, isn't it?" Lisa teased. "You guys are too predictable."

Karen turned to Rafe. "We missed having you around this summer. Did you enjoy seeing more of Canada?"

"Back dirt roads and cheap motels," Jesse offered. "Yeah, I'm sure he hit all the bright lights of our great country."

Rafe ignored Jesse though his cousin wasn't far off the mark. "I had a good time, but I'm glad to be back."

"I bet he spent his summer sleeping in cheesy hotels watching lots of bad late-night cable." Jesse leaned in slightly. "How's your love life, cuz?"

Now that was a taunt Rafe could deal with. He offered an ear-to-ear grin. "Just fine, and about to get a whole lot better. What about you? Anyone left within a three-hour radius of Rocky willing to date you?"

Karen and Gabe let out hisses of approval at the cut. Lisa lifted a hand to her mouth and laughed.

Jesse glanced at them. "What? You think I've been striking out?"

Lisa whistled innocently.

"Hey, just because you're a girl doesn't mean I won't punch you," Jesse informed her. "You're my cousin, and that means the rules go out the window. Be warned."

Lisa shifted her horse away a few paces. "I was going to agree with you."

Jesse looked even more suspicious. "Why does that not reassure me?"

She grinned. "Striking out would imply you got up to bat. Last I heard you'd been benched pretty hard." She stuck out her lower lip. "Poor wittle Jesse. Did my friend Liz tell you to go away?"

Rafe joined in the laughter as Jesse's jaw dropped in disbelief. "Who told you that? And I'm not saying it's true."

"You don't have to admit it," Lisa assured him, pulling out her phone and clicking through a few screens. "Oh good, I wasn't imagining it. I've got video. I was thinking of posting it to YouTube."

Jesse snatched at her, trying to nab the phone out of her hands, but Lisa pulled back and his horse skittered sideways, and the two of them circled until they got the horses back under control.

Karen rolled her eyes at her little sister. "This is very entertaining, but it's not finding those runaways. If you don't mind, could you leave off the taunting for a while?"

"No."

"Yes."

Lisa and Jesse spoke at the same time, and Rafe and Gabe lost it, both of them laughing full-out. Jesse offered a long-suffering sigh then winked before they moved farther downstream.

"What are we looking for?" Rafe asked.

Karen explained. "Couple of my new mares are pretty wild. They're due to foal and they've gone missing. I think I know where they're hiding."

The group broke in two, Lisa and Jesse lazily exchanging taunts as they headed with Rafe toward the far side of the trees in the hopes Gabe and Karen could push the runaways their direction.

"So. You and Laurel Sitko." Lisa changed topic and focused her attention on him. "Tell me more."

He didn't try to deny it. Number one because he didn't want to, and number two, denial would be totally useless in this family. "I'm a little surprised it took you this long. It's been over twelve hours since I kissed her."

"You kissed Laurel Sitko?" Jesse demanded. "What the hell?"

Lisa tilted her head toward Jesse before clicking her tongue. "So sad. Some of us aren't quite as observant as others."

"I noticed that," Rafe answered.

"Of course, since we're talking Jesse here, he has an excuse. He's probably a little stunned from that massive blow to his ego that didn't happen on Friday night."

"Shut up, Lisa," Jesse muttered.

"You know, when he *didn't* strike out with my friend."

"I'm going to end you."

"Man, I have missed a lot." Rafe reached his hand toward Lisa. "Let me see your phone. Who did Jesse strike out with?"

Jesse moved in close enough to punch him in the shoulder. His cousin was no lightweight, and the blow landed hard enough to nearly send him flying out of the saddle, but Rafe didn't care. He laughed and pulled up on the reins, ushering Belle forward.

It was good to be back. Good to return to family and know he was accepted. To know they celebrated with him.

Good to know he had a place to hang his hat, and a woman to learn all over in new ways. Spending time with Laurel and his crazy, mixed-up family would be simple—

Well, he hoped it would be simple. It *had* to work, because he wasn't giving up his family, and he wasn't giving up Laurel. He'd have to avoid bringing her around his father, but the rest of the Colemans were part of his heart and soul.

The frustrations of his morning were erased, replaced by a whole lot of anticipation for when he could see her again.

LAUREL'S FATHER stood at the library reception desk, continuing to exchange pleasantries with Wendy.

Having him show up at work wasn't the most terrible thing to happen, it just wasn't what Laurel wanted to deal with right then. But—he was there, which meant she couldn't avoid talking with him.

She waited for a break in the conversation. "Hey. Were you looking for me?"

"I was running errands and thought I'd stop by. Do you have a few minutes?" her father asked politely.

She glanced at her boss, pretty sure she knew the answer.

Wendy waved them off. "Take your afternoon break. That's fine."

Laurel led him through the main building to the small door off the back that opened onto a grassy area with a picnic table.

"Nice."

"They call it the summer staff room," Laurel shared. "In the winter, we're locked in a tiny windowless room along with the water heater."

"Sounds marvelous." He sat and folded his hands, staring over the grass toward the nearby junior high. Silent, as if he was thinking about what to say, or waiting for her.

Talking with her dad wasn't usually this uncomfortable. She loved the man, really she did, but right now there was potentially a whole lot of awkward about to happen.

He turned to her with a smile. "It's been good to have you back in town."

She joined him on the bench. "It's good to be back. I missed all of you while I was gone away."

"So you've said." He cleared his throat. "I noticed, though, that while you join us for church on Sundays, and you allowed your mother to add you to the music schedule, you're not getting involved in anything else."

And...one of those awkward moments arrived far too quickly. The temptation to offer the "I've been busy" excuse was strong, but if she couldn't lie in general, lying to her father was impossible.

Laurel took a deep breath then answered quietly. "I'm working through some issues."

He hummed thoughtfully. "That wasn't an answer."

"No, it wasn't, but it's the truth." That much she could give him.

It obviously wasn't enough. "Does this have something to do with the decisions you made about your schooling?"

Like how she'd dropped out of her first year of Bible College with three months to go and jumped tracks into librarian training in a totally different province instead? All without saying a word to her family? "It was what I really wanted to do," she insisted, thankful that wasn't a lie.

It wasn't a complete truth either, but at least her face didn't give her away.

Times like this she had difficulty thinking of the man beside her as her father. He was so *Pastor Dave*, sympathetic and yet solemn. Wanting the best for one of the people in his care.

He nodded, understanding in his expression like she'd expected, but also concern. "So, I take it some of those issues you're working through involve the church?"

"Not with you or mom."

"Oh, Laurel. Your mom and I are not the church, and we've never said we were." He rested a hand on her shoulder. "Everybody has doubts at times. It's easier to deal with them if you talk about them with people who share your beliefs."

That was the trouble. She didn't know *what* she believed anymore.

She struggled for a way to share that wasn't going to hurt him. There had to be a way to balance what she'd been taught, and what she completely disagreed with, and still have faith.

Faith in what, though, she wasn't sure.

"Just something for you to think about," he offered quietly. "There are some good, solid people in the church if you'd feel more comfortable talking to them. Or I understand you know Jeff Lawson from school. You could always talk to him while he's here."

It was a good thing she'd turned away before her father said that last bit, or it would've been impossible to keep her feelings hidden regarding Jeff.

She covered her dismay with a cough before asking, "How long is he staying to candidate?"

"He'll be here for just over a week."

Ugh. Hopefully he'd change his mind and decide things were better out East. Maybe *Jessica* wouldn't want to move to a small Alberta town after living in the big city. Anything, as long as she didn't have to face seeing him at church every week. Or accidentally bumping into him in town.

"I'm surprised his wife didn't join him. Isn't it typical for them to candidate together?"

Her father glanced at her quickly. "Jeff's not married."

Suddenly she wasn't breathing very well. The air seemed far too thick. She opened her mouth to say something then realized she had no idea what to say.

Fortunately, her father hadn't noticed her shock and carried on without her.

"I'm quite impressed with Jeff." He rose to his feet, straightening his shirt and tie as he waited for her to stand as well. "I'm encouraged by his enthusiasm, and he has a genuine heart for the youth. Just like you always did."

This whole conversation was like being stuck in the middle of a field full of hidden landmines. There was nowhere safe for her to step. "I have enough on my plate. I don't think I should add anything right now."

Again, thankfully, that wasn't a lie.

"I understand."

Jeff was single. Jeff had *not* married Jessica.

Her mind was reeling, and she was barely aware of her father anymore. So it was another surprise when they were nearly at the door and he paused. "I understand you and young Rafe Coleman have reconnected."

Drat. They'd been so close to avoiding this topic. *Sooooo* close.

Not that she was ashamed of Rafe, and she certainly wasn't going to apologize for him. She never had before.

It was a conversation she wasn't ready to deal with for other reasons, like the relationship was new and shiny, and she wasn't sure exactly where it was going...

She tried to keep her answer as brief and positive as possible. "It's been good to catch up with him."

"Strange that I didn't see him around even once this summer. Since you got back," her dad pointed out.

"He was out of town a lot working for his family. You probably knew that, though, since his mom comes to prayer meetings."

Pastor Dave hesitated then nodded. "You're right, I remember now."

"You've had a lot on your mind." She made a show of checking her watch before stepping toward the door. "Gee, I should probably get moving. I need to do a few things before my break is over."

She walked with him to the front door.

He turned and gave her a hug, pressing a kiss to her forehead. "By the way. Your mother would very much like you to come and join us for supper tonight."

Ha. The invite was *so* unexpected. *Not.*

"Sure." She eyed her father. "I assume Jeff will be there?"

Her father looked as guilty as he possibly could. "Yes, but it's not a setup, or anything."

"Of course not, because I'll be bringing Rafe with me."

Her father's eyes crinkled at the corners. "Dinner's at six, but come earlier if you can. I know your mother would enjoy extra time to chat."

He was out the door, and she turned and escaped to the bathroom. She washed her face with cold water and soaked her wrists until her heart stopped pounding.

Laurel took a deep breath and brought out her phone and called Rafe.

"Laurel?"

"We're dating."

Amusement tinged his voice when he spoke. "Good to know. What brings on this bold announcement?"

"A lot of things."

"Sounds like it. Did you know we're having supper with your parents tonight?"

Okay, that was *really* scary. "How did you do that?"

A low rumble of a laugh hit her ear. "Your mom called. Told me to bring you over at five-thirty."

"Seriously?" How on earth had her dad contacted her mom so quickly that she'd had time to track down Rafe?

The entire "just happened to be in the neighbourhood" thing must have been a cover-up for

90

finding out if she really was seeing Rafe. She wouldn't put it past her father to be sneaky. Or her mom.

"I'm so sorry, Rafe. My parents are going to be a handful. I hope I'm not apologizing for them all the time."

"Your parents are fine. Besides, we have to eat. We'll have dinner with them, and after that, we're going out for real. I've got a plan."

A real date. Anticipation rolled right back in, in spite of her worries. Getting to spend quality time with Rafe felt so right.

"I have work tomorrow," she warned.

"So do I, but we're still going out for a while. Arguing with me is useless."

"I know that. Useless, but entertaining." She checked her watch. "Need to get back to work. Want to meet at my parents?"

"Hell, no. I'll pick you up at five-twenty, if you can be ready by then."

It was a bit of a rush to make it home from the library, into the shower and get dressed on time, but no way she was going out on her first official date with Rafe while wearing what she thought of as her library uniform.

She was putting on lipstick when she realized she hadn't dressed up *just* because of the date, or because of dinner with her parents. It was also a gesture to Jeff as well. A *look what you lost out on, sucker* kind of thing.

Figuring that out wasn't one of her proudest moments, but with Rafe already knocking at her door, it was too late to do anything about it other than feel slightly guilty.

Chapter Seven

IT WASN'T a sight to be rushed over. Rafe savoured every second as he stood in the doorway and admired her.

Her pale blue top mirrored her eyes perfectly, the short-sleeved blouse curving against her body before tucking neatly into the skirt's waistband. Shades of sky and water were layered over each other, the material stopping at her knees and leaving her lower legs bare, toes visible through the straps of her sandals.

When he finally made it back up to her face, her lips had curled into a smile.

"You look edible," he announced.

Laurel's cheeks flushed pink. "Thanks." She twirled, the skirt flaring briefly before she landed then stepped toward him. "Is this okay for whatever you've got planned for later?"

He'd intended to answer her, really he had, but he'd reached around her to offer a quick hug, and the instant his hands made contact with her torso, his ability to think vanished. "So soft."

"Rafe." She pressed her palms to the sides of his face. "Focus for a minute. Do I need to bring something to change into after supper?"

He attempted to restore his brain to its rightful position. "You're perfect the way you are."

"Of course I am, but do I need to bring an extra jacket or something?"

"Nope." He tucked an arm around her and guided her toward the door. "Let's get rolling. The sooner we get there, the sooner dinner will be over—not that I have any objections to your mother's cooking."

He guided Laurel to the driver's side of the truck, lifting her to the seat then waiting for her to slide into the middle.

She was grinning pretty damn hard when he joined her and put the truck in gear.

"What?"

Laurel all but shone as she faced him. "Now I know for *sure* we're dating."

He thought it through for a moment. "Nope. Clueless.

A soft snicker escaped her. "I've gotten in and out of this truck thousands of times, and it's always been me opening the door and climbing in on the other side."

"You've moved up in the world, Sitko." He draped an arm around her shoulders and tucked her tightly against him. "Better get used to it."

It felt pretty amazing to have her cuddled up at his side as another warm fall day came to an end. He figured they'd be at her parents' for about an hour, maybe a little more, and then she was his for the rest of the night.

Laurel made a noise, poking him briefly in the side to get his attention. "Warning. My dad showed up at the library this afternoon. He was grilling me about you."

"What'd you tell him?"

"That I didn't expect him to have to show up at the principal's office to bail me out anytime soon."

Oh, the memories that triggered. "Man, we nearly wore tracks in the floor back in the day. I'm surprised your dad didn't forbid you to hang out with me."

"He wouldn't dare. He and mom have always been adamant we had to make our own decisions and deal with the consequences." She shook her head firmly. "If I want to date you, that's my choice, not theirs."

Discomfort hit as he considered Jeff's warning that Laurel wouldn't appreciate being considered a possession. It had been Rafe's go-to response...stupid and yet automatic.

He pushed aside that thread of concern for now. "I meant more when we were in school."

She leaned against him, tentatively resting her hand on his thigh. "Maybe they hoped you'd be a good example for me."

A burst of laughter escaped. "Yeah, right."

"I'm serious. Don't act like you were always the instigator. I was far too rambunctious and flighty back then. You helped center me, more than you realized."

"That's not the way I remember it, but if you want to give me a halo, swing it over my way. It's sure to get caught on one of my horns."

Her body quivered, and her shoulders shook. As he pulled to a stop in front of the Sitko house, all the signs were there of Laurel having a giggle-breakdown.

A familiar joy struck as he pretended to sigh heavily. "What now?"

"Nope. Can't say."

Rafe narrowed his gaze. "I will get it out of you at some point, you realize."

He climbed out of the cab then reached back for her, placing his hands on her waist and lowering her to the ground between his open legs. For an instant their entire bodies rubbed together.

A soft groan escaped his lips.

Her eyes danced with mischief as she grabbed him by the hand and pulled him up the walkway. "Just remember *that* was your fault."

"My fault entirely," he agreed. "Hang on a second, I need to make an adjustment."

Laurel whirled on the spot, her skirt flaring as she looked at him with wide eyes. He moved in close before casually reaching downward. He stared into her face the entire time.

"You are so bad," she whispered.

He shrugged then bumped her with his shoulder as they headed up the stairs hand-in-hand.

"Is your sister gonna be here with her family?" he asked.

"I'm not sure if Leslie and Jim are coming." She took a sudden breath. "Oh, but th—"

The door opened in front of them to reveal the last face Rafe wanted to see. Coincidentally, the first face he'd seen that morning.

"Come on in," Jeff said, backing into the house as he swung the door wider. "Everyone's busy with last-minute preparations, so I'm the greeting committee."

Awesome. "Good to see you," Rafe lied, accepting Jeff's hand and shaking it firmly but within polite territory. Resisting the urge to crush bones.

Laurel seemed determined to keep Rafe between her and Jeff. He'd moved forward as if to offer her his hand as well, but she ducked away, catching hold of Rafe's forearm and using him to keep her balance as she reached down and adjusted the strap of her shoe. When she popped up, she did so on Rafe's right.

Considering she and Jeff had dated, and the other man hoped to start something up with her again, she didn't seem very thrilled to see him.

Which was A-okay with Rafe.

He slipped an arm around her waist and gave her a reassuring squeeze. "So, hon. You were going to tell me—"

"Is that my mom? Coming, Mom." She wiggled out of his embrace and shot toward the kitchen without a backward glance, abandoning him with his new bestest buddy.

IT WAS cowardly to leave Rafe with Jeff, but since they were standing in her parents' living room, Laurel figured it was pretty safe.

She'd known the evening would be tough, but she hadn't expected that initial jolt at seeing Jeff again to make her quite so tense. Even warned that he'd be there, she was beyond normal levels of uncomfortable, and her childish ploys to avoid looking him in the eye were making the situation more awkward.

Add in that Rafe had moved possessively even though he didn't really know what was going on, escaping was the only option.

I know it was a cheat, and not very mature, she told God, *but really, Jeff cheated in the first place just showing up.*

Walking into the kitchen where her mom was pulling a pot roast from the oven gave her a moment to settle her nerves and get her act together.

"Hello, sweetie. Glad you could come." Her mother rested the pan on the counter and pulled off her oven mitts so she could drag Laurel in for a firm hug. She kissed her cheek and then patted her on the shoulder. "Can you make the gravy, please? I'll get your father to slice the roast in a minute."

Nothing had changed during the time she'd been gone, and Laurel moved easily through the familiar kitchen. She grabbed the ingredients she needed, slipping into position at the stovetop.

There was no sign of her sister, or her family. "Where's Leslie?"

"Amanda has the flu, and Leslie's worried it's going to go through the whole family, so they sent their regrets."

Too bad. Her nieces would have made a great buffer tonight for the testosterone at the dinner table. Laurel pushed aside her concerns. "Getting sick could make it tough for her to sing on Sunday. I hope she avoids whatever bug it is."

"Your sister has the constitution of a bull elephant. She'll be fine." Her mom bustled around, popping vegetables into bowls and adding seasonings. "Or at least that's what I keep telling her. She's not allowed to miss choir. She has a solo."

"It's just choir, Mom. The congregation will sing louder." She couldn't resist. "Or, I bet Mrs. Pfeiffer would jump at the chance to fill in."

Her mother didn't swear, but she certainly made a rude noise under her breath. "We'll have to send up lots of prayers so that doesn't happen." She swung instantly toward Laurel and shook a finger. "Don't you repeat that in public."

Laurel snickered.

Her mom gave her a mock dirty look before pointing at the pot. "Aren't you supposed to stir when you're making gravy?"

She bit down her amusement and turned back to the stove. "Yes, ma'am."

Masculine voices floated in the background, too low to be clearly heard, but so far everything seemed to be going okay. Laurel eyed the clock and estimated how long it would be before she and Rafe could escape.

Her mom was in full kitchen-commando mode. "David," she called. "I need you. Come carve the roast."

"On my way." Her father's answer came instantly, the familiar rumbling tone rolling through the house like an echo, comforting and right.

"Jeff." Her mother waited until he rounded the corner. "I need your help as well. Will you mash the potatoes for me, please?"

That request wasn't nearly as comforting and welcoming.

"Love to."

The room was about to get a whole lot more crowded. With her hands occupied, Laurel was stuck standing over the stove and whisking rapidly as she poured hot drippings into the pot.

Jeff brushed past her as he entered the small kitchen. His reflection was mirrored in the kitchen window as he rolled up his shirtsleeves to reveal strong forearms. His dark hair perfectly in place except for that one spot that always stuck up a little, making him look more human.

The man was attractive, she'd admit it, but it was the sight of Rafe beyond Jeff that set her body tingling and her heart pounding.

He leaned on the doorframe as he took in the domestic activity. From top to bottom he was one fine sight, long legs covered by crisp new jeans, his thigh muscles challenging the fabric. His dark-blond hair was long enough to curl at his neckline, and she was tempted to reach over to slip her fingers through it. He'd put on a dressy shirt, no tie, and the material stretched over broad shoulders, firm muscles pressing the fabric as he folded his arms over his broad chest.

Yup, she was staring, but the view was too good to ignore.

His eyes sparkled at her, and he winked before easing to vertical and approaching her mom.

"You'd better put me to work too, or I'll feel left out. What can I do?" he asked.

"There's silverware to be laid on the table," her mom suggested, pressing the utensils into his hands then turning and pushing him into the dining room. "Napkins are in the top left drawer—"

"—beside the placemats. I remember." He was nothing but polite, but Laurel knew he was holding back from making a comment about how often he'd had dinner at this very table.

Jeff had moved to her immediate left, smiling down as she swirled the whisk through the gravy.

"That smells great," he offered, applying the potato masher to the pot without looking at what he was doing. He was examining her instead, eyes tracing over her in admiration, the way she'd imagined before Rafe had picked her up.

Only it didn't seem to be the expression of a man who was counting his losses. It was someone strategizing to make a move.

Which— *No. Way.*

"My mom did everything. I'm just the unpaid labour," she offered.

"Me too," he whispered conspiratorially, leaning closer. "Am I supposed to add anything? I'm only the manpower, literally."

Laurel got busy as if something vital was happening in the pot in front of her. How was it possible to take this long for gravy to set? "Oh, you'll have to ask my mom. I'm not sure what she's got planned."

"Laurel. You know we love your mashed potatoes. What is it that you always add?" Suddenly her mom stood behind her, reaching around to steal the whisk from her unwilling fingers. "Here, let me take over. You work with Jeff to get those potatoes ready."

Good grief, if Laurel didn't know better she'd suspect that—

No, it was too obvious to deny. Her mom was pushing her toward Jeff even though Rafe was wandering around the table right now, not even ten feet away. She glanced at Jeff who smiled apologetically, but with far too much interest considering she'd shown up with another man.

Nope. Her mom's weird behaviour wasn't Jeff's fault, but he didn't mind them being shoved together one bit.

The only solution was to get out of there as quick as possible. "Let me grab a couple things, but you get to do the heavy labour."

"I'm all yours," he answered quickly.

Which was exactly what she didn't want.

It was like walking through a china shop blindfolded. It seemed there was nothing she could do or say that wasn't going to backfire. As soon as she got everything in the bowl for Jeff, she excused herself, slipping back into the dining room to catch up with Rafe.

He'd been watching the entire thing with amusement.

"Stop it," she muttered.

"I didn't say a word," he whispered back, blinking innocently. "You do make good mashed potatoes."

His expression was completely serious, and she resisted poking him in the ribs. Instead she stepped on his foot as she walked past him, his chuckle rumbling in her ears.

Her mom rushed in and took over, seating everyone with rapid-fire precision—the three of them in their usual family positions with her mom and dad at the head and foot of the table. Rafe sat across her, and Jeff at her side, which was perfect. She'd far prefer to accidentally bump elbows with the man every now and then instead of futilely avoiding eye contact all meal.

Her mom placed the final bowl on the table and whipped right into conversation. "Rafe. I understand you've been gone." She offered the basket of bread down the table to Jeff. "We haven't seen you around lately."

"I was on the road, plus it's been pretty busy out on the ranch," he said. "Gabe and I have been doing a lot of improvements over the past couple of years."

"I've heard good things," she said. "How are Allison and the baby?"

"Doing well. You should come out sometime," he offered "I picked up some new stock, and there should be lambs within the next couple of weeks."

"What else are you working on?" Laurel asked, honestly curious. A flush of guilt swept in for not having asked sooner about that part of his life. The Angel Coleman ranch had been going through some tough times before she left. "I remember you wanted to raise more chickens. I always got a kick out of that. Rafe Coleman, chicken rancher."

His eyes crinkled at the corners as he smiled in response. "Yes, we have more chickens. Turkeys and geese as well—Allison started us growing poultry, and that part of the ranch is doing great.

"How do you ranch birds?" Jeff asked. "Do you use really small horses to round them up?"

"Tiny little lariats," Rafe joked. He turned back to Laurel and shook a finger at her snicker. "I'll have you know it takes a lot of skill to lasso only one at a time."

"Have you ever been on the wrong side of a chicken stampede?" she asked.

"Crushed by chickens. Not a good thing for on a headstone," her father offered.

Suddenly the whole evening felt…different. Some of her tension faded as she looked into Rafe's smiling eyes. He was there for her, his lighthearted, familiar manner making a difference.

When their plates were filled with food they paused for a moment for her father to say grace. She'd never been more grateful their family didn't have the tradition of holding hands while they prayed.

The rest of their dinner conversation stayed generic and light, and other than Jeff squirming oddly in his chair off and on, nothing out of the ordinary happened. No outbursts or troublesome reveals, and she figured she'd dodged a bullet.

She and Rafe were saying their goodbyes far sooner than expected.

"Good to meet you," Jeff told Rafe as they stood at the door about to leave.

"Safe travels back to Toronto," Rafe said, nodding a final farewell to her father. "Pastor Dave."

"I'd love to stop by sometime," her father mentioned. "If that offer to see the lambs wasn't just for Corinne."

"You and Mrs. Sitko are more than welcome. Give me a call to make sure I'm around." Rafe accepted a hug from Laurel's mom, then they escaped to his truck.

They were a few blocks away before he chuckled. An evil sound that was far too familiar.

"What?" Laurel demanded. "I know that laugh. You did something terrible."

"Did not."

"Rafe…"

He shook his head. "Nope. Not me. Just thinking that the Coleman land's got my back."

He wasn't making any sense. She made a face at him then looked out the front window at the passing countryside. He'd left Rocky Mountain House, headed north. "Fine, keep your secrets for now. I'll tease them out of you later."

They sat in silence for a minute, and she closed her eyes. It was fortunate the evening had turned out the way it had. She could easily avoid Jeff during the week, and after next Sunday he'd be gone—hopefully never to return. That part of her history would be gone and forgotten.

The truck slowed, and she popped open her eyes as Rafe took the corner into his brother's place.

While she liked Gabe and Allison, a visit with them wasn't exactly what she'd been thinking of for a date. Still, she put on a good face.

"How are Gabe and Allison?"

"Fine."

He drove right past the house to the opposite side of the new barn.

Okaaaay. "Are you sure I'm dressed for the occasion?"

Rafe caught her by the hand and tugged her out the door after him, the smooth glide of her body against his sending a lovely shot of heat through her system.

"Trust me." He opened the main door and gestured her in.

Light faded to nothing inside the barn. Rafe grabbed a flashlight from the side of the door and offered it to her.

"One for you, and one for me." He clicked his on. "This way."

Chapter Eight

DINNER HAD turned out surprisingly well, considering Rafe had spent most of the evening trying not to say something inflammatory to get under Jeff's skin. Instead he took what pleasure he could from realizing the other man hadn't gone unscathed from their encounter that morning.

It wasn't as good as planting a fist in Jeff's gut, but knowing the stinging nettles on the thistles had gotten to him enough to make Jeff squirm was worth a few laughs.

Coming out to Angel property—far more comfortable. He and Laurel had a lot to discuss, but he didn't want what was their first real date to just be about getting things out in the open.

He'd hurried after getting the invite to dinner and made a few arrangements before going to pick Laurel up. Now he guided her across the floor, her fingers linked in his. The barn smelled like a barn, but a clean, fresh one. Low contented sounds echoed on the air occasionally as she stepped beside him, the boards underfoot clean and white-yellow, not yet aged or stained by years of use.

Laurel swept her arm forward, the light from her flashlight a broad oval ahead of their feet. "Are we spies tonight?" she whispered. "We haven't done that for ages."

He chuckled as he led her to a steep staircase against the sidewall. "We do have lights in here," he said. "But I like how the flashlights feel."

She squeezed his fingers before reaching for the railing. "I don't mind. Let's pretend we're going on a treasure hunt."

"Pretend away."

The staircase was longer than in a regular house, leading up to the second level far above the animals below. The back half of the hayloft was already full, but there was room for a whole lot more bales to be stacked.

He dropped his phone into a speaker set at the top of the stairs and clicked on the playlist he'd made before leading her toward the open area where he'd set a cloth-covered table and two chairs, flickering lights glowing in welcome.

"Rafe Coleman, are those *candles* you left burning in a hayloft?" She sounded panicked and outraged, ready to rush forward and put them out.

"Worrywart." He snagged her by the hand to keep her close until he could pick one up and flip it over to show her the switch on the bottom. "Battery operated."

She flopped into the chair he held for her. "You're crazy. There was no need to leave things lit up."

"I wanted to make a good first impression. And you need to trust me more," he repeated.

"I mean it's pretty, and all, but still." She glanced around the space. "Fancy."

"Private," he countered. "We'll go to Traders later, but we need time to talk, and it'd be nice to do that somewhere no one can overhear us."

She seemed to consider for a moment before nodding. "You should've told me. I would have brought something along for a picnic."

"Good lord, I couldn't eat another bite right now. Your mother cooks like that all the time, doesn't she?" He settled in the chair beside her, kitty corner, instead of across the table. "I didn't come over that often, but the times I did, I remember rolling away from the table even if it wasn't Thanksgiving."

"Hospitality rules," Laurel answered. "I'm surprised she didn't cook your favourites. That's what she tends to do as well."

Mrs. Sitko probably hadn't wanted to choose between cooking his favourites and Jeff's, but he didn't voice the words. No need to make things awkward, not when Laurel was relaxing back in her chair and looking at him with anticipation, a soft smile on her face.

Instead he reached into the cooler beside them and brought out a bottle of fancy pop, placing it on the table along with two plastic cups from his kitchen. "Can I interest you in a drink? One of the finest sugar-coma-inducing food-colouring hits available."

A loud laugh burst out from her. "Brat."

"What? I knew you wouldn't drink anything alcoholic since you're working tomorrow, and I like this stuff too."

She watched as he poured them both glasses. "Since when? I could swear you used to say this stuff tasted like orange Tang gone bad."

"I'm sure you remember wrong." He lifted his glass in a toast. "To friendship."

She touched her glass against his—the hard plastic clinking with a hollow sound—then drank.

Rafe couldn't take his eyes off her. He itched to undo the elastic she'd pulled her hair back with and let the soft strands slide through his fingers. He knew exactly how soft the material was that covered her. He wanted to slip the fabric from her shoulders and press kisses to her bare skin.

Icy-blue heat shone back, and he clutched his glass a little tighter to stop from reaching for her.

"You keep looking at me like that and we're not going to get any talking in," she warned quietly.

"Trust me, I can look at you like this for a long time. Doesn't matter if we're talking or not."

She swallowed hard. "What do we need to talk about?"

He put his elbows on the table and leaned forward, checking for clues of how to approach the topic. The last thing he wanted was for her to be upset, but the elephant in the room needed to be addressed.

Straight up. The only way.

"As far as I can figure, Jeff Lawson either needs to be buried somewhere in the back forty, or I should be sending him a present for whatever it was he did to screw things up with you."

Laurel pressed her lips together. "You just jump right on in there, don't you," she accused, leaning back.

"Aren't you glad I didn't bring this up in the middle of Traders?"

"Very," she said. He gave her a moment as she fiddled with her glass, gathering her courage. Yet she tilted her head and looked him straight in the eye as she answered. "He and I dated for a while at Bible College."

"So he told me."

"What?" Her mouth hung open for a minute. "When did he tell you that? Oh my God, he didn't tell you before dinner, in front of my father?"

"No, this morning." Rafe leaned to one side and came back up with a box of doughnut holes. "Timbit?"

Her eyes narrowed as he opened the box and held it toward her. She sat there, staring, so he picked out a doughnut hole as if it was the most important thing in the world, popped it in his mouth and chewed carefully.

"Tasty," he announced.

A growl escaped her. "You're looking for pain, Coleman."

"Hmmm? Oh, right. Jeff." Rafe wiped the corners of his mouth and licked his fingertips before continuing. "It seemed he figured six a.m. was a good time to share that you two were once an item."

"No. I'm so sorr—"

"—and that he'd like that to be true again."

She sputtered before snapping out the words, "No fucking way."

Rafe blinked in surprise. "Excuse me, Sitko, did you just *swear?*"

"Trust me, Jeff Lawson is worthy of a few prime words that I wouldn't usually utter."

Rafe waited.

"Yes, we dated." She took a deep breath and let it out slowly. "It's not like when I left here I was looking to find someone to spend time with—"

"Hey," he interrupted. "We'd said we weren't going to wait for each other, Laurel. Don't go apologizing for something you weren't supposed to do."

It was easier to say that since he'd had a warning. He wasn't sure how he would have responded finding out without this morning's heads-up.

Gee, he should be thankful to Jeff. Maybe he'd send flowers. A vase full of thistles popped to mind.

Laurel nodded at his words, but it was clear she still felt uncomfortable. "It was strange at first, but it seemed like the right thing to do." Her eyes were glued to his face, as if hoping she wasn't going to hurt him. "I was starting first year and he was in the middle of his four-year program, but we hit it off. He was charming and polite, and he made me laugh." She looked down at her fingers. "This is going to sound really stupid, but in some ways, he reminded me of you."

Rafe wasn't sure if that was a compliment or not. "Considering you can barely look at the man, I hope that's not true anymore."

"No. But we dated, and I thought it was pretty serious, or potentially going to be serious. Then he broke it off with me."

"Idiot," Rafe muttered, catching her fingers in his hand and squeezing them. "You seem a little more choked up about it than just that. Although I'm sure that it hurt, him being your first real boyfriend."

"Yeah, there's more," she said. "He broke up with me right before leaving on a mission trip for a month. When he returned he made a couple of half-assed attempts at getting back together. When I said no, he turned around and started up with someone else. Someone whose father just happened to head an important missionary organization."

"Idiot *and* asshole. Got it." Rafe squeezed her fingers. "Is there more?"

She hesitated.

Huh. "Trust me, sweetheart, while I'd love to take the man apart for upsetting you, I won't go off half-cocked. I want to know how to help make things easier for you."

Laurel avoided meeting his eyes, obviously embarrassed. "To be fair to Jeff, he's guilty of being an ass, but I don't think he meant to be deliberately cruel when he called it off. I had to deal with uncomfortable questions from people asking if he'd called, or been in touch while he wasn't around, but it wasn't terrible. Just...really awkward considering I hadn't expected it in the first place. He straight up told me 'I need time away from you' which made me feel as if I'd done something wrong, or been too smothering or something." She seemed about to say something else, then shook her head as a derisive laugh escaped. "And the fact I can remember *exactly* what he said is pathetic."

"It's not pathetic," Rafe insisted. "You were hurt. It was big and important."

"This is why my parents should have let me start dating earlier, so I could have gotten all this melodrama out of the way back then."

"Hey, dating at any age is no guarantee of losing the crazies. I still get private Facebook requests from Toni Faulk, hoping we can get together."

"Toni?" Laurel blinked. "She moved away in grade nine."

"Yeah, I know, but I guess she's got a job where she travels lots, and she'd love to"—he made air quotes—"'reconnect' anytime I feel like driving to the Edmonton airport for a booty call."

She snorted. "You win. I don't have people DMing me for sex."

"No, you just have them showing up unwelcome in your backyard, potentially working with your father.

"There is that." Misery stole over her expression. "I can't... I don't know what to tell my parents. "

Wait. *What?*

"Oh, shit." Suddenly the awkward tension before dinner made more sense. "They don't know, do they? Because I can't imagine your father willingly inviting around someone who broke your heart."

"Jeff didn't break my heart. Not really," Laurel said. "I haven't told my parents that we dated, though, and I don't think he's mentioned it either."

"Awesome. Very churchy and upright of him."

She offered him a dirty look. "Hey, don't blame him alone. I'm sure he was worried about visiting Rocky, wondering what my dad would say to him."

"Oh, he's a brave man. Totally Captain Canada material."

"Don't be a jerk," Laurel muttered. "I'm just as bad. I'm enjoying the mental picture of Jeff dancing carefully around my father far too much. He had to be totally shocked to find out I hadn't said anything."

"You're not going to convince me you're a villain, Sitko, so give it a rest. A little foolish, but not a villain."

"Hey, Mom and Dad not knowing isn't as foolish as it sounds," she said. "The whole idea was to go away and spread my wings a little. I didn't want to tell my parents everything right as it happened, and by the time we were getting to the stage I thought there was something to tell, there wasn't."

She stared into space, the sadness on her face seeming deeper than just a first love gone wrong.

"This sucks on so many levels." Rafe wasn't sure the whole keeping-secrets-from-her-parents thing was a great idea, and while there had to be more to the story regarding Jeff dumping her for another woman—what he did know confirmed Rafe's opinion.

Jeff was an idiot, an asshole, and Rafe didn't like him one fucking bit.

But it was time to switch topics, and stop wasting their date thinking about the bastard.

Rafe stood and brought Laurel with him to the edge of the loft floor. "Well, I can't change the past, but

112

I'll be there for you. I'll keep him away from you."

"I can deal with Jeff," Laurel said. "What are you grinning like that for?"

"It's date time." The second part of his prepared surprise. "Remember how you always complained about never getting to come out to my place because you were sure there was a fantastic rope swing in the barn?"

"Yeah."

He stepped away a few paces to the wall, unhooking the wooden seat he'd made and bringing it to the middle of the floor where the long ropes had room to hang straight. Rafe waved his hands over it with a flourish. "Ta-da."

"That's not a rope swing," she pointed out.

"Once we put up the rest of the hay, I'll hang a real one, and we can try some fancy jumpin' if you're still game. But in the meantime"—he patted the seat—"your throne, milady."

Laurel eyed the wooden seat. "It's awfully high."

He'd hung the ropes firmly from the rafters but deliberately tied the seat farther off the ground than usual. "Allow me."

He closed his hands around her waist, lifting her into the seat as she wrapped her fingers around the ropes. She glanced at him, her sparkling blue eyes nearly in line with his. "You know this is too high for me to get a push off the ground. You're going to have to help me."

"Not a problem." Rafe stepped into position behind her, slipping his hands over hers. "Got a good grip?"

"Yes. *Oh...*"

Her words faded off into a soft sigh as he pressed his lips to the side of her neck. He leaned his body against her back for a moment, sliding his hands down her arms. Down her sides, finally coming to a rest against her hips.

Heat coiled around them. A slow, gentle simmer he was reluctant to speed up. Not too fast, not too slow…

Whatever history lay between Laurel and Jeff—right now wasn't about that. This wasn't about their history, either, his and Laurel's, even though they had a hundred memories of the past.

He nuzzled the side of her neck, humming happily as he dragged in deep breaths of her scent. "You smell delicious."

"You swing funny," she teased, but she tilted her head to the side and presented him with more neck to nibble on.

"I swing perfectly," he corrected. "Hold on tight."

Chapter Nine

HAVING RAFE pay attention to her like this was...

A shiver rippled over her skin as he kissed her, this time right under her ear, his hard body brushing her back and sending need ricocheting through her core.

This? Was perfect.

Most of the time they'd spent together over the years had been before school and during lunch. Once the school bell rang to end the day, he'd hop on the bus to head home, and she'd walk back to the pastorate, so outside of school hours it wasn't as if they had spent masses of time together.

And they certainly hadn't spent time together like *this*. With that edge of something other than friendship warm and pulsing between them.

When he touched her, a sense of familiar was there. But it wasn't her good friend who gave her hips a squeezing caress before he grabbed the wooden support under her and stepped back, lifting her high in an arc.

Heck, he'd pushed her on the swings before, the two of them talking nonstop about whatever it was that was on their mind at the time.

This was different because they were no longer children. There weren't childish activities stealing though her mind as he pushed her. The swing slid forward smoothly before reaching its peak then drifting back to his strong hands. He caught her on each upswing, pulling her slightly toward him before giving a firm push that sent her soaring.

Beams of light shone through faint cracks, dancing with the dust floating in the air. The heady scents of the ranch filled her on every breath.

But those things faded every time she got close to him. New sensations buzzed through her system. It must have been her imagination because they weren't physically close anymore, not while she was swinging, but it seemed as if the air itself got warmer near him. The hard slope of his body behind her a barrier she could sense.

Laurel pumped with her legs to make the swing go faster, climbing higher as a lovely, dizzying sensation grew. She might not know exactly what they were doing, but this was fun, and she wasn't letting go of a single moment of joy.

A timeless moment later Rafe gave her a warning tap. "My turn."

On the next return swing, he caught hold of the wooden base and slowed her, walking forward rapidly then holding the seat steady so she could slip off to the hard wooden floor.

"You want me to push you?" Laurel asked, moving out of his way as he settled onto the narrow board.

"Nope."

She gasped as he caught her around the waist and tugged her into his lap.

"Rafe—"

"Hold on to the ropes," he ordered, walking backward slightly before leaning back and lifting his feet from the ground.

He had one hand wrapped around her waist, but the other held the rope, and thank goodness, because she couldn't have kept them in place when he increased their speed.

If it had been just her she would have felt slightly off balance, but his iron grip held her in position on his lap, the solid muscles beneath and behind her forming a wall, while the arm around her waist pulled their bodies together tightly.

She relaxed, trusting him to take care of them. "If the swing breaks, you're going to be a pancake," she warned.

A laugh escaped, but there was more than amusement in the sound.

Desire. Need.

Lust.

The heat between them instantly ratcheted up a level.

They fell into a rhythm, moving together. She'd lean back on his chest, their legs extended as they flew forward, glimpses of the fields beyond them dappled with sunlight and shadow visible through the open loft window. Then he'd curl his body forward, stomach muscles flexing as he pressed against her, swinging backward with the weight of her body pressed to his strong forearm. He'd rolled up his shirtsleeves, and her breasts rested on the bare skin of his forearm.

The urge to get naked hit hard.

They moved together in a rhythm that sent her body thrumming. She fought to keep from moaning, but it was impossible to stop a note of pleasure from escaping as he pressed his lips to the side of her neck and murmured. "Comfy?"

"Only you would think about fooling around on a swing, Rafe Coleman."

"Are we fooling around? You've got a dirty mind, Sitko. We're just swinging." But the arm around her body shifted slightly, and his hand drifted higher, brushing the underside of her breast.

They weren't swinging as hard anymore, as if his concentration had broken and airtime was no longer the top priority. They were still solidly seated, but his thumb drifted across her breast, pausing to circle her nipple.

Her body obediently tightened to a hard peak.

It was a heady sensation to press her torso more firmly into his grasp while they canted back and forth, never quite balanced. He adjusted position to cup her fully, a low sound of pleasure escaping as he squeezed.

"We are definitely fooling around," she insisted.

"Okay," he agreed, dragging his feet on the floor to stop them. "We are. Come here."

He stood and turned her at the same time. She ended with her arms around his shoulders, her legs around his hips. Her entire body pressed hard against him, every inch quivering with excitement and...he was kissing her.

Rafe Coleman was a damn fine kisser.

He seemed fascinated with her bottom lip. Licking it, and biting it, and sucking it into his mouth briefly before pressing their lips together completely and stealing her oxygen.

She finally did what she'd been craving earlier that day. Laurel slipped her fingers through the hair at the base of his neck and let the soft curls wrap around her fingertips.

He slipped his tongue into her mouth, and they tangled, bodies rubbing together as he stepped across the floor. She had no idea where he was going. She wasn't sure how he could walk without stumbling because she was blind. Eyes squeezed shut as she concentrated on the blood pounding through her system.

Floorboards creaked, then cooler air struck as he separated them and lowered her on a firm, yet soft surface. Laurel glanced to the side, pressing one hand over age-softened cotton, but she barely had time to recognize the familiar picnic quilt before Rafe was there, crawling over her to stare down with a happy smile.

She caught him by the shoulders, pulling futilely in the hopes he'd settle his weight on her.

"Uh-uh. Not until we set some ground rules," he warned.

He braced his hands on either side of her head, with one knee resting solidly between her legs, only he held himself far enough away their bodies didn't connect. Unmovable, no matter how hard she tugged.

Laurel groaned unhappily. "Tease."

"I suppose. Teasing myself, if I'm honest, but Sitko?" He dipped his head far enough to press a quick kiss to her lips. "We don't need to rush. Trust me, remember?"

He was right. After how long they'd waited, it didn't seem right to go too far, too fast. She was scared to go too far, too fast, but...

She still *wanted.*

Laurel took a deep breath. This was Rafe, her friend since forever. "I trust you."

"Good."

He rolled to the blanket, stretching his long legs beside her. He rested on one elbow as he gazed down, admiration in his eyes.

"See, if I rushed, this wouldn't be nearly as much fun."

"It's well established you have a twisted idea of fun, Coleman."

He trickled his fingers over the buttons on her blouse. "You like me twisted. I want to savour. I want to go slow and appreciate every second of learning you. I've only touched you the one time, you know."

That night so long ago flashed into Laurel's mind. She reached up and stroked his cheek, a thin layer of scruff scratching her palm. He'd been the one to slow them down then, too, and the memory reassured her. "You've got way more willpower than me," she whispered. "Thinking back to the one time."

Rafe slipped the top button on her blouse open before skimming his fingers along the edge, a light, teasing touch over the top swells of her breasts. "I had fun that night."

Just the thought of it was enough to send a flash of desire through her core. "But we didn't have sex. That's what I meant. If I'd had my way we would have."

He was working on the next button. "I didn't have a condom, and no way could I go back into town to grab one." He leaned down and pressed his lips to bare skin. "I got to touch you, and I got you off."

He certainly had. She'd done the same for him, both of them fumbling to find a way to connect intimately without dangerous consequences.

The memories of their one time together were hot, and she'd thought about that night a lot, but right now he was making short work of the rest of her buttons, and staying in the here and now was a whole lot more desirable than trips down memory lane.

Rafe used the backs of his fingers to brush the fabric from her torso, a teasing touch on sensitive skin that made her arch toward him.

"Shhhh. I want to look," he said, stroking up the side of her body and over the cream-coloured bra she wore. He traced his fingers along the lacy edge, down to the dip between her breasts, up the other side. He did it again, only this time he used his thumb on her skin, stretching his hand open until he covered her breast completely.

Oh boy. Laurel swallowed hard. "It's okay if you take my bra off."

"I'll get there," he promised. His voice sounded deeper than usual, and she lifted her gaze to his. Raw hunger reflected back.

"Take off your shirt too," she ordered.

"Later. I'm busy," he informed her, skating his palm over her in a slow, even circle.

Her nipple tightened, pressing against the thin fabric as if desperate to make contact.

He shifted closer, bodies bumping as he pressed their lips together. A slow kiss this time, with gentle pressure and the slightest flick of his tongue. Before she could sink her hands into his hair, he was gone, butterfly-light touches teasing down her jaw and neck. Along the edge of her bra, and over to where her nipple stood at attention as if waiting for him.

He hummed happily, brushing his lips over the peak before tasting her. His tongue wet the fabric and made it cling. He closed his lips around the tip and sucked lightly, and Laurel gasped in pleasure.

A happy sound rumbled up from his chest. "You're as hot as I remember."

"You're driving me crazy," Laurel whispered.

Rafe ignored her. Instead, he slipped his fingers under the edge of her bra, sliding the material aside and tucking it underneath. "But are you as delicious as I remember?" he asked, utter seriousness in the question.

This time when he put his mouth on her there was no barrier between them, and Laurel moaned. "Oh, yes."

He had both hands working now, cupping her slight curves on both sides. Her straps were still in place, but the actual cups were curled under to leave her exposed to his touch. Fingertips teasing. Fingers and thumbs rolling over her nipples and pinching briefly before being replaced by his mouth. His tongue and lips soothing. Stroking. Back and forth from one side to the other.

Laurel didn't know what to expect. One time it was a soft lick followed by a sharp pinch. The next, Rafe sucked, increasing the pressure slowly before putting the edge of his teeth to her in a move that drove a pulse from her nipple straight to her core.

Turned on and aching for more, but willing to follow his lead, she stroked her fingers through his hair and let him play.

His body was hard next to hers, hips pressed tight to her thigh. The thick ridge of his erection nudged her, and she moved her leg, desperately trying to give back to him. She didn't want this to be just about her—this was them, together finding pleasure. Taking the next step.

Rafe lifted himself slightly to gaze down in admiration. "So gorgeous. So perfect, with those tight little nipples that fit my mouth like you were made for me. I could spend all night eating you up, but I want more."

He slid a hand down her belly, fingers swirling for a moment over her belly button before slipping under the elastic of her skirt. "Yes?"

Why was he even asking? "Let's assume from here on the answer is always *yes.*"

"I don't assume. But good to know."

He kissed her, and she was momentarily distracted by his eager lips. Momentarily—because now his hand was under her panties and he was cupping her intimately. Rolling the heel of his hand against the top of her mound.

Not enough pressure for her to come, but more than enough to make her feel plenty optimistic they were on the right road.

"Touch me," she begged.

"I am touching you," he teased, his mouth at her ear as he brought the lobe between his teeth and bit.

Laurel growled. "Touch my pussy."

"Bossy."

"Rafe. *Please...*"

"Well, if you put it that way. How can I refuse?"

He dragged his hand upward, briefly tickling his fingers against her stomach before, with a wicked grin, moving where she needed him.

Chapter Ten

RAFE TREMBLED on the edge of control. As he slipped his fingers through her curls, she all but purred, the sound rising from deep in her throat making him impossibly hard.

He stroked his fingers through her wetness, slipping into her body slightly. One knuckle, retreat, repeat.

He adjusted his thumb until he found her clit and rubbed lightly as on every pulse he pressed deeper and deeper into her body. One finger replaced by two, fingers coated with her response as he fought to keep from frantically dry humping her leg.

It was no use. Laurel rocked against his hand, desperate noises escaping her as he fucked his fingers into her warmth. Distraction. That's what he needed, but the only distraction at hand was her.

Like her pretty little breasts, glistening from his mouth. He reached down to kiss them one after the other, sucking in time with his pulsing fingers.

She made another noise, and he shifted position enough to cover her mouth with his. Capturing the sound of her pleasure and taking it into himself. Their tongues tangled, desperation growing. He was rocking against her, and she was driving her hips up harder, faster, and together they were one minute away from—

Laurel arched under him, body tightening, her moans and little cries escalating in volume as she came.

No way on earth he could stay in control after that.

He pressed his aching cock against her one last time and lost it. Pressure shot from him in a rush, light bursting behind his eyes. He rocked even as he pressed his fingers as deep as possible, Laurel's pussy gripping him tightly in the aftershocks of her climax.

Softer now. Slower, taking her down gently. He kissed her. On the mouth, on the cheek. Over eyelids that fluttered closed a second before she let out a long, satisfied sigh.

She was twirling her fingers through the hair at the back of his neck, and it felt so perfect to lie there wrapped up with her, his hand still between her legs.

"Wow. That was the best swing I've ever had," Laurel offered.

He laughed. He was going home with sticky, wet underwear, and he couldn't remember the last time he'd been so happy. "I told you I knew what I was doing."

"Never had any doubts," she promised, stroking the side of his face as she examined him closely. "Tell me what you need me to do."

"About what?"

She glanced down his body. "About that."

Ha. "Oh, *that*. You did enough already."

Confusion covered her expression for a moment before her eyes widened. "Oh."

He snickered. "You're killing me here, Sitko. Did you not notice I kind of lost control?"

A slightly bemused smile twisted the corners of her mouth. "I must have been busy at the time."

"You need to learn to multitask."

She wiggled up on her elbows, not one bit shy about her bare breasts. "I promise I won't let that happen again."

"What? Me getting so excited about touching you that I come?" He shook his head. "Don't think that's a thing you can make any promises about."

"I want you to have a good time too."

"Trust me, I did."

He trailed his fingers down her body, astonished that he was there with her. That he had the privilege of touching her and making her lose herself in pleasure.

It was a privilege, and more, and he certainly didn't want her getting distracted by things that didn't matter in the big scheme of things.

And as tempting as it was to take her home and start all over, going even farther the next time, that whole going-slow thing had a purpose.

He slipped her bra back into position carefully, taking his time and touching as much as he wanted. "It's gonna be pretty busy around here for the next week," he warned. "Gabe has a ton for me to get caught up on since he's been managing things with hired help all summer. And after that we'll be haying, judging from the fields I spotted while we were out riding today."

"I remember how busy it would get for you in the fall." She stroked her fingers through his hair, patting it into place with a satisfied smile. "I'll email you my schedule for the week—it changes a bit every day. Call or text when you can. No pressure."

"I will. But plan on Friday. Dancing at Traders, if you're okay with that." It was the one place there was sure to be a gathering of the Coleman clan.

Laurel nodded. "I'm helping move Troy's stuff tomorrow, but other than that, I'm yours."

He liked the sound of that. He liked it an awful lot.

They straightened themselves up and headed back to his truck, Rafe ignoring the sensation of his briefs sticking to him best he could.

Distraction helped, like stealing a few kisses after he'd lifted her to the seat next to him. A few more after they pulled up to the sidewalk outside her place, and a final few standing with her in his arms on the concrete slab outside her door.

"I'm going too fast," Rafe muttered, lips brushing together as he let her up for air.

"You don't hear me complaining, do you?" Laurel pointed out, smoothing her hands over his chest as if she couldn't bear to let go either. "It's not as if we met for the first time two days ago."

Another sweet moment, tasting her briefly before shoving his hands in his pockets to stop from grabbing her. "Those weren't years of foreplay, Sitko."

"No, but they were fun, weren't they?" she said, unlocking her door and slipping inside. She offered one final smile. "Thank you. It was a good evening."

"A great evening," he insisted.

He waited until she'd closed the door and put on the safety chain before heading back to his rooms over the garage.

The place wasn't home. It was a bare space, with boxes stacked in piles. Gabe was right—he needed more than this, and he wanted a place Laurel would feel welcome.

The leftover bag from Tim Hortons Jeff had left behind stuck out of the garbage box, reminding Rafe he might have a fight on his hands down the road. Not for Laurel's affections—she'd made it pretty clear who she'd choose between the two of them.

A small trickle of doubt slipped in. They'd been friends forever, and were learning to be more. But they'd both experienced life during the years apart. What if—

Fuck it all, he wanted what was best for her, and what if he wasn't it?

Damn Jeff to hell for putting thoughts into his head. If the man did come back to Rocky, Rafe was going to do everything he could to make sure Laurel didn't have to put up with any bullshit. What would that look like? Hopefully he'd figure it out as they went along.

In the meantime, finding a new place to live moved up his priority list.

He headed to the shower with a whole lot on his mind, his thoughts returning to a certain blonde-haired woman who'd moved decisively in his mind from the *friends* category to *friends plus more*.

HE'D BEEN a hundred percent right—the entire week was a sweat-inducing mess from sunup to sundown and beyond. Forget having time to look for a new place to live, he barely had time to drag off his filthy clothes before falling into bed exhausted.

All the time behind the wheel that summer had made him soft, it seemed, and he dove even harder into work, not wanting to let his brother down.

Gabe and Allison had things well organized, and the half-dozen workers they'd hired to do the simple tasks were great, but the Angel spread was a big chunk of land to care for, even with the combined Coleman efforts.

He'd bumped into what looked like a clan meeting one morning, rounding the corner in the barn to find Gabe chatting earnestly with their cousins Blake, Steve and Karen.

They stopped talking when they spotted him, which wasn't completely out of line—he was sixteen years younger than Blake, and all of them except Karen were in long-term relationships. They didn't have that much in common other than being family, but usually that was enough. To find them hunkered down in the middle of the week seemed as if *secret things* were going on.

"Troubles?" Rafe asked.

"Just making some plans," Blake answered. "Gabe will fill you in when he can. I wanted to talk to you, though. Daniel's boys were helping at the Six Pack ranch over the summer, but they'd like to come out here for a bit." He grinned. "You have more interesting animals or something. Gabe says it's okay. What do you think?"

"If Gabe says it's okay, don't know why you're asking me," Rafe answered.

"You'd have to help supervise them," Gabe explained. "I didn't want to volunteer you without asking first."

"No problem. Will they catch the bus after school?"

"Yeah."

Rafe shrugged. "We can figure it out."

Blake nodded. "I'll let Daniel know. He'll be—"

Shit. "Make sure the boys know to come to Gabe's. We'll meet them here." He glanced at Gabe. "Sorry, but..."

"No, you're right."

Ben never came over to the new buildings if he could help it, and they both knew it.

Hell, the entire family knew what they weren't straight-up saying. Steve and Karen were grim-faced, and Blake was nodding, and it wasn't funny but it was because there was no way he should have to run interference to keep the boys out of his father's path.

Rafe was still thinking about the incident the next morning when he returned to the homestead to complete a few tasks. Terrible screeching noises rose from inside the old barn beside the house, dust shooting from the open doors of the hayloft as if a pack of demons had possessed the place and were ripping it apart from the inside out.

He wasn't too far off the mark.

Rafe parked well away then cautiously opened the door to the old building, confused to find his father tearing apart stall walls, dust swirling everywhere and creating a heavy curtain in the air.

Ben raised the tractor bucket to about four feet, adjusted the blade angle higher and tore out another section. The ripped-up boards landed with a crash, sending more dust flying, the roof creaking ominously.

Holy shit. Rafe ran down a side path, desperate to get into his father's line of vision as quickly as possible. He stayed back as far as he could, shouting over and over as he waved his arms until his father stopped flinging the bucket around.

Ben's face was folded into a scowl as he put the tractor into low gear, as if Rafe had done something absolutely terrible. "Get out of my way," he shouted over the engine roar.

"What the hell are you doing?" Rafe rushed the tractor and yanked the keys from the ignition. The sudden quiet as the engine died made his final words extra loud, and they echoed in the open space. "You can't take down walls without a plan. The next post over is the support beam for the main roof—are you trying to kill yourself?"

Ben shot to his feet and out of the tractor, eyes narrowing. "I'm not an idiot, and I'll thank you to remember that when you're talking to me."

"Don't act like one, then. And I never said you were an idiot, but that move you were about to make was damn stupid. What's going on? You're making a mess—"

"Last time I checked this was still my place. Even though your brother likes to boss us around, this barn is *mine*"—Ben smacked his fist down on the tractor frame—"and I don't need anyone's permission to make changes."

The fear that had driven Rafe became anger. Blood pounded, and his ears rang, and the thing he wanted most at that moment was to wipe the indignant expression off his father's face.

"You might not need permission, but it'd be good to have a structural plan in mind," he shouted back, flinging a hand to point at the support post his father had been mere feet away from dislodging. "Or at least if you want to bring the whole thing down on your head, give me enough time to get the animals and equipment out so they don't get hurt by your stupidity."

Ben's face had gone bright red, and his hands were clenched in fists by his hips. "I don't like your tone, young man. I'm still your father, and you will speak to me with respect."

"It's not disrespectful to try and save your life, but if you think it is, fine. That's the last time I'll interfere."

He tossed the keys at Ben, not even watching to see if they were caught. Instead, he stomped away, heading into the house to grab a drink before returning to the other side of the ranch and getting as far away from his father as possible.

The interior of the house was well worn, but clean and tidy, little signs of his mother everywhere. Today there was a reason for additional warmth as he wandered past his mom at the stove and squatted beside the high chair where Micah was strapped in and chewing on a baby cookie.

Rafe took a deep breath and shoved aside the anger and exasperation of the past minutes with his father. His nephew didn't deserve second-hand frustration.

"Hey, big fella. You living the life of leisure today? Getting spoiled by your Grammy?"

His mother appeared at his side, handing him a chocolate chip cookie warm from the oven. "Allison's not feeling well." She frowned. "I didn't expect to see you. I thought your father had a whole bunch of tasks he wanted your help with."

Rafe wondered exactly how much to say to his mom. "He didn't say anything. Although I didn't give him much of a chance because we were too busy shouting at each other about him being an idiot."

"Oh, Rafe." His mom sat next to Micah, absently brushing the hair off the toddler's forehead. "You two are so alike at times."

Fuck—exactly what he didn't want to hear. "Great. You think I'm an asshole?"

His mom whirled on him, eyes flashing. "Watch your language, Raphael Coleman. And no, I meant you're both stubborn when you get an idea in your head. It's like beating rocks with my bare hands to get you to change your mind. And now you've both set yourselves on paths where you're like oil and water."

"That's not what I intend, but the minute I see him—" Rafe cut himself off, slightly mollified by her explanation.

Wisely, his mom changed the topic. "I heard something interesting today."

Anything to not have to talk about Ben. "What's the latest gossip in Rocky?"

She smiled coyly. "I hear there's a new lady in your life."

Rafe was tempted to lean his head on the table. Great change of topic—from one thing he didn't want to discuss to another. "That wasn't the kind of gossip I expected."

"I like her. She's solid and yet fun, and you've been friends for years." Dana waggled her fingers as she seemed to consider the matter a little more then nodded. "Yes. I think she'll be good for you."

"I really don't want to talk about this with you, Mom."

"Which is why we're not talking. I'm simply offering my opinion, as mothers do."

He chuckled. "As mothers do—you got that right."

"You two always did get along so well." She eyed him. "Too well at times. I never expected the pastor's daughter to be such a troublemaker, but all those detentions couldn't have been your fault for so many years.

"This is starting to sound an awful lot like a conversation."

Dana leaned back in her chair and examined him as Micah stared between them, brown eyes blinking as he gummed his cookie into a sloppy mess. "And that would be an absolutely terrible thing? To have a conversation with your mother."

"About Laurel, yes. That would be a terrible thing to talk about right now," he teased.

His mother's eyes brightened. "Oh, I *like* that. If you don't want to talk about it, that means you must be in that first giddy falling-in-love stage, where everything is new, and you just want to keep it to yourself."

Rafe pinched the bridge of his nose. "Mom..."

She laughed at him, patting his shoulder as she got up to get a cloth and a toddler sippy cup from the counter. "Relationships are important. Every mother wants to see her kids happy and settled down, and with Gabe and Allison doing so well, of course I would be thinking about you."

He really shouldn't have asked, but she'd brought up the topic of relationships...

"Why do you stay?"

A stillness settled over the kitchen, sounds of the fire in the wood stove and the ticking clock on the kitchen wall loud as his mother stared out the window. Micah banged his fist on the highchair tray, but Rafe waited. It was rude that he'd asked, but since he had, he wanted to know the answer.

She faced him, an unreadable expression on her face. "I promised. I made a vow to stay with him. It's not always easy to keep our promises, and sometimes we make mistakes, but this is one that I can keep, so I have."

"He made promises too. I don't think he's keeping them," Rafe complained with a grumble.

His mom took a deep breath. "But my behaviour is not based on somebody else's. What I do needs to be the right thing, even if everyone else is failing around me. I promised for better or for worse—"

"But lately it's all been worse," Rafe pointed out.

Dana shook her head. "I know your father isn't the easiest man to get along with. He's got…troubles, especially when it comes to you boys, but as far as I know he's never done anything that's beyond the line. That means something. That means enough to keep trying, and keep hoping."

They stared at each other. Rafe heard it in her voice— Ben had never crossed the line, but if he ever did, she'd leave.

It was the most he could hope for.

All afternoon he kept thinking about her words as he worked. Right before supper he slipped into the quiet of the new barn outside Gabe and Allison's. He settled onto the bale beside Gabe, wondering why his thoughts had gone so morose. "You ever think how different life might have been if Mike hadn't died?"

A grunt escaped his brother. "All the time."

They sat in silence for a long moment, Rafe throwing bits of straw to the floor in front of them in a steady rhythm. "Sometimes I get jealous. When I look at what the other guys have—at their relationships with their dads. I mean, at least with Uncle Mike and Uncle

Randy." Uncle George was more a mystery, choosing mostly to hang out at the Whiskey Creek ranch to "get things done" since he didn't think his girls could do it without supervision.

"I know. I've felt it too," Gabe admitted. "The good thing is while they're not our dad, they're willing to listen, and help, and they're family."

Which was good, but it wasn't the same.

Gabe laid a hand on his shoulder before they both headed out without another word. Too many shared wishes that would probably never come true closed off Rafe's throat and made him need a dose of happiness.

Luckily, he had a date that night with his own personal prescription for feeling better, and it couldn't come soon enough.

Chapter Eleven

IT WASN'T as if Laurel had never been to Traders, but she'd never been there on a date. And just to mock her, fate arranged it so she had to come straight from work.

Rafe was waiting for her on the steps, uncoiling himself from where he'd been leaning on the railing. He stepped down toward her, all long legs and lazy movement.

Dark jeans stretched over firm leg muscles, the edge of a grey T-shirt visible at his neckline under the open collar of his checkered flannel shirt. Cowboy casual, handsome enough to make her mouth water.

"When I got your text, I thought you were canceling on me." Rafe met her at the bottom of the stairs, tucking his fingers under her chin to tilt her head and press a quick kiss on her lips.

"Wendy wasn't feeling well, so I had to stay on until closing. Sorry I made you wait."

He kissed her again as if he couldn't stop himself, before wrapping an arm around her and guiding her up the steps. "No worries. I'm looking forward to showing you off."

"Are we meeting anyone? Because I'm not dressed

137

up, or anything."

Rafe looked her over with approval. "You look like a naughty librarian. Want to help me check out a book later?"

She rolled her eyes, and he grinned.

"A couple of my cousins are bound to be here. It's Friday night, and this is the easiest place to find us." He pushed open the door and gestured her in. "Less now than before since a bunch of them need babysitters to get away and have fun."

He brought her into the drinking section of the pub. There were tables to sit at to shoot the breeze, with dartboards and pool tables at the far end of the room for playing games. A quick glance through the crowd proved the Colemans were gathered in the back corner.

Rafe caught her fingers in his and led her across the floor, weaving between tables. He smiled over his shoulder at her. "I think you know them all. You're not scared, are you?"

Laurel laughed. "Scared? Who you think you're talking to, Coleman? I ain't scared of anything," she said, drawling out the last sentence, imitating his voice the best she could.

Masculine laughter broke out on her left. "I could've sworn that was Rafe talking." Jesse Coleman came forward, his lips twisted into a cocky grin.

"I heard that line enough times during school," Laurel offered. "It echoes in my brain at times."

"What she's not telling you is I would usually utter it a couple seconds after she taunted me into doing something that would get us in trouble." Rafe stepped beside her and waved a hand over the crowd. "Laurel, meet...everybody. Let me know if you need introductions."

"I'm good," Laurel insisted. "Honestly, I know your family."

"Bet you can't name them all," Jesse dared her.

"I'll take that bet," Rafe interrupted.

Jesse raised a brow. "I wasn't talking to you, I was talking to the beautiful lady."

Laurel fought to keep from snickering. The man was as much trouble as the rumour mill said. Also, just because she'd only spent time around the Coleman family in passing, it didn't mean she was clueless.

"What's the wager?" she asked.

"You name everyone, I'll buy your drinks tonight."

"And if she makes a mistake?" Rafe demanded.

Jesse looked her over with approval. "I get a dance. A slow one."

Rafe stiffened, disapproval written on his entire body, but Laurel laid a hand on his arm and patted it reassuringly.

"Trust me," she said before turning to Jesse and raising a brow. "My drinks *and* Rafe's."

Jesse chuckled. "Sure, since you're not going to win."

"Get your wallet out." She stepped closer to Rafe, easing against him as she checked out the gathering. Then she turned back and named them without a second glance. "Travis, Ashley and Cassidy at the pool table with Melody. The Whiskey Creek girls are holding court at the end of the table beyond Trevor and Becky. Steve and Lee are straight behind us, and an empty chair, which means Rachel's probably in the bathroom."

Jesse didn't seem annoyed that she'd rattled them off so easily. He turned to Rafe. "I thought Becky might throw her."

"Librarian, remember? We met more than a few

times this summer," Laurel admitted.

"And the rest?"

"How long have you lived in this town, Jesse Coleman?" Laurel demanded. "Oh, right. All your life, kind of like me."

"You were gone for a few years."

"And now I'm back." She shrugged. "It's pretty easy to get caught up, between the library and the prayer list at church."

"Where I'm sure Jesse's name appears on a regular basis," Rafe taunted.

She laughed, but didn't admit or deny anything.

"I figured you could do it." Jesse offered a wink. "I just wanted to push Rafe's buttons."

Rafe rolled his eyes. "Come on, Sitko. Since it's on Jesse, we'd better start drinking." He smacked Jesse with his shoulder as he stepped past him, sending his cousin stumbling back.

His grip on Laurel's fingers demanded she join him, and she followed along, giggling softly. Jesse might've been teasing, but Rafe wasn't taking any chances.

He pulled out a chair for her next to Trevor and Becky, and she sat, offering them both a smile.

Trevor stared at Rafe, his expression somewhere between disgust and admiration. "So. You're not interested in trying to date Laurel because she's *forbidden fruit*. She would *never* look at someone like you because you don't travel in the same circles...or what was your bullshit excuse?"

Rafe shrugged. "Not my fault you're gullible."

Laurel took pity on Trevor. "If it makes you feel better, I didn't go out with him for over fifteen years."

"I never asked," Rafe pointed out.

"You were my best friend. Dating you would have been creepy."

The spot across the table from them was filled as Jesse joined them. "Once you get bored of him, you can take me as an upgrade."

"I'm younger, better looking, and I already know her ticklish spots," Rafe said. "Upgrade? No chance, old man."

Jesse leaned back in his chair, folding his arms behind his head and grinning easily. "You keep telling yourself that. You know I hold back on the charm because if I didn't, none of the rest of you would even have a chance."

Becky leaned in close to whisper in Laurel's ear. "Trevor tells me he's okay, but Jesse kind of scares me."

Laurel snuck her hand under the table and caught Becky's fingers in a reassuring squeeze. "Picture him as a big puppy with a lot of tail wag and enthusiasm. Absolutely certain everybody loves him."

"Because everybody does."

His comment jerked their attention back across the table to where Jesse was leaning forward on one elbow, chin propped up on his fist, listening to their conversation.

"What?" he drawled. "You shouldn't talk in front of a man if you don't want him to know you're admiring him."

Laurel snorted then pretended not to have heard him, speaking to Becky as if they were alone. "I'm sure you know how to deal with a puppy that gets too eager..."

"Pet them?" he suggested.

"...a firmly rolled-up newspaper," Laurel offered, and Becky finally smiled.

Across from them, Jesse snapped to attention,

admiration drifting over his features. "I like you."

Rafe growled. "Leave my girlfriend alone, asshole, or I won't crate train you, I'll take you over to the vet's and get you fixed."

Laurel joined in the laughter, but she noticed Becky had tucked herself a little tighter against Trevor for protection. On the other side, Rafe wrapped himself around her a little harder as well.

A change of topic was in order.

She glanced down the table to where the Whiskey Creek girls sat. They'd finished their serious discussion, and she didn't think interrupting was a problem. "Hey, Lisa. You're second up on the wait list for that book you wanted."

Lisa came around the table, tapping Rafe on the shoulder. "Move it. I need that seat."

"I'm sitting in it," he pointed out.

"Which is why I told you to move."

Rafe shifted into the empty chair to his left, but he dragged Laurel after him, keeping her by his side. It opened a space for Lisa to settle between Becky and Laurel.

The three of them talked quietly, the rest of the Coleman conversation swirling around them. They chatted about books for a while, Lisa and Laurel comparing favourites as Becky nodded—making notes about the ones she wanted to try. Becky was still learning how to use a computer, and when Laurel couldn't answer a question off the top of her head, Lisa offered to help.

"You guys can use the computers at the library if that's more convenient," Laurel proposed. "I'll let you into the classroom so you have some privacy."

"I like the library," Becky said.

"Works for me," Lisa said. "Great idea."

Rafe had been absently stroking his fingers over hers as he chatted with Karen and Lee, and he adjusted his chair to let her slide in closer as she and the girls rejoined the conversation at the main table.

"We've got to make plans. Snow is expected early this year—" Karen cut off as all the guys at the table groaned. She shrugged. "If you don't like snow, you're living in the wrong province."

"It's only September. We don't want to talk about it until it happens. Besides, it's not supposed to snow until after Halloween," Rafe insisted.

"Awww, you gonna be sad because you have to wear a coat over your Halloween costume?" Jesse teased.

Rafe made a rude noise as he rolled his eyes. "Yeah, I'm totally bummed when that happens."

"I bet Jesse's the type to design his costume to have the coat included." Laurel scratched at her chin as if she was thinking hard.

"You're right." Rafe grinned at her, figuring out where she was going. "He was a Stay Puft Marshmallow Man one year, wasn't he? Loved that costume—it was so him."

"The yeti was my favourite," Laurel confessed.

"Not the year he went as a Teletubbie?"

"Very funny, guys," Jesse offered with a smirk.

"We're just trying to help," Laurel insisted. "If you need an idea for this year, I hear you can get Pikachu onesies in your size."

Jesse's eyes flashed with amusement. "I'll say it again, I like you."

Another rumble of annoyance drifted from her side, and Laurel decided she'd better stop taking the bait Jesse was tossing before Rafe had kittens.

She turned to face him, placing her palms against his cheeks and looking him in the eye. "You know what happens when we go places together in public. It's a free-for-all—it's just for fun."

"As long as my family isn't getting in your face too much, and by family, I mean one annoying cousin."

She slid her hands into Rafe's hair and pulled him toward her so she could plant a deep, passionate kiss on his lips. An apology, and a claiming.

As anticipated, the Coleman crowd at her back let loose with wolf whistles and noises of encouragement. She pulled away to find Rafe staring at her hungrily.

"We good, baby?" she asked.

"We're great," he murmured. "You do know that kiss is going to get back to your parents."

"Yup, I figured. Along with the fact I'm at a bar, drinking and dancing." She took a sip of the beer in front of her. "Someone will feel the burden to inform them of my transgressions. Good thing my daddy's church isn't one of the strict ones."

"Are you going to be in shit?" he asked. "Because we don't need to—"

He was headed into a ramble, so she cut him off and kissed him again. It seemed the fastest way to stop his protests.

"Hmmm, okay, we don't need to talk about that anymore." He brushed his lips against her neck. "You said dancing?"

"Yup," she repeated.

He finished his beer, motioning for her to do the same, then he rose to his feet and took her by the hand, waving their farewells to the rest of the table. "We're off. Anyone else headed to the other side for a while?"

Trevor shook his head, and Becky waved goodbye,

obviously content to stay in place. The others seemed happily occupied as well.

The only one to take him up on the offer was Jesse. He rose to his feet, his grin only getting wider when Rafe tugged Laurel to his side.

"Don't get growly," Jesse said with a laugh. "I'm not going to poach."

"I'll break your eggs if you try," Rafe warned.

Laurel snickered at the pun, then let herself be led to the opposite side of the building where the music was a lot louder and the wooden floor was crowded with bodies.

Another first. She hadn't actually been on the Traders dance floor before.

Rafe didn't hesitate. He pulled her into his arms and guided her around the room.

It was nice to be held, but it had been a long time since she'd done this. "I'm not going to be very good."

"You're fine. I already know you like stepping on my toes," Rafe reminded her. "We need some practice to remember what we learned during our high school phys ed classes."

"My sister was so jealous I had you as a partner. All the guys in her year had two left feet, and the fact you had a sense of rhythm made you nothing short of a miracle."

He pressed her closer, twirling them for a moment as they smiled at each other.

Rafe wasn't the only Coleman on the floor. Joel and Vicki were there as well—Jesse's twin and the youngest member of the Six Pack family—dancing with his long-time girlfriend. They moved smoothly like a couple that'd been together for a while, and they looked happy.

But according to the rumours Laurel had heard, trouble was only moments away.

She glanced over her shoulder, wondering where Jesse had gone. "This isn't going to end well," she warned Rafe.

They'd finished a few more turns before Rafe realized what she'd seen. He sighed. "Dammit, I wish Jesse and Joel would get past whatever the hell happened between them."

It was like watching a giant tsunami wave roll toward them. Laurel spotted Jesse a few seconds later. He whirled the woman in his arms and came face to face with Joel and Vicki.

They froze for a second before Jesse's smile tightened, then he turned and danced the couples apart.

"Better than usual," Rafe muttered.

"Nobody knows what happened?" Laurel asked.

"Not unless you do." He adjusted her tighter against him as the music slowed. "You seem to know everything else about my family."

"Small towns," Laurel offered as an excuse. "I was gone at the time, so I really don't know what's wrong. I'd like to find out, though..."

He kissed her. "You're a busybody. Admit it."

"I'm curious," she corrected him. "Not the same thing."

They danced on, Rafe's hold on her possessive, yet right. It wasn't about getting turned on, but about being together. Being connected.

They stayed on the floor for nearly an hour before Laurel begged off, making their way outside into the cool fall night.

"I'll walk you home. When you said you'd be coming straight here from work, and you didn't have

your car, I left my truck outside your apartment."
Which meant they'd be at her place...
Maybe the night wasn't over yet.

Chapter Twelve

THEY HELD hands and strolled along, chatting about nothing. Laurel soaked in happiness like a sponge.

Rafe let out a contented sigh. "I needed this."

"Friday night at Traders?"

"Time with you, at Traders or anywhere." Rafe squeezed her fingers but kept walking. "It's been a tough week, but the entire time I was thinking about you, and it made it easier to get through the day."

"That's sweet." The warm glow in her heart increased. "Anything in particular make the week tougher than usual?"

He hesitated before answering. "Sometimes I get caught up wishing for things I can't have—and the biggest of them is a father I can look up to."

Sadness swept over her. "I know, and I'm so sorry."

"I don't begrudge you your dad, or Jesse his, or anything like that, but..." He sounded so worried, Laurel tugged him to a stop.

"What? Tell me."

"What if I end up like Ben?" Rafe held up a hand to ward off her protest. "What if, even though I plan to do things differently, I turn out like him? I've got him inside

148

me, and I've grown up with him around, and even if I want to make different choices, they say we become our parents."

Laurel thought for a moment. Of all the things for Rafe to worry about, becoming his father was not on the list. Not as far as she was concerned. "Gabe isn't like him, and he's got the same blood as you."

Rafe made a rude noise. "My brother is a way better man than me. He's walked away from trouble far more often than I ever have."

"Yeah, because you're totally out there, brawling the nights away," Laurel teased. "Not to make light of your concerns, but do you really think you're some kind of town bad boy?"

"No, but—" He made a face. "I'm not telling you what I'm most worried about." Rafe looked away, lowering his voice so much she had to listen carefully to hear. "He gets me so mad I literally see red. I want to hit him, and keep hitting him until he learns a lesson. Feeling that kind of rage scares the shit out of me. What if I go too far?"

"But you don't." Laurel curled her arms around him. "Even when you're absolutely furious with him, and I know that's happened before, even then you don't act on it. You don't knock his head off, and you don't let his anger overwhelm you."

"So far."

She nodded, linking her hands together behind his back, and letting her body press against his, warm and soothing. "Because you've decided that's not you. You made the choice, and that's what makes you who you are. I think you can trust yourself. The Rafe I know is a pretty good guy. Even-tempered. Cool. I've hung out with him a time or two—and I like him. I trust him."

He tucked his fingers under her chin. "I never want to break that trust."

"Then don't. Keep trying. That's as much as we can do...our best."

He kissed her and she leaned into it, accepting the contentment pouring from him.

"You make me a better man," Rafe said.

Laurel snorted without intending to break the serious moment, because his comment was too funny to ignore. "Yeah, I'm pretty sure that's not what Mr. Taylor said back in seventh grade. I think he said something to effect of 'Miss Sitko seems determined to ruin your chance to excel in this math class.'"

"God, how can you remember these things?"

"Am I right?" she demanded.

He laughed. "Yeah, something like that."

They'd reached her place, and this time he accompanied her down the stairs.

"You're coming in?" she asked.

"Definitely." Rafe stepped through the doorway, locked the door behind them then tugged her toward the couch. "I want to neck with my girlfriend."

"Okay." His girlfriend. She was such a dweeb that the word on his lips gave her shivers.

He sat, pulling her into his lap. "You're agreeable tonight."

"Why wouldn't I be? Kisses? Fooling around?" She tugged on the button shirt he wore so she could get her hands underneath his T-shirt. She pressed her palms to his warm stomach, tracing the lines of his six-pack with her fingertips. "You never did take off your shirt the other day."

"I was busy," he reminded her. "Here, let me. I want your hands on me."

Instant shiver. She sat back while he made short work of his shirts, pulling off both layers at once to reveal his broad chest and muscular shoulders. His left arm was darker than the right, and she traced her fingers over the line where his T-shirt had left a farmer's tan. "You drove with your window down and your arm on the sill this summer."

Rafe nuzzled her neck before nibbling on her earlobe. "The AC in the truck died in mid-July, and I wasn't sure repairs were in the budget. So, yeah. I red-necked it the rest of the summer."

He was so warm under her Laurel was ready to strip off a few layers herself. Whatever he was doing to her neck was sending goose bumps down her skin, and she alternated hot and cold as he touched her.

Their lips met, and she joined in enthusiastically as he kissed her. Twisting her in his arms as she dragged her fingers through his hair then lowering her to the couch so he could lever himself over her.

When he lifted up for a breath of air she moaned in approval. "You like being on top. I'm good with that."

His entire body shuddered for a second. "Fuck it. I'm trying to go slow."

"I can tell, although I'm not sure why." She lifted her free leg and wrapped it around his hip, sliding their bodies together more firmly. "This couch is too small. I have a perfectly good bed in the other—"

"Laurel..." he warned, his voice gone deep. "You're killing me. No beds. Not yet."

She squeezed her eyes shut and fought to keep from complaining. He was right. She didn't want him to be, but he was.

"Slow. Right. Sucky idea, by the way."

Rafe chuckled. "Why does it not surprise me that

my best friend, the churchy girl, is the hottest ever to fool around with?"

"You've had lots of experience since high school, then? To compare me to?" Laurel didn't mean to sound jealous. Heck, she had no right, especially considering her relationship with Jeff.

Ugh, *Jeff.*

Fortunately, Rafe kissed her thoughts back into line, only letting her up once she'd relaxed against him.

"I'm not saying you're some *Footloose* cliché or anything. You're *you.* Enthusiastic whether you're teasing my cousins, or making trouble, or driving me crazy." He took control, leaving her breathless, ears ringing. He paused the kiss only to confess, "I like that about you. I always have."

What she wanted was to strip them both, but since that seemed off the books, at least they could take things to the next level.

Tracing her hands over his body seemed a good start. Scratching lightly with her nails as they kissed and rubbed together. He went reluctantly when she pushed on his chest, rolling to one side of the couch and giving her room to move.

She was determined he get the message. "You like it when I'm enthusiastic?"

"Of cours— *Hell*, woman."

Laurel finished peeling her shirt off over her head, tossing it aside. She straddled his thighs then reached behind her and undid her bra. "Then shut up and kiss me."

He stared as the fabric fell away. "I'm on a thin rope here, Sitko."

"Let's make it snap." She swayed forward and pressed their bodies together as she reconnected their lips.

He kissed her urgently, as if the fate of the world depended on this moment. Or his sanity—one of the two. Laurel hummed her approval as he brought both hands up and cupped her breasts, playing with her nipples for a moment before sliding his hands lower.

Undoing the button to her dress slacks as he deepened the kiss.

It wasn't the time to tease about how his version of slow seemed to be rapidly accelerating. She was totally on board, wiggling to vertical to let him peel off her pants. He took her panties with them, and she was naked sooner than expected.

Naked, except for her socks.

Embarrassment slipped in far too quickly. As much as she wanted this, the urge to place her hands strategically over a few areas was difficult to ignore.

He didn't seem to notice her wavering. Instead he held her hand, swallowing hard as he looked her over, mesmerized, raw desire in his eyes. "Sweet angel."

Standing motionless in the buff as he stared got more difficult by the second. "Your turn," she whispered.

He caught hold of her hips and dragged her back into his arms. It was a heady sensation, bare-ass naked against his jeans, her breasts rubbing the fine hairs on his chest. Heat enveloped her, inside and out.

"Since you seem to be extra needy tonight, I'm going to do what I've been longing to do since the last time."

He lifted her skyward, standing her over him. He leaned on the backrest and smiled up at her.

Standing on the soft cushions meant she had to work to keep her balance. Plus there was that whole *naked* thing going on. "I'm dying here, Coleman."

"We can't have that. I'm dying for a taste. Let's both get happy."

He pulled her toward him and suddenly his mouth was on her and standing seemed like a bad idea. How on earth was she supposed to keep her legs from buckling with his tongue doing terribly wonderful things to her?

Laurel planted her hands on the wall, closed her eyes and let herself enjoy the moment. "If I fall over, it's your fault."

He didn't answer, for which she was very grateful, because it meant his tongue was occupied with more important matters, like teasing her clit. And licking her, and covering her with his mouth, and suddenly there were stars floating before her eyes. A clear midnight sky full of them as tension gathered in her core, whirling in a circle like a cyclone about to go off.

Rafe hummed happily, the vibration tipping her further to the limit. And when his fingers slipped into her, and he sucked on her clit, she lost it, rocking helplessly against his face before her knees gave out.

He caught her as she tumbled downward, cradling her in his arms. His grin was both cocky and teasing. "Shaky ground, Sitko?"

"Didn't you feel that earthquake that rumbled through here?"

A low sound of amusement escaped him as he pulled her closer, going to his feet. Still holding her, he drifted toward the back of the apartment.

Giddy hope rose, cutting through the endorphins raging in her system. "You taking me to bed?" she asked.

He shouldered the door at the end of the short hall. "*Putting* you to bed."

Soft sheets met her skin, and a moment later he'd

pulled the quilt over her. She wiggled up on her elbows, the fabric barely covering her breasts. "You're leaving me?"

"Yup." Rafe knelt, leaning in for another kiss.

He pulled away when she attempted to put her arms around his neck, slipping from her grasp to stand over her. His erection pressed the front of his jeans, the thick length clearly visible as he adjusted his stance. Hands resting on his hips for a moment as he seemed to be trying to memorize her.

Unbelievable. "You're leaving me. When you're like *that*. And I'm like… *this*. Naked, *this*."

His smile never faltered. "Night, Sitko. Sweet dreams."

He turned and walked away.

Laurel collapsed back onto her pillow, satisfaction and frustration warring within her. Stupid stubborn ass. Just like always.

The familiar connection between them coloured with something *more* warmed her as she rolled over and stared at the clock until it blurred and vanished.

WALKING AWAY?

Forget being an angel. Right then he was a fucking *saint.*

Rafe held the steering wheel tight enough he swore the hard surface creaked under his grip.

Part of him wanted to turn the truck around, hurry back to Laurel's apartment and finish what they'd started. But driving away was the right choice no matter how much he wanted her.

It hadn't even been a week yet. It didn't matter that they had tons of history together. In the long run taking their time wasn't going to hurt them. Heck, he wasn't sure if Laurel was a virgin. They had to have a talk about that at some point, soon, so he could be ready.

God. Even the idea of Laurel with another man was enough to set his teeth on edge, which was all kinds of twisted considering he wasn't a virgin, and he knew damn well she didn't expect him to be.

So what if it was chauvinistic. Still set off something caveman-like in his gut to think of her with anyone else.

He hit the edge of town and pressed his foot to the floor, tires spinning briefly before he checked himself. No use getting a speeding ticket on top of being sexually frustrated. He slowed to the speed limit, breathing carefully to settle his nerves.

Coming over the rise of the hill and down toward the Coleman property, he laughed when he spotted the speed trap set up at the side of the road. He slowed even further, rolling down the passenger window so he could wave at his cousin, Anna Thompson.

She offered him a grin, then refocused her attention on the radar gun.

Amusement lingered as he drove past the house he'd shared with his cousins not that long ago. Jesse's truck was parked outside, and he was sitting on the tailgate, throwing a ball for his dog.

Rafe turned in the driveway and parked next to his cousin. Slipped out and joined him, jumping up to sit at his side.

Jesse indicated the case of beer resting behind him, the box cracked open and a couple of empties already slid back into place. "Help yourself."

Rafe took one and popped off the lid, drinking deeply as he relaxed in the silence. The golden retriever raced back with the ball in his mouth, resting his paws on the metal tailgate and depositing the ball at Jesse's side before dancing off, glancing back optimistically toward his master.

"You ever wish people were as easy to understand as dogs?" Jesse asked.

"Never really considered it."

Jesse picked up the ball and stared at it for a moment. "They're pretty simple when you come down to it. A dog's goals, I mean. Take Morgan, here. He wants to be fed and watered. A warm place to sleep, and a whole lot of activities that make him happy. And he doesn't care if those are rabbits to chase, balls to return—"

"—balls to lick," Rafe offered.

His cousin gave him a dirty look before whipping the toy into the yard. Morgan took off after it like a shot. "I'm trying to have a serious conversation, if you don't mind."

"How many beers you had tonight?"

Jesse shrugged. "Not that many."

Rafe nodded. "Okay. You're right. A dog's goals are pretty simple. Anything in particular bring on this deep and philosophical discussion topic?"

"Don't you think our goals should be just as simple?"

He resisted making another joke about balls. Jesse probably wouldn't see the humour in it. Not tonight.

Instead Rafe gave it a bit of serious consideration. "What makes you think our goals *aren't* that simple? We like food and drink and a roof over our heads. And I'm all for a whole bunch of things that make me happy."

"Dogs don't do things deliberately to make other people unhappy," Jesse pointed out. "Humans do that. And sometimes we do things we completely hate because we know somebody else wants us to. Dogs don't do that."

"We can make a pretty long list of things dogs don't do." Rafe took another drink. "You really want us to spend the night at it?"

His cousin shrugged. "Hell, no. Just figured you'd like something inane to discuss to get your mind off your troubles."

"My troubles?"

Jesse lifted the bottle to his lips and took a long drink, a slow smile curling his lips. "Laurel get off to bed okay?"

Rafe's entire body tightened. "Shut up."

"Seriously, cuz, I figure you're destined for sainthood."

A grumble escaped him before he could stop it. "Already told myself that tonight, but it's worth it."

"She's a fine-looking woman, and she's sharp."

He really didn't want to talk about Laurel anymore. "On a different topic, how come you're home early? And alone?"

Jesse popped the lid on another beer then used the bottle to gesture into the yard. "I'm not alone. I've got Morgan. Finest companion a man could ever want."

"He doesn't look tall enough to dance with."

"Got enough of that in earlier tonight." Jesse stared into the distance, his feet kicking gently as they hung from the tailgate.

Rafe stayed quiet as well, thinking things through as he waited for more answers to spill.

"I get restless at times," Jesse said. "Feels as if nothing ever changes here. We get up every morning and

158

work the land, and on Fridays we go to Traders and see the same people."

"Maybe you need a hobby."

Jesse snorted.

"Maybe you need a holiday," Rafe suggested

"Maybe."

"Why not? I'm pretty sure you could get away for a while. After harvest, before winter really sets in. Doesn't have to cost a lot." Rafe thought back to how he'd spent his summer. "It was good to get away these past months. You teased about cheesy hotels, but hell, I slept in the truck a lot of nights. Or in a hammock in the trees. Talk about a simple life."

His cousin made a rude face. "Don't think I can do that come November. I'm attached to my balls. Don't want to freeze them off."

"If you head far enough south your balls would be safe. Talk to your brother. Maybe Blake's got some reason for you to hit the road. Take a look around for stock, or some such."

"It's an idea."

Rafe glanced over his shoulder at the dark house. "Nobody else moved in with you yet?"

His cousin shook his head. "I figured you'd be coming back pretty soon."

Bastard. "You did, did you?"

He got treated to a cocky grin. "I know this place isn't much, but it's a whole hell of a lot better than the room at your folks. Move back any time."

"Sometime this week. Won't take me long. I never did unpack." Rafe didn't hesitate to offer a warning, though. "I'll be bringing Laurel by at times, and you'd damn well better be on your best behaviour."

"What's that supposed to mean?" Jesse demanded.

Rafe held up a hand, counting off on his fingers as he rapidly listed items. "You will not flirt with her. You will not make her feel uncomfortable. You will not try to join us at any time when we're fooling around. You will not—"

"Really?" Jesse leaned an elbow on one knee as he pulled a disgusted face. "I'm not allowed to *flirt?*"

Rafe punched him in the shoulder. Jesse responded by laughing, popping off the tailgate and grabbing the rest of the beer. "Oh, and you're lucky I didn't move yet into the master bedroom like I considered."

"Yeah, I'm lucky you're a lazy son of a bitch."

"Don't push it. I could move my stuff tonight before you can get back."

Yeah, right. "Highly doubt it. That would require you to pack up your shit, and mine is still in boxes."

Jesse swore. "Fine, it's yours."

Rafe patted his cousin on the shoulder, firmly, following him into the house. "So what are we doing for the rest of this fine evening? Cards?"

"We can play crib for money."

"Sure." He dropped into a chair at the kitchen table, reaching for another beer. A slip of paper followed it, clinging to the bottle. He glanced closer at the narrow strip, cackling evilly as he realized what it was. "I guess you didn't notice that Anna wasn't at Traders tonight."

Which Rafe *had* noticed, which meant their cousin was probably working, which was why he'd guessed there was an extra good reason to not drive home like an idiot.

"Shut up," Jesse complained. "I swear that woman sets up her speed traps deliberately to catch as many Coleman relatives as possible."

"Probably. She's damn smart."

Jesse joined in laughing reluctantly. "Yeah, she is. Now prepare to get beat. I need money to pay the fine."

"At our usual twenty-five cents a game? You *are* a dreamer."

Late-night card games with his cousin wasn't what Rafe really wanted to be doing, and yet...it was.

Spending the night, *all* night, with Laurel was something he looked forward to, but this time with one of his family was also important.

Morgan wandered in and settled at Jesse's feet, resting his muzzle on his paws as he stared up adoringly at his master before letting out a contented sigh.

Sometimes life was simple, no matter which way Rafe looked at it.

Chapter Thirteen

SUNDAY MORNING, seated behind the piano keyboard at the side of the church, was when Laurel felt the most as if she knew what she believed. Familiar worship songs rolled over her one after another and took her to a different place. A place where the sensations of belonging and acceptance were still pure and sweet.

Pure, unlike the thoughts drifting into her mind about what she and Rafe had done two nights before, and the decidedly un-sweet things she wanted to get up to with him the next time they were together.

Guilt shot through her for daydreaming about sex in the middle of church.

You shouldn't have made it so much fun, she chastised God. *The fooling-around stuff. If it was more like doing calculus, not as many people would get in trouble.*

She definitely needed to apologize to God later.

But in the meantime, she listened to her father as he preached with conviction, each word uttered with deep compassion. He believed with everything in him. His love for his family, and for the people of his congregation—his love, *period*—was genuine.

Another source of guilt. She simply didn't have his kind of faith.

No, focusing on the music was easier. It allowed her to get lost in memories of when things were simpler. This is what she was told, so this was what she believed. Music, and the voices of the congregation, albeit slightly less than angelic at times, let her slip back to where she knew one thing.

There was love in the world.

She stopped after service to grab a cup of coffee and chat with a few of the church members, lulled into a good mood by the joy she'd experienced.

There was a reason she was supposed to be on guard. Jeff caught her before she could escape, good mood still intact.

"Laurel. I was worried I'd missed you." He smiled apologetically at the woman he'd interrupted. "Tracking her down is like trying to find the end of a rainbow, but just as rewarding."

Gag.

But the ladies were charmed. The ladies had no troubles cutting their conversation short. The ladies *obviously* thought Jeff was one of the most amazing creatures in God's creation.

Laurel didn't blame them too much—she'd been pretty impressed with him herself once.

"I'm heading home later today, but before I go, I'd like to talk," he said quietly. "Somewhere private."

Hell, no. She barely kept from blurting it out. "I'd prefer not, thanks."

He let out a heavy sigh. "Laurel, I want to make sure there're no misunderstandings left between us."

Against her better judgment, she tilted her head toward the hall off the kitchen. Half a dozen volunteers were cleaning up and dealing with the coffee cups, but at one end of the room the tables were empty. It was private enough, yet public. She marched quickly to the back of the hall, taking the chair on one side of a table where the only other place for Jeff to sit was on the opposite side.

Putting lots and lots of barrier between them.

He settled in, looking all impressive and friendly. "I've been meaning to get in touch for a long time."

"It's been two and a half years," she pointed out. "Oh, wait. You were with Jessica for some of that, right? I suppose you couldn't really talk to me then, could you?"

"I wanted to apologize," he said. "Things didn't end well between us, and I'm sorry."

She waited.

He'd gotten the expression just right—contrite sadness. "My timing wasn't very good."

She waited some more.

Jeff glanced away. "You know, you might consider giving me a clue of what it will take to make a difference."

"There's no difference to make. We dated, then we stopped, end of story. So if that's all you have to say... Goodbye. Safe travels."

She made as if to stand, but he caught her by the wrist, pinning her hand to the table. "Laurel, I—"

"Let go of me, or I will break your fingers," Laurel snapped before clenching her teeth.

Shock slid across his expression, but he let go. "That's a little extreme, isn't it?"

"Jeff, what do you want me to say? That I forgive you for leading me on?"

"I never led you on," he said softly. "What was between us was real. We liked each other, and we were attracted to each other. That didn't stop."

He was being deliberately obtuse. "That's what breaking up meant, Jeff. That we *stopped*."

"No, what it meant was we were getting too serious, too quickly, and I felt for both our sakes we needed some time away from each other."

The numbness inside her grew heavier. She'd dealt with this once—with all the stresses she'd had to face without him. Why was he dragging her back into hell? "So, you *didn't* break up with me?"

"I certainly didn't plan on it. I wanted us to slow down. Once we'd taken a breather, I figured we'd start over, only with a little more restraint..." He gave her a wry smile. "I'd never been in the situation I was with you before, and I lost control. I'm sorry for that."

The irony of Jeff telling her they should've gone slower contrasted with the iron control Rafe had displayed, years earlier and years younger.

But that wasn't the point right now. Her mind reeled at the idea he was presenting.

"I'm confused. It sounds as if you intended for us to be together, but I'm pretty sure we didn't just take a break. You were with someone else. In fact, my memory must be really terrible, because I seem to remember an engagement announcement."

"That was long after." Jeff reached across the table as if to take her fingers again. He paused, then sat back and folded his hands, resting them on the table. "Laurel, I don't understand what happened. I told you we needed to take a break, then I left for my trip. Before we could fix things, you left school with no warning, months before classes were done."

She didn't need the play by play. That part she remembered. "I did leave. And how long *before* I left did you start going out with Jessica?"

165

"That's not really fair," he complained. "All the clues said you wanted nothing to do with me."

"And what clues were those? Were you reading my mind?"

"Laurel." He lowered his voice. "I know it doesn't make it better, but we aren't the first couple to get carried away on the physical side of things. I thought maybe you were punishing yourself for us...going too far."

"Having sex, you mean," she said.

Jeff glanced into the room as if making sure no one had overheard her bluntly spoken words before he turned back and nodded. "I think we both agree we needed to slow down. That's all I intended. I'm sorry you misunderstood."

Her brain was on overload. That most certainly wasn't how she remembered things.

Had she been wrong?"

"Everything I did was because I cared for you," he insisted.

"Dating Jessica was because you—?" No, definitely didn't make sense.

"You made it clear you didn't want me anymore." He leaned forward. "I cared too much to hurt you more by forcing myself back into your life."

A cold laugh escaped her. If he'd shown even a fraction of this much attention to her at the time, things might have turned out very different. "But you're totally trying to force yourself back into my life now. So does that mean you *don't* care about me anymore? I'm confused."

Jeff let out a long sigh. "This isn't helping. The details are too clouded by time, and what happened after isn't what we need to try to remember."

Strange—she might not have the same memories of their breakup as him, but she could remember what happened after like it was yesterday.

He didn't give up. "I'd like it very much if we could wipe the slate clean. I'm going home today, but there's a good chance I'll be asked to return. If I come back, I'd like to know we'll be friends."

"And that's all. Friends?"

A smile curled his lips. "I'd like more, but we should let it grow naturally out of our renewed friendship. I think we could be good together, but we can't even start until we move beyond the past."

On top of everything else, him totally ignoring the fact she and Rafe were together was rude and annoying.

Laurel folded her arms over her chest. One rude behaviour deserved another. "What happened with you and Jessica?"

He blinked. "Pardon?"

She shrugged. "I saw an engagement announcement, yet here you are, not married. Why?"

Jeff didn't hesitate. "I called it off."

Uh. "Why?"

His gaze danced over her face for a moment before he spoke. "You can't marry someone when you're in love with someone else."

The hard knot of pain that formed in her stomach whenever he was around tightened even further. She didn't want to listen to this. She didn't want to think about him, or have to waste brain cells deciding if he was being honest, or the most spectacular liar on the face of the earth.

She'd spent two years getting to a new place in her life, and it was *bullshit* that he could march back in and effortlessly drag her emotions back to a darker time.

She got to her feet, and he rose, hope in his eyes. *Hell, no*—and she didn't feel one bit blasphemous for thinking it.

"Thank you for telling me. But I really hope you decide the best way to be a true friend is to never step foot in Rocky Mountain House again."

She turned on her heel and walked rapidly toward the kitchen.

"Laurel…"

She ignored his pleading call, because up until now she'd been polite. She'd been…proper. The sheer amount of control she'd displayed shocked even her.

No name-calling, no swearing, no planting her fists in his face.

But she'd reached the limit to what she could take. And the one thing she really needed was a dose of Rafe. Stat.

Laurel was pulling into the yard at the Angel Coleman's before she even thought to call Rafe to warn him she was coming over.

She'd beat Dana Coleman home from church, and she hesitated for a moment before parking outside the barn where an oversized truck was awkwardly positioned at an angle.

Even taking the time to make the call didn't help—she got no answer. But there was noise coming from the barn, so she made her way inside, looking around with confusion at the broken stalls and what seemed to be abandoned machinery.

"Hello?"

Sound echoed from an upstairs corner, and she picked a path cautiously to the ladder leading into the loft. She wasn't dressed for crawling around, but her curiosity got the better of her. Fingers wrapped tightly around each of the ladder rungs, she made the climb.

The thumping noises stopped as she reached the upper floor, stepping to one side and staring into the dimly lit space, one hand clinging to the long length of rungs that extended above the loft floor.

"Hello? Rafe?"

"What're you doing?"

Laurel tightened her grip, shocked by how close Rafe's dad stood. "Mr. Coleman. Hi. I'm looking for Rafe."

He spat out a laugh. "He's not here. Don't know why you'd want to find him, anyway."

"Because he's my friend," Laurel answered instantly only to be interrupted.

"Bullshit."

She snorted before realizing he was serious. "We've been friends for years, Mr. Coleman."

"Girls like you don't make friends with someone like my boy."

"No, of course not." She'd had too much to deal with that day already. Holding her tongue was impossible. "I'm lying because it's entertaining to drive into the country, wander into a strange barn and start conversations that have no purpose. I'm actually here selling cookies."

The man stepped back half a pace, blinking hard. He seemed stunned. "Are you sassing me?"

"Probably. Although you could pretend I'm looking for Rafe like I said in the first place."

His eyes narrowed.

Her give-a-damn was well and truly broken. She planted her fists on her hips, raising one brow as she stared back.

"Get the hell out of here," he snapped.

She waited a beat or two to prove she wasn't scared, then turned to the ladder and made her way down, muttering evil things under her breath as she went.

How on earth Rafe had grown up around that man and not given in to the urge to badmouth him every chance he got—

Rafe was *far* more of an angel than he gave himself credit for. He was worried about losing his temper? It was a good thing *she* didn't spend more time around his old man, or she'd be the one committing murder.

She made it outside just as Dana Coleman pulled into the yard, and she hurried over to help open the door.

Mrs. Coleman examined her with curiosity. "Did I forget something at church?"

"I'm trying to track down Rafe. Mr. Coleman didn't seem to know where he was."

The other woman's eyes widened for a moment as she glanced toward the barn. "I see."

Yeah, she probably did at that. Laurel took pity on her, pulling the basket from her hands and walking them toward the house. "Did you have a good morning at service?"

"Yes, thank you." Mrs. Coleman tilted her head. "Will you come in for a cup of tea?"

Laurel was torn. "I'd love to, but I really need to get in touch with Rafe. You have any idea where he is?"

Mrs. Coleman took the basket from her and placed it on a table just inside the door. "I'm not sure, but Gabriel and Allison would probably know. If you head over to their place, I'm sure they can help you."

"Thank you."

She turned as if to go, Mrs. Coleman caught her by the arm. "If you ever need help, you should probably head over there. Straight off," she said with a perfectly expressionless face.

All the things Dana wasn't saying rang through loud and clear. Laurel surmised far more than the other woman probably wanted her to, which is why even though she'd been longing for Rafe to pet her and listen to her complaints about Jeff, a change of plans was needed.

Talk about a saint. Dana Coleman had put up with that mean bastard as a husband for how many years, now?

"You know what? My throat is dry after the singing this morning. If you have time for me to stay for a while, I'd like that cup of tea very much."

Mrs. Coleman's lips curled upward, and a touch of Rafe's familiar smile shone back. She glanced at the barn then stepped back to welcome Laurel in. "Let me take your coat. If you don't mind sitting in the kitchen, I can get things started for lunch while we have a visit."

Laurel passed over her jacket, but refused to sit and be served. "Let's work together, then we can both relax."

She picked up a knife from the counter and set to peeling the potatoes she found waiting in a pot by the sink. The other woman's gaze rested on her for a moment, but Laurel ignored it, working without comment. Finally Dana moved to add water to the kettle before gathering the things needed for the meal.

By the time Mrs. Coleman put two cups and some baking on the table, lunch was simmering on the stove, and they sat together, all awkwardness forgotten as their easy conversation continued.

It wasn't what Laurel had expected to find that morning, but the shared time with the gentle-hearted woman was exactly what she needed.

Chapter Fourteen

RAFE DROVE over the rise of the hill, coming to a sudden stop as he spotted the second of their ATVs waiting beside one of the small pole barns where they kept supplies.

He hadn't expected Gabe to be in the area, not today. There was no sign of his brother as Rafe got off his ride, pulling off his gloves and leaving them on the seat.

"Gabe?"

It was most definitely not his brother's head that popped around the corner post.

"Hey, you." Laurel strode toward him, hands reaching forward as she offered a happy smile.

"Hey. I didn't expect you."

She curled into his arms, clasping him around the waist as she rested her head on his chest. "I tracked you down."

He took a second before answering, enjoying the feel of her in his arms as he squeezed her tight. "I'm glad you did."

Laurel wiggled free, catching hold of his hand and pulling him toward the far side of the building. "You haven't had lunch yet, have you?"

"Was going to take a break in a while." He eyed the food-covered blanket she'd guided him to. "Wow. A picnic?"

"Sort of. But don't go giving me all the credit." She sat on one corner of the blanket and patted the spot next to her. "Everybody else has been taking care of me today."

From the looks of the spread before them, eating was going to take a while. "I don't care who made it. I'm not going to complain."

He reached for the thermos and opened it, taking a cautious sniff. The rich scent of strong coffee filled his senses.

"Sweet mercy, it's not that nasty fancy pop."

Laurel shook her finger at him. "I knew you didn't really like it."

He shrugged. "I like making you happy. If drinking weird fizzy drinks goes along with that, it's not the worst thing ever. But I do love my coffee." He glanced over at her, a moment of confusion hitting. Something was out of place. "How come you're wearing Allison's boots?"

"I'm also wearing her jeans and shirt," she confessed. "I ended up out at your place without a change of clothes. She offered me stuff when I told her I wanted to bring out your lunch."

"And Gabe popped you on the ATV and told you which direction to drive."

"Something like that." She took a bite of her sandwich then stared over the land as if she wasn't really seeing it.

Rafe examined her for a moment more before putting down his drink and reaching for her. He caught her fingers and gave them a squeeze. "Hey. What's up?"

Laurel shook herself before glancing back at him. "Oh, nothing. I mean..." She wrinkled her nose. "Something, but it's not as all-fired important as I thought it was."

That made no sense. "You had something to tell me before you set up the picnic, but you don't have anything to tell me now?"

She moved aside the few things between them so she could switch positions, settling herself close enough she was right beside him and able to lean against his chest. "Basically. I was upset this morning, but after talking with your mom for a while I feel much better."

"My mom is a pretty cool lady."

"She is." Laurel looked up with a smile. "She's very proud of you, you know. Thinks her youngest son can pretty much do anything he puts his mind to."

"Only with a lot of help," he said. "I'm glad you guys had a nice visit after church. But I don't know why you didn't go home and get changed before coming out here."

She made a face. "We actually had tea at her place. After church."

His spine stiffened, and he fought the frustration and worry that struck instantly. "I don't really want you going out there."

"I figured. But it's okay." Laurel laid a hand on his thigh and pressed down reassuringly.

"No, it's not," he insisted. He took a deep breath and let it out slowly. "I don't want you around my father."

"I know, but I'm telling you it's okay. I mean, I won't go out of my way to get in his face, but I like your mom, and I plan to visit her more."

"Dammit, Laurel, your face is red. What are you not telling me that's close enough to a lie to set you off?"

"Noth—" She slammed to a stop and covered her mouth.

"Yeah, you watch yourself, because you were *totally* about to lie."

"I kinda bumped into your dad this morning, but everything is okay, really," she rushed to assure him. "And I won't get in his face...anymore."

Shit. "Laurel...?"

"I was lippy." The words escaped in a rush. "It was wrong, and if he mentions to you that *the Sitko girl is a rude creature*, he's not lying. But it was my fault, not his, and afterward I had a great visit with your mom. Let's focus on that part, okay?"

She looked so hopeful—the expression she used when playing down how bad they'd been because they weren't *ever* going to try that particular bit of mischief again.

There were downsides to knowing each other so well.

It was on the tip of his tongue to order her to never go near the homestead, but he couldn't. Couldn't boss her around when it was very clear she was aware of the problem. "While you're on a streak, you got anything else you want to tell me about this morning?"

"How about you eat first?" Laurel grabbed another sandwich. "Or more importantly, let me eat because I'm starving."

"Laurel..."

"I'm serious. Don't you hear my stomach rumbling?"

Enough. He rolled her over his body, ignoring her squeal of protest as he kept them going until he had her pinned under him, mostly off the picnic blanket and resting on the soft grass of the hillside.

He plucked the sandwich from her fingers. "I'm very impressed you didn't lose that."

"I *told* you I was hungry."

"And we'll eat in a minute. Now, spill."

She seemed to be thinking hard before she spoke. "It's nothing," she insisted.

"I'll spank your ass if you keep lying to me," he warned.

Some sort of gibberish escaped her lips, as if she couldn't figure out what words to say.

He grinned. "Was that a *no way on earth, don't you dare*, or are you secretly wanting me to paddle you?"

"Have you done that?" she demanded. "I mean, no, don't tell me. I don't even want to think about that, yet at the same time I want to know. And that's not a yes or a no to you doing anything to *me* that involves my bottom."

This time a snicker escaped. "Your *bottom*? Really? So proper."

Her lips twitched into a smile.

"You're not distracting me," he warned. "We're not going anywhere until you confess."

It took a moment before she nodded. "Fine. You probably want to let me up, though."

"That serious, huh?"

"Kind of?"

He didn't let her go far. Just back to vertical so they could look each other in the eyes as he kept hold of her hands. "Tell me."

She took a deep breath. "Jeff leaves town today, but he decided before he goes he should clear up the 'misunderstanding' between us."

"Bastard."

"No, he's definitely the acknowledged first son of his father," she muttered. "Let's stick with *asshole.*"

"Genealogy aside... Spit it out, woman."

"He insists he didn't really break up with me. That it was a misunderstanding on my part when he decided we should slow down."

"*Asshole.*"

"Right? Because it wasn't possible for him to actually make it clear that he wanted to be with me because I was 'being difficult' to get a hold of." She made more air quotes.

Rafe was missing something here. "Because he broke up with you."

Laurel paused for a moment. "I *didn't* make it easy on him. I was upset, and I didn't want him to get back together with me because it was easy. I wanted him willing to work a little." She wrinkled her nose. "I'm sorry, this whole conversation is weird considering you and I are going out."

"Do you not remember the conversations we used to have back in the day when I was dating, and you weren't?"

"But that's the point, *we* weren't dating then."

He shrugged. "I told you everything. Heck, you found out the morning after I lost my virginity." A terrible thought flashed into his brain. "Oh my God. You and Jeff—that's what part of what this is about, isn't it?"

She looked absolutely miserable. "If you're asking if we had sex, yes. We did."

Rafe liked the guy even less. "Do you think he's already left town?"

"You're not going to rip his arms off, so settle down," she muttered. "He didn't force me or anything. I told you, I thought things were serious between us, and we were attracted to each other." Laurel covered her face with a hand. "This is embarrassing."

"Because you had sex?" The idea wasn't sitting comfortably with him, but it wasn't right for him to have double standards. "Don't beat yourself up over something that's pretty natural. And fun," he grudgingly admitted.

"I've had way more fun fooling around with you," she said quietly.

Oh, hell yeah.

"Way to stroke my ego."

She flashed him a grin but her amusement quickly faded. "The point is, I thought something real was happening before he called it off, so when he came back, I wanted him to *prove* he was serious." She shrugged. "He didn't. Not in my books, and I was dealing with…some other stuff at the time, and in the end, that's when I realized Bible College wasn't for me."

"You never wanted to see him again?" he guessed.

"Partly, but it was more than that." She sighed unhappily. "I knew my parents were going to be disappointed, for so many reasons, and so I didn't tell them either."

"Not that I want to keep bringing it up, but you seem to be keeping a lot of secrets from your folks."

"I wasn't off living under a bridge or anything. I went to my aunt's in Winnipeg. I was supposed to go there for the summer, anyway. I just went earlier without saying anything to them."

"And changed your school plans, and everything else without discussing it." Rafe held up a hand before she could protest. "I know, you're a grownup, and you don't have to tell them everything. But they're decent people, Laurel. I think they would've understood. They probably could have helped you talk things out."

"Maybe if they were less perfect it would've been easier to share. I didn't want to disappoint them, and I couldn't..."

She still wasn't telling him everything, but it wasn't time to drag it out of her.

He cupped her chin with his fingers and made her look him in the eye. "Here's the only question you need to answer. Whether your whole breakup was a misunderstanding or not, what do you want now? Do you want to give Jeff another chance? Because—"

"No," she snapped so quickly he knew it was the honest truth.

Or at least the truth she wanted to believe.

"Then I don't think you have anything to worry about," he assured her. "Not as far as your parents go. You've got a good job, Laurel. And you're back here, and you like spending time with them— Whatever it was you set out to do, I think you accomplished it. You're standing on your own two feet."

She nodded slowly.

"You do want to be in Rocky, don't you?"

"Yes. And I want to be with you—about *those* things I have no doubts."

And there it was. A hint of what might be wrong. He scooped her into his lap and held her close, cuddling her for a moment. Her heartbeat rang through him as she leaned in harder, circling her fingertips on his chest as she relaxed.

Laurel had grown up in the church, with a pastor for a father, and bible studies and bedtime prayers and whatever else came with the territory. *Doubts* to her had to be about the things she'd been taught.

It was a terrible time to bring this up, but he had to know. "I'm never going to be an upstanding member of the church," he warned her gently. "That's not part of who I am, or what's important to me."

"I know."

"Is that going to be a problem?"

Laurel tilted her head until she could meet his gaze, her eyes filled with moisture. "It's not what *you* believe that worries me. I just don't know..." She took a deep breath. "I've spent all my life standing firmly in one spot, but the last three years shook me up pretty good."

"You got doubts about what you believe?"

"Yeah."

Which would have totally thrown her into a loop. Made sense.

Whatever else they'd done over the years, Laurel had always had a solid sense of who she was. She'd never preached at him—not with words. But he'd always known what was important to her, which was another reason why he'd been able to hold off that long-ago night when they were first tempted to get involved.

"Hey. It's not *that* terrible," he teased, rubbing his thumb over her lower lip. "If you knew everything now you'd have nothing to learn for the rest of your life. That'd get pretty boring."

"I suppose."

"You okay? You need me to do anything?"

She shook her head. "You keep being you. I'll figure it out."

"I know you will."

This time when her stomach complained, he heard the rumble.

"Can I eat now?" she asked plaintively. "Next time I'll know better than to start talking before we've eaten."

Rafe handed over a fresh sandwich. "Right. Feed your stomach. I don't want you to pass out later."

Laurel gave him an amused glance. "Why? Are you making me help with chores?"

"I'm working you over," he announced happily. "It's one of the last fine fall days, and I don't think you've had a chance to fool around outdoors yet. Have you?"

She didn't answer. Just stared at him with her sandwich halfway to her mouth.

"I didn't think so." He nudged her sandwich with his. "Get munching. You'll need your strength."

AFTER EVERYTHING that had gone on that day, and all the wild swings of emotion she'd experienced, right there and then with his eyes on her...

Intense.

Forget the physical reactions like *fight or flight*, guilt or frustration—lust had them beat by a country mile.

Laurel remembered her momentary discussion that morning with God while seated on the piano bench. Maybe she was supposed to feel a whole lot guiltier for being physically intimate with Rafe, but it was too right to be wrong. As if out of all the people in the world she could've gotten involved with, He'd known Rafe Coleman was the one for her.

She'd told the truth. While she and Jeff had gotten along, and there'd been an attraction there, it wasn't the fire and deep-core-melting, body-shaking need she experienced having Rafe around.

He made a picnic on the grass seem like the most erotic of experiences.

She was too hungry to play around before satisfying her stomach. Only with each bite he seemed to focus on a different part of her body, his gaze trickling over her. Intense enough she swore she felt it. A stroke across her cheek. Another trickling over her collarbone. Lower. Each moment more intimate.

She rushed to get down her sandwich, picking up a bottle of water and drinking it thirstily, all the time ultra-aware of his gaze on her.

Rafe ate rapidly as well, somehow consuming twice as much as she did during the same amount of time while never missing a beat.

"You had enough?" His voice a deep, needy rumble.

"It's a little cold to strip," she warned.

He dropped the few remaining sandwiches back into the basket, pretty much tossing the rest after them. "Trust me. I can get you hot enough not to worry."

Of that she had no doubt. "So, how's this going to work?"

He shifted into the middle of the blanket, patting his lap. "Have a seat."

She crawled over eagerly, letting him help her settle, one knee on either side of his legs as he draped her arms over his shoulders. When he placed a hand on her back and tugged, their bodies came into contact, and she lazily drifted her fingers over shoulder muscles, enjoying the soft touch of his flannel shirt.

They touched innocently for a long while. Slow, with curiosity. As if they'd never met each other before and it was the first time to explore one another.

In some ways, it was true. Every day changed their relationship enough for Laurel to have to think hard about the man she was involved with.

He wasn't the boy she'd laughed and played games with. He was more than the innocent, childish trouble they'd embarked on back in the day. The fact he'd grown up was carved into his muscles—in the strong line of his biceps, the firm curves of his chest, and the rigid edges of his six-pack as she stroked a hand over his abdomen. The hours of labour he'd put in on the Coleman ranch had been written onto his body.

His physical body had matured into the man he'd always had the potential to become. But his words earlier had said it wasn't only his body that had changed.

She'd faced dealing with Ben for a moment, and failed miserably. For Rafe to have come through the past years without choosing the bitter path said a lot about the strength of his convictions.

Even the way he touched her now was perfect. She'd shared things that could have upset him, but instead of taking revenge, he was being nothing but gentle. Stroking her, caressing her—pretty much petting her as if she was precious, and he wanted nothing more than to care for her.

The secrets she held buried inside moved closer to escaping. Could she trust him with *all* her fears and doubts? With everything she'd faced alone over the past three years?

Soon, but not this moment.

Not when he was touching her as if he craved her.

So when he stopped stroking and took a firm grip on her hips, she went willingly. Kneeling upright as he nudged her breasts through her borrowed shirt.

"Undo your buttons for me," he ordered. "That's it. Slowly. Let's see you get bare one inch at a time."

Laurel took her time slipping the buttons free, but she had no intention of making him wait too long. She had the shirt undone, the tails hanging loose as she enjoyed his gaze following her fingers, heat tracing over each newly exposed bit of skin.

When she would've shrugged the material from her shoulders, he told her to stop.

"Do that thing you girls all know how to do. Remember—you showed me in junior high. Leave the shirt on, but take off your bra."

She bit her lower lip to stop from laughing, reaching into her sleeves and pulling the shoulder straps free while leaving the rest of the bra in place. "You thought this was the neatest magic trick."

"I don't know what impressed me more. That you could take off your bra, or that you wore one in the first place."

Their fingers met at the back of her body under her shirt as she reached behind her. He stroked his fingertips down her spine, waiting for her to finish undoing the hooks

The bra fell to the ground.

"*Oh...*"

Rafe'd caught her by the hips and lifted her, bringing her to his mouth so he could lick her nipple. She expected him to tease for a while, but after that first slick motion, he closed his lips around her and sucked, tongue flicking hard as he applied enough pressure to make her squirm.

Laurel let her head fall back. The warmth of the sun shining on her bare skin sent a delicious sensation of mischief through her. They were outside where it was private, and yet not.

He only had eyes for her.

She tossed his cowboy hat on top of the basket before stroking her fingers through his hair. Rafe's grip tightened on her butt, squeezing in rhythm with the pulses of his mouth.

He brought her down onto his lap, dragging her forward until the thick ridge of his erection was directly between her legs. He took her lips as he rubbed her over his length, heat and pressure building as he teased with his tongue and lips.

It was natural to rock with him. It was impossible not to, it felt so good, and yet nowhere near as good as the other day when they'd been skin on skin.

Laurel tugged on his shirt, but he pulled away her hands. "You keep trying to get us naked, woman."

"I know a good thing when I see it," she teased.

"You're on fire," he retorted.

"You're not cooling me off any, just saying." She accepted the next kiss without trying to deepen it. Soaked in the sensation of him touching her. The privilege of touching him. "I want to make you feel good."

"You have no idea." He'd returned to nibbling on the section of her neck under her ear that he seemed fascinated with. "You have no idea how hot you make me. Getting to be around you. Knowing I can touch you whenever I want—it doesn't mean I have to keep pushing it harder. It's too damn good to rush."

Laurel let loose a sigh of pleasure mixed with frustration, and it kind of came out like a hiccupping moan.

Rafe jerked to attention. "Well, *that* was interesting."

She giggled. "Shut up."

He peered at her, laughter dancing in his eyes. "No, seriously, that was a cool noise. Let's see if you can make it again."

Like a signal to begin a free-for-all, they teased and touched and played for the next fifteen minutes. Rolling on the blanket as they tickled and kissed, pausing every now and then to stare at each other.

Laurel stroked the back of her hand over his cheek. "At some point I want to do more than just fool around."

"We will," he promised. "When the time is right."

Huh. Yeah. *The right time* probably wasn't after that weird conversation about Jeff and faith and life that she'd dragged them through not even half an hour ago. "How'd you get so perfect?" she asked.

"I had this amazing friend back in school," he told her. "She taught me a lot about having fun."

It was like a bell went off.

That's what she kept forgetting. That's what went missing whenever her brain got tangled up in the past. The idea that life was supposed to be fun kept slipping from her fingers.

"I'm so glad you're you." Laurel wrapped her arms around Rafe and gave him the most enormous bear hug she could. An intimate connection that wasn't sexual, even though her shirttails hung open, her naked body pressed to his. His shirt was untucked and his hair was a mess, and the two of them ached with sexual tension, but this was—

Almost magical.

It took a while to find their feet, what with all the helping each other get dressed. Most of Rafe's attempts seemed borderline groping instead of helping, which set her off laughing.

He strapped the picnic basket to the back of her ATV before glancing over and offering a cheeky grin. "You got plans for the rest of the day?"

She thought it over. "Not unless I want to redecorate my apartment. Which would take all of five minutes."

"Come help me do my chores?"

She grinned at the invitation. "You're such a slacker, Coleman. Sure, I'll come along. But you know this means you have to be a librarian someday."

"Deal." He waited for her to mount up before kissing her firmly then retreating to his bike. "I've always wanted to fool around in the stacks," he teased.

Hmmm. The perfect thing to daydream about as they headed farther into Angel land. Overhead, the sun was shining, and the land seemed to stretch endlessly in front of them, and they were together.

Funny how much better the day had gotten.

Chapter Fifteen

WHILE HE'D thought life would get busier now that he was back at the ranch, he'd underestimated exactly how stinking busy. Not just Gabe, but the entire Coleman clan were determined to keep him going from before sunrise to well after dark.

They'd always shared tasks, but this year it seemed everyone had more work than workers, and every day he had to make a choice. When he got a few minutes free, he could use them to move into the house with Jesse, or he could steal away and spend time with Laurel.

It was a no-brainer.

They met in the strangest places, but Rafe didn't mind. He'd text her a warning, and if she was free, they'd meet in the middle somewhere between the field or the barn he'd been working and wherever she was at. They fit in a couple of fast food restaurants, and another picnic, this time with a lot less fancy sandwiches—peanut butter that he'd tossed together before leaving his place.

If it had been up to him, he'd probably have been living above the garage at his folks when the snow flew. Laurel, it seemed, had other plans.

Rafe: *you at work?*

Laurel: *you done? Coming up for air?*

Rafe: *not done. My tractor broke. Gabe is making me take a break while they fix it. Then I get to work until midnight.*

Laurel: *awesome. Come to the rental.*

He wasn't sure where she was talking about.

Rafe: *your place?*

Laurel: *no, yours. Your new place, with Jesse. Which is your old place, I guess.*

He had no idea what she was doing, but he hopped in his truck and made the short trip, pulling into the yard to discover his cousin Trevor's overgrown beast of a truck backed up nearly to the door.

He peeked into the truck bed surprised to recognize the half dozen or so boxes in the back.

"Hey, you made good time." Laurel slipped out the front door and into his arms, giving him a big squeeze as she pressed a quick kiss on his lips. "Only a couple more trips, then you have to do the rest of the work, because I'm not unpacking for you."

Rafe looked around in confusion. "Where's Trevor?"

"I don't know. Your cousin and Becky must be out in her truck, because I stopped by and the house was empty."

He caught himself chuckling. "You stole Trevor's truck?"

"Can't steal something he keeps giving away," she pointed out, elbowing past him with an oversized box balanced precariously in her arms.

That was true. Trevor left the keys in his truck as if he were begging someone to steal it. *Borrow it*—since this was his girlfriend with the goods and all.

"I'll put in a good word for you when my cousin the RCMP officer shows up to arrest you." He lowered the box he'd carried to the living room floor. "How'd you get this stuff here?"

She shrugged, pushing him back toward the door so they could grab the final two boxes. "I had the afternoon off, and you were busy. It didn't seem like you were going to get to do this anytime soon, so I figured I'd help."

Which meant she'd been over at the homestead without him. It seemed kind of stupid to be scolding her after the fact, but he really didn't like her going there.

She must have read his face. "Hey, it was okay. I barely even saw your parents."

Shit. "My dad didn't say anything to you, did he?"

Tension spiraled upward as he waited for her response.

She was far too relaxed about the whole thing. In fact, she seemed determined to not answer his question. "I grabbed the boxes, and got a great leg workout in at the same time. Those stairs are brutal."

He followed her down the hall into the master bedroom where she put the last box beside his bed.

Bed.

Which meant his furniture, as limited as it was, had also been moved. "I didn't realize Trevor's truck was good at lifting."

A bright grin broke free. "You can thank Jeff for your furniture being here."

What the hell?

She didn't make him wait for an explanation. "While he was in town candidating, he mentioned to my dad the 'willing hands' list he'd come up with at college. They popped up a new bulletin board at Jeff's suggestion.

191

I posted a couple of days ago that I'd need help for about half an hour at some point. A couple of the youth came out. It only took twenty minutes, and I gave them movie passes as a thank-you, so they were happy."

"You've had this planned for a while," he said with a smile.

"You've been working like crazy. I know you'll be happier out of the yard, so, yeah." She shrugged. "It's just a little thing."

"Means a lot to me. Thanks." He caught her under the chin and gave her a kiss.

He meant it to be short and sweet, but the instant they made contact his plans went out the window.

He'd been busy, but that didn't mean he hadn't thought about her almost constantly. Driving a tractor required only so much concentration. The rest of it he'd spent thinking back to touching her. The sounds she made as he caressed her skin.

How she tasted...

Addictive. That's how she tasted. He wrapped a hand around her, palm to her lower back. He pressed their bodies together and dipped in for another sip. Teasing his tongue over her lips until she opened to him.

Any moment he could get called back to the fields, but until then he had no deadlines. Nothing dire waving at him, or clanging, or demanding his attention.

Nothing but her. And he had every intention of giving in to sweet temptation for as long as he had.

Laurel didn't seem to mind. She crowded against him, slipping her thumbs into the belt loops at his side, her fingers draped over his butt. She held on tight as if afraid he would vanish.

Not a chance. Not going *anywhere.*

He tilted her head sharper so he could get at her lips, stroking their tongues together, heating them up. His cock lay trapped behind the thick material of his jeans, yet he felt the softness of her belly where he pressed against her.

Kissing was hot, but far less desperate than their previous encounters. Mostly because he knew they couldn't take this past a certain point—not with him taking off at a moment's notice.

It gave them the freedom to savour each other.

Laurel tightened her grip on his belt loops, using them to tug him as if to get his attention. He reluctantly broke the lock between their lips, smiling down at her, his breathing unsteady.

Her lashes fluttered for a moment. "I'm glad I can do something to make you happy. I'm pretty happy these days too."

"Except I bet you're jealous of my new digs," Rafe teased. "There's a spare room. You're welcome to move in."

A laugh burst free. "Don't make offers you're not serious about."

Her living down the hall from him? That would be awesome, and dangerous, and...*dangerous.* "I didn't say it was a *smart* move, but hell, you want it? It's yours."

She loosened her grasp so she could rearrange her hands, sliding her fingers under the edge of his waistline. Easing forward and brushing his abdomen. "I'll take that offer into serious consideration, but right now? I have something else on my mind."

"Want to grab a bite—?"

He sucked for air as she undid his belt and pulled it free.

"Don't think you want me to *bite*." The words came out rather breathlessly.

Her gaze dropped from his as she focused on her fingers, undoing his button, sliding his zipper down. Each click as the metal rasps released rang loudly in his ears.

"Laurel?"

"I'm happy," Laurel said. "And I want this. You would not believe how often I catch myself..."

She lost concentration as the material opened and allowed his package more freedom. His cock strained against his cotton briefs, and he eased his jeans downward until they slipped from his hips to bunch around his ankles.

A happy sigh escaped her as she pulled his briefs down as well. His cock rejoiced the instant she set it free, snapping upward to the ready position.

Ready for *anything*.

He was so busy watching her face he missed the instant she planted a hand in the middle of his chest and pushed. Off balance, he fell backward onto the mattress.

"I've had the dirtiest daydreams about this." Laurel looked at him as if he was on the menu and she was starving.

"About my cock?"

She crawled onto the bed. "About all of you. But yes, about your cock."

He let her explore, folding his arms behind his head as she pushed his shirttails higher.

Laurel stroked her fingers over his abs, mesmerized. "Do me a favour. Pretend you're going to do a sit-up. I mean, don't pretend, just do little ones."

Rafe did as ordered. "Don't know what this has to do with my cock."

She hummed happily as he curled partway up then relaxed a few times, her fingertips tickling his skin as she traced the edges of his six-pack. "Everything moves when you do that, including this."

He swore, because the hand that had been drifting over his stomach was now decisively lower, her fingers wrapped around his rock-solid length.

"So soft," Laurel murmured.

"Not the adjective a guy likes associ—*fuck*."

She finished running her tongue down his entire length, then up the other side before she answered. "It is soft, baby. And I want to rub it all over me. Hmmm..."

One tantalizing swipe of her tongue sent his muscles tightening. When she paused to spend time working the sweet spot under the head of his cock, her tongue moving in slow, never-ending circles, he moaned her name.

She laughed. "You really need to think of a pet name for me. *Sitko* isn't really sexy."

"It's fucking sexy," he insisted. "Put your mouth on me now, *Sitko*, and suck me hard."

She shivered, moving to obey. Pumping with her hand before angling him higher and surrounding the tip with her lips. She sucked him in an inch at a time before retreating then doing it all over.

The wetter he got, the more of his length slipped into her mouth. Her grip tight around his base, her lips meeting her fist on every stroke. Rafe's vision blurred every time she added a bit more powerful suction, or dragged her tongue just right over the sensitive spot under the head.

A soft caress passed over his sac as she cupped him, fingers brushing the area between his balls and ass, and a flash of white-hot heat set every nerve tingling.

"*Damn* it."

She moved over him harder, deeper. Rafe was being dragged to the edge of the precipice where the slightest bump would send him over.

One movement went a little too far, and she gagged before pulling back, a moan rushing from her as if she was ready to explode as well.

That electrifying rush hit, but he tightened his grip on her hair. "You're about to blow my mind. Don't push it."

Laurel panted as she looked at him with those icy-hot eyes. "What if I love your cock more than breathing?"

Fuck.

Rafe closed his eyes and fought for control.

The mattress bounced, and he twisted to find her lying next to him, her head by his hips. "Get up," she ordered. "I want to try something."

The few seconds it took to curl to standing and turn to face the bed were far too long. She'd stripped off her shirt and bra, and the sight of her naked tits nearly did him in. Perfect little mounds with erect nipples just calling his name.

"*Jeez.*"

Laurel offered him an upside down smile as she wiggled closer to the edge of his bed. Her head fell back slightly as she reached for him, pulling his hips forward and placing his cock at her mouth. "I want to play."

She licked her lips, and temptation was too strong. He took control, pressing forward so her tongue passed over the head of his cock, wet heat wrapping around him.

The new angle let him go deeper than expected, and he slowed his stroke. Moving carefully even as his legs shook with need.

Laurel caught him by the hips and encouraged him. She dug in her fingernails and refused to let him stop. Pulling him toward her, deeper than he thought possible. Faster. He reached down and played with her nipples. The countdown to him finishing accelerated at an alarming speed until—

"*Coming.*"

Rafe pulled out, seed spurting free. He pumped his cock hard to keep the pressure going, long lines of white landing on her breasts and face. A stripe crossing her lips.

She snuck out her tongue and licked it up, and another, harder jolt escaped him as he moaned.

...and the front door slammed.

Jesse's voice echoed clearly through the open bedroom door. "Hey. Trev? Rafe?"

Laurel didn't waste a second. She was off the bed and flying for the master bathroom. Rafe measured the distance between him and the door, the bed in his way, and made an instant decision. He dove for his ankles, jerking up his briefs and pants as fast as he could, Jesse's loud footsteps marching down the hall.

"Be there in a second," Rafe warned, as if he hadn't just shoved his semi-erect cock into his pants.

The bathroom door closed a second before Jesse's head appeared in the doorway. "Hey, you're back."

"Yeah." Rafe dragged a hand through his hair and attempted to force his brain to work. It was tough, considering all the blood in his system was still pooled in his lower body.

"Well, good. I didn't even have to help." Jesse scanned the room, and Rafe cursed as both their glances fell on the clothes tossed on the bed.

The T-shirt could have been his. The bra? Not so much.

Jesse met his gaze, his grin widening. "You'll have to do something special to celebrate moving back in."

Rafe was going to kill him. "Hey, I was going to ask you about that thing in the living room."

His cousin went willingly enough into the living room, but he snickered the entire way. Rafe closed the bedroom behind him with a solid click so Laurel would know it was safe to grab her clothes.

"That *thing* in the living room, eh?" Jesse teased.

"Shut up." Rafe was usually more on the ball than that, but considering he'd been in the middle of the most brainless moment a man could experience...

"Glad you're back, though," Jesse said. "It'll be good to have company in the evenings."

"I'm not done tonight," Rafe warned.

His cousin snorted. "I figured."

"Shut the fuck up," Rafe ordered, but this time he couldn't stop from laughing as well. "I meant I'm headed back out to finish a few more hours haying."

Jesse plopped onto the couch and reached for the remote. "Well, if you have more fields to do, I'll find something else to entertain me. *House* marathon, maybe."

The bastard was going to make him outright ask. Which was pretty much what Rafe would have done if their positions had been reversed. "You're such an asshole. Do the decent thing and get out of the house for a while."

"I hope you don't plan on making me leave every time Laurel is ready to go home, because I won't do it." Jesse got to his feet, though. "She's your girlfriend. It's not a walk of shame unless you want it to be."

"We won't. I won't—only give her a little space this time."

"Sure. I can be a gentleman. By the way, you're flying low."

Rafe glanced down involuntarily, hands going to his zipper, which was in the proper position. "You're such a jerk."

An evil chuckle escaped Jesse. "Do we really want to discuss *jerking* or—"

"No," Rafe snapped.

Jesse seemed to find this pretty entertaining. "Don't leave me openings like that, cuz."

Rafe offered him the finger. "Anytime you want to leave..."

"No prob." Jesse sauntered to the front door, whistling happily. He paused with his hand on the doorknob, the door halfway open. "Oh, hey, just in case. You might want to think about this for the future..."

Rafe waited.

His cousin pulled the door toward himself. "Open," he said with a grin that grew wider by the second. Then he pushed the wooden barrier the other direction. "Closed. Open—"

"Get out, *now*," Rafe said without heat.

Jesse left, obviously entertained, and Rafe returned to the bedroom to let Laurel know it was safe to come out. He hoped she wasn't too traumatized.

Still, he had to chuckle as well.

Welcome home, indeed.

Chapter Sixteen

RAFE CAUGHT himself thinking often about what Laurel had shared with him during the picnic. It wasn't the bits about Jeff, or even the admission she'd had sex with the guy that bothered him the most, although he wished he could have offered the man a firm kick in the pants to send him on his way back east.

No, it was the fact Rafe was completely unfit to help Laurel deal with her worries about faith that sent his brain through endless loops.

The dilemma teased at him in the quiet moments between tasks. During the mindless repetition of driving the swather, and the baler, and moving the harvest into storage. He didn't want there to be *anything* he couldn't help her with.

The topic got shoved to the top of his attention when a message from Pastor Dave showed up on his phone, asking for a tour. Rafe called back to confirm a time. A couple hours later, he left the fields and headed toward Gabe's to get some work done there before he met the man.

The school bus was pulling away from the entrance to the ranch, Lance and Nathan Coleman beginning the long walk toward the barns.

Rafe stopped his truck beside his Six Pack nephews.

"Want to drive?" he asked Lance.

The kid's eyes lit up. "Don't have my learner's yet."

Rafe pushed open the driver's door and climbed down. "Then you need practice, don't you?"

Lance swallowed hard then eagerly got behind the wheel.

Nathan was up on the back bumper with a leg over the tailgate before Rafe stopped him. "Sorry, bud. In the cab, with your seatbelt on."

He got a massive eye roll in response. "You're not serious? That's so lame. We're on the driveway."

"Not lame," Rafe assured him, "It's called self-preservation. Your father would take me apart if he found out I let you do stupid shit on my watch."

"My dad's not scary." Nathan gave him a dirty look, teenage attitude dripping from every word. "He won't mind. He doesn't make stupid rules."

He didn't have time for this. Rafe shrugged. "Have it your way."

He got in the cab, locking the doors before Nathan could get in.

Lance glanced over, hands clutching the wheel at ten and two. "You letting him ride in the back?"

"Hell, no." Rafe rolled down the window. "Don't even think about it," he warned Nathan who had one hand on the side of the truck box as if he was about to jump over the edge. "You can walk. We'll meet you at the far barn, and if you plan to have more trouble with your hearing around me, you can sit yourself down outside and wait for your 'not scary' dad to come pick you up early. I'll be happy to call him."

Nathan snatched his hand off the truck and backed up rapidly, all trace of rebellion washed away. "You don't have to do that."

Rafe closed the window and motioned for Lance to drive, hiding his amusement best he could. His cousin Daniel was a great dad—Nathan wasn't scared of him in a bad way, but he obviously had a healthy amount of respect for the man.

Which is what Rafe desperately wished he felt for his own father.

He shoved his frustrations down as Nathan got smaller in the background. "When can you take your test?"

Lance's focus on the gravel road never faltered as he drove far slower than necessary. "I'm fourteen in November, but my mom's making noises about me waiting until the spring."

"Let me guess. She doesn't want you driving in the snow?"

Lance sighed, the noise rattling around the cab with the kind of long-suffering intensity only a teenage boy could put into it. "Yeah."

"I get it. I wonder if she's nervous because of her accident. She was hurt pretty bad, wasn't she?"

Lance was quiet for a minute. "I'd forgotten about that."

Because teenage worlds revolved around a small radius.

"Well, whatever you and your parents decide, there're always vehicles on the ranch if you want to practice driving in bad conditions. On Coleman land—off the main roads." Rafe held back a laugh, keeping as straight-faced as possible. "If we have a big snowfall, maybe you can help clear."

"Can I?" Lance blurted eagerly.

This must have been what Tom Sawyer felt like. "Well, it's a pretty big machine, the tractor with the blade, but I bet you could handle it. I'll ask your dad."

"Sweet."

They were pulling up to the side of the barn. Rafe pointed to where he wanted Lance to park, then sent him on ahead to get started on the stalls.

He waited for Nathan to join him, ignoring what had happened minutes earlier. "You interested in some digging?"

Nathan made a face, but didn't grumble out loud. "I guess."

"I need a pretty deep hole. You'll have to use the backhoe."

The kid went from zero to sputtering with excitement in under three seconds. "You're joking."

"If you're not interested I can teach—"

"I'm interested," Nathan all but shouted.

Rafe smiled as he led the boy around to the back where they needed another burning pit. "I'll get the backhoe in position then show you how the controls work."

Fifteen minutes later he left behind a far happier helper. Nathan was eager to make a mess and one hundred percent on Rafe's side, at least for the rest of that day.

The old backhoe was bombproof. The gears moved slowly, the footing was rock solid, and the only way the kid could get hurt was if he literally threw himself from the seat into the hole he was scooping in the soft soil. Rafe made sure Nathan was belted in tight before promising to check in on him in a while.

He liked kids—always had. Gabe might have joked about him being the annoying little brother, but as his cousins had children, he'd ended up babysitting off and on for all of them.

Laurel likes kids.

The thought hit hard, and for a second he had to shake his head. Except...

He'd dived into dating Laurel because it felt right. They'd been friends forever, and it made sense to take it to the next step.

Kids? That was a step farther than they'd ever talked about.

Don't you think she's thinking about more than just fooling around and having fun?

The fact her father was stopping by only added to his sudden mental turmoil. Was this a forever path he was headed down with Laurel?

If *his* father weren't an issue, that answer would potentially be a whole lot simpler. Maybe if Rafe knew for certain he wasn't going to turn into the bastard at some point in the future...

You're so much like your father.

How many times had he heard that when he was growing up? Not as much lately, but then he'd made a point of not hanging out where too much gossip got tossed his direction.

Lance was hard at work, so Rafe slipped around to the back room, intending on sorting through tack until Pastor Dave arrived. Hopefully sorting out his brains at the same time.

Instead he bumped into another clan gathering, this time with a few of the older generation. He'd caught them during a break. Uncle Mike and Uncle George were peering out the window to where he'd left Nathan while

204

Gabe was sorting through what looked like a pile of maps on the table.

"You spot a sasquatch in the yard?" Rafe asked.

Uncle George twisted to face him. "That kid hasn't stopped grinning since you plopped him in the seat. What's he being rewarded for?"

"Being lippy," Rafe admitted.

A chuckle escaped his uncle. "Interesting system you got going, but if it works..."

Gabe slid the pile of papers into an envelope and passed it to Uncle Mike, ignoring Rafe's raised brow and offering a slight headshake before changing topics. "They're good workers. I'm surprised you didn't want to keep the boys over at the Six Pack land for longer," he said to Mike.

"I wouldn't mind," Mike said, "but Gramma Marion was spoiling them rotten, and Lance has a major crush on Vicki, so it's time to get them some fresh territory."

Rafe and Gabe exchanged glances before snickering. "Vicki?" Gabe asked.

Mike shrugged. "She shows up to help out where she can. Lance walked into a barn wall, he was so busy staring at her."

"How's Joel handling that?" Rafe managed to get out through his laughter.

"He's at the still-amused stage, but there's no use in making any of them suffer for longer." Mike folded his arms and leaned back on the wall behind him. "Hear you've got a new girlfriend."

"Old friend, new as a girlfriend, yeah."

"Marion speaks well of her," Mike said. "Her whole family, in fact."

Rafe eyed him for a moment. His Aunt Marion went to church, but Mike didn't—but it didn't seem to have caused them trouble over the years they'd been together. He wondered if maybe he wasn't seeing the big picture. "Pastor Dave is coming over, if you want to say hello," Rafe offered.

Gabe bumped him lightly on the arm. "Sounds serious. Isn't this a little fast, bro?"

Confusion hit hard. "He's coming over to see the new lambs. What's wrong with—?"

Oh.

"You're an ass," Rafe said.

"You should see your face right now," Gabe taunted.

"Jerk."

"I told you some day it would be payback time for all the teasing you did about me and Allison."

"Butthead."

Mike turned toward Uncle George. "It's so much fun to listen to the children argue, isn't it?"

George laughed, patting Mike on the shoulder. "They're quieter at it than my three girls. Of course, Tamara isn't around as much anymore. And Karen only argues with me, which puts me in closer range. Increases the volume."

"That girl takes after her old man," Mike said. "Stubborn, good with horses."

"Stubborn." George cracked a grin. "Yeah, she's that, all right."

Rafe checked his watch. "I should look in on Nathan before Pastor Dave gets here."

"We'll take care of the boy," George assured him, peering out the window at a car pulling into the yard. "Go on."

206

"Yeah, don't make Laurel's dad wait," Gabe deadpanned. "You never know what he'll do."

Uncle Mike leaned in closer. "Have him put in a good word for me."

"With who?" Rafe glanced over his shoulder as he hurried toward the door. All three men were pointing a finger toward the ceiling, angelic expressions twitching into grins.

He ignored the lot of them as he exited the barn and went to meet his girlfriend's dad.

Pastor Dave got out of the car and looked around, a pleased smile on his face as he took a deep breath before answering Rafe's hello.

"Thanks for indulging me," he said as Rafe led him toward the barn.

"Any time. Although, if you stay too long, I'll have to put you to work."

He chuckled. "Seems a fair trade."

Rafe unlatched the side door and led Laurel's father in by the back way. "I forgot to ask earlier, but did you want to get out on the horses today, as well?"

"No. Thank you, though. I don't want to keep you from your work for too long. And my wife would never forgive me if I got to go riding and she didn't." Pastor Dave followed closely after him deeper into the barn. "If the invitation still stands, maybe you can take both of us out some other time."

"How about when Laurel can come along? I could arrange that."

Pastor Dave nodded, his expression indicating he was thinking hard.

Was he worried about Rafe's involvement with Laurel? Trying to come up with a polite way to tell him to back off and leave his daughter alone?

Rafe attempted to keep his concerns under wraps as he led the man deeper into the barn to where the most recent arrivals were. The barn was quiet, his uncles, brother and nephews vanished into thin air. Either they were hiding, or they'd high-tailed it for safer ground.

He kind of wished he could do the same.

But if he and Laurel ended up making a go of it—and his brain was still adjusting to thinking beyond simply dating—this man would be involved in his life in some capacity.

Rafe didn't want to place walls between them. He also didn't want to invite in a lot of judgment or, well, *preaching*. Which was probably a bad thing to expect to avoid when conversing with a man who made his living as a preacher.

Fifteen minutes later it appeared Pastor Dave didn't have much of an agenda other than thoroughly enjoying his visit with the newborn lambs.

"There's something inspiring about birth and the changing seasons." Pastor Dave leaned his elbows on the low gate as he checked out a pen that held an ewe with two tiny lambs, barely hours old. "You've got a pretty good job, getting to experience this firsthand."

"It's great at ten in the morning, and four in the afternoon. It's a little less exciting when it's dark and cold and you're not heading for shelter or supper for another couple hours."

"I can see that." Pastor Dave smiled. "I get to work more civilized hours, and usually indoors."

He asked a few more questions, mostly about what Rafe had on his plate for the next while, never once veering into territory that made Rafe uncomfortable.

Which was uncomfortable in a whole different way.

He hadn't planned on it, but it seemed the most natural thing to raise a few questions of his own. Laurel loved her family. It would be good to be forewarned if there were changes on the horizon.

"How long are you planning on staying in Rocky?" Rafe asked, jerking to a halt as he realized the question came out wrong. "I mean, don't most pastors move around a lot? You and Mrs. Sitko have been around Rocky for a lot of years."

"Depends on the church," Pastor Dave said. "Some like their pastors to move often, but in Rocky we've got a community that has roots that go deep. It's better to keep a man here that knows the people, and cares for them."

"Makes sense." Rafe cleared his throat. "And I wasn't asking because I hoped you'd leave, or anything. I just know Laurel likes having you around."

Implying *he* didn't? Man, he was on track to win all the awards for making a fool of himself.

Fortunately, the other man smiled. "We plan on being around for a long time. Rocky Mountain House is our home, and the people here are in our hearts. Including you, and your mom, and the whole lot of your family, if you want to know the truth."

Rafe chuckled. "That's a pretty big list. Just saying."

"I've got a big heart. Just saying." Pastor Dave leaned a shoulder against the outer pen wall as he looked Rafe over. "You got something on your mind?"

The words burst out before he really thought them through. "You know I'm seeing Laurel."

The other man nodded.

All his possible follow-up sentences seemed over-the-top rude as he considered them in turn. He wasn't asking permission. He wasn't going to stop, so there

209

didn't seem to be any reason to ask if Pastor Dave had a problem with it.

So he went on a completely different tack, ignoring the fact he was wildly changing the topic back to something safe.

"Well, that's good you'll be around. People can get pretty set in their ways after a certain time. Hard to change what comes naturally like that."

"What comes naturally?" Pastor Dave hesitated. "You're talking about character. The *who you are* when the going gets tough."

Rafe shrugged. "I suppose."

"I'd say that's not set in stone, not even when people get old." Laurel's father considered his words carefully. "People make decisions all the time about who they're going to be, and it doesn't matter if they're eight or eighty—people can change. A person can decide he wants to be a man of strong character, but he won't get there by wanting it to happen. He'll get there because it's a part of him through and through. It's a goal, and more. It's what he believes in, and more."

Belief. *Damn.* This was where Rafe was going to lose any goodwill he'd built up with the man, but the point had to be made. The image of his Uncle Mike flashed to mind. His brother, for that matter. "I know a whole lot of men who don't go to church who have strong characters I admire, so it's not just about believing."

Pastor Dave raised a brow. "I didn't say that. You don't have to believe in church, or religion, but you need to have faith in something."

"...or I'll fall for anything?"

"No, without faith, a man gets cold inside and dies."

The words struck with the impact of a sledgehammer. Rafe could picture his father standing before him. Eyes—cold. Soul—brittle.

Pastor Dave went on, seemingly oblivious to the fact Rafe was fighting to stand. "Whatever you believe about how we got here, men need certain things to keep alive. Air, water and food for the physical body. The brain needs challenges. But the heart, our *soul*'—he tapped a fist against his chest—"that needs a connection to others, and a reason to go on. That's the road that gets narrow—picking which path you'll walk through life, and who you'll walk with. If you step into bitterness, it'll coat your boots like cowshit. You can scrape it off, but the odor lingers. Clings to you, even if you look clean and shiny on the outside. And every step you take, you leave traces of shit behind."

As if he'd been passed something a little bigger than he knew how to handle, Rafe stood in silence for a minute before eyeing the other man. "You're not exactly how I remember you."

"Because I said *shit*?" Pastor Dave laughed. "Been preaching for nearly thirty years to men who work the land. Shit comes up fairly often."

Rafe nodded, not sure what to say next.

Fortunately, Laurel's father patted his shoulder, turning them both toward the door. "I've taken up enough of your time. And Corinne will be expecting me home soon."

"Tell Mrs. Sitko if she'd like to come see the lambs, she's welcome."

There wasn't much more said after that. Pastor Dave got in his car and headed into town, and Rafe stood motionless in the yard, feeling a little like he'd been run over by a semi.

He must have been out there long enough to get Allison's curiosity up. He blinked and discovered his sister-in-law next to him, head tilted to the side as she looked him over, amusement in her eyes.

"What?" he snapped.

"You're pretty cute, all embarrassed from talking to your girlfriend's daddy," she teased.

"I'm not embarrassed," he protested.

"Shell-shocked, then. Did he ask what your intentions were?"

Rafe rolled his eyes. "I'm glad this is so amusing to you. And no, we didn't talk about Laurel."

"Interesting." She backed up. "Come join us for supper. I made lasagna."

He wasn't about to turn that down, even knowing he'd have to put up with a whole lot of comments through dinner.

He didn't mind. The distraction was appreciated, although he knew he'd be thinking about Pastor Dave's words for a long time to come.

Chapter Seventeen

"It MADE sense to carpool," Laurel said to her friend, somewhat apologetically. "We're going the same direction."

Nicole shrugged, adjusting her seat so she could pop her feet up on the dash. "I don't have a problem with it, but a shopping trip with the four of us is a funny combination. That's all I'm saying."

Laurel turned into the driveway at Trevor Coleman's place. "Becky's often in the library going through magazines and books. When she heard we were sneaking away midweek to Red Deer for the day, she asked if she could come along."

They'd hit it off, her and Becky. Laurel had been honoured when the other woman opened up and shared some of her past, but the rough life Becky had faced until recently wasn't common knowledge. Nic wasn't in the know about a lot of the details, and she didn't need to be.

And Laurel's struggles with her issues of faith paled when she considered the hell Becky had lived through. The woman had come out the other side without breaking. It was inspiring, and it was humbling, and it made Laurel all the more pleased to be counted on Becky's list of friends.

"Oh, I get the connection with Becky. I think Ashley Coleman is a bit of a stretch, even for you," her friend said with a smile. "Although, you do seem to have developed the ability to make just about everybody fall in love with you."

Laurel pulled to a stop beside Trevor's big truck. "Except a few, you mean."

Like Ben Coleman, who glared at her as if she were possessed every time he spotted her, even from a distance.

"It's your puppy-dog eyes," Nicole said as they got out of the car and headed for the front porch of the old house.

Becky was waiting on the porch swing, and she wasn't alone. Her boyfriend Trevor Coleman from the Moonshine clan had an arm stretched along the back of the swing, and she was tucked against him, her legs curled up on the bench. He was making it rock, and the two of them looked as if there was nothing more perfect they could be doing at that moment.

It wasn't the freshly painted house trim, or the clean-scrubbed porch boards Laurel was a little jealous of. The two of them were obviously together, on so many levels.

Becky turned toward him. "I'll miss you today."

He kissed her, fingers cupping her chin as he took his time, lips moving slowly but thoroughly over hers.

Hot. *Very* hot.

"Tick-tock, tick-tock, haven't got all day," Nicole teased, clapping her hands rapidly. "Enough with the kissing, already."

Trevor didn't stop what he was doing, just let one hand drift upward, raised middle finger aimed toward Nicole as he silently continued to kiss Becky.

Laurel laughed. "And that's all he's got to say on the matter."

Nicole leaned toward Laurel as they ignored the couple on the swing. "So was Ashley hanging out at the library when you issued the invite as well?"

"Yes," Laurel answered primly. "You'd be surprised how many people actually *read* in this town."

"Hey. I read," Nic protested. "Especially since you started the wine and chocolate nights."

Too funny. "I notice you remember the wine and chocolate parts, but not the *reading club* part of it."

"What was Ashley reading? How to survive testosterone overdoses?"

"She's doing an art mural for us in the children's area," Laurel said.

Her friend snorted. "Your idea?"

"Yes."

"Hiring Colemans—isn't that against some kind of nepotism rule?"

Laurel resisted the urge to roll her eyes. "I don't see me married to her, do you? This is why you need to read more—you've been watching too many cheesy sitcoms."

The two on the swing finally broke apart, a flush colouring Becky's cheeks. "We're supposed to wait here for Ashley. I guess she wants to drive."

A moment later another enormous four-by-four truck joined them, Ashley waving from behind the steering wheel before she popped out and marched up to them, jamming a cowboy hat on top of her long blonde hair. "Hey, ladies. Everybody ready to burn the place down?"

Nic jerked a thumb over her shoulder. "If those two are finished kissing…"

Ashley folded her arms over her chest, looking Becky and Trevor over with interest. "Oh. In that case, no rush." She gestured for them to continue. "Go on."

"I'd say we were done, but it wouldn't be true. Never going to be finished kissing my Rodeo," Trevor murmured.

Becky rose to her feet, fingers tangled with his as she made her way to the top of the stairs and to the truck. "Down, boy."

He chuckled, lifting her into the back seat as the rest of them climbed into the enormous beast of a vehicle. "You sure you want to drive this monster, Ashley? Because you're welcome to take mine, you know."

"As if yours is any smaller."

Nicole snickered.

"Shut up, you," Ashley said with a laugh. "It's okay, trust me—*I* know how to drive big beasts. Lots of practice. *Ahem.*"

Another snicker escaped Nic.

"Don't start up yet, Ash, they're kissing again," Laurel warned.

Becky's soft laugh carried through the truck cab as she whispered goodbye to Trevor. He closed the door and backed away, waving to them, then stood there and watched as Ashley turned around and headed out.

"Sorry about that," Becky said.

From her position behind the wheel, Ashley made a rude noise. She glanced in the rearview mirror at Becky. "What did I tell you the last time we talked?"

"Too much for me to be able to remember?" Becky admitted.

"Never apologize for kissing. At least remember that one," Ashley said.

Nicole twisted in the front passenger seat, one arm on the backrest so she could see all three women. "Okay. I'm tour director. Shopping is on the agenda. And lunch. Who needs to go where?"

"I need a craft shop and a lumber mill," Ashley said. "Oh, and the junkyard."

Laurel couldn't resist. "Doing some decorating?"

Ashley looked both ways before turning onto the main highway. "I'm starting on Christmas presents."

"At a junkyard?" Becky was obviously amused. "You have way *way* more artistic ability than me."

"Says the woman who makes pictures with teeny tiny bits of fabric."

"You quilt too," Becky pointed out.

"Mine are different," Ashley insisted. "I throw fabric at the wall then stick uncomfortable things to it. Your quilts are soft and pretty, and I'm going to cheat this year during the Coleman Christmas exchange and make sure you get my name."

"You guys pick names?" Nicole asked.

"Have you seen the size of the gathering on Boxing Day?" Ashley said in a shocked tone. "I had no idea that getting involved with Travis and Cassidy meant I was signing up for a biannual dose of insanity."

"It can't be that bad," Laurel protested.

"Oh, really? You can let me know down the road if you change your mind about that, little Miss Freshman Coleman Woman. By the way, Becky, Laurel's taken over newbie status from you. You're off the hook for teasing— it's her turn."

Heat rushed Laurel. "There's nothing official between me and Rafe."

"Yet." Three voices echoed back simultaneously.

She turned to Becky. "I expected them to be terrible teases, but you too?"

Becky answered the question with another question, pressing a finger to her lips as if considering before speaking. "Hmmm, how come I've seen your car drive past our place so many times in the last month? You know, headed toward Angel land?"

"Wow, and I've seen her car parked outside Rafe's rental at least a few times. A few *dozen* times," Ashley deadpanned.

"And here I was wondering at how often Rafe's truck was outside her apartment." Nicole twisted a little further to offer a cheesy grin. "Yeah, you two aren't spending *any* time together. None. Nada."

Laurel let the happy feelings inside bubble before trying to change the topic. "So where else do we need to go? After the thrill of the junkyard?"

"Where do you need to go, Becky?" Nicole asked.

The young woman flushed bright pink. "Ummmm..."

Ashley chuckled evilly. "Does this mean you want to hit another toy store?"

"Ashley," Becky whispered in shock. "I don't... I mean, don't talk about... I mean—"

"What? I think it's safe to talk about sex in this group. Nicole is living with Troy Thompson, and I'm damn sure that boy's got the moves. Laurel is seeing Rafe, who is a Coleman, which means the man's got the libido of a bull, which means with all the time they're spending together there is surely some *spectacular* hanky-panky going on. You are with a Coleman, ergo, ditto on the tomfoolery, and me..." She tilted her head to the side and batted her lashes at Becky in the rearview mirror. "Okay, you're right, then there's me, pure as the driven snow. Oh, horrors, don't mention the s·e·x word."

"You're so bad," Becky said with a smile.

"Just spit it out, woman. We're all friends here."

"Not toys, but something pretty to wear, is that right?" Laurel asked, the magazine articles she'd found Becky peering at a dead giveaway.

"Ooooooh, like lingerie?"

Becky nodded. "Yes. I want to get some pretty things. I want to surprise Trevor."

It wasn't a bad idea, although Laurel was stumbling a little mentally over Ashley's assumption that she and Rafe were already a lot more sexually involved than they were.

The fooling around they'd been doing was fun—*really* fun—and Laurel had no intention of complaining. Except it seemed Rafe was a touch *too* intent on keeping them going slow. It was October already—they'd been a couple officially for a month, after she'd been dreaming about him all summer.

Maybe she needed to push the agenda a little harder.

The hour-long drive to the city passed quickly enough with shared stories and laughter about nothing in particular. They hit a half a dozen places and had a nice lunch before finding a parking spot at the mall where Ashley led them straight to Victoria's Secret.

Trying on lingerie with Ashley was a full-out production. Bra shopping usually involved Laurel hauling a couple hangers off the rack at Walmart then hoping they fit.

She got measured this time, and suddenly there were a lot of pretty bras that made the limited amount of chest she had look spectacular.

The other difference was she usually went shopping by herself. By the time they'd been in the store for half an hour, Ashley wasn't the only one walking out of their private change rooms into the larger area with the mirrors to show off what they were trying.

"Holy moly." Laurel elbowed Nicole to get her attention as Becky shyly stepped out to get their thoughts on an outfit. "It's illegal to look that good."

Becky didn't quite seem to know where to put her hands as she stood before them wearing virginal white. Little bows were attached to the barely-there garment in strategic places that would be perfect to drive Trevor wild.

"It's beautiful," Nicole said.

"*You're* beautiful," Laurel added. "You've got to get that. Trevor won't know what hit him."

"You think?" Becky wiggled on the spot before lifting her gaze to Laurel's. "It makes me feel like a present waiting to be unwrapped."

"You buy that and if you wear it often, you'll never have to give Trevor another gift for the rest of your life."

"Not that she'll be wearing it for long," Nicole pointed out.

"True." Ashley joined the conversation as she slipped into the room. "You're a knockout, Becky. Sweet, *sweet* and sexy. And I think Laurel here needs to follow your example."

"What are you...*ohhhhh*. Whoa." Laurel stuttered to a stop as Ashley held out a pile of clothing to her. A very skimpy pile.

Ashley smiled. "Similar to Becky's, but more what you need."

Laurel lifted one of the silky straps, and the miniscule amount of fabric that followed shimmered in a seductive red. "Should I assume the colour choice means something?"

"You've made one of the Angel Colemans fall hard and fast." The woman waggled her brows. "Go, try it on."

It took a couple minutes of wiggling to slip everything on, including the garter belt and stockings Ashley added to the collection at the last second. Laurel glanced down. Thinking about Rafe seeing her in the outfit was enough to make her legs start quivering.

Outside her change room, the coaxing began.

"You have to show it off," Nicole insisted. "Come on."

"You saw mine," Becky teased. "I should get to see yours…"

On the other side of the door, Ashley snorted with amusement. "I'm so proud of you, Becky. That was terribly naughty."

Laurel gathered her courage. It was true. If Becky could manage a show-and-tell, then so could she. She left the change room and stepped forward, suddenly the center of attention.

Nicole's eyes widened. Becky had wrapped a nearly transparent white robe around herself, and the contrast with the pale fabric made her cheeks darkening to deep pink even more noticeable.

Ashley was the only one who didn't seem at a loss for words.

Although the first few things out of her mouth were swears that she apologized for immediately. "Travis warned me to watch my language around you guys, but holy *shit*, that is the kind of outfit that makes a person break a few rules."

"I look okay?"

Becky shook her head. "Better than okay. Wow? Whoa?"

"Hot to the nth degree," Nicole agreed. "Merry Christmas and happy birthday, because I'm buying that for you if you don't get it yourself."

She felt pretty, and she *felt* hot, and she had an idea Rafe would like the outfit as well.

"One thing, though." Ashley dropped to her knees and undid the garter belts, fingers moving quickly as she adjusted them to lie under the narrow edge of the panties. "Garters first, panties second." She glanced up. "Means a certain someone could take off only one layer if he wants."

Oh.

Ohhhhhhh.

"I knew that," Laurel insisted.

"That was a lie...I think," Nicole said. "It's hard to tell because your face is so red in the first place."

"Go away, you brat," Laurel told Nicole.

The others laughed, but as embarrassing as the whole situation was...it wasn't. Laurel felt accepted and cared for, and knew they only wanted what was best for her.

And the best seemed to mean seducing Rafe.

Which, okay by her.

He'd been holding back a whole lot. A wild idea hit—maybe it wasn't that he needed a nudge to get him to take the next step. Maybe she needed to convince him they were *both* ready.

All four of them walked out of the store with new purchases.

"I don't think it's fair you saw what we bought, but you didn't show us," Becky complained to Ashley.

"I didn't want to shock the children," Ashley mock-whispered to Nicole.

"After what we *did* see you try on?" Laurel licked another bit of ice cream off her spoon. They'd stopped at Dairy Queen to grab treats for the ride home. "Now you have me curious. What could possibly be more scandalous than that see-through, seductive underwear you were wearing?"

"Never mind."

"I know," Nicole said smugly.

"They're so mean," Becky said with a laugh. "How're we supposed to learn if you keep secrets from us?"

"Getting an education in sexual adventuring works on an escalating scale. You know how it's fun to have the guys talk dirty to you?"

"I like it better when he can't say anything at all," Nicole admitted.

"Speechless is good too," Ashley agreed.

Becky giggled. "Oh. I thought you meant when they had their mouths...busy..."

"Becky Hall. You *are* a naughty girl," Nicole said approvingly.

"I didn't just say that," Becky insisted, but she was smiling as she rearranged the bag with her new outfit. She folded it carefully, straightening the corners as if she was planning something special.

Laughter continued to ebb and flow the entire trip. It wrapped around Laurel, comfortable yet fresh and new as she got to know the others better.

They were nearly home when Becky leaned toward her. Ashley and Nic were chatting in an animated fashion in the front seat, busy with their own conversation.

"I've tried to figure out why being intimate with Trevor doesn't feel wrong, even though it's against everything I was taught while I was growing up," Becky said. "I think you know what I mean."

Boy, did she ever. "That sex is a sin unless you're married?"

Not that her father had ever preached brimstone-and-fire sermons specific to that topic, but the sentiment was there. Self-control and chastity were highly valued.

It was one of the areas Laurel had struggled through after leaving college. After dealing with Jeff, and the fallout from their intimate relationship.

"Did you come to any conclusions?" Laurel asked.

Becky nodded. "I think God has a lot of good things planned for us, and sometimes people get in the way of those good things. I really don't think it was his idea for me to end up where I did, treated the way I was. The God I believe in wants me to be with Trevor, and he's not about to punish me for loving a man who would give up *everything* for me."

Which was pretty much where Laurel had hung her hat. She reached over and caught Becky's fingers with hers, giving them a squeeze. "I'm so glad you have Trevor. I'm so glad to know that you're happy."

Becky smiled. "I'm glad to have you as a friend. Thanks for always being willing to talk to me. Trevor is there, but he doesn't understand this part."

Laurel nodded.

Becky rejoined the conversation with the women in the front seat while Laurel let her thoughts drift a little longer.

Coming back to Rocky hadn't just been about coming back to Rafe. She had her family, and she had new friends, *and* she had Rafe.

224

It was pretty amazing. She might not know exactly where she stood on a whole lot of issues, but like Rafe had told her—life would be pretty boring if she didn't have things to learn.

One of which...how to seduce a man. She resisted peeking into the bag holding her pretty, seductive outfit and planned for the best time to make her move.

Chapter Eighteen

A WEEK later the weather was holding. Contrary to Karen's prediction that winter would come early, October temperatures dropped slowly which made finishing tasks in the fields a whole lot more enjoyable for Rafe than it could have been.

And when he wasn't working, he and Laurel were having a blast dating. Nothing unexpected there considering their background. But at the end of each night, he went home and she went home, which even with the fooling around they were doing meant he spent a hell of a lot of time in the shower jacking off.

Keeping under control was going to kill him.

Dead.

Soon.

But that impromptu sermon from Pastor Dave had hit hard. Rafe was still working through what he believed in, but he knew pretty well where some of Laurel's lines lay, and it made zero sense to blow past her limits without regard.

Until he knew for sure what he was offering her... What he *had* to offer. Doubts struck over and over, made even worse every time he bumped into his father.

Canadian Thanksgiving weekend meant a change-up in his and Laurel's typical last minute "do whatever fits into the time allotted" routine. If they'd been any other couple dating as long as they'd been, it would have been a simple thing. They'd attend their own family dinners without worrying about inviting the other along.

Only as long-time friends as well as dating, it made sense to join the other family, except both families had arranged to celebrate Sunday.

Add to that—both families had *issues*, so figuring out where and when they'd have their holiday get-together was anything but simple.

"This is a rude question," Laurel warned as they sat together at the picnic table outside the library, stealing lunch together, "but I honestly want to know. Do you really *do* holidays with your family anymore? I mean, just the Angel Colemans? Considering..."

He knew exactly what she was asking. What a mess.

"Considering my dad is an ass? Yeah, it's awkward, but my mom shouldn't have to miss out on things because of him, especially now that she's got a grandson. Since Allison and Gabe got married they host most of the time, and Mom and I join them. Ben rarely shows up, and the couple times he did, he mostly behaved. Just glared the entire time then left after he ate."

"I'm sorry." Laurel rested her hand on his arm. "It's not right that's what family's like for you."

It wasn't, but it was his reality.

Do I have any right to make it hers?

Rafe shoved the negative thoughts aside. "We deal with it, but considering how well you and he get along,

Ms. Lippy, you probably don't want to take the chance he shows up this year."

She stuck out her tongue before offering a warning back. "And I don't think you want to come to my house. Jeff starts work this coming week, so he's back in town."

"What's that got to do with your family dinner?"

She grimaced. "My mom invited him to stop by for dessert once he arrives."

"Gee, all the more reason for me to come with you. Me and Jeff, we're best buds. I totally need to be there to welcome him back to Rocky."

Laurel snickered. "You remember we talked about this?"

Rafe sighed as dramatically as possible before raising a hand in the air. "Yes, Sitko. I promise not to lay a hand on the man."

"Or...?"

"...or a boot," he finished reluctantly. "Fine. I'll go to my brother's and put up with my dad. But you need to call me as soon as you're done, and I'll come rescue you."

Turned out Rafe was the one who needed rescuing.

He showed up at his brother's only to find Gabe coming out the door, Micah in his arms.

"Change of plans," Gabe announced, his expression twisting reluctantly. "Allison isn't feeling well enough to have people in the house, so Mom said she'd take over."

Rafe held back from cursing. Dinner at the homestead meant the odds of Ben being there were high. He was doubly glad Laurel hadn't come along.

He considered going home and warming up leftovers. He'd have a better appetite without Ben around.

Still, his sister-in-law feeling shitty took precedence over his hurt feelings for having to spend time with his father. "Allison's been under the weather a lot this fall. She okay?"

Gabe hesitated. "She's expecting."

Hot damn. "Well, that's good news. So, it's morning sickness."

"All-day sickness," his brother shared. "She doesn't want to tell anyone yet—so keep that under your hat."

"No problem." He eyed his brother. "You're looking tired. Is that from worrying about Allison?"

"More to worry about than usual, yeah."

The answer was a strange one and seemed not just about Allison. Rafe thought back to the clandestine meetings that had been going on—he'd run into another the day before. "You got anything else you need my help with? Like ranch stuff?"

Micah gave a shout and waved his arms excitedly as Gabe lowered him into the car seat. "Not yet. Soon, okay?"

"Whenever. You know I'm there for you," Rafe insisted.

"I know. It's not my choice."

The comment just piqued Rafe's interest further, but he held his questions, heading over to the homestead in his own truck and striding ahead of his brother to open the back door.

The scent of ham and stuffing and apple pie hung thick in the air as their mom hustled forward to take Micah from Gabe's arms.

"Thanks again for taking over, Mom." Gabe snuck in and gave her a hug and a kiss.

"I hope Allison's feeling better soon. There're a lot of people down with the flu already this year. With any luck the rest of us can avoid it." Dana placed Micah on the small kitchen tabletop to remove his tiny wool jacket.

Gabe shot a glance at Rafe.

Deflection seemed wise. "You should consider getting the flu shot, Ma," Rafe suggested. "It's one of those things that can help—"

Their mom glanced toward the living room before giving them both a pointed stare.

Right. Vaccinations were another topic to avoid discussing when his father was around. According to him they were all one step away from the apocalypse because of modern medicine.

Ben didn't move out of his chair when they entered the room, just glared with disapproval. His gaze lingered on his grandson as Dana placed the little boy on the floor beside a box with a few toys in it. "He sure doesn't look like a Coleman," Ben muttered.

Rafe wasn't sure what his dad was implying. He bristled on Gabe's behalf, ready to snap something rude.

His brother played it cool, far less annoyance in his tone when he spoke than Rafe could have mustered. "Micah's my son. He's definitely a Coleman."

Ben grunted then turned back to the television.

Fine by Rafe. The only reason he was here was for his mom's sake. He settled on the couch beside her, the three of them—her, Gabe and himself—chatting while Micah dragged the toys out of the box then threw them back in.

A ball rolled under the couch, and Rafe fished it out, spinning it in his hand then balancing it on a fingertip in front of his nephew.

Micah laughed with delight, his face lit with excitement.

Ben turned up the volume of the television.

A buzzer went off in the kitchen, and his mom rose to her feet. "That's the last thing. We can take everything to the table."

Gabe reached for Micah, but Rafe waved him off. "I got him. You help Mom."

Rafe picked up his nephew and brought him to the highchair, strapping him in as he chatted with the kid. Ignoring his father who seemed content to ignore his family.

But he couldn't overlook it completely. That deep cutting hurt inside was there, no matter how much he wanted to pretend it wasn't.

Laurel had insisted Rafe's decisions were his own. That he'd never step too far and let loose the anger he felt inside. Only Pastor Dave's comment about character being what wanted to come to the surface first didn't bode well, because his first impulse was to walk over and give his father a smack across the head and tell him to smarten up before he ruined any chance he had of making things right with his family.

The meal was tolerable. For once Ben didn't start in on a rant, and the silence from his end of the table let the rest of them continue to talk as they passed the food.

Only the bastard was there. Silent and judgmental. Silent, and irritating the hell out of Rafe. He stared at each of them in turn, chewing his food angrily. And when he looked at Micah, Ben's brow furrowed as if he was attempting to solve a puzzle.

They were nearly done the main meal before he spoke. "The kid doesn't look like anyone in the Parker family, either."

The out-of-the-blue comment took a moment to understand, but when it clicked, Rafe was speechless. What the *hell?*

He opened his mouth to demand what exactly his father was implying, but before he could snap angrily, Gabe soothed the situation, although even his angelic brother looked at the end of his rope.

Rafe couldn't take it anymore. He got up and gave his mom a quick kiss on the cheek as he muttered his thanks. Carried his plate to the kitchen, stacking it beside the sink before heading for the door and escaping into the cool air.

He wasn't feeling very thankful at the moment. Spraying gravel as he left the yard didn't make him any happier, nor burning rubber as he turned into the yard of the rental. He skidded to a stop in front of the house and glared at nothing.

It took ten seconds to decide to pull out his phone and send a text. She'd be at dinner now with her family, so he wouldn't hear from her for a while, but *dammit*, he needed to touch base with Laurel.

Rafe: *I should have come with you. Call when you're done.*

She texted back right away. *That bad?*

Rafe: *Fuck.*

His phone rang almost instantly, and he felt like a fool for having interrupted her. His dad was a jerk, but Ben hadn't even been that terrible that day. Not really. There'd been no shouting, or temper tantrums, or anything truly shitty.

Just not a family. Not a time of thanksgiving by any stretch.

Guilt struck. "You didn't have to call me. I shouldn't have complained."

"Are you kidding me? Your timing was perfect. I got to look all concerned then excuse myself from the table." She sighed happily. "I might even be able to get out of doing dishes if I leave soon."

Great. Her words reminded him he'd abandoned Gabe and his mom to clean up. He mentally promised he'd make it up to them. "Don't get me in trouble with your family."

"They don't care. Well, yes, they care. Leslie was looking forward to doing dishes with me so she could hound me the entire time in the hopes I'd cave to her latest request."

Rafe laughed in spite of his inner frustrations. "Your sister never gives up. What's it this time?"

"She wants me to take over teaching Sunday school for the next three months. Which—no way."

"You having a good time, otherwise?" he asked.

"It was fun, but now it's time for *us* to celebrate. Where are you?"

He glanced around. "My place."

"Give me a few minutes and I'll call you back. I have an idea."

"Don't get us in trouble, Sitko," he warned jokingly.

"Nothing you can't handle, baby," she promised. "Sit tight. I won't be long."

Laurel hung up before he could make a comment about the pet name she'd started tossing his way. The term wasn't really what he'd expected, but damn if it didn't make him grin every time she said it.

As if she were the one taking care of him. Him, who towered over her, and outweighed her, and could easily pick her up with one arm. And she called him *baby*?

It was twisted enough to make him grin.

He headed into his place to wait to see what new mischief she was concocting.

LAUREL RACED through a few ideas of how to redeem the day for Rafe, and ended up calling her best friend.

"Hey, you. Done stuffing yourself like a turkey?" Nicole asked.

"Just. What are you and Troy doing? You okay to get together with Rafe and me to do something? He needs a bit of a pick-me-up."

Nicole made a rude noise. "Let me guess. Family dinner?"

It was sad everyone jumped to the correct conclusion so quickly. "Yup. Tell me you're free."

"Sort of free. We had the Thompson family meal yesterday and the Adams' one isn't until tomorrow. We're joining Vicki and Joel Coleman for a bonfire. Want to come?"

"Perfect. Need me to bring anything, or call to warn them?"

"Nah. Joel and Rafe are family, and Vicki always cooks enough for a crowd. I'm sure it'll be fine."

As much as she'd enjoyed the time with her own family, Laurel was eager to go help Rafe feel better. She stepped back into the dining room and offered a reassuring smile.

"Sorry for disappearing like that. If you don't mind, Mom, I'm going to head out early."

"Is anything wrong?" her father asked.

"Nothing much, but Rafe and I are getting together with some friends for a bonfire."

Her mom nodded, rising to her feet and offering a hug. "I'll save you a piece of pecan pie for later this week."

"Thanks. I'll promise I'll eat enough at the bonfire to make up for missing dessert." She kissed her mom's cheek then her dad's. "Happy Thanksgiving, everyone."

"Pass on our good wishes to Rafe," her father said.

Laurel left the family at the table, gathering her things from the living room before hurrying to the front door. She pulled it open and jerked to a stop.

Jeff stood in the doorway, an armload of flowers on one side, his free hand raised as if to knock.

Drat. She'd forgotten about him.

"Hi." His smile partially vanished as he took in her outfit, car keys dangling from her fingers. "Running out to get something? Need a hand?"

"Date with Rafe," she said clearly, stepping aside so he could enter the house. "Mom. Dad," she called over her shoulder, since he hadn't had a chance to ring the bell or knock. "Jeff is here."

"Wait." Jeff stopped her before she could escape. "These are for you."

He held out a bouquet of white and yellow blossoms.

Frustration roared back to high. What did he think he was *doing*? Only hours back in town, and already trying to get together with her?

Before she could blast him, her mother entered the room. "Jeff. So glad you could make it. Everything go okay with your move?"

"Yes, thanks." He adjusted position to grab another set of flowers. "Happy Thanksgiving. These are for you," he said, offering a batch to her mom.

"Why, isn't that sweet? Thank you." Corrine took the bouquet, glancing at the remaining sets in his hand and under his arm.

"Your other daughter is here, isn't she? Leslie?" Jeff asked, pulling out the third bunch. "These are for her."

Laurel sighed. He'd brought a bouquet for each of the Sitko women, which meant if she refused hers it would look bad. To everyone else he was being friendly, that's all.

She didn't believe it for one minute. He'd tied her hands. *Asshole* echoed in her head loud enough she was sure her parents would hear it as the rest of the family filed into the living room.

She escaped in the middle of the chaos after a simple thank-you to Jeff, racing out of town to where Rafe waited.

She pulled the notecard from the bouquet, tempted to trash it, unread. But maybe she'd misjudged him. Maybe he'd realized the error of his ways while he'd been gone...

And maybe pigs would fly.

See, this is me being optimistic, she pointed out to God, *but if Jeff's still being stupid, I'd appreciate a little more backup support.*

She pulled the card from the teeny envelope, glancing around to be sure she wasn't going to run anyone over if she took her eyes off the road for a second.

Giving thanks for the good memories we have, and the better ones we will make in the future. I'm glad God brought our paths together again.

And...no. So much for optimism.

It was wrong but had to be done. Laurel rolled down her window and dropped the flowers one by one, pulling them from the bouquet with sharp jerks before letting them fall to the asphalt.

Organic material wasn't littering, was it?

She crumpled the note and the empty paper wrapper that had been around the stalks into a ball and tossed them on the backseat. Then she pursed her lips and whistled a happy tune in the hopes the music would be enough to change her mood before she arrived.

Rafe was sitting on the front steps waiting for her. He rose as she put her car in park, all long and lanky and sexy-to-the-max as he strode forward.

Maybe they should forget the bonfire. There were a few other ways they could heat up the night. A few key things on her agenda...

Only, Jesse might be out of the house now, but he'd be back soon enough, and while Laurel was getting used to the idea of the other man guessing she and Rafe were fooling around behind closed doors, the first time they had sex, she did not want an eavesdropper.

Rafe caught her in his arms, squeezing tightly. He buried his face against her neck and took a deep breath. "Hmm. You smell delicious."

His lips skated over her skin making it tough to concentrate. "Eau de la turkey?"

"Sweeter."

"Can't be the pecan pie, I didn't get any—"

He swallowed her teasing words, and kissing him back was far better than baiting him.

Distraction finally set aside, she shared their plans. Rafe looked so pleased her momentary thoughts about a private party were forgotten.

He took the back roads to the trailer where Joel and Vicki lived, pulling into the yard at the same time as Troy and Nicole. Noisy greetings and hugs followed— gentle ones for Troy who was recovering from his accident.

"You okay grabbing the drinks?" Joel asked Vicki. "We're going to get the bonfire going."

"We'll be out in a few minutes," Vicki answered waggling her fingers at him as the door closed firmly behind the men. "I love that fire pit area," she said, turning back to Laurel and Nicole with a smile. "Wait until you see the changes Joel made."

Laurel didn't bother pointing out she'd never attended a bonfire there before. Not that she wasn't welcome, but...

She considered the friendship she'd made that summer with Nicole as a turning point. She'd always been on good terms with everyone in town, but that label of *preacher's daughter* made more than a few people shy away from asking her to social gatherings, especially those of a wilder variety.

Nicole's previous party-girl rep might be gone, but the fact she and Laurel were now tight had made a few people less prone to avoidance.

"Do you want me to put beer bottles in the bucket?" Nic asked, "or are we doing something different?"

"I offered to make Joel something more festive, but he said anything other than beer was wasted on him." Vicki glanced at Laurel. "And I wasn't sure if you drank, and I know Troy doesn't, so I limited our options.

Hot cider, wicked or otherwise, and beer for those who are too boring to get into seasonal joy."

"I do drink, but not much," Laurel said. "Definitely a lightweight, so if you're spiking anything, pretend I'm about the size of a pixie, and top me up accordingly."

Nicole eyed her. "Maybe we need to get you tipsy so we can see what happens."

"I've been tipsy. That's how I know I'm a lightweight, and trust me, you want to keep it that way."

"Do tell," Vicki ordered. "I take it this is part of your wild and wicked past?"

"Would that be during Bible College, or librarian training?" Nicole teased.

A laugh escaped Vicki. "Because both those strike me as wild and wicked endeavours." She offered a wink along with the words, but Laurel already knew she was joking.

"See, there's your problem. What you don't understand is exactly how much mischief the supposedly good people get into."

Vicki's smile twisted slightly. "I know exactly how much trouble people assume a person can get into when they're *not*, so it wouldn't surprise me to find out the badness is actually occurring somewhere else."

"Kind of like a karmic teeter-totter?" Nic asked.

Vicki shrugged. "The world's gotta stay in balance."

Maybe there was something to that. It stayed on Laurel's mind as she joined the girls, obediently carrying everything put into her hands to where the guys had the bonfire blazing cheerfully.

Instead of lawn chairs, long benches with thick cushions were arranged in a circle around the pit. Sitting room for more than a dozen people was available, but the guys had arranged themselves on the upwind side in a semicircle. Rafe patted the spot next to him, tugging her closer as he wrapped an arm around her and held her.

A long sigh of satisfaction escaped him.

She glanced into his contented face. "Happy?"

"This is what I needed. Thanks." He pressed a quick kiss to her lips before joining in the conversation, his grip on her sure and possessive.

Good call on her part—giving him a positive dose of family and friends to fill the gap he'd felt that day.

Small talk. Quiet conversation. Laughter and gossip flowed, but it was positive stuff for the most part. Friends who wanted to enjoy a night with people they cared about and trusted.

"When's the Six Pack gathering?" Rafe asked Joel at one point. "Jesse never mentioned."

"Today." Joel poked the fire.

Laurel frowned. "This morning? You had a brunch?"

"No, right now." His expression grew more sober, but he seemed satisfied. "Vicki and I aren't going this year."

Beside her, Rafe tightened like a spring being wound. "Did Jesse—?"

"Oh, it's not his fault," Joel insisted quickly. "This was my idea. I know Vicki and I didn't do anything wrong, but I don't want Jesse left out of family events because he's avoiding us."

Vicki laid her head on his shoulder, her expression a mix of adoration and sadness.

"I suggested to my mom that we'd come over for dinner this week so Jesse could join in the family dinner without us." He pressed a kiss to Vicki's temple. "There's enough mayhem in the place they won't really miss us, and Vicki made me a pumpkin pie, so it's all good."

"That was sweet of you," Laurel said. "He's lucky to have family who care so much about him."

Joel offered a cocky grin. "Don't go hanging too big a halo on me. My oldest brother told me he's kidnapping Jesse for the night. Seems there're boxes of junk left in his old room. He's been putting off the job for years, and Jaxi's not letting him leave the house tomorrow morning until he deals with the mess."

"Good for Blake," Rafe said. "Jesse's notorious for leaving his shit everywhere." He paused. "I've tried to get it out of him what's wrong, but it's like talking to a brick wall."

Laurel slipped her fingers into his and gave them a squeeze.

"Hey, he's better than before," Vicki pointed out to Joel. "He talks to you sometimes. And you've worked together more this past year again—those are all good things."

"Fine, I'll be happy about the cup being half full."

Laurel was impressed with Joel's efforts, but the serious moment was making Rafe's contented mood slip away—probably worrying about *his* father and family.

So she leaned forward and deliberately made a fool of herself. "That phrase always confuses me. I mean, one of the best things about a cup is that you can always refill it."

As she'd hoped, Rafe snickered. "Way to mess up a motivational saying, Sitko. Want to go and rip a few silver linings out of the clouds while you're at it?"

"Not motivational, but why do people searching for lost items always tell us they found it in 'the last

241

place they looked'? Of course it's the last place...they found the stupid thing. They don't need to look anymore."

Nicole and Troy exchanged glances. "She's as bad as you," Troy proclaimed.

"Why do you think we're best friends?" Nic demanded.

A shot of pure joy hit hard. Rafe had relaxed, pulling her into his lap as the fire blazed higher. The others were talking with each other, lost in private conversation.

"You're grinning," Rafe murmured.

"I'm happy," she admitted. "Nic's my best friend."

"I caught that," he said. "Good. *I'm* glad too. If I have to give up the title, I can't think of a more worthy person. I'll get the trophy off the shelf and give it to her later."

"Goofball," she teased.

He took a deep breath, nuzzling her neck. "Still can't figure out what you smell like, but it's making me hungry all over."

"There's more pie," she offered, a shiver racing over her skin as he nibbled on her ear.

"Hungry for something sweeter," he murmured, the words rumbling up from deep in his chest. A sexy, needy tone that made her entire body ache, and a rush of heat strike deep in her core.

An idea grew rapidly—tempting and dangerous.

Tempting, and perfect.

Except...she was missing one key ingredient.

She cornered Nicole alone for a minute, blushing furiously as she quietly stammered the question. "Do you have any condoms?"

Nicole's eyes widened. "Whatever are you planning? I know! You want to make balloon animals for a late-night activity."

"You know exactly what I'm planning, but I need to have one on me when I..." She made herself finish. "Well, I don't want us not to have one, okay? And I bought a box, but they're at my place, and I didn't think to bring any with me to my parents'."

"You're killing me here." Nicole was fighting her amusement hard. "I'm not laughing at you, really. But I'm sorry, I can't help you. We stopped using condoms when Troy moved in with me."

Well, now. "That's exciting."

She grinned. "Scary and exciting, but it doesn't help with your issue. Don't you think he's got some at his place?"

Laurel frowned. "What if he doesn't? He's not about to go buy some at the 7-Eleven with me in the car."

Nic snorted. "Yeah, that would end well." She hesitated. "Give me a second. There might be a backup stash still in the truck."

Her friend vanished, and Laurel slipped back to the fire, settling beside Rafe who curled himself around her instantly. Nicole returned a few minutes later, giving her a secret thumbs-up that set her cheeks heating.

It was nearly midnight before they gathered the bowls and glasses and called it a night. Laurel gave the girls hugs, the guys did that pound-each-other-on-the-back thing, and all three couples headed in different directions.

Nicole patted the pocket of Laurel's coat on the sly, and she slipped her hand inside to discover a half-dozen thin, square packages.

Oh boy.

The lights were out at the rental—and Jesse's truck was nowhere to be seen.

"Think Blake and Jaxi tied Jesse to something to keep him there for the night?" Rafe asked with a laugh.

"They probably just offered him food."

"Ha, yeah. You're right." Rafe slipped her out the door and headed toward her car. "That was a great evening. Thanks for making my day end better than it started."

He had no idea what she was planning. "No prob."

"You want to get together tomorrow?"

"Why don't we decide when we wake up?" Laurel suggested.

Rafe shrugged. "Sure, I guess. I'll call you then."

She took a deep breath. She ignored the open door he held for her, slipping into his arms instead. "How about you roll over and tell me? Since I plan to stay the night."

Chapter Nineteen

FOR THAT spilt second before his brain caught up with his hearing, he must've looked like the dumbest son of a gun, staring as if he'd lost his mind.

"*What?*"

She didn't answer with words. Instead she wrapped her fingers around the back of his neck, tugging him down until their lips met.

The sweet taste of her slipped into his system and raced through him as if she'd pulled a starting cord. He'd heard what she said, and he was pretty certain he knew exactly what she intended.

Sleeping?

Sex.

Even as his brain fought to decide if this was the right time, his body was shouting it was the most perfect fucking time, and he needed to stop with the brain bullshit and let the smarter parts of his anatomy take control.

Hallelujah and amen. Yes to the *hell, yes* on sex.

Rafe picked her up. She wrapped her legs around his hips, kicking the car door closed before he raced toward the house. The heat of her body against his fried his senses. He'd wanted to go slow, not just getting to this moment, but once they'd reached it. Slow? What the hell did he know about going *slow*? They were rubbing together like two crazed animals as he stumbled his way into the house, slamming the door shut behind them. He whirled and jammed her against the wall. Holding her there with his body, frantically kissing his way down her neck. Laurel dug her fingernails into his shoulders, scratching hard. The most amazing noises escaped her lips as she encouraged him on.

Thank God for casual clothes because he didn't think he would've survived dealing with tiny buttons or delicate lace. She had on pretty things, but he could barely see them, his gaze lust-filled as he somehow dragged his hands off her and lowered her to the ground. He reached to grab the bottom of her shirt, and their hands tangled.

Laurel laughed. "Take off your clothes, baby. First one naked wins."

He caught her wrists in his hands. Pausing for one last moment. "Are you sure about this?"

His voice rasped like a mad man on the edge of control. Maybe that's why she didn't give him hell, or start in on how she should know her own mind.

She licked her lips as she looked him up and down, dirty anticipation in her eyes. "Oh, I'm *sure*."

The low lusty sound rang in his ears. "Good enough for me."

Only her idea of racing to get naked? Not going to fly. He was in charge of this. It was his hands that stripped her shirt over her head. It was him who reached behind her and undid her bra, pulling the fabric down slowly so it teased her nipples.

The tiny points sprang upward, and he hummed

246

happily, staring at them, but not touching.

He undid her pants. Button, zipper. Pressing his palms to her ass before trickling his fingers down the backs of her legs as he sent the fabric to the floor. Her shoes and socks came off at the same time as her pants, and she stood there in nothing but a pale blue pair of panties, the rest of her naked. Smooth, pale and mouthwatering.

There. He'd gone slow.

Rafe took a step back, as he stripped away his shirt, ridding himself of the rest of his clothing in ten seconds flat.

They stood there, breathing heavily as they ate each other up with their eyes.

"You're so beautiful," Laurel whispered.

Rafe chuckled. "That's what I'm supposed to say."

She stepped forward, trailing her fingers over his body, and everywhere she touched sent electric zaps through his system. "You're a work of art," she insisted. "Carved out of marble, like the statue of David."

Her fingertips brushed his ass cheeks, and he shivered, willing himself to allow her this moment because once he started the next stage, no way could he stop. "Not planning on fighting any Goliaths tonight," he teased.

She'd finished her perusal, stepping back in front of him. "The only thing you need to fight are my panties."

"I can handle them."

He dropped to his knees, glancing up for a second before catching hold of the edge of the material and dragging it down an inch at a time until she was squirming on the spot and his mouth was watering to taste her.

Not in the front foyer, though.

He picked her up, the smooth heat of her in his arms enough to make him crazy. They were halfway down the hall when she interrupted him with a soft curse.

"My coat—"

Her coat? Last damn thing he was worried about. "It's not going to be cold in the bedroom, I promise."

"There are condoms in my pocket," she whispered.

A laugh escaped, but Rafe kept walking. "Are they *special* condoms, or can we use mine?"

She pressed her hands to his cheeks. "Only special in that they had your name written all over them. I wanted this to happen tonight."

He kicked his bedroom door open. "If it means that much to you, I'll run back and get them."

Laurel kissed him eagerly, pulling him over her once he'd lowered her to the bed. "Don't stop," she ordered. "That's all—don't *stop.*"

The final word turned into a moan as he settled between her legs and covered her with his body. Every inch of air between them vanished as their skin met. His cock rested against her belly, rock-solid and already wet at the tip. Their frantic rush forward slowed enough he could take a breath and actually look at her.

Her eyes shone, her lips glistening as every breath shook both their bodies.

He rocked his hips, dragging the length of his cock over her mound, and another moan drifted from these perfect lips. "*Rafe.*"

Another rock, and this time she bent her legs, knees rising on either side of his hips. Intimate, yet separate. He watched her expression, moving again, slower, ever slower. His muscles clenched tight as he held himself high enough to stop from crushing her.

Aching to make that final adjustment and press into her fully.

"You know what I'm thankful for?" he asked.

Laurel's eyes flew open from half-mast where they'd fallen. "What?" Her voice tinged with amusement.

"Did I say something funny?"

Laughter hovered between them. This was Laurel—laughter *always* hovered nearby.

"List of things to do on Thanksgiving. Eat dinner—*check*. Get naked—*check*. While naked, list the things you're thankful for—" She stroked her fingers over his shoulders. "Go ahead. I'm not doing anything else right now."

Her serious expression was ruined by the giggle-snort that followed when he nipped at her chin. "I'm thankful for the perfect pair of tits pressed against me. The ones with pale pink nipples that taste like cotton candy."

Rafe twisted far enough he could lick them one after another, swirling his tongue around the tips before closing his mouth over her and sucking until she wriggled, pressing closer even as she quivered.

"Ahhh. It's a *dirty* thankful list. That makes more sense." Laurel drove her fingers into his hair, scratching his skull lightly as he teased.

"What other kind of list is there when we're naked?" Before she could answer, he put his lips to one side of her nipple and blew a raspberry.

She curled under him instantly, laughter escaping as she struggled to push him away.

He moved farther down. "I'm thankful for this beautiful belly that I get to lick"—he licked—"and nibble"—teeth to her skin—"and, oh look. A bellybutton." He circled it with his tongue before stabbing inward.

"Practice target."

Laurel gasped. "You are *not* fucking my belly button."

"Am too. With my tongue."

"I'm dying here," she complained.

"Don't do that. I have plans," he said. "And they require you to be alive."

Rafe sighed happily, slipping lower. He used his shoulders to press her legs apart, stroking his fingers quickly through her curls and opening her to his vision. "It's as if you're made up of every shade of pink there is, and every one of them tastes different."

He glanced up to find Laurel staring at him, the hint of a smile curling her lips. She leaned on her elbows, waiting with anticipation.

He dipped his head lower, turning aside at the last moment to kiss the inside of her leg. "I'm thankful for how much fun it is to tease you."

Down again, another last-minute kiss, this time on the other leg.

Her thighs quivered as her belly shook, and she was laughing even while she complained. "Your *thankful list* needs to include 'I'm thankful Laurel didn't kill me when I teased her too much'."

"Dead men can't do this."

Rafe finally gave in and placed his mouth over her pussy. He feasted greedily, tasting and licking until he found the spot that made her squirm the most, all semblance of control gone as he stabbed his tongue deep then rasped over her clit.

"Oh my—oh, yes..." Laurel planted her heels on the mattress and pressed upward, searching for more.

He shot a hand over her belly to stop her from squirming, pinning her to the mattress as she fought his grasp. She bucked against his mouth, panting with excitement, and while it was hot as blazes, he wanted more control.

Rafe grabbed her by the hips, shuffling them both around until he could kneel on the mattress. Then he lifted her to his mouth, fingers digging into her ass cheeks, holding her precariously in midair. He fucked her with his tongue in earnest as the taste of her ricocheted through him. Her fingers were tangled in his hair, tugging as she attempted to rock against him. Her soft groans escalated as he concentrated on her clit. His cock ached, and he needed to be inside her, but not until she *came*.

He put his lips over her clit and sucked.

"*Rafe...*"

Her squirming directed into one solid thrust against his face, body arched in midair, noises of pleasure rolling from her as she shook wildly.

Finally. Sweet fucking Christ, *finally*.

Rafe had a condom out, his cock covered, and was back between her legs before she'd time to protest he'd been gone. He pressed the head of his shaft to her sex and took a deep breath.

Their eyes met as he pushed, barely entering her. Her sex tightened around the tip of his cock as aftershocks rocked her. Forward more, even more. Impossibly hot, impossibly tight. The only thing that let him inch his way in was how wet she was.

Gazes connected, he pushed forward steadily, not stopping until he was buried as deep as possible. Her eyes widened as he moved, her mouth falling open in a soundless gasp.

He wanted to make some sexy comment. Or a sweet one. Hell, he wanted to say *something*, but he was two seconds away from completely losing it.

Rafe closed his eyes and fought to keep everything from being over right then and there.

SHE WAS stretched to the maximum, tingling with energy and excitement.

Her heart was filled to overflowing at taking this step with her best friend. Her brain was so full it was a tangle, happiness whirling through her system.

And the physically full part—oh, *yeah*, they fit together perfectly, which meant things were snug enough it was possible Rafe could feel her heart pounding with his cock.

"I'm thankful you're not nearly as patient as you wish you were," she teased.

"You should be thankful I don't fuck you through this bed," Rafe said through gritted teeth. "I mean, you'd enjoy it, *trust* me, but sweet fucking *Christ* you feel so good around me."

"Rafe..." she warned, slapping his shoulder.

"Fucking... *hell?*"

Laurel laughed, wrapping her legs around him so she could dig her heels into his ass. "Fuck me all you want *without* the swearing."

He rested his elbows on either side of her head, their bodies connected, the heat of him like a brand over her.

"How do you feel?" he asked quietly. Calm in the middle of the storm.

"You're incredible."

A cocky smile shone down at her. "Yeah, I knew

that."

Laurel dragged her fingers through his hair, catching hold at the back of his neck and pulling him closer so they could kiss. Speaking against his lips before they connected fully. "I've wanted this for so long."

"Me too."

Their lips brushed. Innocent—almost. Sweet and soft as their lips met and their tongues tangled, except for the fact that their bodies were joined and he kept his hips in motion. Dragging his cock over sensitive skin.

She'd already had one orgasm. The next seemed queued up and waiting, pleasure rushing her with his every move.

"What you need me to do?" she whispered. "I want to make this good for you."

He shook, his strong arms quaking as he stroked forward. "It's good. Trust me, it's so good I want to…*swear.*"

Pleasure mixed with amusement, tingling through her system. The sensation she felt—it wasn't just lust, it was *more.* It was all the days they'd spent together to this point. Talking and sharing and occasionally crying—all of that was a part of what they were doing right now.

But it was time to drive him crazy. She tightened her core.

Rafe sucked for air.

Evil thoughts whispered temptation to her. "*Interesting.* So that does work."

"*Sitko,*" he ground out. "For fuck's sake, you're pushing me too far—"

Laurel did it again, adding pressure with her legs to make sure he went deep, and Rafe cursed under his breath. She timed her next squeeze with his thrust, and he finally broke tempo.

Rafe sped up. Stretching his arms and angling his body higher for leverage as he pumped into her. Fast, hard, nerve-tingling and wonderful.

The mattress bounced under her back. What they were doing was deliciously dirty, with barely enough time to suck in air between each of his drives. Laurel clutched the quilt, fingers tangling in the fabric as she tried to lock herself in position.

Another curse escaped him, this time louder, and he dropped to one elbow, shoving his free hand between them. Fingers slicking over her belly until he reached her clit.

Laurel gasped as he rubbed, and thrust, and leaned in to cover her lips and steal her breath away. Bodies sliding together, his fingers teasing the way she desperately needed as his cock commandeered the extra spots she hadn't been aware of needing before.

Pressure rose, faster and faster. He linked his free hand with hers, their fingers tangled as he pressed them to the bed. "*Sitko...*"

He groaned, and she lost control, another orgasm sweeping her away as she stared up at him. His eyes went glassy, or maybe it was her vision blurring as she came hard, her sex clamping down on his cock as if she was never letting go.

Rafe pulsed his hips rapidly—small strokes. His abdomen brushed hers as he rocked, and whatever else he was doing dragged out her climax until her ears were ringing and she was gasping for air.

Then he pressed his lips to her neck, growling as he came. His body tight, like an iron sculpture over her, trapping her, caging her...

Freeing her.

She slid her hands through his hair, whispering his name. Brushing her lips over his face as he twisted toward her. Chests heaving as they fought to come back down to earth.

Then mostly silence, although she swore she heard bells ringing. The rasp of his moan of approval sounded as he rolled to one side, slipping from her body but taking her with him until she was draped over him.

Laurel laid her head on his chest, listening to his heart pound. "Wow."

"Right?" He trailed his fingers over her back, stroking gently. "You good?"

"Great."

"Perfect."

"Yeah—I knew that." Laurel bit her lip to keep from laughing, but it trickled out anyway, her words tumbling together as she tried to keep her voice steady. "That was so much fun."

"It was." He tilted her head so he could kiss her lips before rolling them apart. "Give me a second, then we can cuddle."

"Hmmm, a man who likes to cuddle. This is why I'm with you." His ass flexed as he stepped toward the bathroom, and Laurel sat up to appreciate the view.

"I know. You had this theory back in tenth grade. Only losers wouldn't figure out that cuddles were three steps away from sex..."

"I never said that," Laurel protested.

The water turned off, and he stuck his head around the corner to grin at her, his gaze dropping over her body. Lingering on her breasts. "Sure you did."

"Did not." She narrowed her eyes as he marched back to the bed. "And how in the world are you still hard? You just came."

"This?" He wrapped a hand around his cock and stroked it.

She swallowed, a shiver rippling over her.

"You don't think once is enough when you're in my bed, naked, do you?" Rafe dropped to the mattress, trapping her under his body.

She took a deep breath. "*Good.* I was worried I'd worn you out."

His blue eyes flashed. "I don't have anywhere to be until nine a.m. tomorrow. You?"

"Same."

"Good." Rafe leaned in close. "I think you were perfect, but *I* need more practice. We'd better start now."

"In the interest of perfection, by all means." She laughed against his lips.

Rafe let out a huge, long-suffering sigh before he inched back to smile at her. "What?"

"I'm thankful for you," she admitted. "My slow, yet impatient, fuck-me-through-the-bed, not-at-all-able-to-hold-back boyfriend who *still* called me *Sitko* when he came."

His smile widened. "Told you. Not yet perfect. I'll work on it."

She could handle that, arching against him and letting herself fall into pleasure as he worked on being perfect.

Chapter Twenty

RAFE DRIFTED between awake and dreaming, debating which he was experiencing. If he was dreaming, it was the best one he'd had in his entire damn life. His bed was full of soft, supple woman, and he had one hand draped over her, his hand cupping a breast as he kept her tight against him.

They were both warm from sleep, both naked. If it wouldn't have scared the hell out of her, he considered letting loose a shout of joy. Not a dream.

Laurel Sitko, naked in his bed. Life didn't get much better than this.

He lay as motionless as possible, waiting for her to wake, ignoring the fact his cock had come alert well before his brain. Pressed together tight as they were, it nestled against the crack of her ass, happy in its cozy nest. Or as happy as it was going to get until she rolled over and announced she was ready for more.

He'd worked her over pretty damn hard the night before. Still, he couldn't resist tucking his nose against her hair, breathing deeply to fill his head with her. She was all spicy innocence and sated sex, and if he could bottle her scent and sell it, he wouldn't have to work another day in his life.

A purr of contentment escaped her.

"What time is it?" she asked, twisting toward him.

He brushed the hair off her face, tucking it behind her ear. "Early."

"Good." She finished rolling, draping her arms over his shoulders. "There's something I want to do."

He went willingly enough as she pressed him to his back, leaning across him to grab one of the last condoms from his stash. "You're going to be sore," he warned.

"Worth it," she rebutted. Suiting him up before she crawled on top, slowly sinking onto his length.

They both sighed happily.

Yeah, he had a hell of a lot to be thankful for. He slid his hands up her waist to cover her breasts, rubbing his palms over her nipples. "I could get used to waking up like this," he warned. "You want to leave your shitty apartment and move in here?"

"We're going slow, remember?" She gave him a sweet, seductive smile. "Don't move too fast, baby. You'll get whiplash from changing gears that quickly."

He didn't care. "There's a room down the hall. That's not moving in with me."

"Concentrate," she teased, rolling her hips and blowing his mind.

He pushed aside everything else so he could focus on her and how amazing this felt. She must have come to the same conclusion because conversation faded to noises of satisfaction as she rode him until they both collapsed, bodies pleasured to the max.

She hijacked the shower first, and Rafe decided to give her a break, because even after everything they'd done, if he joined her, she'd end up plastered against the wall with his cock deep inside.

He got breakfast started. She came into the kitchen with her hair wrapped in a towel to trade places with him, and fifteen minutes later they were grinning at each other across the table. Talking comfortably about not much in particular.

That's when he remembered something. "Isn't the library closed today?"

She nodded, refilling his cup from the coffee pot. "I figured I'd go in and do a little work while it's quiet. Wendy will be taking time off soon to have the baby, and I'd like to get ahead of the game if possible."

Kissing goodbye at the door before heading different directions seemed...weirdly right. Rafe stared after her car as she turned toward town, waving happily at him.

It had been a damn fine Thanksgiving after all.

Rafe wandered to his truck with a stupid grin on his face, refreshed and eager to get to work.

A couple days later the first snowfall arrived, thick and heavy enough it was clear winter intended to stay.

The change in seasons meant a refocus of what they worked on around the ranch as winter chores switched in. The time they spent in the barns was all about warmth, the sounds and scents of contented animals heavy in the air. In contrast, the constant chill and snap of the wind that accompanied working outdoors had a beauty of its own, yet sharper and more dangerous.

Rafe enjoyed both extremes as he prepared for the weather outdoors to get even colder.

A week later he was in town to grab something for Allison, and the temptation to track down Laurel was too much to resist. He slipped into the library, the scent of books and the rumble of voices making him smile. It really was the perfect job for her—so much like her character. A quiet setting that had the potential to burst open with life at any moment.

Ever since the night she'd stayed over, they'd continued to steal moments together, fooling around fairly innocently at times, sometimes doing more. Enough to keep him on the edge, wanting to rush forward yet satisfied with taking one step at a time.

Laurel seemed happy as well, visiting with her family and hanging out with her girlfriends. He wasn't able to join her every day, but when they did get together, it was pretty damn good.

Testing the waters. Moving forward. He still wasn't sure where they were going, but this thing between them felt right.

Although, if he was willing to admit it, the possibly of sex was a little distracting.

Like now. Rafe paused just inside the doors, glancing around until he spotted Laurel disappearing behind some library shelves. He detoured to the back of the stacks so he could sneak up on her. He peeked around the corner to spot her as she squatted to return books to a bottom shelf, the curve of her ass teasing him under the short skirt of her straight-laced librarian outfit. He moved forward, checking to see if anybody else could see them, but they were tucked out of sight, neat and tidy.

His mind went to a dirty, dirty place.

He drifted behind her as she stood. When she would've turned to face him, he sidestepped, keeping her back to him as he snuck a hand around her body and pulled her tight against him.

"Oh—" A gasp escaped her, then she laughed, twisting her head as she peered down the long opening between the bookcases. "I seem to have been accosted by a pirate. Whatever shall I do?" she murmured.

He nibbled on her neck, his cock thickening rapidly as he breathed her in. "I'm looking for a treasure to steal. Maybe you can help me find it."

"*Treasure Island* is in the fiction section, or we have 'How to bury treasure for dummies' in the non-fiction," she announced proudly.

"It's not my treasure that needs burying," he growled, rocking his hips forward.

"Oh, my." Laurel wiggled naughtily. "Well, in that case, I think I can help, but you can't tell my boyfriend."

Rafe laughed. "Brat."

Her body shook against his. "You're going to get me in trouble."

"Why do you sound so surprised?" He took hold of her earlobe between his teeth, nipping lightly before soothing the sting with a kiss.

"You know, two can play this game," she warned a second before leaning over and placing both hands on the book cart. The movement stuck her ass toward him, pressing them together harder.

Jeez. If she were naked, in that position?

"You don't fight fair," he muttered, "but then again, neither do I."

Rafe reached around and between her legs, cupping her over the fabric of her panties. The heat of her sex hit his palm, and he pressed down, rubbing the heel of his hand hard against her clit. She moaned, shivering in his grasp. Arching upward so her torso connected with his. She caught hold of his neck, arm stretching overhead so she could guide him closer until their lips connected.

Someone coughed.

Rafe nearly jumped out of his skin.

Laurel straightened and twisted all in one motion, turning her back toward the far-too-familiar newcomer before quickly tugging at her clothes and pulling herself together.

Rafe stood and let her hide her face against his chest as he stared back at Jeff. The other man's brow was furrowed, but at least he had the decency to leave without saying anything.

Decency. Like how *decent* Rafe had just behaved?

"He's gone," Rafe told her, pressing a kiss to her cheek.

"I don't know which is worse," Laurel confessed. "Getting caught fooling around by my boss, or by *him.*"

"He's an ass," Rafe reminded her, but the dose of guilt got stronger. They were at her job place, for fuck's sake. He wasn't some kind of animal that he couldn't keep it in his pants for a few hours. "But I promise to be good from now on."

Laurel glanced up from under her lashes. "Whatever for?"

She offered her hand as they walked to the front of the library, waving at Becky and Hope Coleman who stood at the checkout, arms full of library books.

His cousin-in-law had her armful resting on top of her enormous pregnant belly.

Okay, some traditions had to be maintained. Rafe clicked his tongue. "Haven't you had that kid yet?"

Hope narrowed her eyes.

He grinned evilly.

Laurel stepped past, tapping him on the back of the head. "You're going to get in real trouble one of these days. Don't you know better than to taunt pregnant ladies?"

"Especially ones who are—" Whatever Hope had intended to say vanished as her eyes widened and her mouth popped open.

Shit.

It got very quiet for a moment as they glanced down at the wetness staining her maternity pants.

Laurel recovered the quickest. "Hope? Did your water just break?"

The other woman nodded, passing her armload of books to Becky so she could cradle her belly. "Whoa. Didn't expect that."

All other plans went out the window as Rafe got pulled into the action. It was weird how much coordination and effort it took to get one pregnant woman and her husband to the hospital at the same time.

Hope refused to let them call an ambulance. "I'm not in that much of a hurry, but I suppose someone else should drive."

Becky's eyes widened in horror. "I can't do it. You've got a standard."

In the end, Laurel was drafted to help, the three girls taking off in one vehicle with Rafe racing off in his truck toward Six Pack land in search of his cousin Matt. Ranchers and phones were notoriously unreliable, between dead zones on the cell grid or having their hands full of shit—sometimes literally—that made answering impossible. Matt hadn't responded to Hope's text or phone message.

Rafe drove as fast as he damn well wanted this time. Figured, though, that the first time he had a good excuse to burn rubber, his cousin Anna was nowhere in sight.

It took a while, but he found Matt's truck outside the main Six Pack barn, rushing in at a dead sprint to discover Blake helping a horse foal. Matt knelt at his side, calming the mare.

Break the news gently, or not?

"Hope needs you," Rafe announced with as much calm control as possible. "Every—"

Matt shot to his feet, twisting so quickly he lost his balance and fell to the ground.

Blake chuckled, one arm buried nearly to the shoulder in the horse. "Smooth."

As if he'd hit a trampoline, Matt was back up, his eyes wild as he patted his pockets frantically. "My keys. Where the hell are my fucking *keys*?"

Blake made soothing noises, but he caught Rafe's gaze as he tilted his head to the side. "You two go ahead, I'll finish up here. But, Matt, maybe it would be best if Rafe gave you a ride. Would save you wasting time looking for—"

Matt was across the barn and in Rafe's face. He caught hold of the front of Rafe's shirt and half dragged him out of the barn without another word, Blake's laughter echoing off the walls behind them.

Obviously his cousin was not in his right mind, and when Matt held out his hand, Rafe tightened his fist around his keys. "No way in hell are you driving. Get in. I'll get you there as quick as possible."

They flew down the highway, Rafe listening as Matt went off on twenty different tangents about everything Hope had been doing the last few days that he'd warned her not to. "I told her this would happen, stubborn woman."

"I think the kid is ready," Rafe pointed out. "It's been nine months, at least."

Matt had both hands clenched tightly in his lap, his knuckles going white. "*I'm* not ready," he muttered.

While Rafe concentrated on getting them to the hospital in one piece, his cheeks hurt from grinning so hard. "You want to call to see where you need to go?"

Wrong suggestion. Another frantic set of patting ensued as Matt checked every one of his pockets before dragging his fingers through his hair and swearing loudly. "Where the *hell* is my phone? Dammit, why is everything happening to me?"

Obviously fatherhood destroyed brain cells, even before the kid arrived. "Relax," Rafe ordered. "I'll get you to her."

He was grateful Matt seemed willing to stay by his side as they left the parking lot and strode toward the main doors. Rafe texted Laurel for information as they hurried forward, and her instant response let him guide his cousin straight to the second floor where Laurel met them.

"You've got lots of time, Matt," she assured him, holding him back from sprinting down the hall. "Becky's with her, and the doctor, and everything's going great." She sniffed, then pushed him toward the nearby public bathroom. "First you need to wash your hands. With soap."

"Soap. Right. And water." Matt was wide-eyed and breathing fast.

"Water is a great idea," Rafe agreed, failing to keep his amusement hidden. He looked forward to teasing Matt about this for years to come.

Laurel glanced between them, her nose wrinkling. "And Rafe's going to give you his shirt."

"My shirt?" Oh hell. Rafe hadn't even noticed. Matt had come straight from the barn, and there was straw in his hair and other not-so-fresh things on his clothes. "Yes. My shirt, *and* my pants," Rafe offered.

Matt was ready to strip right there in the hallway, but between him and Laurel, they got Matt into the oversized bathroom with the door closed and Laurel safely on the outside before anyone got naked.

A whole lot of imaginative cussing escaped Matt's lips, and by the time he was clean and dressed in Rafe's clothes, his cousin had reached his utter limit and was spoiling for a fight.

"I want to see my wife *now*," he demanded as he burst into the hallway.

"Right here." Laurel stood halfway down the hall, and she pushed open the door beside her. Matt took off at a dead sprint, skidding around the corner and into the wall before he vanished.

"Good luck," Rafe called, stopping outside the door to give them some privacy. Laurel hung back as well, the two of them exchanging huge grins.

"Well, *that* was exciting." Laurel tucked her fingers around his arm, guiding him back toward the elevator.

"For a second there, I thought I was going to be delivering the kid, right there in the middle of the library," Rafe said. "Grabbing Matt was a whole lot better."

"You would have done fine if you were needed." She sniffed, glancing at him and shaking her head as she backed away as far as she could. "Now *you* stink."

"Think Hope will appreciate Matt not smelling like a cow's backside?"

"I think so." Laurel laughed with him. "I need to get back to work. Becky said she'd call when there's news."

Rafe kissed her goodbye in the parking lot, watching her go.

It seemed he'd barely made it back to Angel land when his phone vibrated and an email came through. Sent to the entire list of Colemans—Becky was using Hope's phone, and she still hadn't figured out the concept of BCC, adding one name one after another.

Hope and Matt are pleased to announce the arrival of Colton Coleman. Eight pounds, fifteen ounces, twenty-three inches. Everyone is healthy. Matt says Colt will be at Traders, dancing and breaking hearts by this coming Friday. Hope just rolled her eyes.

He's beautiful!

Love from Becky.

p.s. Someone has to tell me what "Got ya, Blake" means.

The attached picture showed a bundle of quilted fabric around a crinkled little face, the baby's eyes open, but not focused on anything. Typical kid—he looked like a tiny, wrinkled gnome.

Newborn animals were far prettier, but maybe if it were his own kid, Rafe might feel differently. Maybe if it were a baby girl with ice-blue eyes and fair hair like her mama...

The thought kicked his butt for a long time as he tried to decide what to do with it.

Back at the start of summer it had seemed so simple. Even in September, but now? Now there was a whole lot more history to their story, and *friends plus more* might not be enough.

Might not be nearly enough,

NOT A week after the excitement of Colton's arrival, Troy Thompson called Laurel out of the blue. "Need your help. Since you're Nic's best friend, and all, I figured you'd like to get in on this."

"What are we doing, surprise party? You know it's not her birthday, right?"

"We're getting married,"

"*Seriously*? She never said a word—"

"She doesn't know yet," Troy said with a laugh. "Here's the deal..."

Laurel listened eagerly as he explained his plans for a sneak elopement less than a week away. She dove into helping with preparations, thrilled for her friend.

The hardest part was making sure she avoided meeting Nicole in person because keeping Troy's secret would be impossible if Nic got suspicious and outright asked for information.

The planning also gave her something different to focus on other than spending time with Rafe, or dodging Jeff.

The man was being a royal pain in her side—more than usual—but she didn't want to get Rafe riled up by complaining.

Jeff wasn't...

Well, he wasn't *deliberately* rude. He hadn't come right out and asked her for a date, but he seemed to show up like a shadow every time she turned around. At the grocery store, asking if she had any recipes to share. At the library, looking for books for his research topics, and what was she reading these days?

At the frickin' gas pump. *Could he help check her tire pressure?*

It was annoying as hell, and yet could be

explained away as just small-town life where it was common to bump into people all the time.

Yes, having something as exciting as a wedding to help plan was a welcome distraction.

"I've found these perfect candles—like the ones you had in the hayloft," she told Rafe, when they talked on the phone at night, right before it was time to crawl into bed.

"Told you my brilliance would help you someday," he gloated. "You're not overdoing it between work and this wedding, are you, Sitko? You sound tired."

She wasn't about to explain about her sleep troubles, either. Another side effect of having Jeff around so much. Her brain insisted on going back over the troubles she'd faced in her past, like some twisted sitcom on repeat loop. "Had a rough night or two, but I'll be fine. The wedding is in a couple days, and once it's over, this weekend you and I can enjoy a lazy day together. Maybe even catch a nap."

"A real nap," he insisted. "You're pushing yourself too hard."

"Don't get bossy, Coleman," she warned.

Only the Friday morning they were due at the wedding site, Laurel got a five a.m. call from Rafe, and he was the one who sounded exhausted and lost.

"Sorry. I can't make it."

"What's wrong?"

"I'm holding down the fort. Allison's in the hospital. She lost the baby last night. Gabe's with her."

Laurel's throat tightened. She could barely speak as a rush of memories threatened to take her under.

"I'm sorry. I'm so..." She fought for control, looking down at her hands. She was gripping the edge of the table tight enough her fingers were going numb. "I'll pass on your good wishes to Troy and Nicole, and I'll stop by the hospital as soon as I can."

It was a mixed-up, crazily emotional day. Everything at the sunrise wedding was beautiful, the fresh white snow reflecting the flickering light of battery-operated candles. The entire area seemed filled with winter fireflies as Troy and Nicole stood in front of friends and families to exchange their vows.

It wasn't right to add any sorrow to a day that should be nothing but wonderful for two people who had come through their own moments of hurt. So Laurel held in her sadness, smiling at the appropriate times, hugging Nicole fiercely while pretending she wasn't grieving over Gabe and Allison's loss.

She skipped out of the celebration breakfast early, heading to the hospital to see if Allison needed anything.

Laurel found Gabe leaning against the wall outside Allison's room, face held stiff, dark shadows under his closed eyes. He'd clearly been crying, and to see the strong man reduced to such misery churned her gut all over again.

She must've made a noise because he glanced up, offering a wan smile. He opened his arms and she rushed forward to hold him tightly. "I'm sorry."

He patted her back, and she stood there until he let go.

"Thanks for coming," he said. "Not much we can do, though."

"Just knowing she's not alone will help." Laurel hesitated only for a second. "Do you need someone to talk to? I mean, maybe not me, but my dad, or anyone else? I'll help however I can."

Gabe brushed at his eyes before nodding slightly. "I'll let you know." He cleared his throat and tilted his head toward the door. "Let me check if she's up to seeing you."

Laurel waited in the hallway as helplessness overtook her. The next strongest emotion was that cold, aching rock inside of sadness and guilt that she'd worked so hard over the past couple years to move on from.

There is nothing anyone can tell me that will make me believe that this is part of your plan, she told God. *I refuse to believe it. The world is broken, and bad things happen, and it sucks, but this as your will for two people who wanted their baby so badly?* Never.

The door opened and Gabe gestured her in, guiding her to the bedside. He leaned over and gave Allison a kiss. "I'm gonna grab a coffee while Laurel's here."

"You should go home and get some sleep," Allison insisted, adjusting the blankets higher.

"Just a coffee. Doctor said he'd be back by noon. I'll stay until he sees you."

Gabe left reluctantly, Allison sighing deeply as the door closed behind him. "That man is going to break my heart all over if he's not careful."

"He loves you," Laurel said quietly.

Allison nodded rapidly, tears in her eyes. "Thanks for coming."

The despair on the other woman's face threatened to choke Laurel. "I'm so sorry. I know it doesn't help, but there's nothing I can say that will make this better."

"I know." Allison reached for the box of tissues, grabbed out three or four then passed the box to Laurel who did the same. They took a moment to blow their noses and calm down before trying to talk.

"It's funny, I didn't feel as if things were going well this time. I had a miscarriage before Micah, and the whole time I kept denying that this pregnancy felt the same as that one."

Laurel shook her head. "Sometimes there are no warning signs. Our bodies shut down, and there's nothing we can do to stop it."

And if she'd given away too much by sharing that, she didn't even care. Right now was about Allison, and if Laurel's secrets needed to be laid out in public to offer even a touch of comfort, she'd face whatever fallout came with it.

Only Allison hadn't caught Laurel's slip of the lips. She sat with her eyes closed, her face twisted with emotional pain.

"You know what's the worst? Knowing I'll have to deal with the stupid, hurtful comments. The well-meaning people who say things like 'you're young, you can have more babies'. Or the ones who tell me to be happy with the little boy we already have. Because as much as I love Micah, it doesn't mean I haven't just lost a piece of my heart."

Laurel held her hand and let Allison talk.

"She was a girl," Allison shared, her voice shaking as she continued. "And damn if it isn't the stupidest thing ever, but all I keep thinking of is now I have two babies in heaven with my mom, and I know she's taking good care of them for me."

They both lost it.

Laurel wrapped her arms around Allison, and the two of them cried. Cried for what might have been. Cried for the pain of having nothing but questions instead of answers.

Allison and Gabe had lost something precious that day, and Laurel wept for them. But she also wept for herself, because while she'd vowed that she was strong enough on her own, she really wished Rafe knew everything. That sometime before today she'd told him her secrets so he'd be able to comfort her and hold her tight.

To whisper that she hadn't done anything wrong.

"Do me a favour?" Allison spoke softly, her soul-deep tiredness coming through in the words. "If they keep me in for another day like they were talking about, can you go stay at my place and take care of Micah tonight? I know Gabe is there, but he's going to want to be with me, too, and Dana will offer to help, but I don't want Micah over at the..."

Laurel nodded. She wouldn't want her child in the same house as Ben for any length of time either.

"I'll take care of everything," she promised. "You take care of yourself and Gabe, and I'll do the rest."

Allison let out a low, slow sigh, and they fell into silence, their hands linked until Gabe came back.

It was time to let them have some privacy, so Laurel got ready to head out. She pressed a kiss to Allison's cheek. "Let me know if you need me. I'll be waiting to hear from you."

The other woman nodded, her gaze darted to where Gabe was hanging up his coat on the far wall of the room before whispering to Laurel. "I don't care if it's not official, but to me you're already a sister. Thank you."

Laurel didn't remember leaving the room or heading to the parking lot. Everything vanished into a white-cold haze until she dropped into the seat of her car and sat there, numb, staring into space. It seemed as if every hard and hurtful thing she'd dealt with over two years ago rushed back with a vengeance.

If she hadn't miscarried, *her* baby would have been over a year and a half old now. And the guilt inside, and the sadness she'd faced on her own, sprang up again.

Allison would never have to deal with being alone, and for that Laurel was grateful.

Her phone vibrated in her hands as a text came in.

Rafe: *you okay?*

Laurel thought about the different answers she could give him. She could share how broken she was seeing Gabe with his heart on his sleeve. She could say how much guilt rolled through her at the choices she'd faced before they'd been torn away from her.

How did you text a million doubts? How did you put into a few words and an emoticon that the world sucked, and yet...

Gabe had wrapped Allison in his arms. That was love. Allison trusted her with baby Micah—that was love as well. For all the hurts they faced in life, when there was love, it made a difference.

But there was no way to express that to Rafe without telling him things that weren't his burden to bear. So she wrapped the dark, painful emotions up like she'd done so many times before and pushed them into as small of a bundle as she could.

Laurel: *I'll be okay.*

It wasn't completely a lie, but it sure wasn't the entire truth. Not yet.

Chapter Twenty-One

IT TOOK a while for things to turn around. Winter days might move at a slower pace at the ranch, but Rafe worked his ass off to give Gabe as much time as possible to spend with Allison and Micah.

The secretive family meetings seemed to be put on hold, and there wasn't as much laughter in the Angel Coleman household when he stopped in, not until later in December when Allison insisted on having him and Laurel over to go cut down a tree.

Gabe fussed over Allison until she gave him hell.

"I'm bundled up more than Micah is. I'm not an invalid," she snapped before offering an apology. "If you want to make my day, how about you hook up the sleigh? We can ride out to get the tree."

So they hitched up a pair of horses, festive bells on their reins. Micah's eyes widening as Gabe lifted him up to show him the horses' holiday trim.

Rafe and Laurel sat in the front to drive, Gabe in the back holding Allison and Micah in his arms as they took the sleigh over the hills to the east of the cozy log home in the trees.

"Where are we going?" Laurel asked.

"We tagged some trees in Gabe's Folly last

summer," Allison said. "They should be the right size to pick from."

"Gabe's Folly?" Laurel questioned Rafe.

Rafe held the reins in one hand so he could loop the other around her. "The chunk of land we traded with Uncle George a few years back, while you were gone. Everybody thought it was as bad an exchange as buying Alaska, but it turned out pretty good. We got to go organic there the following spring instead of having to wait like on the rest of our land."

Little bits of history shared. Little memories built. They loaded up a couple of Christmas trees and brought them back to decorate, sharing time together as the season turned.

For once Gabe put down his foot and announced there would be no Angel Coleman gathering on Christmas Day. "Not this year. We'll do something simple with Ma, and we're going to get together with Allison's brother and sister at the restaurant so there's no cooking or cleaning for any of them."

Rafe considered doing something more official on Christmas Day to make his mom happy, but when he thought about deliberately spending time with his father, the idea choked him.

Ben rarely showed up to work these days, and never over at Gabe's anymore. It just meant that Rafe's workload was heavier, and every time he did run into his father on the ranch he got an earful about how stupid every decision Gabe made was, and how Ben would have done things differently.

Rafe got good at turning around as fast as possible to escape anytime he spotted his father.

He was concerned about Laurel. Her usual cheerfulness seemed dimmer these days, as if the grey days of winter were taking a toll. Then she'd perk up and he'd have his sunshine back—joining him for television in the evenings, or dancing at Traders on Friday nights.

It was Laurel who came up with the idea that saved the holiday. "There's a Christmas dinner at the church on Christmas eve," she suggested, holding up a hand before he could protest. "Your mom will feel comfortable there, and if you show up, that can be your Angel Coleman Christmas time with her."

The church was the one place Ben would never come.

Rafe leaned in and kissed her. "Brilliant woman."

He wished he'd have thought of it years sooner. The food was delicious and plentiful, and his mom glowed with happiness as people around her offered good wishes and exchanged little presents.

They were done the main meal and heading toward dessert when his mother leaned in close. "Thanks for coming," she said. "I know this isn't your thing."

He kissed her cheek. "I'd do anything for my best girl."

His mom offered a soft laugh. "I don't think I have that title anymore."

Rafe looked around as if in shock. "What, you think you see someone who can replace you? Never."

His mom's laughter faded rapidly. She poked him in the side before gesturing across the table to the far side of the room, her hand discreetly hidden under the table. He followed the line of her finger to discover Laurel, her hand full of plates, trapped outside the kitchen door by Jeff.

A flash of anger filtered through his Christmas cheer. "Excuse me."

"Rafe," his mom warned. "Be nice."

He rose to his feet and smiled down on her. "I'll be nice. I'll be so nice he won't know what hit him."

"That's what I'm afraid of," his mother offered before shooing him away and turning back to her neighbour.

Rafe figured that was her signal to tell him she wasn't watching. Which meant he could do anything he wanted.

Jeff had to be the most oblivious son of a gun out there. The man refused to give up. Rafe marched up to him and slapped a hand on his shoulder, squeezing hard. He might've heard bones creak.

"Jeff, my man. Merry Christmas." Another squeeze.

The young pastor gingerly twisted to remove himself from Rafe's grasp. "Rafe. Good to see you."

Yeah, bullshit on that.

Jeff held his hand forward, and this time Rafe gave into temptation, shaking harder than necessary.

Only the bastard fought back, dirty. Jeff casually wiggled his fingers at his side, but made a dig the only way he could. "Laurel and I were discussing the plans we have this year for different ministry opportunities. We're going to do one of the studies we worked on together."

"That's nice," Rafe said as casually as possible. "Plans you have...together?"

"I'm hoping she'll come on board as one of the teachers." Jeff offered his most professional smile, and Rafe wondered if the man practiced in front of a mirror. "We've worked well together in the past."

"I need to get these to the kitchen," Laurel excused herself, giving Rafe a warning glance before she pushed the door open with her back and escaped.

He didn't need the warning—

Well, maybe he did, because it was tempting to lift a hand to Jeff's chest and slam him into the wall. Not the wisest move, and definitely not the proper place. Right smack dab in front of a gathering of over fifty, some of whom were watching with great curiosity.

Figures. Their little "situation" couldn't have gone unnoticed with the small-town gossips. He refused to call it a love triangle like he'd overheard at one point, though. There was nothing love-like about either Laurel or his relationship with the man.

Now if they could convince Jeff of that. He was like a dog with a freaking bone...

"I think I'll slip into the kitchen and help." Jeff tipped his head, his eyes flashing slightly. "You go ahead and rejoin the visitors. I'll take care of Laurel."

Rafe caught himself a second before he nabbed the other man around the throat. Instead he leaned in and placed a hand on Jeff's shoulder. Gentle, though. No smashing him into anything.

"You want to go somewhere to have a private discussion?" Rafe asked, casual violence in his voice. "Or do you have plans for the rest of the holidays that require your teeth?"

The other man narrowed his gaze. "Threats?"

"Promises." Rafe stepped back, tipping an imaginary hat before stepping around him and entering the kitchen. He joined Laurel at the sink, hip checking her lightly to get her to move over so he could take over the washing.

She stared at him with suspicion. "What're you doing?"

"Washing dishes," he said innocently.

"Good grief." She tucked herself against his side and lowered her voice. "You're supposed to be having dinner with your mom."

"I was, and as soon as you're ready, we can both go have dessert with her."

"You're a pain in the butt," she noted. "This is about Jeff, isn't it?"

"Who?"

"Don't tempt me, Coleman. I've got a sink full of soapy water only two inches away from you."

He chuckled. "Just get your chores done so we can go spend time with my mom."

It was only a few minutes later when Laurel took him by the hand to guide him out of the kitchen, choosing a side door that brought them into the hallway outside the banquet room. Private. Quiet.

Laurel stuck a finger in his face. "I don't need you to defend me," she scolded him, and then before he could protest, she caught him by the shirtfront and tugged him toward her, "but I appreciate that you care."

She kissed him gently. Lips brushing his before she pulled away and offered him a brilliant smile. "Let's go eat some pumpkin pie with your mom."

Rafe didn't even bother gloating when they walked past Jeff, hand in hand en route to the dessert table.

Well, maybe he gloated a little.

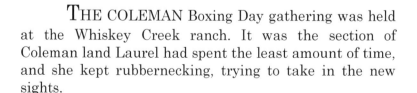

THE COLEMAN Boxing Day gathering was held at the Whiskey Creek ranch. It was the section of Coleman land Laurel had spent the least amount of time, and she kept rubbernecking, trying to take in the new sights.

It was difficult with the sheer number of people in the area. Ashley hadn't been joking when she mentioned the celebration would be chaos. There were only a couple dozen direct relatives, but everyone seemed to have brought along a friend or two, and their children, and extra parents, until the whole place was noise and laughter.

The oldest of the Whiskey Creek girls approached her, a pitcher in one hand and cups in the other. "Hey, Laurel. Want your cider with a kick?"

"Think I'll stick to the plain stuff."

Karen gestured toward the sidewall. "Over there. We've got enough visitors around today we decided to keep tabs on the alcohol. Don't need the Six Pack nephews sneaking their friends into the spiked drinks."

"Spoilsport," Laurel teased.

She got a burst of laughter from the other woman in return. "Rafe said the same thing a few minutes ago." Karen paused. "By the way, he's headed outside with some of the kids. I think they mentioned the tobogganing hill."

Laurel had insisted on coming on her own—her family didn't do a big official Sitko gathering on Boxing Day, but she'd gone over to her mom and dad's that morning and made them pancakes. Just a quiet meal with the three of them, easy and comfortable.

At least until the topic veered into dangerous territory.

"It was good to see Rafe join us at the church for dinner Christmas Eve," her mom mentioned innocently between sips of her coffee.

"He and his mom, yes."

"Dana Coleman's a good woman," her dad said. "One of the pillars of the community."

"Is Rafe planning on coming to church this year?" Corinne adjusted the plate in front of her. "It would be nice to get to know him better."

"He doesn't have to come to church for that to happen," Laurel pointed out.

"No, you're right." Her mom and dad exchanged glances, her father shaking his head slightly. Warning her mom off?

Maybe, and perhaps she should be grateful for that, but it bugged her that the only thing they seemed to hold against Rafe was the fact he didn't belong to the church.

But she definitely didn't want to get into that conversation today, so she ignored the issue like she'd done before, and concentrated on safe, generic topics, like the plans her parents were making for a short winter getaway.

She left them with hugs, that slightly uneasy sensation lingering as she drove away. They were her parents, and she loved them, but she wasn't a little girl anymore. The world kept changing, and she still wasn't sure how to fit the pieces together.

And now as she headed outside wrapped up against the cold, that strange sensation continued. She knew these people to some degree. All the generations of the Coleman clan, from Mike and Marion, to their son Blake and his wife Jaxi, and the growing family they were raising. And the Moonshine clan, and the rest of them, tangled up with familiar members of the community who'd been invited to the gathering.

Laurel knew them, and at the same time...she didn't. They had faces, and they had names, but the real people inside?

She wasn't the same person she'd been when she

left Rocky, and ever since she'd returned there'd been a wall around part of her. Secrets kept because they needed to be—

Were all of *them* the same? Hiding parts of themselves?

Her ponderings were interrupted as a strong pair of arms wrapped around her from behind and lifted her off her feet.

"Rafe?"

No answer.

She twisted in an attempt to see which Coleman male had picked her up, because it had to be a guy since she was now floating effortlessly over a foot off the ground.

A masculine chuckle sounded in her ear.

She realized her mistake the instant she spotted Rafe running toward them, his gaze narrowing as he approached.

"Jesse, he's going to murder you," she warned.

"All's fair during a family snowball fight," Jesse insisted, tugging her to the right and backing up rapidly.

Laurel laughed. "You're using me as a shield?"

"Yup. Great idea, right?" Jesse interrupted himself to shout at his cousin. "Put the snowball down, and nobody gets hurt."

Rafe kept coming, arm raised high.

Laurel spotted it now, the solid circle of white held in his grasp. "Don't shoot," she begged even as laughter bubbled free.

"Don't worry, Sitko. I've got good aim."

"Not that good," she protested, and he winked.

"I won't go willingly," Jesse warned.

Laurel twisted a leg behind her, wrapping a foot around Jesse's knee as she threw her weight backward, tipping them both to the ground.

She landed on top of him. Jesse let out a grunt, but he didn't let go.

A second later Rafe had her free, nudging her behind him so he could stare down at his target.

Jesse held up his hands in mock horror. "You wouldn't hit a defenseless man, would you?"

Rafe sighed before lowering the snowball and shaking his head, "Nah, you're right. I wouldn't." He glanced at Laurel and tossed the snowball to her. "But I bet she would."

"She totally would," Laurel agreed, stepping toward Jesse with an evil grin.

The free-for-all ended a long while later as a whole lot of the Colemans joined the scramble. Rafe's toque sat askew, and Laurel had snow melting down her back, but she was warm inside as Rafe took her by the hand and guided her toward the nearest barn.

"That was fun." She stepped into the warmth with a sigh of contentment. "But the ice running down my back is killing me."

"I can do something about that," Rafe said, his voice going deeper. "Come on."

He led her past stalls filled with horses, the fresh scent of clean hay and contented animals adding to the warmth. "What beautiful animals," she whispered.

"Karen and my Uncle George are geniuses when it comes to breeding," he offered, marching them past too quickly to really admire the beasts.

"In a hurry, Coleman? You have a schedule to meet?" she teased.

"More like an agenda." He brought her to the nearest ladder that led to the loft.

She twisted to face him, making sure she wore her

most serious librarian expression. "Mr. Coleman, are you taking me somewhere for nefarious purposes?"

He laid a hand on his chest and attempted to look shocked. "I can't believe you asked that question."

Laurel snickered. "I notice you didn't say no."

Rafe grinned and turned her to face the ladder then patted her on the butt. "Right. I just couldn't believe you had to ask. You *know* what terrible mischief we get up to in hay lofts."

This one wasn't guaranteed as private as the one on Angel land, but there was a shiver of excitement running up her spine—or maybe that was the melting snow. Whatever it was, she made the decision to go along, climbing the ladder with him crowded close behind her. Letting him guide her when they reached the top. He brought her through the sweet-scented air toward a corner filled with stacked bales.

At the very edge a narrow path had been left open, and he guided her down it toward the far wall.

"Are we going to disappear like magic?"

"I had something to show you," he insisted innocently.

She thought he was kidding, but he led her to a small platform on the west wall, unlatched the wooden partition in front of them and swung it open.

The height gave them a view of the entire Whiskey Creek house and yard, the enchanting building with its wraparound porch perched at the top of the hill, the backyard sloping to the south until it leveled off where it met a wide bend of the river. Grazing land beyond the house and the garden on the east was snow covered, but it was probably the prettiest of all the Coleman houses, except maybe for Gabe and Allison's.

Laurel rested her arms on the windowsill and

leaned forward. "Wow, I didn't know they had such a great view."

"Tamara and Lisa used to bring me up here when I was little. We were figuring out the best places to build jumps to go off with our sleds, but I've always remembered being jealous they had a hill and we didn't."

"Everyone else in your family built on level ground, didn't they?"

"Whiskey Creek's got more of the rolling hills right in their backyard. The rest of us have them scattered over different portions of the land."

"Well, it's pretty." Laurel twisted to face him. "Did you really bring me up here to show me the view?"

Rafe blinked. "What else would we do in a hay loft?"

She fought to keep from smirking. "I have no idea."

Leaning past him to grab hold of the window let her deliberately brush their bodies together as she closed and secured the latch. He chuckled, but didn't step out of her way.

Didn't make a move to ravish her, either, more's the pity.

She slipped her fingers into his. "We'd better rejoin the party. It looked as if there were some free sleds."

Playing for the rest of the afternoon allowed some of her earlier concerns to fade. They went up and down the hill a dozen times, the Six Pack nieces stealing rides with her. Rafe joined some of the teenage boys on the oversized inner tube, which tended to bounce everyone into the air and leave them in piles on the snow.

Inside the house there was food and laughter, and with Rafe's hand around her waist, keeping her close,

Laurel realized maybe it didn't matter that she didn't know these people inside and out.

So what if everyone had some secrets? The people she saw on the outside were still worth spending time with.

She was valuable as well—it was a truth she reminded herself of daily as she fought to keep from falling into sadness.

A wonderful, blessed sense of peace flowed through her as Laurel took Rafe home, slipping into her tiny apartment and guiding him directly to the bedroom.

He curled himself around her, stroking his fingers through her hair. He tightened his grip and tilted her head back. "Did you have a good time?"

She nodded as she tugged his shirt free from his jeans so she could slip her hands underneath and press her palms to his warm skin. "I like your family."

"They like you," he returned, dragging in air as she brushed a fingertip over his nipple. "I want to stay the night," he murmured.

"I want that too." She glanced over her shoulder at her bed. "You have no idea how much I'm regretting that twin mattress."

Rafe swept her up in a tight embrace before rolling onto the bed. "I don't know. I kind of like the fact there's not enough room for you to get away."

She pulled at his shirt until he stripped it off, pressing her lips to his chest. "Hmm. Warm. And tasty."

He chuckled as she licked him. "You're tickling."

"Am I? I didn't mean to. I meant to turn you on."

"Oh, you got that part right, as well." Rafe wiggled her shirt up and off, swearing softly. "Long underwear? Seriously?"

"We were going tobogganing," she explained. "I

wasn't about to wear anything dainty. I don't like the cold." She gasped as he slid his hands beneath her layers. "*Rafe*, your hands are like ice."

When she attempted to squirm away, he flipped her over and pinned her under him, his palms warming against her skin. "You make a great hot-water bottle."

Laurel opened her mouth to teasingly give him hell—and a long, low moan of lust escaped instead. He'd placed his mouth on the bare skin he'd exposed at her lower back, and as he stripped away her pants, he nibbled and kissed and licked his way down her body.

Brief caresses sent her senses reeling. Shivers rolled over her skin in anticipation of his tongue's attention. Sensitive spots, like the edge where her thigh and butt met, heightened the pleasure. He laved his tongue along the crease there, and she wanted to beg for more.

Even as she wanted him completely and fully at her mercy—like in any great friendship.

She twisted her head to the side, cheek resting on the mattress so she could gaze down the bed at him. "Hey, baby?"

He nipped her butt. "Still insist on using that nickname, do you?"

"Until you figure out something better than *Sitko*, um, yeah."

Rafe pressed a kiss to her bottom before kneeling to strip off his shirt and undershirt. "Sweet Cakes? Princess? Like one of those?"

She fake-gagged then went back to the topic at hand. "Hey, you ready for your last Christmas present now?"

His hands were back on her body as he stroked and caressed and drove her mad. One move lifted her hips in the air, then he was behind her, hand between her legs, stroking his strong fingers between her folds and over her clit. "It's a lovely present. Just what I've always wanted."

Laurel shivered as he pressed a thick finger in deep. Slowly, carefully...

"It's all yours. Oh, and by the way, we don't need wrapping paper anymore." His fingers hesitated, and she kicked herself for her bad timing. "Don't stop," she complained.

The bed bounced slightly as he landed beside her, his eyes fixed on hers with a question.

"Too many sugar cookies today to concentrate? Or was I pushing it with the Christmas analogies?" Laurel asked.

"Just want to be crystal clear," he said, his voice gone a tone deeper. "No condoms?"

"I went on the pill. And it's been long enough, we're good to go."

His gaze trickled over her lazily, heated intent rising. "Oh, well now. Merry Christmas to me."

Rafe leaned closer and kissed her, his tongue sweeping in and stroking hers before he broke away to kiss a path down her back again. This time he didn't stop until he'd reached his target. His strong hands gripped her hips as he stroked his tongue over her sex. Dipping deeper, sliding higher.

She gasped when he licked between her cheeks, face hot enough she'd forgotten she'd ever been cold. "Fuck."

Rafe chuckled. "No swearing in bed, Sugar Plum. You know it distracts me."

"Fuck, *please?*" she tried, a gasp of amusement slipping out.

"Hmmm, so polite. Hard to resist a sweet request like that, Snuggle-bug."

Only he did. For the next umpteen minutes that blurred together into one ball of pleasure, one stroke of need, one touch of rising urgency until his rapid licking and caressing with his fingers sent her hurtling into an orgasm.

"*Rafe...*"

He rose behind her, hauling her hips up a second before he pushed her torso down. She was wide open to him and his cock was between her folds and—

She expected a long, hard thrust. One stroke that would join them rapidly and send her flying.

Rafe slid into her. Inch by inch, his cock thick and hot, with his body rising over hers. She was filled to the brim, covered by him, and she should have been one small gasp away from being overwhelmed.

Instead she found herself grounded. Anchored. He kissed the back of her neck so sweetly tears threatened to gather.

Until he whispered lovingly— "You good, my Darlin' Lambchop?"

Laurel lost it, laughing out loud. "Way to break a moment."

"Were we having a moment?" He kissed her, then hummed softly. "I'm planning on having several moments. If *someone* could concentrate."

"How am I supposed to concentrate with you calling me stupid pet names? Oh, *yes*—do that again," she begged.

He'd slipped out, angling higher as he stroked in. Teasing her, and priming her pleasure higher with each motion.

"Boo-bear? Pum-kin? Hot *damn* this feels good."

"So good," Laurel agreed, fists clenching the quilt as she rocked back to meet his every drive.

"Does Cutie-Pie like my cock?" He snorted at the same time she did. "Nope, even I can't say that one with a straight face."

"Coleman?" Laurel muttered.

"Yeah?"

"Shut up and fuck me already," she ordered.

His grip on her hips tightened. His answer didn't come with words, it came with actions. Long hard drives, slow teasing stokes. Every time she was on the verge of coming he'd shake it up until she was making so much noise her throat was going to be sore the next day.

Rafe was over her, riding her hard when she broke, and a second later he joined her, hips tight to her ass as he wrapped himself around her and pressed her to the mattress. Heavy, but perfect.

Their breathing was fast and hard, and her entire body tingled. Rafe was kissing the back of her neck, stroking his fingers down her arms as if he couldn't get enough of touching her.

Her face was sore from smiling so much.

This was where her joy was—with him. They were laughter, and they were light, and they were...

More.

Together they added up to so much more, and she was beginning to think that something might equal forever.

Chapter Twenty-Two

JANUARY CAME and went. Laurel found herself staring at the bulletin board in front of her without really seeing it.

On a scale of one to ten, she'd grade the time she got to spend with Rafe as a solid nine. Every day she looked forward to going to her job, and her friendship with Nicole was amazing.

Church, on the other hand...

After Jeff had started holding weekly meetings with the worship team, she'd asked to be taken off the music schedule. Bumping into him that often just brought up painful memories—and it was past time to move on.

Actually quitting the church was more difficult than she'd imagined, even if it would have meant not seeing Jeff's face on a weekly basis.

Why was she doing this? Why was she being so wishy-washy about church? They were well into a brand-new year, and still she hadn't found the solution to her dilemma.

Sticking to her *no* and not teaching for her sister was the most Laurel could do. Helping put up a few decorations had seemed like a safe alternative to keeping the peace, but being back at the church midweek, stapling snowflakes around the edges of the board for her sister seemed to trigger all the things Laurel hadn't wanted to think about too hard.

A few doors down voices were raised in song. Words of praise from a group of seniors who met every Wednesday night to pray for Rocky Mountain House and everyone who lived there.

Why was she there?

Where did she fit in?

God? This place doesn't feel like home anymore. That's not really a complaint, by the way, more like a comment, but... Okay, it's a complaint. I'm mad I don't feel the way I used to about church. I don't think that's fair, do you?

"Laurel?"

Shit.

Very funny, she muttered to God. *You had him hidden around a corner to send out as an attack dog if I got cheeky, right?*

"I'm glad to see you," Jeff offered, leaning on the wall next to the project she was dillydallying over. "I'm finished with the youth group. You want to get a drink and chat for a while?"

"Not really." Laurel grabbed a random piece of paper off her pile and held it against the board, trying to look as if what she was doing was absolutely vital.

"The café downtown is open for another half hour," he teased, poking the snowflake out of her grasp with a finger. "Pie and hot chocolate."

Really?

She turned slowly to allow herself to control a flash of temper—the temper she seemed to only develop around *him*. Although, maybe he wasn't being stupid and annoying—no use jumping to conclusions. "Is there a group going?"

He smiled enticingly. "Just us."

Or...maybe he *was* still being stupid and annoying. "I don't want to go anywhere with you alone. I have a boyfriend—why is that so hard to understand?"

"Laurel." He shook his head. "When are you going to stop pretending?"

She looked him over carefully for more clues because he wasn't making any sense. "You think I'm *pretending* to go out with Rafe?"

"No, I think you're dating him, but he's obviously just a temporary rebellion."

Something clattered to the floor. She glanced down, shocked to discover the stapler lying on its side, sprung open, on top of the snowflake that had fluttered to the ground earlier.

Rebellion. Rafe was her *rebellion*? She could hardy wait to tell him.

But in the meantime, she had to deal with Jeff. Politely.

Notice I'm still trying the polite thing. Maybe you could suggest he do the same.

"There is nothing temporary about my relationship with Rafe. *He's* never told me we needed to stop seeing each other. *He's* never left without a word for a month."

Maybe not as polite as she'd hoped. Oh well.

Jeff stared at her, a frown creasing his forehead. "When are you going to forgive me for that? I've explained it was a misunderstanding."

"Misunderstanding or not, you called it off between us, left town, and when you returned, you got together with someone else who you thought would help your career. It wasn't about caring for me, it wasn't about doing what you were 'called' to do."

Maybe she'd feel pity for him if she weren't so tangled up with other emotions.

"I've confessed I was wrong. And I was even more clear about why things didn't work out between me and Jessica." He folded his arms, looking at her sternly. "You seem to think you're the only one who's suffered in this situation. There was a lot of emotional baggage that I've had to deal with—"

She snorted.

Nope. He lost her the instant he tried the sympathy route. She had zero for him.

"I can see how that must have been so terrible to think you'd be part of a family who could help launch you to the top." *Huh.* Laurel wondered if Jessica had called off the engagement.

"This isn't you," Jeff said. "So bitter, and so cold. You need to forgive and forget, and move on."

No, she needed to keep control of her temper before she hit him with something blunt. "I'm not God. You can confess your sins to him, and I'm sure he'll accept. But me? I'm not that awesome. I can forgive you, to a certain extent, but I can't forget."

"You choose not to forget."

"Damn tooting, I don't," she snapped.

"So you're going to ignore what's best for you out of spite? That makes no sense, Laurel. Please don't do that to yourself."

She wanted to laugh in his face. "And I suppose you think you're what's best for me?"

"Yes," he retorted. "And if you would stop being childish and start using your brain, you'd see that. Being unequally yoked with that redneck rancher is the last thing you need."

She went even colder inside.

Jeff must've taken her silence as agreement, because he carried on. "You know, we had good times together. We're compatible, and we share common passions and interests. We'll make a great ministry team, and if none of that seems important right now, consider that your parents think we're a good match."

"They like liver and onions too, but you don't see me jumping up and down to join them when they order it."

He seemed shocked at her out-of-the-blue comment, but it was make a bad joke or scream at him for continuing to put her through this. She wanted it over. Needed him to get the hell out of her life.

Jeff caught her fingers in his. "Your parents want you to be happy, and have a place where you can grow strong. A place for you to be protected from the storms of life, and I want so much to be on your side for all of that. For the good, and the bad, and—"

Laurel backed up so quickly she nearly tripped over her own feet. "What do you know about being around to support people through the good times and the bad? I've seen no examples of you being supportive. In fact, what I saw was you focusing on your own needs to the exclusion of everybody else. Protective? More like tossing somebody into a storm and leaving them without a life preserver."

Damn. She'd said more than she wanted to, but he was such a self-centered *bastard*.

"I have no idea what you're talking about," Jeff insisted. "But I want to know. I *want* to be there for you."

She shook her head. "You had your chance. I'm not such a glutton for punishment that I want to ever risk trusting you again. Oh, and besides, I don't need to. I *have* someone else in my life who has never let me down. I'm not about to throw away what I have with Rafe just because you've suddenly decide to develop a conscience."

"I didn't suddenly—"

"Jeff, stop." Laurel was suddenly exhausted. "I don't want to fight, and more talking isn't going to change my mind. I forgive you, for everything you think you did, and all the things you don't even know you did and I won't tell you because it doesn't make any difference now. The only thing that will make a difference is to move forward, and that means *you* need to move on without me."

He looked kind of stunned. Speechless, for once in his life.

Thank you for small mercies, God.

She dove back into it, praying he would get it this time. "I might see you because you work with my father, but if you have any feelings for me, stop going out of your way to put us into awkward situations. You will not arrange setups where we'll be alone, and you will *stop* trying to run my life."

Jeff stared at her for a long time, his lips pressed together into a thin line.

Then, *hallelujah*, he nodded briskly.

Laurel grabbed her sweater from the nearby chair and left without looking back.

She *had* grown strong. That was the point. Her world had turned dark and colourless for a while, but she'd survived and come out on the other side.

This was the moment she wanted to be with Rafe and let him know everything. It was time for *all* her secrets to come out—because she'd said a mouthful to Jeff.

Rafe had never let her down. She could trust him, and she needed to tell him that.

Leaving the church and heading to the rental, she felt an amazing cloud of calm surround her, and for the first time in a long time she was sure she was doing the right thing.

She felt...peace. And hope. And joy.

Okay, it's up to you to deal with Jeff from here on, because I'm done, she informed God.

The lights were out at the rental, both Rafe's and Jesse's trucks missing from the yard. She was so full of plans she didn't even care if Jesse knew she was sleeping over. It was past time pretending—as far as she was concerned, she and Rafe belonged together.

She let herself in and made her way to his room to grab a shower. When he wasn't home by the time she'd dried her hair, she borrowed one of his T-shirts and crawled into his bed with her book to wait.

GABE HAD given up, but Rafe insisted they could get the job done without having to call in any of the cousins.

His brother shrugged. "Maybe, but not tonight. We're done."

"It shouldn't take that long," Rafe insisted.

"You want to be stubborn—fine, go ahead. I'm calling it a night and going home to my family." Gabe pulled his winter gear back on for the trek to the house.

"If you were smart, though, you'd go find Laurel and spend some time with her."

"In a bit," Rafe said. "No use leaving when I'm so close to having it finished."

Only, fifteen minutes later he'd broken a sprocket, which in turn had made fixing the connection between the trailer and the truck impossible with the equipment he had on hand. He went looking through the older pieces of equipment in the yard, the icy cold of the February evening stealing into his entire system. No luck—nothing matched with what he needed.

His hands were cold as ice, even through his gloves, and he wanted nothing more than to go home and fall exhausted into bed. Instead he dragged himself over to the main barn at the Angel homestead because now if he didn't fix it, Gabe would get up in the morning to find a small job had become way bigger.

The door Rafe should have used to access the barn was covered past the doorknob with hard-packed snow. He cursed as he stomped around to the far side of the building through thigh-deep drifts, wondering what the hell his father was thinking to push the snow from the road up against the barn. Bloody fool.

Only he'd been staying away from Ben, and if his father wanted to do stupid shit, so be it.

Except when he finally got into the barn, he discovered the trailer he needed parts from was nowhere to be found.

"Pain in the fucking ass," Rafe muttered, hitting the light switch. Maybe if he searched hard enough there'd be—

The lights stayed off.

"What the hell?" He flipped the switches, as if that would help. Nope. Whatever weird shit his father was doing, it included shutting off the power to the place. Or at least to part of it. A small light shone in the distance, and Rafe made his way through the darkness, frustration rolling forward with him like a wave.

He rounded the corner to discover his father glaring at a blank wall, his hands full of torn old rags, a single bare light bulb hanging on a long wire from the ceiling.

Rafe was tired, and he was pissed, neither of which made for good decision-making. He stepped into his father's line of vision and spoke sharply. "Are you trying to burn the place down?"

Ben jumped back, his slack expression twisting into a frown. "I don't need your lip."

"I didn't come here to give you any. Just need to know where the spare trailer is."

"Hell if I know," Ben snapped. "Go ask your brother. He's the fucking king of the heap around here, not me."

Let it pass, he told himself before trying again. "Not one of the horse trailers, but the one for the flatbed."

"I told you I don't bloody well know. Didn't think you were stupid as well as a slacker."

Okay. That was a little harder to ignore, but Rafe tried. He walked past his father, snatched up a flashlight from the workbench and clicked it—

Nothing. No batteries, or dead.

He whirled on his father. "Is there anything you haven't torn apart or broken on the entire ranch? I'd like to finish my fucking job tonight."

Ben snorted. "Right, as if you're worried about getting things done. Ungrateful bastard." He stuck a finger in Rafe's face. "One of the stupidest things your brother has ever done is let you have a free ride."

For fuck's sake. "What the hell does that mean?"

Ben coughed for a moment, tapping his chest before turning a derisive look Rafe's direction. "You don't know what hard work is. Sure, you show up and do the chores, but you don't have a lick of sense when it comes to making long-term decisions. That's why you're doing stupid things, like hanging out with Sitko's daughter. Can't you see the woman's only using you to upset her family?"

If that was the best insult the bastard could come up with—? Rafe wasn't laughing, but it wasn't enough to make him blow his top. "Whatever."

His father couldn't leave it alone. If he had, Rafe might have walked away, but Ben kept talking, and his ranting got worse by the minute. "Damn stupid choice in women, both you and your brother. Pastor's girl is using you like a patsy, and that other one with Gabe—thinks she can tell the men around her how to do their jobs? She can't even fucking do her job as a woman."

Blood roared in Rafe's ears. "Her *job?*"

"Don't know why we're trying to save the ranch. Ain't going to be any of our blood to pass the place on to, the way that woman can't keep a child going—doubt if that one they got already is even theirs in the first place."

Rafe could not believe his ears. "Micah is Gabe and Allison's son. What the hell are you smoking? Or are you fucking drunk to come up with this bullshit?"

"Don't you talk to me like that," his dad roared, shaking a fist at him. "Wet behind the ears. You're lazy,

you're rude, and you need to shape up, right now, because I don't want it ever said that one of my sons—"
Rafe broke. "I wish to hell I wasn't your son."
Ben stuttered to a shocked silence.
Fuck it all. Rafe's temper flashed to white hot. The fuse had been lit, and there was no stopping this time. "I wish to hell you were even a fraction of the man that Pastor Dave is. I don't know how Gabe ended up so damn perfect when you were constantly in his face telling him he wasn't good enough."

He expected his father to interrupt at any moment, but the man just stared at him, face drawn with anger. Clutching the rags in his hands so tightly his knuckles had gone white.

"It's nothing you've done that's turned this family around. Folks call this the Angel land. Well maybe there was some divine intervention going on that helped Gabe pull us out of the hell you had us headed toward."

Ben opened his mouth, but Rafe didn't let him get a word in. He was on a roll, and everything he'd been holding back for the past days, and months—hell, for *years*—it spilled out of him.

"And if Gabe's an angel, I have no trouble with you judging me and calling me a devil, because I sure the hell ain't wasting my breath praying for you. You can act *holier than thou* all you want, but it doesn't change the truth. I know who's responsible for saving our land, and that's my brother. And Allison, and the rest of the family. It's Mom, who's put up with more heartache and *bullshit* than any woman ever should have to."

Rafe stepped closer and stared his father in the eye. "You don't like how I'm doing things? I don't give a *damn*. You're not the one I'm trying to impress anymore. I gave that up when I was twelve years old, the first time you got so stinking drunk you threw your empty beer bottle my direction."

Ben's lips were pressed together into a thin white line as his gaze flicked to the scar beside Rafe's eye. The one he'd gotten from a flying shard of glass. The scar on his body was small—the hurt inside was far *far* greater.

His volume faded. He wasn't shouting anymore, but there was just as much intensity in the words. Just as much anger and frustration for all that Rafe spoke barely above a whisper now. "You've walked too close to the line, and you can't ever come back. Not with me. Maybe Gabe and Allison are waiting for you to come to your senses and wake up to everything you've got right in your hand. Maybe Mom still prays for you, hoping you'll go back to being the man she married. But I'm *done*. You're not my father. As far as I'm concerned, you never were my father." He took one last look into Ben's ash-white face. "And you can go to hell."

Rafe stood there, expecting Ben to take a swing at him. He wasn't sure if he'd fight back, or not. His mouth tasted vile, as if the words he'd spat out had somehow left a taint behind.

Ben just stood there and stared, trembling. His mouth hung partially open, but nothing came out. No curses, no counter accusations.

Rafe turned on his heel and stomped away, slamming the door behind him and heading to his truck. Even knowing Gabe would find the abandoned mess in the morning, there was no way Rafe was going back to his task, not tonight.

His phone rang as he climbed behind the wheel— Laurel's ringtone—and he swore. The rage burning in his veins left him hot and dirty inside, and the last thing he wanted to do at that moment was dump this crap on her. Seeing Laurel right now was out of the question.

He ignored the message. He was in such a stinking foul mood, he didn't even want to think about her—she was going to be so fucking disappointed in him when she heard he'd lost his shit.

He didn't want to think—*period.*

So he wouldn't. Rafe took the back roads into town and swung by the local off-sales to pick up a bottle of whiskey. Skipped going to his own place—he didn't want to deal with Jesse tonight either. Just headed into the back hills to one of the small shelters dotting the land.

Twenty-four hours—that's all he was looking for. Time by himself to forget that his dad was a piece of shit, and while they deserved better, this was as good as it got.

Chapter Twenty-Three

A LOUD crash woke her, the bedroom door slamming into the wall. "Rafe, get up, man— What the fuck?"

Laurel struggled upright on the bed, blinking hard as her heart pounded.

"Jesus, what are you doing here?" Jesse demanded.

"What—?" She looked around in shock, waking up enough to discover she was alone in the bed. "Where's Rafe?"

Jesse dragged a hand through his hair and cursed loudly, stomping back down the hall before rushing back. "Get dressed. All hell is about to break loose, and you probably want to go home before anyone finds you here."

"I'm not hiding my relationship with Rafe," Laurel insisted, but she scrambled out of bed. "What's wrong?"

He stared down the hallway, pointedly looking away from her. "I'll tell you in the living room."

Then he was gone, and she was struggling to get into her clothes. She seemed all thumbs, her clothes tangled in knots, and the entire time her mind raced, picturing terrible things.

If something had happened to Rafe—

Laurel shoved the thought away violently, jerking her jeans over her hips and doing them up as she glanced at the alarm clock beside the bed.

No wonder she was groggy. It was only five forty-five in the morning.

She pulled on her sweater as she rushed into the living room, desperate for answers. "Jesse, what's going on? Is Rafe okay?"

Jesse had calmed down, which was good because she was frantic enough for both of them. "He's fine. I mean, I don't know for sure because I thought he was here, and he's not."

Her heart was pounding hard enough the blood rushing past her ears made it hard to hear. "Then what?"

He shook his head. "Uncle Ben—he's dead."

Laurel gripped the back of the couch as the room started spinning. "D-d-dead? But how?"

And where was Rafe?

Jesse guided her around the couch and made her sit. "I'm sorry for busting in on you like that, but I honestly thought I'd find Rafe. Aunt Dana went out this morning to start chores and found Ben. She called my mom, who called *me* because Rafe didn't answer his phone."

Poor Dana Coleman.

Only the smallest amount of guilt struck that her first thought wasn't that she was sorry to hear Ben was dead, but that Mrs. Coleman had been the one to find him. "But why isn't Rafe here?"

"I don't know."

Laurel dug in her pocket for her phone, checking if there were any messages. Nothing. She sent a followup to the one he hadn't answered.

Fear rose in her gut—

She wasn't worried that Rafe had done anything terrible, but that he'd *experienced* something terrible. That he was hurting.

She glanced at Jesse. Afraid to ask, yet even more afraid not to. "Do you know how Ben...?"

Her whispered words faded into nothing.

His face folded into a terrible frown. "Not yet."

Laurel shot to her feet. Didn't matter that it wasn't even six a.m.—she needed to do something, not least of which was find Rafe. "Where could he be? I can go look—"

"Laurel, think," Jesse interrupted. He reached out and caught her upper arms. "What're you going to do? Drive your teeny car in circles on winter roads in the dark? Rafe could be anywhere, and we don't even know what's going on. Hell, for all we know, he got stuck over at his brother's for the night, and they're having breakfast at Gabe's. Don't go off half-assed."

"I need to find him," Laurel insisted, fear closing off her throat and breaking up the words.

"For now you need to go home. Go to work like normal. Maybe Rafe will call you. If he does, make sure he knows to get his ass home."

It might be logical, but it made her crazy to think of simply going about her day as if nothing had happened. "If you hear anything, will you call me?"

He passed her his phone. "Punch in your number."

She did so with shaking fingers, the first rush of adrenaline wearing off. When she passed his phone back, he shoved it in his pocket then caught her close, squeezing her tightly in support.

He was big and strong. A wall of Coleman, but as sturdy as he was, it was *Rafe's* comforting touch she craved. Rafe's arms she wanted around her so she could offer him support in return.

That instant confirmed what she'd thought the previous night—her world had changed. What she felt for Rafe was no longer based on childish games, or even long-time childhood caring. The depth of emotion was so much richer because it was sorrow as well as laughter. She wanted to be with him in the good times, and in the bad. She wanted to share it all.

Now she had to find him and make sure he knew.

Jesse gave her shoulder a final pat before peering into her face. "You okay to drive?"

She nodded. "Call me," she insisted, preparing to head home for before hitting the library.

Only once she was in the car and about to make the turn south back into town, she changed her mind, manoeuvering carefully down the snow-covered gravel road toward the Angel homestead. She wasn't sure what she'd find, but on the off-chance she could do some good, she made the slow trip.

The snow in the driveway to the old house was well packed down for the time of day, a couple of extra vehicles parked by the back door.

She felt a little foolish as she pulled into a space next to them, but the outdoor light was on, and people were visible through the window, moving in the light of the kitchen.

Laurel made her way to the back door, wrapping her arms around herself as she waited in the cold. The door opened, and the matriarch of the Six Pack Colemans, Marion, stood gaping at her for a second before gesturing her in.

"Laurel Sitko? What on earth?"

She peeked around the woman, wishing words of comfort had magically escaped her instead of the tongue-tied nothing she offered instead. "I heard."

As she spoke, Dana Coleman rose from where she'd been sitting by the kitchen table, sorrow in her eyes. "Oh, child. What're you doing here at this hour?"

Only she opened her arms, and Laurel stepped forward to embrace the older woman, offering the only comfort she had to give.

She hadn't liked Ben very much, for a lot of different reasons, but Dana still had to be hurting. This wasn't about Ben anymore; it was about those left behind.

Maybe Laurel didn't have the right words to say. Maybe she didn't have a good explanation for why she already knew Ben was gone without admitting she'd spent the night in Rafe's bed, albeit without him.

And maybe her being there was all wrong... But as she held on to Dana Coleman, it seemed as if this was exactly where she was supposed to be.

The whole time, though, one question rang in her mind like a haunting echo.

Where was Rafe?

Chapter Twenty-Four

RAFE FELT as if he'd been taken out behind the barn and beaten black and blue.

His head ached from the hangover rocking him. He swore his back was bent double from crashing on the hay bales in the rustic shelter with the sleeping bag from his truck as a lousy blanket. His eyes itched, his fingers were freezing, and his mouth tasted like ass.

Hell, if he had to make a list, it would be shorter to say what didn't hurt than what did.

He swung his legs toward the ground and sat up, closing his eyes as the building spun.

The nearly empty whiskey bottle taunted him from where it lay one hay bale over.

The anger and frustration he'd felt the night before had peaked at some point, and he'd decided he should go back and actually tell his dad to shape up or ship out. Fortunately by that time he'd been too drunk to find his keys.

Keys. *Shit.*

Rafe patted his pockets, momentarily reminded of his cousin Matt, but the slapstick-routine didn't seem as funny this time around.

Not much seemed funny, between his dad being a stupid jerk and the fact Rafe knew that by running off and getting drunk he'd acted even stupider.

He was an idiot.

He'd sworn long ago to never do things just because he'd been provoked, and what had he gone and done? Lost his temper and then lost his goddamn mind.

Rafe grabbed his phone, certain by now he must have a ton of angry messages from his brother. He wasn't sure if he should be happy or sad the battery was dead. Just meant the shit he was in would be delivered face to face.

The only good thing was that Laurel didn't know how he'd screwed up. After all the times she'd told him to ignore Ben—she'd be so disappointed.

He stumbled to his truck, cranking the heater to high and letting it warm up enough he could feel his feet on the pedals before driving straight to Gabe's. Might as well get the punishment over and done with—since he damn well deserved it.

Only no one was around. The house was empty, there were no trucks in the yard, but when he checked the animals, they'd been fed and watered recently.

He hated to do it, but he had no choice. He made his way over to the Angel homestead, his crappy attitude changing to worry when he spotted the vehicles crowded into the yard. Both Gabe and Allison were there, along with his three uncles.

Shit. What had he done? If Ben had gone and hurt his mom, he'd fucking kill the man with his bare hands.

He rushed in the back door and skidded to a stop. His mom stood by the stove, and his heart started beating again. "Mom."

Her face twisted when she spotted him, and leaving the wooden spoon in the pot, she turned to offer her hands.

"You look like something the cat dragged in." She pulled him against her with a quick hug before pushing him away and patting his chest. "Oh, Rafe. You *smell* like something the cat dragged in. Where have you been?"

"Never mind that." Rafe glanced past her toward the living room. Gabe and his Uncle Mike were fast approaching the kitchen. He looked down, meeting her eyes straight on and watching them fill with tears. "What happened? Why're you crying?"

She swallowed hard. "It's your father. I'm sorry, but he's gone."

The words *good riddance* were on the tip of his tongue, but considering the serious expressions on his uncles' faces, and his brother's, Rafe held back. "Gone?"

Uncle Mike answered. "He's dead, Rafe. Massive heart attack from what the medical people told us. Probably died after he finished chores last night."

Rafe froze. Fucking froze—and it wasn't just an expression, it was real. As if all the heat and fire from the previous night had burned away so utterly, there was nothing left in his soul but ice.

"I didn't find him until this morning. I figured he was—" His mom let out a soft little sob. "Well, sometimes he does his own thing. I thought he was sleeping in the guest room."

"It's not your fault, Ma," Gabe insisted, wrapping an arm around her and guiding her toward the table. "There was nothing you could have done. Remember? The doctor told you that."

"I should've known," she murmured, reaching into her pocket for a tissue.

Rafe had to be still slightly drunk. "He's *dead?*"

His uncle had an arm around his shoulders now, settling him in the chair next to his mom. "I know it's a bit of a shock. Just sit for a minute."

Rafe stared across the table, not really seeing anything. At least not until his brother's face came into focus. Gabe looked worried, sad *and* royally pissed off, all at the same time.

Yeah, Rafe was in deep shit.

It wasn't until later that he found himself alone with his brother. He'd managed to shrug off his absence from everyone else, although his Uncle Mike had given him some pointed looks.

Once they were safely outside and out of hearing range, Gabe didn't beat around the bush. "What the hell happened to you?"

There was no way he could tell the truth. "I'm sorry."

His brother grabbed him by the front of the jacket, hauling him in for a split second before making a disgusted noise and pushing him aside. "God, you reek."

"I got frustrated with that repair. I'll go finish it now."

Gabe gaped at him. "You really think I give two shits about the repair job? Yeah, you should have either stopped when I told you to, or at least left me a note explaining what went wrong. But that doesn't explain why you're showing up at noon smelling like a still."

"I got drunk, okay?" Rafe shouted. "It was a bad day, and I'd had enough, and I screwed up. There, happy?"

"Not remotely," Gabe bit out. "Jeez, Rafe. I've never known you to act up like that. Fucking terrible timing."

His brother didn't know the half of it.

"Go home," Gabe ordered. "I don't want you around everyone until you get it together."

"I don't need a lecture," Rafe started.

"You're weaving on your feet," Gabe snapped. "And I'm at the end of my rope. Go. Home. Ma needs us to be there for her, and right now you look as if you're barely one step out of the ground yourself."

There was no use fighting when his brother got stubborn. Rafe marched off to his truck and got in. Slamming his door shut was stupid—the resulting pain punished him more than anyone else. He turned his truck toward home with a head that was one step away from exploding.

He stood under the shower with the water as hot as possible, the scalding liquid steaming against his face until a few loose strands of pain washed away, only to be replaced by something newer.

Guilt so cold it burned.

What had he done? What had he *said*? The night before was enough of a blur he wasn't sure anymore what was real and what he'd imagined, but even then what he did know for sure—it was bad. It was real bad.

The water had gone cold by the time he left the shower, stepping out and vigorously rubbing himself dry. He pulled on sweatpants and marched into the kitchen—

She stood by the stove. His angel, shining like innocence as she stirred something in a pot, the scent of it on the air making his mouth water.

"Laurel?"

She whirled, eyes wide. "Rafe. Oh my God, you're okay. I was so worried."

She was across the room and holding him, and for a moment everything *was* okay. An angel in his arms— he had her, and he was never going to give her up.

Laurel murmured soothing words against his neck, telling him about how she'd come to see him last night and he'd been gone. How she'd slipped away from work, and he'd been in the shower, so she'd made soup, and was he okay??

The heat from her body warmed the cold spots inside, and then some. Her shirt was silky soft under his touch, and a pulse of eager desire flared.

Desire? *Urgent need.*

A need as desperate as a drowning man fighting for his next breath.

He slipped his hands under her shirt and over her belly. Palms pressed hard to her warm skin so he could savour the heat as he caressed up her sides. His body lit up.

Her lips met his, and they kissed, desperately trying to get closer. It was fucked up, and wrong, and he couldn't have stopped if the house had caught fire.

Rafe lifted her to the table and stripped away her pants. Jerked off her underwear and brought her hips to the edge so he could bring his mouth down on her and feast hungrily.

Her fingers were in his hair. Part of him wanted her to tighten them to fists so she could jerk him away. Push him back in disgust and demand answers.

She did neither, her feverish moans driving him on as he thrust his tongue into her. As he slipped fingers into her wet heat and fucked her rapidly, his tongue devastating her clit.

Seconds later...or was it hours? She damn near screamed his name, sex clamping down on him as her legs quivered.

Rafe stood and dropped his sweatpants, his cock springing free. Hard and needy like the rest of him, he stepped between her legs and lined them up. The head of his shaft slipped through her folds as she fought to take a breath.

One motion, that's all it took to thrust in, their foreheads pressed together. Laurel's eyes went wide, but she clutched his shoulders, nails digging into his skin as he shoved his cock deep then stopped.

She was still pulsing around him.

He closed his eyes to hide himself in the feel of her, in the scent of her wrapping around them as he waited until her orgasm calmed before catching hold of her right knee. He lifted it high, opening her farther to his frantic plundering.

"Oh my God," she whispered. "Rafe. Baby. *Yes.*"

He watched his cock disappear into her body. One, and connected. The two of them completing each other. The gasps from their lips mingling to create a whirlwind between them.

Emotional overload hit, and the trembling pulse in his heart acknowledged this was because of her.

It was Laurel who gave willingly as he stole pleasure. Didn't matter that she was moaning along with him, digging into his bare back with her nails. This was because of *her*, not him, and he felt selfish and dirty—

—but not enough to stop.

Not when the rush of pleasure up his spine was roaring loud enough to drown out the other voices in his head. The guilt and disgust and anger and...all of it vanished as he buried himself in her body. Used her, gave to her.

Took everything she'd give before he broke completely.

"*Rafe.*" She dragged her nails down his back hard enough to leave stinging trails, hips pulsing wildly as she came. He buried his face against her neck and let himself fly apart.

The floor was unsteady under his feet. Hell, the entire house could have been shaking for all he knew as he clung to her, trying to hold on to every good and pure thing she'd given him for one final moment.

Their desperate fuck had been perfect. *She* was perfect, and he was about to get kicked out of paradise because there was no way he belonged anywhere near her.

Never going to give her up? What an idiot he was. Being with her forever was what he wanted, and exactly what he couldn't have.

Rafe released her leg and gently lowered it to the table. Then he pressed his fists to the hard wooden surface, because if he kept them there, he wouldn't catch her in his grasp and hold on. Wouldn't cling to her and never let go.

Because he had to let her go. After what he'd done? He couldn't trust himself ever again.

Laurel was kissing him, her lips brushing his face. His eyes. Butterfly-slow blessings dusting his heated skin. Her hands danced over his shoulders, his cock still buried inside her warmth.

He didn't want to move, because the next step was away from her.

Saying goodbye was going to kill him, but hell, better him now than her someday in the future. Better to never spend another hour with her than to someday become like his father, and have a family who were better off with him dead.

He pulled back. Stole one final touch as he scooped her pants off the floor and held them for her. Laurel rested a hand on his shoulder as she lifted one leg, then the other before standing motionless as he pulled the waistband over her hips.

That was all he could bear. Rafe stepped away and did the hardest thing he'd ever done in his life. "Go home."

He turned his back on her.

She curled herself around him. "I'm here for you," she insisted. "Let me in, Rafe. Let me help you."

He laughed, the sound escaping hard and brittle as he carefully wrapped his fingers around her wrists and removed her arms. "After what I did?"

She didn't move, or at least the old wooden floorboards didn't squeak, which meant she wasn't going to make this simple and walk away because he asked.

"I'm not mad at you," she whispered, stroking a hand down his back. Touching the places she'd left her mark on his body. "The sex was—real. That was being alive, and being real. Shutting me out and not talking to me isn't being alive, baby. Ben died, not you. Don't punish yourself."

Her fingers traced the marks on his body, but her voice—her words—they tore at the places inside where she'd left her mark even deeper.

"I need you to go away." He faced her and hardening his resolve. Tightening his voice so he didn't simply break down and beg. "I need time away from you."

Her sudden intake of air struck him razor-sharp. He met her pain-filled eyes, and that's when he remembered—Jeff had said the same thing to her.

He wanted to take it back. Wanted to ease the hurt he'd caused, but there was no turning back. "Just go."

Laurel searched his face, concern deepening as she reached out a hand then jerked it back before they touched. She took a deep breath, then without a word rushed to the front door to pull on her coat and boots.

He waited silently for his heart to walk out of his life.

Only she stopped with her hand on the doorknob, glancing up so the fire in her eyes was clear. The hopelessness was gone and what remained was one-hundred-percent stubborn-ass Sitko, the girl who'd leapt fearlessly on the class bully in spite of being out-gunned.

Laurel lifted her chin and spoke like she was the one in charge. "You need some time? You've got it, but don't think you can run from me forever, Coleman. Running doesn't change things."

She checked him over from top to bottom before meeting his gaze, so direct and powerful it took everything in him to keep from looking away.

"When I do come back? We're going to talk about a whole lot of things, and once we're done, we're going to bed for a solid week, so save up your strength and get whatever it is out of your system, because even best friends only put up with bullshit for a short time."

Laurel reached above her to snatch his favourite cowboy hat off the hook on the wall. She jammed it on her head, then marched out the door, slamming it after her.

Chapter Twenty-Five

THE FUNERAL was set for Saturday. Even with the things they had to deal with because of Ben's passing, Rafe had had a lot of time on his hands, especially since he was actively avoiding Laurel.

Her words rattled in Rafe's brain for the next couple days. It was in the empty moments he especially felt her absence. The times when he would have reached to text her, or talk to her. Hell, every time he reached for his damn *hat* he thought about the flash of passion in her eyes.

And just because he wasn't texting her didn't mean *she* stopped. He considered blocking her number for about two seconds before realizing he'd sooner cut off his balls.

It hurt to read the messages, but it would hurt more to not.

Laurel: *Your cousin pulled me over for having a broken taillight. I'm glad she wasn't one corner earlier or I'd have been nailed for speeding too*

Laurel: *Made pizza tonight and put pineapple on it because you're not here. You're welcome to come pick it off and make rude comments about how fruit isn't a dinner item*

Laurel: *I'm wearing your T-shirt to bed. It smells like you. Well, a good you, not after you've been shoveling manure*

Laurel: *This bed seems empty without you hogging the covers*

Laurel: *I've got room saved for your stubborn ass*

Laurel: *Baby? It's cold without you*

She wasn't making it easy to move on without her, that was for fucking sure.

So he looked for ways to fill the time. He certainly didn't want to spend it over at Gabe and Allison's, and have to face questions about why he was there and not with Laurel like usual. Jesse was nearly as bad company these days as he was. When Rafe had mentioned that he and Laurel were over, all his cousin had done was grunt.

He figured his mom was probably lonely. Plus, making his way over to the homestead between chores was also an excuse that let him salve his conscience slightly.

And if his mom was confused at how often he showed up, she didn't mention it. Not right away.

He walked in to find her leafing through a pile of pictures on the kitchen table. "What's up?"

"You again? You were here only a few hours ago." Dana glanced at him suspiciously. "Wait. Are you and Gabe keeping an eye on me?"

Rafe settled into the chair next to her. "Course not. You have homemade cookies, though. It's like ringing a bell."

She was focused on the photo in front of her again. "Help yourself. The neighbours have been bringing around food like crazy. I don't know what they think I'm doing with my time that I can't make a meal for one person."

"It's what people 'round here do when someone dies." Rafe pulled a picture from under her fingers. "Who's Gabe with in this shot?"

She laughed. "That's not Gabe, it's me and your father."

No way. He picked the photo up to examine it closer. "But you're so..."

"Young?" Dana sighed mightily. "Did you think I was born this age?"

"I was going to say *happy*," he said, unable to tear his eyes off the picture. His father had an arm draped around Dana's shoulders, her head thrown back as she laughed, hands clutching a small bouquet of purple flowers.

Ben was staring at her with adoration on his face.

Rafe looked again—he could have sworn it was a shot of his brother, right down to the expression. It was exactly the way Gabe looked at Allison, as if she were his entire world.

His gut twisted. "You guys were in love."

Dana took a deep breath. "I know you two didn't get along, especially toward the end, but yes. He was a good man for a long time. The man I fell in love with..." She smoothed the picture under her fingers. "He was sweet and caring. Gruff with everyone else, but with me? Ben made the hard work seem easy. Even when we were working ourselves silly, there was always time for laughter."

But that wasn't who he'd been—not for many years. That wasn't the father Rafe remembered having. Not since Mike had died.

And if Ben could change that much...

Rafe closed his eyes and took a deep breath, willing his fists to unclench before his mom noticed. No, this proved even more clearly he was right to stay away from Laurel.

As if he'd summoned her name by thinking of her, his mom spoke.

"Since you're here already." She looked him over. "Why don't you call Laurel and ask her to come join us for supper?"

"No." The word snapped out of him like from a slingshot, and his mom's eyes widened in surprise.

He felt about two years old, pulling a tantrum even as he was being offered what he wanted.

"I'm not seeing her anymore," he admitted.

"What? Are you—?" She stumbled to a dead stop. "Did she break up with you?" Dana asked far more gently.

Rafe hated to admit it. "No."

The fire was back in an instant. "Raphael Coleman, what on earth were you thinking? That girl is the most perfect person for you. You call her up this instant and apologize for whatever you've done."

"No," he said again, feeling childish. "Mom, it's over. Drop it."

"Not likely. You have that 'I'm being heroic' look to you that men get." She leaned in closer and glared like only a mother could. "Call her."

"Mom."

"Then I will. I need to talk to her—"

He snatched the picture off the table and shook it. "This? This is why it's over between me and Laurel."

Dana settled back in her chair, utter confusion on her face. "Because your father died?"

A bolt of guilt straight to the heart. "Because my father wasn't the man you married. There's been no laughter in this house for years, no joy. I can't stand the thought of doing that to Laurel down the road."

"Oh, Rafe." His mom laid a hand over his. "It's not that simple, and yet it is. You're not your father."

"I hate that I'm his son. I hate that the same thing might happen to me—that I'll grow cold and sharp, and all the good things in my life will be torn apart."

"You're not him," Dana insisted. "I shouldn't need to tell you that, you stubborn child."

Nearly twice the size of her, and still a child. Felt it, right then. Felt like a damn baby, crying at shadows.

"Don't try to tell me I'm like Gabe, because we both know that's bullshit."

She narrowed her eyes. "Watch your language, young man. You're not too old for me to wash your mouth out with soap. But you're right—you're not Gabe. And you're also not Ben. Both you and your brother have made your own choices since you were young."

But this wasn't just about making choices, or even about losing his temper. It was because he'd ridden the knife's edge so long, but when push came to shove, he broke. Fucking broke in the wrong direction—the same path his father had taken.

His mom seemed to have zero sympathy for him.

"Well, you make your choice about who you spend time with, right or wrong, same as always, but I think you're acting a fool, Rafe. When you've got love in your grasp, you don't toss it away. I wish *all* the years I'd had with Ben had been filled with laughter, but that wasn't our lot." She rose to her feet and stared down at him from her towering height of five foot nothing. "I wouldn't give up a single minute of the good days. Not a single one."

Then she kicked him out. *His mom* kicked him out.

"You want to be an idiot, go do it at your own place." She picked up her book and pointedly ignored him.

Rafe stumbled to his truck and drove home. Even the meager penance spending time with his mom had offered was now in tattered shreds.

And the one thing he wanted most, he couldn't have.

He pulled into the yard to discover Jesse leaning against his truck, an old horse trailer hooked up behind. Morgan sat by his feet, tail thumping into the snowy ground as Rafe approached.

"You holding that door up with your backside for a reason?" Rafe asked.

His cousin dropped a treat to the dog, then shrugged. "Just finished loading up Danger. Thought you might be home soon."

The strange comment pulled Rafe from his gloomy thoughts. "Where are you taking your horse at this time of year?"

Jesse ignored the question. "Laurel phoned me."

Rafe swore.

"Yeah. Gave me an earful, by the way." Jesse looked him over. "You want to talk about it?"

Not really, but...

Rafe examined his cousin. Out of everyone in his family, Jesse was the one person he figured he could trust not to say anything if he shared.

"I'm no good for her," he said.

Jesse made a rude noise, uncoiling himself to vertical. "I could have told you that. I offered to be her upgrade, remember?"

"Fuck off," Rafe muttered without any force behind the words. They walked side by side toward the small stable where they could look over the Coleman holdings to the east.

Thick snow covered the land—nothing growing, nothing moving, at least not within eyesight. The far fields were pristine and beautiful in spite of the cold.

Yet all he could see was Laurel's face as she stared back at him with pain in her eyes. Pain he'd put there.

"For someone who's supposed to be no longer your girlfriend, she had a lot to say about you," Jesse shared. "Told me to keep an eye out so you didn't do anything stupid."

"I'm not—"

"Actually, she said 'so he doesn't do anything *stupider* than he already has', which I assume means the trying-to-break-up-with-her bit. Or the getting-drunk-and-not-coming-home. Either works."

Rafe leaned his arms on the top railing. "Breaking up with her isn't stupid. I'm trying to protect her."

"She doesn't want to be protected," Jesse pointed out.

"She doesn't know what I'm capable of," Rafe snapped. "It's not that simple."

"It never is."

They stood in silence for a moment before Rafe confessed. "All my life I've tried to not become my father. Laurel knows this—she knows how much I hated what he'd become at the end."

She'd also stood up to his father fearlessly more times than he'd liked. Maybe she was strong enough...

No.

Maybe his mom wouldn't give up the good moments, but the truth remained that Ben's final years had sucked the joy from all their lives.

Jesse interrupted his thoughts. "If that's your worry, you've never been anything like your father. You get quiet at times, but usually you're just out there, working hard and living hard. You and Laurel make me think of yard lights."

"Seriously? A fucking *yard light?*"

"Its not an insult, you ass. Yard lights are constant. They never get in anyone's faces like Travis or Jaxi, looking for attention, but when it comes down to it, you rely on them a hell of a lot—and yes, I knew you two were friends back in school. She makes you happy, so why the hell aren't you with her, you dumb jerk?"

"Because someday I'm going to become my father, and I can't bear to be the one who makes her light go dim," Rafe said.

"Oh, bullshit. You're not your father," Jesse insisted. "And while it doesn't excuse him, my dad said the change started when your brother died. That Ben felt guilty, and that's what made him cold."

So, asshole behaviour was triggered by guilt. *Great—*

"All the more reason I'm done."

Jesse let out a rude snort. "Right. What the hell have you done to feel guilty about?"

"Because I'm some sweet, innocent yard light, is that what you think?"

"Shut up. Because you're *you*, asshole. You screw up at times, but you turn yourself around and make it right."

"Some things we can't make right. Some things we can't take back."

Jesse froze. His expression as he looked Rafe over was suddenly far less snarky and more wary. "What did you do?"

And this was where it all hit the fan.

"Ben and I fought the day he died. Hell, he could've been having a heart attack while I was shouting at him about being a shitty father, telling him how much I hated him, and that he should basically roll over and die."

"Jesus." Jesse's tone was a lot more sympathetic this time. "Okay, that's fucked up. I'm sorry."

"Yeah, me too." Rafe stood motionless, the cold winter blowing around them fitting his mood nicely. "Thus, guilt."

"I'm not going to argue with you about that. But I still say you belong with Laurel, man."

"For fuck's sake," Rafe snapped. "You've never been in a relationship with anyone for longer than three nights. Why the hell would I take advice from you?"

"Because I know exactly what amounts to taking things a step too far, and you didn't cross the line."

"Oh, now you're the expert on what's real guilt and what's bullshit?"

"Yeah, as a matter of fact." Jesse glared at him. "I'm the fucking king of guilt." He slammed a boot on the bottom rail, staring out over Coleman land, his expression icy.

Rafe stilled. All the anger and frustration and fears whirling around him quieted as he watched his cousin battle his own internal demons.

Silence reigned for the longest time until Jesse finally spoke, his voice little more than a whisper. "Everything changed. Joel and me were a team, then suddenly Vicki was there, and I..." Jesse snorted derisively. "I acted like the biggest fucking ass."

Not a ghost of a word had come out over the past two years about what had torn apart the twins. Rafe almost didn't want to speak for fear Jesse would stop talking about the one thing everyone wanted to know. "You resented her."

"Resented, envied." Jesse made a rude noise. "I hated her guts."

Shit. "You hated her?"

"Only for a while, and then I hated myself."

"Because you were jealous."

Jesse turned back, sorrow on his face. "Because I crawled into bed with her—"

That's all he got out before he was spinning on the spot, a grunt of pain escaping. Rafe had moved instinctively, stepping forward, his fist swinging hard. The smack of his knuckles into Jesse's jaw was immensely satisfying, the second blow even more so.

Jesse hit the ground without raising his arms in defense. Just sat there, blood pouring from his nose, his eyes haunted.

Rafe cursed, sick to his stomach for so many reasons. The anger whipping through him tasted like blood and death, and it wasn't about Jesse, it was all about his own damn feelings. His *own* fucking faults.

He looked down at his hands still clenched into merciless weapons. He could hit his cousin again. It was clear Jesse would accept whatever punishment Rafe passed out, but it didn't remove Rafe's guilt.

Because he'd done it again. Struck out with anger, and it had been easy, and sweet, and the first thing he'd wanted to do.

Had Ben's death been the turning point Rafe couldn't come back from?

Like he'd feared?

Rafe willed himself to unfurl his hands, taking a deep breath before reaching down to his cousin. Strong fingers curled around his forearm as he hauled Jesse to his feet. He shoved aside his frustrations and focused on the other man and his confession.

They stood quietly for a moment before Jesse spoke. "I didn't sleep with her."

The words cut into the silence.

"Not for lack of trying." Rafe heard the disgust in his own voice. "What the hell was getting into bed with her going to accomplish?"

Jesse pulled a handkerchief from his back pocket and pressed it against his face. "I thought I'd get my goddamn brother back. Instead, Vicki thought I was Joel, and..."

"Sick bastard," Rafe muttered. "I'm surprised Joel didn't kill you."

"It wasn't like that." Jesse visibly swallowed. "Well, it was, but it wasn't."

Cryptic, much? Yet Rafe didn't want to push. Whatever happened that night had clearly...*destroyed* something inside his cousin.

"She was barely awake—hell, she was mostly asleep, for all I know—and she fucking *gutted* me. She wasn't even aware of what she was saying, but it hit me so hard..." He wiped his face then shoved the handkerchief away. "It changed everything."

By now Jesse's jaw was rigid and Rafe's churning gut had turned into a solid block of pain. "What'd she say?"

Jesse shook his head. "It broke me, Rafe. All thoughts of...hell, I don't know. Whatever childish ideas I arrived with vanished right then and there. I'd gone to prove to Joel that..." He trailed off.

"That what?"

"Fuck." Jesse groaned. "It doesn't even matter anymore. All I know is that I screwed up. Big-time."

"They've never said a word," Rafe said in disbelief.

"They don't know."

Holy shit.

Jesse paused before rushing on. "I swear nothing happened. Not really, and I got the hell out of there before Joel got home. Vicki obviously doesn't remember a thing."

Rafe eyed his cousin. "This went down two years ago, but you're still being an ass. Why?"

"*Why?*" Jesse turned and gripped the fence rail as if he were ready to rip it to shreds. "Because no matter how much I plan to make a move to fix things, I take one look at Vicki, remember what she said in her sleep, and guilt hits so hard I can't breathe. I can't fucking *breathe*, Rafe, and it's killing me."

Guilt. Rafe understood that one in spades.

They stood together silently for a minute, staring over the land that held no answers. Just the wind moving endlessly over open spaces.

Rafe took a deep breath. "So, what do we do?"

Jesse tilted his hat back, motioning to the truck and trailer. "I didn't mean for this to come out right now, but I'm leaving."

"Leaving...*Rocky?*"

His cousin nodded.

A flash of his earlier anger returned. Rafe couldn't change what he'd done, but Jesse could. "Leaving won't fix anything."

"And staying won't either," Jesse retorted. "You didn't do anything wrong. Not really, but you still feel like shit, right? I can tell you it doesn't get any damn easier, no matter how much time passes. You're going to look into your mom's eyes from now to fucking eternity, and every time you see her hurting, you'll think about how *you* might have changed things."

Laurel's voice echoed in his head, and Rafe found himself repeating the words out loud. "Can't change things by running."

"And I fucking can't change the past," Jesse roared. "That's why I'm leaving."

"Running," Rafe snapped back.

"Call it whatever the hell you want, I don't give a shit."

In the midst of the shouting Rafe saw the truth all too clearly. He lowered his voice. "Only you do give a shit, and that's the problem."

Jesse damn near vibrated as he stood there. An icy wind curled around them, the sun buried behind washed-out grey clouds. Snow lay against the side of the barn, hard packed from the wind, with dirt and straw mixed in. The path they'd made stomping their way into the building pocked with dirt as well.

It wasn't the clean, fresh aftermath of a snowfall, where everything seemed pristine and hopeful. It was jagged ice and ruined plans, and right then Rafe felt so damn empty inside he wasn't sure his heart was still beating.

His cousin turned to him, his face grim. "Yeah. Yeah, you're right. I care. Which is why I'm leaving, because it's the right thing to do. The only person this hurts is me. But you? Don't throw it all away. Don't hurt Laurel as well as yourself."

He slapped Rafe on the shoulder then turned and walked toward the truck that would take him even farther from the people who cared about him.

Rafe called after him. "Joel loves you. Hell, all the Colemans love you, you ass."

Jesse kept moving. "I know."

Rafe didn't try to stop him. Just watched him go, hoping his cousin's road turned smoother. Hoping it would turn around and someday lead him home.

The house was deafeningly quiet.

There'd been four of them living in the place at one time, and now it was just Rafe. Gone was the raucous laughter, piles of dirty dishes, sporting events played too loud. No more arguments about who ate the last piece of pizza, or finished off the milk without buying more.

The cousins who'd moved out to settle down—that was life. But Jesse? If the stubborn asshole had talked to Joel, so much pain and sadness could have been avoided over the past couple of years...

His phone signaled a text from Laurel, and he could hardly bear to look.

Laurel: *Your mom invited me to dinner. We're discussing the stubborn men in our lives*

Laurel: *You should show up to defend yourself*

Laurel: *btw, she knew about the time we got in trouble for throwing the water balloons. Or if she didn't before, she does now. Oops*

A smile twitched to his lips before he could stop it. Damn it, he missed her so much. She was strong and fearless, and too sweet for her own good.

Strong enough to deal with his sorry ass?

Fueled by frustration, and with too much energy to be contained, Rafe went outside and made toothpicks of the woodpile, swinging the axe like a mad man. Hours later, his muscles ached and he was sweating in spite of the freezing temperatures. His brain whirled through options until he was tired enough to drop into bed exhausted.

Chapter Twenty-Six

HE WASN'T at the funeral.

There was still time until the actual service got started because the family always gathered early. But with half an hour to go, and no sign of Rafe, Laurel was pretty sure he wasn't late but being stubborn.

Stubborn? Try a complete and utter jackass.

There she'd been, all ready to make a huge move forward with him, and *pfffft*. Nothing.

While his father's death had been unexpected, the way Rafe'd been acting ever since, anyone would have thought he'd lost the most important person in his life. Like he'd been rocked off his foundation—and that made no sense because she knew exactly how much Ben had frustrated him.

Maybe he felt guilty. Maybe the fact he *didn't* miss his father as much as he thought he should playing into this.

Laurel understood guilt. Heck, she understood it at whole lot more than he'd probably give her credit for, and if they ever got a chance to *talk* she was prepared to tell him everything.

But after he'd all but shoved her out of the house, he'd raised every wall possible between them. He'd gone

335

from ignoring her phone calls to ignoring her completely. She was torn between stalking him so she could give him a piece of her mind or letting him be a jackass, alone and miserable, because that seemed to be what he wanted.

If only it was that simple. Because what *she* wanted was to make him better. To find out why he wasn't acting like the man she knew.

Like the man she *loved*...

Stupid timing on her part. Falling in love wasn't supposed to be this frustrating.

She'd put up with his bullshit over the past few days figuring he'd have to show up eventually, and when he did, she'd duct tape herself to his side if that's what it took to make him talk.

Tough to duct tape herself to a person who didn't show up, though.

I could be running off on a wild-goose chase, God, but maybe you could do me a favour? Keep the stubborn man where I can track him down easily?

She'd had it up to here with Rafe's suffering in silence. She headed for the door, trying to call in case he was just late, but when he didn't answer, she sent a warning text then grabbed her winter coat.

"Going somewhere?"

She twirled. Her dad stood there, a suitably solemn expression on his face.

"There's someone I need to track down," she informed him.

He glanced at her outfit then back into the family waiting room where the Colemans continued to gather. Gabe and Allison stood at Dana's side. The older woman looked delicate, yet her spine was straight and she held her composure as she waited for the ceremony to start.

It was pretty clear which of the Angel Colemans

wasn't there yet.

She looked into her father's eyes and saw understanding. He cupped her cheek with his hand. "You can't make someone do something they don't want to do."

"I know. But I can stand beside him. I can let him know he isn't alone." She offered the faintest hint of a smile. "I can tell him what I believe."

A momentary flash of curiosity and hope lit her father's eyes. "Maybe you and I can have a discussion later about some of those things, but for now, might I suggest different footwear if you're going out?"

She glanced down at the delicate shoes she'd slipped on at church. Her boots to wear to the graveside weren't much better. While she didn't know for sure where she was going, she had a pretty good idea Rafe'd be somewhere a little less than civilized. "Suggestions?"

He pointed to a pair of oversized Uggs on the shoe rack. "Borrow mine."

She snickered. "Oh, those will totally work. I don't even have to remove my shoes."

"I can't delay the service," he warned, "but people will understand if you're late. Or there's the graveside later, if that helps."

Laurel darted in and kissed his cheek, accepting the quick hug he gave in return, along with his comforting smile.

Having her father's blessing made heading out on her task easier. She was going to be okay. *They* would be okay, she was sure of it. Even if she couldn't knock sense into Rafe fast enough to make it back for the funeral, she'd make a difference where it counted.

In forever.

She paused with the keys in the lock of her car, the piles of snow pushed up at the edge of the parking lot making her hesitate. She'd be safer in something a little bigger and broader. One glance around the parking lot made her choice clear.

She hauled open the door on Trevor Coleman's enormous truck and climbed inside.

The seat was still warm, the keys dangling from the ignition. She smiled as she started up the big beast. A moment later she had the truck in gear and headed toward Rafe's.

Her frustration slid all over the place, a lot like the tires under her. It wasn't easy to get a grip with the heavy winter snow and ice that lay on the highway, but she was in a solid enough vehicle that she felt safe. She might be having difficulty, but she was controlling it, if just barely, and that made the difference.

Maybe control was an illusion.

She slowed before she twisted the wheel to take the driveway into Rafe's rental, pleased to find her first guess accurate. Rafe wasn't hiding. He was sitting there in broad daylight, tailgate of his truck lowered...

...a six-pack of beer at his side.

Laurel saw red. She had no issues with him being twisted up over how to feel about his father's passing, but he could be miserable without the alcohol.

Thanks for keeping him here, God. Excuse me if I shout at him a little for his own good. I might need to use a few bad words to get through his thick cowboy skull.

She pulled to a stop, the heavy truck shimmying under her as she offered Rafe a dirty look. It took three seconds to get out of the truck and march over to him, slam her fists down on her hips and give him a death glare.

Temperatures were below zero and the idiot was sitting there in his suit, cowboy boots dangling toward the ground. His second best hat was jammed so far down on his head the brim nearly cut his eyes off from view.

Nearly.

She could see enough to know he was watching her closely. Weighing her reactions as he picked up the beer beside him and lifted it toward his lips.

He wanted it to be like that, did he?

She snatched the bottle from his fingers. "Don't you have somewhere to be, Coleman?"

"Yup." He grabbed the bottle back, taking a good long drink before meeting her stare with a "what are you going to do about it?" attitude. "Right here."

You're right, God. Sometimes it's not patience we need to pray for, but courage. Help me help this stupid man get his shit together.

Laurel snatched the bottle from his fingers. This needed something big. Something epic to get his attention and prove she meant business. She twisted and threw as hard as she could, the bottle flying nicely through the air to slam into the half fence beside the parking area.

She had to stop from gasping in surprise when the bottle didn't just break, it shattered into a million pieces, falling like green rain onto the undisturbed snow.

She could hear God laughing at her. *You don't remember your laws of physics, do you?*

Fine, maybe not, but it was as good as blowing a bugle to get Rafe's attention. She snatched up the remainder of the six-pack before he could get any ideas.

There was something very satisfying about swinging her arm back then sending the box flying in a smooth arc. Up and up then down, vanishing into the deep, soft snow.

Laurel faced him again, fighting to stop herself from shaking out of her oversized boots.

"You're going to that church, right *now.*" Although if he refused to cooperate, she had no idea what she'd try next, because, holy moly, he looked big and imposing sitting there. Completely unmovable.

They exchanged long glances, Rafe's expression hard and unreadable. What she wanted most was to crowd closer and wrap her arms around him. Comfort him and kiss him and tell him…

Well, she wasn't going to tell him she loved him until he got his head out of his ass and smartened up.

It took all her courage to stay in one spot when he hopped off the tailgate and stepped into her personal space. Tall. Very tall—and *big.* Had she mentioned big?

Still, chutzpah could take a person a long way. "You don't scare me," Laurel said with as much conviction as she could muster. "Get your ass in gear."

One brow rose in surprise, but he didn't tease her about swearing. Instead he looked nearly scared to death for a moment. At least until he stepped closer, his muscular body brushing hers.

She was airborne a second later, held in his firm grasp high enough she could look him in the eyes and see raw emotion. Desire as well as a whole lot of fear.

His fingers slipped around the back of her neck and then his mouth crashed down on hers, and he was kissing her as if he expected her to vanish between one breath and the next. Kissing her as if this was the last thing he was going to do before wandering out to meet a firing squad.

Kissing her as if she were the only thing in the world he had, and he was desperately afraid he was going to lose her.

She didn't fight him, just pressed herself tighter against him and gave. Gave her willing friendship from all those years. Tried to give some of the joy that they'd built up through laughter and troublemaking and everything that had come before.

And over it all she laid a thick layer of love. The kind of love that took years to build, sneaking in when you weren't aware of the walls rising higher and higher. Built on a rock-solid foundation so that when storms like this hit, things could shake, and things could rock, but they weren't going to fall.

They could stand firm through anything together.

He had her up the stairs and into the house, and for a second she thought he was headed to the bedroom. Instead he plopped himself down on the couch, arms like iron bands around her as he refused to let go and just held on tight. Kissing her, caressing her, whispering words she struggled to hear.

She couldn't take it anymore. She threaded her fingers through his hair and tugged him back so she could look into his face. Tears threatened, but the rest of his face seemed almost emotionless as he struggled to stay in control.

He didn't need to be in control around her.

"I love you," she whispered.

His eyes widened, his jaw dropping open a little.

"Stupid timing to confess that, but, hey, this is *your* Sitko. The girl who blurts out things as soon as they come to her—although honestly this one I've pretty much had in me for most my life." She stroked her fingers through his hair, soothing it to lie straighter. Soothing him. Soothing herself by touching him.

He looked dazed. "You don't know. You don't know what I did. What I could do in the future— You *can't* love me."

Okay, that was one-hundred-percent horse hockey. She looked at him sideways. "Excuse me, Coleman. Did you just tell me I'm *not* allowed to do something? Because you know that's the surest way to make me want to do it."

His lips twitched for a second before he grew serious again. "This isn't something to joke about. I can't do it. I can't go to that funeral and listen to people talk about Ben without wanting to stand up and tell them it's my fault he's dead."

And he told her what happened that night, and by the time he reached the final part of his confession, her heart ached at the pain in his voice.

"When he started in on you and Allison, I lost my temper. We fought... Actually, I was a coward and a bully, and called him every name in the book before I left him to die. He must've had his heart attack right after that."

Guilt. Hoo boy, did she know what a number that could play on a person.

"I lost control, Laurel. I didn't take my fists to him, but I as good as killed him with my words." Rafe sounded wrecked. "It's what burst out of me, and I can't help but think... What if I do that? Maybe Ben deserved it, I don't know, but what happens when, down the road, *you* do something, and I get pissed off? What if we're together and raising a family—what's going to stop me from turning into Ben and lashing out at our kids someday?"

"You won't," Laurel promised him. "It's not you."

"It certainly was that night," he insisted. "Easiest fucking thing in the world to rake him over the coals."

"Oh, Rafe. Trust me, I know exactly what kind of

frustration your father could trigger. Ms. Lippy, remember? You and me both lost our tempers with him. He knew exactly which strings to pull to piss us off."

She stroked his shoulders, made hopeful by the fact that even though he was trying to convince her that he needed to leave, that he wasn't good enough for her, he was clinging to her like a lifeline.

"I'm sorry that's your last memory of him." Laurel considered her words carefully. "Remember the doctor told your mom he was surprised it didn't happen sooner, considering how bad Ben's heart was."

Stubbornly, Rafe didn't say anything.

"Ben was broken," she said. "Maybe you should have— No, you're right, you *should* have kept your temper, but your father chose a path that made him miserable, inside and out, and *that's* what killed him, no matter how much you shouted."

"I don't know that for sure. I *can't* know that—so this guilt is mine to bear."

"Then let me help you carry it," she offered. "Because you don't have to be alone, Rafe."

He pressed his face to her neck and held her tightly. "I don't know if I'm strong enough, and I don't want to hurt you. I don't want to make you have to carry this burden, either."

"Because you're protecting me?" she asked.

He shrugged.

Laurel curled her arms around his body and held on tight. "Because I'm someone who means a lot to you, and you don't want to hurt me. And I understand that, and I appreciate it, but I'm not made of tissue, baby. I'm strong enough to be there for you."

"It's like there's a fire inside my gut," Rafe whispered. "And my brain keeps going in circles with all the different options that I didn't pick. In spite of the fire, something inside feels cold and broken—"

"—and it feels like every person who looks at you has to know exactly what you've done, and you can't figure out why they're not backing away from you in disgust."

Rafe's grip loosened until he could pull them far enough apart to look into her eyes. "How...?"

"How do I know what guilt feels like? Soul-shattering, heart-breaking guilt?" Laurel took a deep breath. "I have to tell you something that no one else knows, and it might be tough to hear, but I need you to listen."

Maybe it was the lost tone in her voice that got through, but Rafe sat silently, waiting, his body tight under her.

"Long story short. Jeff broke up with me then took off for a month. That's when I discovered I was pregnant."

A soft curse escaped Rafe's lips.

She hurried on. "I didn't tell him because I didn't want him 'doing the right thing' for the sake of the baby. I wanted us to be together because we loved each other, but he blew me off, I swear he did. So I left school and went to my aunt's to decide what came next. I miscarried the baby at four months."

"I'm sorry." Rafe brushed his fingers over her face, his expression going sorrowful. "God, I'm sorry I didn't know this back when Allison and Gabe... That must have been so hard." He let loose another softly uttered curse. "Now I understand better why seeing Jeff threw you for a loop in the first place. Why you have doubts."

"I should have told you sooner," she admitted. "But ever since, I've been struggling to find my way back

344

to happiness. It's been tough."

"Nothing you did made you miscarry," he reminded her.

Laurel hesitated. She didn't want this to be about her, but he needed to know she understood guilt and regret. "I know, but it could have been. Rafe." She looked him in the eye and let out a long slow breath. "I had made an appointment at an abortion clinic."

His eyes widened slightly, and his grip tightened, but he didn't speak.

"I don't think abortion is absolutely wrong, but it's not something to do without thinking it through. Jeff had made it clear he didn't want to be with me. He was already seeing someone else, and I didn't want to trap him into marriage, which is what would have happened. I couldn't have the baby without someone figuring out who the father was. It seemed like my only option. So I made the appointment."

She closed her eyes, the fear and sorrow and hope and guilt she'd felt in that moment as fresh as it had been yesterday.

"I went to the clinic that morning, and I walked through those doors, and I *still* didn't know if I was going to go through with it or not. If it was the right thing for *me* to do. Over an hour I waited, the whole time debating and coming to no decision. I was so nervous I had to stop at the washroom, and that's when I found out I'd starting bleeding, and..." Laurel forced herself to finish. "I don't know what I would have done, Rafe. If I'd actually had the abortion I think I'd be less conflicted and guilty, because I would have *made* the choice, but I never got to. It was out of my hands, and I've had to live with that ever since."

They stared at each other in silence.

Rafe stroked his fingers down her cheek, cupping her chin then leaning in and touching their lips together. A brief, tender caress that went all the way down into her soul.

He pulled back and stared at her, his blue eyes like a calm, moonlight sea. "Does it get easier? Does the guilt ever fade? Do the fears ever go away?"

"Not completely," she said quietly. "Not yet, but there's joy in the world, Rafe, and we deserve to experience it."

"It's hard to believe," he said.

Laurel might agree with him, but this moment was a fresh start for both of them. "That's the good part about faith. That even in the middle of doubting, we can believe it will get better."

"Belief." Rafe gave a soft laugh. "Your father talked to me once about how important it was to believe in something."

"Trust me, he talks a *lot* about believing," Laurel teased. "Comes with the job description, I suppose."

She stroked her fingers over his shoulders. A slow confidence building as his body relaxed slightly. The tension easing away.

They were going to make it. If she had anything to say, they would.

"You want to know what I believe?" Laurel caressed his cheek. "I believe everyone deserves another chance. That there really is a plan for our happiness if we're smart enough to open our eyes and accept it."

"Even stubborn-ass cowboys?"

"*Especially* stubborn-ass cowboys," she agreed. "But Rafe? Most of all, I believe in you."

He kissed her then, deeper and harder this time than the last.

Talking time seemed to be over, but he wasn't letting her go. In fact, his hands were drifting over her body, igniting the flame that constantly burned in his presence.

"I need you," he whispered. "As desperately as I needed you the other day. The same way I've needed you every fucking second since."

"Then take me," she answered, rising for a moment so she could wiggle out of her panties.

She settled in his lap, undoing the top buttons of her dress until he could see the lacey edges of her bra. Then she offered him a cheeky smile. "Do your worst, baby. Take me for a ride."

Rafe lifted her, tracing his tongue along the edge of her bra. He closed his teeth over where her nipple pressed to the silky fabric, nipping sharply and making her gasp.

"You said something about spending a week in bed," he reminded her. "After we'd talked. We've talked..."

"Later," she promised, reaching between them to undo his button and zipper.

Rafe helped her, shoving the material of his jeans aside so he could pull his cock free. Their fingers tangled as she stroked him, his hand engulfing hers as he moved their hands over his length, her palm touching velvety-smooth skin over steel-hardness.

A groan escaped him, and he took her lips, their arms bumping as they kissed, tension building.

It seemed only a second later he stopped her hand, chest heaving as he sucked for air. "Now," he ordered.

Begged. *Prayed*.

Laurel lifted up far enough he could slide his cock

to where she was ready and wet. His body trembled as she stared into his eyes and sank onto his hard length until there was nothing between them.

His blue gaze fixed on her face as if he were memorizing her.

"That feels so good," Laurel whispered. He might have needed her, but she'd needed him just as much.

Rafe pressed his hands to her hips and lifted her easily. Small motions, as if he couldn't bear for them to be apart. It was enough to tease her aching nerves, every one of them sending out urgent cries for more.

The springs on the old couch creaked as he increased tempo, bringing her down hard enough they bounced slightly. Again, and again, the rhythm like an old-time squeezebox, metallic rattles mixing with the sound of their uneven breaths.

Pleasure swirled around them, and it was more than physical. They were there for each other. In the touch of their fingers. The sound of a gasp. The taste of his lips on hers. Sensory overload. Filled to capacity.

They came together, the explosion in the middle of the room tightly contained as she wrapped herself around him. Rafe's arms like bands of steel—as if he was never going to let go.

Never, and that was just fine by her.

Now she had to figure out how to help him get through the rest of the day—although she had a pretty good idea of one thing that would help.

With a little luck they wouldn't get arrested.

Chapter Twenty-Seven

RAFE STRAIGHTENED his clothes reluctantly as he waited for Laurel to finish fixing her hair. "Are you really going to make me do this?" he complained. "Because...week in bed. Just saying, that's an option."

"You're not attending the funeral for his sake. Funerals are for the ones left behind." Laurel pushed him out the front door. "Stop whining."

"It's not whining, it's expressing a viable option. One that doesn't require clothes." Instant evil eye. "Wow, you're good at that. Very scary."

She broke into a smile and took his hand, but when he would have guided her to his truck, she pointed the other direction. "I need to return Trevor's."

"Would serve him right to have to catch a ride out here to pick it up. Don't know what it is with him leaving the keys in the ignition all the time."

But he wandered obediently to the other truck, pulling back sharply when instead of sliding to the middle, she set herself firmly behind the wheel.

"Sitko?"

She jerked her head to the other door. "I stole it, I'll return it. Get in. We've got somewhere to go."

He thought she was talking about the church, but

she turned a half-dozen blocks early, on the road that led to Traders Pub. "You taking me to the bar?"

"You already had beer for breakfast, which, by the way, I'm only going to say this once—*never* again. Got it?"

He chuckled sheepishly. "I wasn't planning on drinking it all."

"No, of course not. You were practicing your juggling." She drove past the bar.

"We're going to be late," he warned.

"We need to do this."

"I thought you wanted me at the funeral."

Laurel focused on the road. "I want you there for your mom and your brother, and that doesn't have to be at the church. Although you should text Gabe that you're okay so he doesn't worry. I have an idea."

She was up to something. "I don't want to accuse you of anything, Sitko, but you're wearing that same expression that used to get us in a lot of trouble in the old days."

Her lips twisted into a wry smile. "Yes, but it'll be worth it," she promised.

"I trust you."

And that was the truth right there. Whatever mischief she wanted to do, she had a reason and it was something she thought was right for him, for them, so he was willing to go along with it.

Except he hesitated when she pulled into the back alley behind the Principal Jamieson's house, her gaze darting like a cat burglar's as she crawled out of the truck.

"What are—?"

She pressed a finger over her lips to demand silence, eyes going wide.

He shut up.

Laurel pulled open the back gate cautiously, glancing toward the house before tilting her head for him to follow her. Rafe obeyed, not quite sure how getting arrested for breaking-and-entering was going to be helpful.

Only, she slid to the side of the garage and started rooting in the snow, and he was one second away from bursting out laughing in spite of everything. The Jamiesons' backyard was a sea of lost-and-found items, and garage-sale trinkets that never quite made it to the dump. They'd nailed solo gloves in layers to a telephone post, old skis to the fence, and flower pots full of artificial flowers filled every available bit of space between the garden gnomes and driftwood.

She made a low noise of triumph before twirling toward him, a big bouquet of plastic prairie crocuses in her fist. The pale purple flowers were dusted with snow, but she shook them wildly as she headed for the alley at a dead run.

Rafe chased after her. He lifted her into the cab, pushing her over so he could get behind the wheel and take off, tires spinning in the snow. "B&E charges. Was that really the next thing on our to-do list, Sitko?"

"I'll find them new ones," she promised. "But I figured this was one time it was okay to ask forgiveness instead of permission."

He knew exactly where this was headed. "Those are for my mom, aren't they?"

Rafe kept his eyes on the road as she laid her head on his shoulder, pouring her warmth and strength into him. "When I had dinner with Dana last night, there was a picture on the table. She said they used to go for walks when your brothers were young, and he'd give them to her. It sounded as if the memory meant a lot to her."

He nodded. "I saw it."

Laurel twisted to face him. "I know Ben was a bitter old man, but he was once a loving young man, and that's who she's remembering today. Isn't it worth letting go of some hurtful memories for her sake?"

There was no answer to that, because she was right.

The church parking lot was mostly empty, and Rafe took a deep breath then continued on to the graveyard. The sick feeling in his gut was horrid, mostly because he knew he should have been there earlier.

But Laurel took his hand and walked beside him to where his family was gathered. Her fingers in his warm and strong. Grounding him enough to keep him putting one foot in front of the other.

He'd expected condemnation or anger. What he got was acceptance as his mom offered her hands and pulled him in tight for a hug. He held her, meeting Gabe's eyes over her shoulder. His brother nodded slowly then patted his back.

Rafe choked out the words. "I'm sorry, Mom. I should have been there for you."

She kissed his cheek, turning a wan smile his direction. "Yes, you should have been, but you're here now." She glanced beside him at Laurel. "And you're not being a fool anymore, so I forgive you."

Laurel stepped forward. "I'm sorry for your loss," she said quietly. "Do you need anything?"

"Just for the morning to be over," Dana said.

Someone called for them to gather, and Rafe found himself standing with his mom on his left, and

Laurel on his right. Gabe and Allison and the rest of the family gathered close as Pastor Dave spoke.

The words didn't register, but Rafe was hyperaware of everything else around them. Sorrowful expressions, moisture-filled eyes. A blast of wind whipped past

His uncles came forward, and it finally registered what this day meant to them as well. Ben had been their brother. He might have gotten mean and broken by the end, but they'd climbed trees with him. Plowed fields, and done chores, and—

For a second he could barely breathe, remembering the pain of losing Mike. Thinking of losing *Gabe*.

The only thing that stopped him from breaking down and weeping like a baby right then and there was the warmth of Laurel's hand in his.

Pastor Dave finished speaking, nodding to the attendants. The casket lowered on its rigging, moving out of sight. Someone—his cousin Steve?—began singing, and slowly more voices joined in. Even after his long absence from the church, he recognized *Amazing Grace*, and Rafe stood and listened.

The tune was familiar, but this was the first time he'd really listened to the lyrics in years, and he caught himself squeezing Laurel's fingers tightly as her sweet voice rang out as if she were singing to him.

'Twas Grace that taught my heart to fear.
And grace, my fears relieved.
How precious did that grace appear, the hour I first believed.

Maybe being afraid something would happen was enough to make sure that it never would. Rafe was still worried that he'd fail Laurel, but he figured there was a good chance she'd kick his butt anytime he stepped out of line.

It wasn't grace but Laurel he believed in, and at that moment, it was enough.

And when the service was over, they waited until it was only the immediate family at the graveside, the rest of the Colemans drifting away as Dana stared at the place where the headstone would go.

Laurel bumped Rafe's side. "Flowers," she whispered.

Right. It seemed too little, too late and somehow wrong, but he trusted Laurel, so he pulled the little batch of purple plastic from under his coat and turned to his mom. "I know it's—"

Dana's instant gasp cut him off, sending him into a near panic as she pressed her fingers to her mouth, eyes filling with tears.

Then, *thank God*, she spoke, and while her voice was shaky, it was clear she was happy. "Oh, Rafe." She took the bouquet and stroked the flowers. "Thank you. Thank you so much."

Gabe glanced between him and Laurel, a small smile coming on as his brother nodded his approval.

The day wasn't over. All Rafe's worries weren't gone, but right then he felt as if he'd finally stepped onto the right path, and pretty much knew why.

He wrapped his arm around Laurel's shoulders where he planned to keep it—forever.

Chapter Twenty-Eight

BEN'S DEATH brought changes. Big ones and little ones, not only in what went down between Rafe and Laurel, but around the Angel ranch. During the early days, sadness always swept in when they gathered, but also a sense of purpose—something fresh and hopeful.

The aunts came and helped his mom go through the house from top to bottom, clearing away bitter memories of Ben's later years. Rafe and Gabe helped fix things up, listening to Dana chat about the things she brought out to display on freshly painted shelves.

Laurel stopped in often. She and Rafe ate dinner with his mom at least once a week, and he'd drop by the ranch house at other times between chores to discover his girlfriend's car in the yard, cups of tea between her and his mom as they chatted. Or Laurel holding knitting needles awkwardly as Dana tried to teach her.

Rafe teased as he drove her home after supper one night. "I swear you're going out with me because you like my mom."

"And your point is?" she asked in a completely serious tone.

He laughed. "Brat."

She curled up a little tighter to his side. "Your mom's happy. You've done good things for her, and you should be proud."

"There's a long ways to go to get the ranch the way we want it, but yes, the house is looking much better, and I'm glad Mom is comfortable. Still think it's a big place for her to take care of on her own." Which gave him ideas and made him want to have a certain *discussion* with Laurel, but the timing sucked to rush into things. "This spring we're going to be extra busy," he warned, wishing it wasn't true.

"Maybe you'll be busy enough to stay out of mischief, then."

"Look who's talking about mischief? I'm not the one who stole the cookies out of the staff room."

She gasped in mock horror. "Seriously? You're willing to go *that* far back to find the one bad thing I did on my own?"

"You still did it."

"Never got caught," Laurel pointed out. "Therefore, it never happened."

He laughed, walking her to the door and dropping her off with a kiss. Long, slow and tender, pulsing heat there between them, under the surface. The temptation to stay with her for the night, every night, was strong, but she'd made it clear she didn't want them to push too fast.

Only the rental was getting lonely to ramble around in on his own, and crawling into bed without her in his arms was nearly unbearable.

By the time the winter weather broke, it was the tail end of March, the month going out like a lamb for the first time in years. It made him think ahead to springtime flowers and green growing grass.

New starts. New beginnings.

It was time to make the next move.

Rafe marched into the barn, eager to track down Gabe. Instead he bumped into another Coleman meeting, this time just breaking up.

His Uncle Mike was the last to leave, stopping to offer Rafe a solid man-hug-slash-pat-on-the-back. "I was telling Gabe I think you two have done a fine job taking care of your mom over the past while. I'm glad she's got you."

Mike looked older than Rafe remembered, his smile slower to come. "Thanks. You doing okay?"

His uncle shrugged. "Feeling my age, I guess." He glanced at Gabe. "We'll talk soon."

"Yes, sir. Try not to worry," Gabe added. "I'm sure he's doing all right."

Uncle Mike tipped his hat then left without a word as Rafe watched him go, heaviness in his soul. "Jesse?"

Gabe sighed. "Yeah, partly. Still can't believe he up and left like that."

"You did," Rafe said bluntly. "Oh, sorry. You waited until *after* the funeral to leave. That made it so much better."

His brother gave him a dirty look.

"And if you spout some bullshit about how it's not the same thing, I'll prove that you're my big brother in age only these days," Rafe warned.

"You're right, I was an idiot, like Jesse is being now." Gabe slapped him on the shoulder. "Did you need something? Or did you stop in to be annoying?"

Rafe pushed aside the other issue for a minute. "When are you going to tell me what's happening with all the sneaking around? You starting a secret Coleman society? Because I'm getting paranoid that I wasn't asked to join."

"I didn't mean to keep it from you this long, but then life got pretty chaotic."

Rafe shrugged. "It's never going to be calm around here, so spill."

"We're working on getting the ranches together more. It was a fine idea they had to split things up back in the day, but the families didn't really turn out even, did we? If we split the Angel ranch between us, and the Six Pack clan divvies theirs up—you can see it's not going to work. But there should be room for *all* our family as far as I'm concerned."

Not what Rafe had expected. "What brought this on?"

Gabe leaned back on the wall and folded his arms. "We started talking a year or so ago when Uncle Randy got sick and Steve didn't know if they could keep things going at the Moonshine ranch. We'd been struggling over here, hoping the choice to go organic would work. And Karen—well, that woman can ranch circles around us, and Uncle George will never see it. It seemed like we needed to find a way to put on paper what we know already—it's Coleman land. It doesn't matter if it was given to Randy or Mike or Ben, it belongs to *all* of us, or it should."

"You think that will make a difference down the road?"

"You tell me. What if Uncle George thinks it's Blake calling the shots on Whiskey Creek land? Making decisions about breeding animals and crop rotations? Would he let him?"

Sadly, the answer was too clear. "In a second."

"So if Karen actually makes the decisions for Whiskey Creek, but it's down in the books as *Coleman* planning, the best decisions can be made without a fight. Although—we're thinking more of everyone using what they're best at. So Karen works with the breeding animals, and Joel helps us use those crazy computer programs of his for crop rotations, and we share what we know about going organic."

It was actually rather brilliant. "I could see this working. It's a good thing this isn't like *Downton Abbey* with those third cousins inheriting," Rafe said.

Gabe laughed. "God, Allison and Laurel are crazy about that show, and every time they put it on that's the first thing I think of. Inheritances are crazy, bro."

"They're not watching it for that part," Rafe pointed out. "Be glad neither of them have asked us to start dressing in suits."

His brother shuddered.

Rafe got back to the point. "So this land business. Everyone in the family needs to approve?"

"Legally it has to start with the stakeholders—which means all three uncles—Mike, George and Randy. They needed to know we wanted this, without any of them knowing the parts about them—I mean, Uncle George thinks we're doing this because the families didn't breed evenly."

Rafe snickered. "Yeah, he'd think in those terms."

Gabe grinned in return. "We're getting closer, but there's a lot to figure out, including if Uncle Mark wants to be a part of the final agreement."

Their mysterious uncle who'd never returned after dropping off Becky at his house and basically giving it to her. "The whole thing sounds pretty twisted, even for the Coleman clan."

"You cannot believe the paperwork," Gabe complained. "Anyway, when Ben died, one problem vanished—I can decide for Angel without it causing a rift like it could have. I won't do it if you tell me not to, but I sure hope you can see farther than our own pocketbooks."

"You don't want Micah and your future kids to inherit?"

Gabe's face twisted slightly, and Rafe felt like a shit for reminding his brother of sad memories. "He will, or they will, but if we do this right, *all* the family who want to work the land will be able to, for generations to come. Even the kids like Lance and Nathan who don't have rights anymore because Daniel did a buy out."

"And those that don't want to ranch, like Daniel?"

"They won't be tied up in the finances the same way."

It was brilliant, and twisted, and if he'd known about this before shouting at his father—

Rafe's gut rolled, but he took a deep breath and thought of Laurel. Thought of her promise that things would work out in the end, but it would take time.

Reminded himself all over that she believed in him.

He was still thinking about it that night as they sat together on the porch of the rental, both of them wrapped up against the cold, but it was too pretty an evening to spend indoors. Laurel swung her feet back and forth as she leafed through a seed catalog, her fuzzy topped boots looking as if she had strange animals hugging her shins.

She was popping sticky notes on the pages, so focused and intent on her task she didn't notice he was staring at her, the warm sensation in his heart washing over him familiar and—

Shocking as he recognized it for what it was.

How had he not seen it earlier? Or more to the point, why had it not registered in him? They'd been friends forever...and maybe that was part of the problem. This thing he felt inside wasn't brand new. It was the same sweet sensation he'd always felt when he thought about her. Only *now* he had a name for it.

Stubborn, stupid-ass cowboy that he was to not notice he'd fallen in love.

Thinking of stubborn, stupid-ass cowboys...

He hauled out his phone and texted his cousin like he did at least once a week, the opening message the same as always.

Rafe: *Come home, you jerk*

Jesse: *Back off, cuz, or I will hurt you*

Rafe: *You need your head examined. Your dad is a mess, dude. Call him, FFS.*

Jesse: *Fuck, I'm sorry. Tell everyone I'm fine. I emailed you my contact info in case of an emergency, but I'd appreciate if you keep where I'm at quiet. This is best for everyone.*

Rafe: *When you get your head out of your ass, we'll be waiting*

Jesse: *jerk*

Rafe: *butthead*

He caught himself smiling at the stupid banter even as he wished Jesse had made a different choice.

It was strange. Years ago he'd always wondered how everyone in the family seemed to gravitate toward Gabe, asking for advice and sharing their troubles.

He'd never dreamed that he'd end up in the same type of situation. Rafe considered all the secrets he'd learned over the past while. It was a privilege to know people trusted him.

It was a privileged burden to bear—

He glanced over at Laurel. This time she looked up and caught him watching her, and her slow smile made his insides melt. Burdens were easier to carry when there was someone he loved at his side.

Now to make sure that she stayed there.

He pulled out his phone and made a few plans...

SWEET, SPRINGTIME air flowed through the open windows at the library, and Laurel took a deep, appreciative breath. The change in seasons made her glad, and not only because they were finally able to put away the thick winter coats.

Time was passing, and time brought healing. She knew Rafe worried off and on. She figured he would for a long time, but he was happier now. He'd joined her family for dinner a few times, and even gone ice fishing with her dad before the melt set in.

She'd teased him about trying too hard to impress her father. "You don't have to haul him into the wilderness. Just go out for a coffee or something if you want to talk."

Rafe had laughed. "You're right about that. Know what he said when I kept trying to make conversation out on the ice?"

She waited.

"He was polite and all for a bit then finally told me to shut up and fish."

Laughter came quickly again, returning from wherever it had vanished to for that brief time—or maybe it had never really left. It was a part of them, and always had been. It had just gotten a little dusty for a while, in both their souls.

Laurel was determined to keep joy close to the surface from here on. Close to her heart.

She was already in her car before she noticed the note tucked under the windshield wiper. She popped out and grabbed it, letting her grin break loose at the oh-so-familiar message.

Do you want to build a racetrack?

They were going back in time, and while she wondered what Rafe was up to, she drove slowly to let the happiness soak in hard.

He was where she'd found him nearly ten months earlier, arms stretched on the picnic table, his legs out in front of him. She admired the view as she strolled up, stealing his cowboy hat and plopping it on her head. "Hey, stranger."

Rafe rose and kissed her. He curled one hand possessively around her to hold them tightly together. Sweet, passionate heat rising.

Her heart was pumping hard when he finally let her go.

"Good day?"

"Great day," she said. "Want to hear a secret?"

"I'd love to."

"Someone is transferring to a different church."

He blinked then grinned. "Okay, for a second I thought you were talking about your parents, and I couldn't figure out why you were smiling. But this? Great news."

"Don't say anything to anyone. I might have been eavesdropping." Her cheeks instantly heated up. "Fine, I was eavesdropping," she hurried as he waved a finger in her face. "But it's still good news."

Rafe tugged her with him into the playground. "I wish him well, wherever Jeff lands."

She snorted—couldn't help it. "So now that he's leaving he's *Jeff* again instead of you calling him Pastor Ass?"

"I'm forgiving that way," he deadpanned. "Although you have to admit it had kind of a ring to it."

He dropped to the ground beside the sandbox and Laurel gasped as he pulled her into his lap. "Rafe."

"Can't build a racetrack from way up there," he admonished her. "Oh, look, there's already one here."

The sand was pushed into piles and dips, a far fancier setup than they'd managed years earlier. She curled an arm around his neck and leaned forward to admire his work. "You've improved your technique. I like the corners—much smoother than I remember."

He stole a kiss. "I've gotten more experience dealing with *curves*," he whispered, his hands brushing over her body.

Hmmm. "Naughty sandbox time. You're going to get us in trouble, Coleman."

"I certainly hope so." He nipped at her lips. "Want to race?"

She ignored the playground and focused on him, straddling his legs and easing her body against him as she offered up a word of thanks there were no kids around. "I don't have any cars with me."

"You can share one of mine."

The soft texture of his hair teased her fingers as she stroked him, soaking in his kiss. He tugged at her elbow, and she slid her hand down until their fingers met, confused when he pressed something cold and hard against her palm.

Laurel pulled back, concentrating as hard as she could with her senses still reeling. "What's this?"

"Can't race without a truck," Rafe said, a lilt in his voice, and something else.

She glanced into his eyes, seeing—nervousness?

"Baby? What's up?"

"It's my favourite truck, and I want you to have it."

He lifted her hand between them, and she finally looked down.

It was an old battered Hot Wheels truck. Black, vaguely familiar. It could have been the same one she'd given him all those years ago. Only in the tiny truck bed, something sparkled, and Laurel caught her breath.

A bit of twine held the ring in place, but it was clear this wasn't a childish trinket.

She held the truck tight and lifted her eyes to his.

"I love you," he admitted. "I think I always have, but now I love you so much I can barely breathe without you."

"I love you too."

His eyes shone with hope. "Then say you'll marry me. Say you'll stick beside me for the rest of our lives. You can kick my ass when I step over the line, and kiss me when I'm good, and all the while remind me to get in the right kind of trouble."

She laughed through happy tears. "What's the right kind of trouble?"

Rafe got the ring free and held up her hand so he could slip it on her finger. "Any trouble I get into with you—that's the perfect kind."

Laurel paused for a second. "I'll marry you, but I have one condition."

He grinned even as he pressed kisses to her fingers. "What?"

She put on the most serious expression she could manage. "You've got to figure out a better pet name for me than *Sitko*. Deal?"

"For you, anything."

Then she wasn't worried about pet names or the fact the school bell had just rung, and there was about to be a mess of children running into the schoolyard wondering why the pastor's daughter was kissing her cowboy in the middle of the playground.

Although if anyone did ask, she'd say they were celebrating building a racetrack.

Epilogue

Early summer

"I THOUGHT you'd like this."

Laurel smiled as she let Rafe lead her along the river's path—the same one they'd walked so many years before on the night of Grad. Giddy with excitement, buzzing with lust...

Okay, so things hadn't changed that much in the years between. She still quivered at the thought of being with him. The fact she now got to touch him any time she wanted—that she got to be with him for the rest of their lives—made it so much better. There was something more in everything they did these days.

A connection beyond friendship. Far *far* beyond, but she was so grateful it had started there.

"You sure I'm dressed for this?" she asked, holding her pretty dress shoes in one, the fingers of the other hand linked with his strong grip.

"Yup. Although you might..." His words faded away.

She laughed. "I heard that. So I'm not going to be wearing anything for long?"

"Not if I have my way."

The look in his eyes was familiar, and so was the picnic blanket he'd laid on the ground near the tree where she'd sat so long ago.

"Why, Coleman. You got something dirty on your mind?"

"Not dirty at all," he protested. He tugged her into his arms and held her close as he smiled down on her. "Making love to my bride is the nearest thing to heaven there is on earth."

"Smooth talker," she teased.

"Come here." He brought her to the blanket, lying beside her. The sun filtered through the trees, dappling the ground in a moving kaleidoscope of gold and tan.

They'd come straight from her parents'. Her father had performed the ceremony for them, standing in the backyard under the flowering apple tree. She'd seen tears in her father's eyes, but he'd smiled and given his blessing, along with the rest of the family.

She and Rafe had a couple hours before they needed to return to enjoy their wedding dinner. Her family and his would gather at the Angel homestead. They'd both wanted a small gathering—they'd party with friends and the rest of the Coleman clan on Friday at Traders.

But now they kissed and touched and fooled around rather innocently for the longest time before things heated up to the point Laurel got worried.

"Public place," she reminded him. "That feels good, but Rafe, *baby*, you've got to stop."

He stroked his fingers along the insides of her legs, over her sex, slipping under the edge of her panties. "No one is going to interrupt us. I put up the warning markers, and a couple of my cousins are watching the side paths as a favour."

Laurel flushed, shocked far more than she thought possible. "Your cousins know we're having sex?"

Rafe threw back his head and laughed so hard his body shook. He pulled her over him, still chuckling. "Sitko, we just got married. I'm pretty sure everyone in town assumes we're about to have sex."

He had a point. "I guess..."

He stilled her worries by giving her something else to think about. Or not think about as he rolled her under him and got them both naked.

It was deliciously dirty to have him over her, sunshine on his strong body. Rafe kissed and teased and touched until she shook with pleasure. Sliding in deep and connecting them physically as he whispered how much he loved her.

Pressing his forehead to hers as he came—shared pleasure she couldn't get enough of.

She'd wanted a lifetime with him, and now she had it.

LAUREL STRETCHED beside him, her white-blonde hair tousled on the blanket. Rafe stroked a strand off her face, her blue eyes capturing his.

"I was so scared that day," she said softly.

He waited.

"My first day of school. Everyone else had started a week earlier, and they all seemed to have already found their friends. I was one second away from crying."

"You sure didn't look it."

She stared up at him. "I was praying as hard as I could that God would give me a friend. And not just someone to be with so I wouldn't be scared, but a *forever* friend."

Rafe lowered himself to the blanket and curled an arm around her. Unable to speak—her expression so bright she was nearly glowing.

"I believed like a child *you* were the answer to that prayer, and you really were."

"Even with all the trouble we've gotten into over the years?" he teased.

"That proved you could keep up with me," she said, cupping his cheek. "And now— *Now* you're the answer to my grown-up prayers, and dreams, and wishes, and while I don't know all the answers, I sure know this one thing—I love you, baby."

There was nothing he could offer in return except what was pouring out of his heart. "If anyone was an answer to prayer, it was you—I love you, Sitko."

She laughed against his mouth between the teasing kisses that followed. "That's not my name anymore. Say it," she whispered.

"Pussycat—ouch." She'd nipped his lip, and he chuckled. "Sweet cheeks?"

"*Say it...*"

Their tongues stroked together, and he was ready for another round, rolling her under him to the blanket.

He stared into her eyes. "My all. My everything. My *love.*"

Laurel nodded with satisfaction. "That'll do."

New York Times Bestselling Author
Vivian Arend

invites you to meet the Colemans. These
contemporary cowboys ranch the foothills of
the Alberta Rockies. Enjoy the ride as they
each find their happily-ever-afters.

───────────────⌒⌒───────────────

Six Pack Ranch
Rocky Mountain Heat
Rocky Mountain Haven
Rocky Mountain Desire
Rocky Mountain Angel
Rocky Mountain Rebel
Rocky Mountain Freedom
Rocky Mountain Romance
Rocky Retreat
Rocky Mountain Shelter
Rocky Mountain Devil
Rocky Mountain Home

With over 1.6 million books sold, VIVIAN AREND is a New York Times and USA Today bestselling author of over 50 contemporary and paranormal romance books, including the Six Pack Ranch and Granite Lake Wolves.

Her books are all standalone reads with no cliffhangers. They're humorous yet emotional, with sexy-times and happily-ever-afters. Vivian pretty much thinks she's got the best job in the world, and she's looking forward to giving readers more HEAs. She lives in B.C. Canada with her husband of many years and a fluffy attack Shitzu named Luna who ignores everyone except when treats are deployed.

Made in the USA
Middletown, DE
20 September 2016